Dear Reader:

It is my pleasure to present yet another engrossing novel from best-selling Allison Hobbs. Hobbs is the author of *The Climax, A Bona Fide Gold Digger, The Enchantress, Double Dippin', Dangerously in Love, Insatiable* and *Pandora's Box*; all published by Strebor Books. A "Queen of Erotic Fiction" in her own right, Hobbs now puts a new spin on her previous works by taking her talent to the next level in *Big Juicy Lips*.

Get ready for the dramatic ride of a lifetime as you enjoy this loosely based sequel to *Double Dippin'* in which a young lady decides that controlling men is the most powerful high. But when the men comply, it turns into a deadly game of lust and despair. Chocked full of surprises, you will not be able to put this book down after the very first page.

I first met Allison at the Baltimore Book Festival several years ago and was immediately impressed with her talent. Not everyone has a natural writing ability, but Allison was born to create masterpieces like the one you are about to read. She is ever positive and determined, much like myself, and will go far in this industry as her next three books are already scheduled for publication.

Thanks for supporting Allison's efforts and for supporting my imprint, Strebor Books. I am overwhelmed by the legions of avid readers who genuinely appreciate not only my personal work but the works of the dozens that I publish. For a complete listing of titles, please visit www.streborbooks.com

If you are interesting in making extra income, please email dante-feenix@gmail.com to be sent an "Opportunity" packet. Now sit back in your favorite chair or, better yet, chill in the bed, and be prepared to be tantalized by yet another great read.

Peace and Many Blessings,

Zane

Zane
Publisher
Strebor Books International

ALSO BY ALLISON HOBBS

Pandora's Box
Insatiable
Dangerously In Love
Double Dippin'
The Enchantress
A Bona Fide Gold Digger
The Climax

ZANE PRESENTS

Big Juicy Lips

A NOVEL

ALLISON HOBBS

SBI

STREBOR BOOKS

NEW YORK LONDON TORONTO SYDNEY

Strebor Books
P.O. Box 6505
Largo, MD 20792

ISBN-13: 978-1-60751-436-7

Cover design: www.mariondesigns.com

Manufactured in the United States of America

THIS NOVEL IS DEDICATED
to My Precious Little Diva
Kapri T. Johnson

Acknowledging Sisterhood

Five years have passed since the publication of my first novel. Now, eight books later, I'm as thrilled and as grateful as I was the first time I saw my name on a book cover. Still, I'm very much aware that the angels who've touched my life in a number of ways have all had a hand in making this writer's life such an amazing journey.

So, here's a shout-out to all my sistahgurl/angelfriends:

Karen Dempsey Hammond, Shari Reason, Aletha Dempsey, Chanelle Sealy, Elysha Perry, Charmaine Parker, Tandace Wilson, Tina Brooks McKinney, Jessica Holter, Janet Stevens Cook, Kimberly Kay Terry, Radiah Hubbert, Tiffany L. Smith, Michelle Coates, Locksie, Anna J, and of course, my publisher and friend, Zane.

The best and most beautiful things in the world cannot be
seen, nor touched…but are felt in the heart.
—HELEN KELLER

Beauty is not in the face; beauty is a light in the heart.
—KAHLIL GIBRAN

That which is striking and beautiful is not always good,
but that which is good is always beautiful.
—NINON DE L'ENCLOS

CHAPTER 1

"I wonder if those creams really work." Misty trailed a finger over Brick's soft penis, trying to caress the sagging appendage back to life.

Lying on his back, his head resting on his clasped palms, Brick jerked himself upright. "What kind of cream?"

"Stay-hard cream," she said nonchalantly, knowing Brick would become incensed.

"What the hell do I need that for?"

"It's supposed to make you stay hard...last longer." Misty sighed, withdrew her finger, clearly giving up on any hope that Brick would become erect.

"Cut that shit!" Brick scowled, further distorting his face, which was already disfigured by a cruel scar that ran jagged from his hairline down to his chin. "I pounded on you for two straight hours—killing that pussy. But I held back, didn't bust 'til after you did." Brick gave Misty a look of disbelief. "What? You expect my jawn to stay hard for two, three days?" Brick gave a little chuckle, but the sound lacked mirth. "Come on, Misty, stop being so greedy. I gotta get some sleep." Brick rolled over on his side. He pulled the top sheet over his mountainous body and also over his head. His back, broad and hard as granite, was turned stubbornly toward Misty.

"You claim you love me, but you're so selfish, sometimes!" Being spiteful, Misty plucked Brick in the back of his sheet-covered head.

"Stop frontin'; you know you got yours," Brick mumbled, his face buried in the pillow.

"No, I didn't. I didn't get shit; I faked it! I knew you were tired, so I faked it so you could bust, rest up and start all over again. I didn't think you'd lay your selfish ass down and try to get your snore on." Growing more resentful by the minute, Misty swatted Brick with her pillow.

He threw the sheet off his head. "Stop lying. After all these years, you think I don't know when your lil' ass is faking?" He flung the pillow she'd hit him with, but used much more force than he'd intended. The sound of the thumping sound made by the pillow, as it connected with Misty's face, resonated inside the bedroom.

Misty's mouth dropped open, stunned that Brick had hit her. It didn't matter that it was just a playful smack of a pillow and that no real harm had been done. She was furious at his audacity. The five-foot, one hundred and five-pound little dynamo pummeled Brick's hard-as-concrete arm and shoulder, but quickly realized that he barely felt the blows from her small fists. "Are you fuckin' crazy?" she yelled and then, using all her strength, she elbowed him as viciously as she could.

Brick laughed and said, "Ow! I might need an ambulance."

Misty rubbed her cheek. "I don't see anything funny about a big-ass man whipping my ass and leaving welts all over my face."

"Whipping your ass? Is that what you gon' tell the po-po?" He laughed even harder, his loving eyes adoring her, despite her fury.

"It's not funny, Brick! My face feels like it's starting to swell up."

Brick sat up. His unattractive, scarred face was frowned in confusion and concern. "I didn't mean to throw the pillow that hard. Misty, baby. I'm sorry, aiight?"

"No! It's not aiight. You threw that jawn like it was a football; acting like you Donovan McNabb or somebody."

Gently, the giant of a man pulled Misty's small, delicate hand away from her face. With increased concern, he scrutinized the right side of her undeniably beautiful face and then he inspected the left side. "It's aiight, Misty. Ain't no marks," he said, genuinely contrite. "I didn't mean it. You know I forget my strength. I'd hurt myself before I'd put a mark on your pretty face." Involuntarily, his hand touched the gruesome, jagged scar on his face, taking both him and Misty back to the dreadful night it happened.

Shaking away the memory, Misty refused to dwell on the past. "You gotta stop playin' all the time. If it wasn't for me—the way I look—we couldn't make any money. Shit, we wouldn't get in all those clubs for free or nothing." Misty sighed, giving Brick a look of disgust. Suddenly, she grimaced and clutched her stomach.

"What's wrong? Did I go too far up in you?"

"No," she uttered in a pained, raspy whisper. "Cramps." She bent at the waist and commenced to rock and moan softly.

The worry lines that intermingled with his jagged scar made Brick appear more grotesque than he actually was. "I didn't know you had cramps. Why didn't you tell me?"

"You were acting all sleepy and everything, so I was going to try to get you in the mood—trying to get you aroused."

Brick's eyes saddened. "Misty, baby, why'd you let me fuck you so hard if your stomach was hurting?"

"It wasn't that bad, yet."

"So, why you have to come at me all shady, pretending that you were horny? If I banged you again, you'd be in worse pain." He looked in her eyes intently. "You gotta let me know, when you feeling bad. It don't matter how tired I am, I'd never go to sleep and leave you laying awake, in pain. And you know it." His voice rose in anger.

"I said that I'm sorry for not telling you, so stop yelling. That's not making it any better." Annoyed, Misty sighed and rolled her eyes.

"Can I get something off of my chest?" he asked, voice lowered.

She nodded, her expression becoming increasingly pained.

"Why you got so much game, Misty? You be trying to get over when you don't even have to?"

Misty smiled sheepishly. "I'm sorry, Brick. You know that I have a big problem with honesty."

"I know." Brick caressed her silky hair. "It's all good, though. You were a born scam artist. Real talk; your game is tight. But you act like you in this by yourself." He shook his head. "I'm on your side. How many times I gotta prove myself? I'm ride or die." Brick nodded emphatically.

"I know you're on my side, Brick," she said, and tenderly traced his scar with her fingertip, silently acknowledging the sacrifice he'd made for her.

"This is our crib," Brick went on. "This is where you rest your head at night. When you come home, you gotta leave all the game at the door."

Pretending remorse, Misty lowered her head, while Brick continued to adoringly run his fingers through her long hair. Misty spoke softly. "I hear what you're saying, but don't get it twisted. I like you and everything, but there ain't nothing but larceny in my heart. That's how I keep us living good. My brain is working overtime, always figuring out new ways to scam mufuckas. I don't have time for that lovey-dovey shit. Feel me?"

He nodded, head bowed in sorrow.

"Don't take it personally, Brick. It's hard doing what I do," she said, pouting.

"I know, I know." Brick raised his head, reached up and massaged Misty's shoulders.

"And tonight…dealing with all this pain—" She winced and pressed her hands against her stomach. "I can't think straight. Brick, you gotta make a run to the store. Get me some Midol for these cramps."

"Midol! You don't need that! Whatchu think you got me for? I got the best remedy for your cramps."

"Well, do something. I'm in pain," she whimpered, biting her lip as if fighting unbearable agony.

Brick repositioned Misty, pulled her to the edge of the bed, allowing her legs to dangle. He bent low and crouched between her thighs.

Misty shivered when she felt Brick's rough facial hairs scrape against her thighs. "I'm sorry for lying to you, Brick," she murmured, speaking in the fake, tiny voice she used on tricks, Brick, and her mother to get what she wanted.

She could feel Brick's semen starting to bubble outside her pussy, slowly saturating her pubic hairs.

"Hold up," he said. "I'll get a washcloth and clean you up."

"Ow!" she blurted and rubbed her stomach frantically.

Brick looked in the direction of the bathroom and back at Misty. "You hurting, real bad?"

"Yes," she whimpered. "Oh, God!" she cried out, and tried to sit up as if the pain had gone up a notch. The extra effort exerted inadvertently caused more semen to erupt and trickle out. Misty pressed her thighs together, while moaning in pain. "Hurry up, Brick, go get the washcloth," she said pitifully. She knew he disliked the sour taste of his own semen and only ate her cum-drenched pussy under extreme emergencies. But watching him suck his thick ejaculation out of her coochie aroused her like crazy; gave her a body-quacking orgasm.

She pretended to cry.

"Don't cry, Misty, baby. You know I gotchu, girl," Brick assured her with eyes filled with love.

Playing her part to the hilt, Misty continued to twist and writhe, all the while rubbing her stomach and moaning, "It hurts. Oh, Brick. Help me, it hurts so bad." She could feel a thick stream of his semen, trailing down one of her thighs. Just in case the sight of it repelled him, she cunningly took her theatrics to another level, sobbing as if she were in critical condition.

"Relax, Misty. Open your legs."

Misty wanted to break into a wide grin, but she grimaced as if in excruciating pain. Brick tenderly parted her thighs. She could feel the slimy ejaculation, now stuck on both thighs. Brick's loving lips went straight to the center of her semen-saturated honey pot, sucking and kissing it; showing her coochie mad love. He gently separated her cum-stuck pussy lips with his moist tongue. Once he had her pussy wide open, he sucked on her snatch—healing it—giving it mouth-to-mouth resuscitation.

He went from sucking to licking. His tongue strokes felt so good, so soothing, it took an enormous amount of willpower for Misty to resist wrapping her legs around his neck and grinding her slushy coochie all over his scarred face. "Mmm," she uttered spontaneously. "Oh, baby. I feel so much better," she moaned, twisting and shuddering, no longer able to restrain herself.

"You sure?"

"Uh-huh." She sounded tentative.

"Go for it, then."

"For real?"

"Yeah," Brick said huskily. "Don't worry about me. Do you. Get your thing off, baby."

That was all Misty needed to hear. She placed frantic pussy rotations on Brick's lips for a few moments. Then crudely, disrespectfully, she slid her cunt up and down his face, abusively smearing cum and pussy juice on his forehead, eyelids, nose, mouth, and chin, all the while crying out and calling Brick horrible, degrading names.

Seconds later, Misty felt her coochie walls contracting. Heightening her arousal, she called Brick an ugly monster, a beast, and every other deplorable name that seemed fitting. Squeezing her eyes tightly, she geared up for an erotic explosion that would soon gush out and splatter Brick's ugly face.

CHAPTER 2

Misty's body shook from the final, orgasmic tremor.

"Feel better?" Brick's face was shiny, glazed from her juices. Misty sat up and looked at him. She turned up her nose. She scooted backward. "Eew! You stink, Brick. Your face smells rank; like cum."

Misty's spiteful words stung badly, but Brick kept the hurt from appearing on his face. "Yeah, you're feelin' better," he said as he got off his knees. "You're back to your same ol' evil ways."

Recoiling, Misty grimaced. "Back up, away from me! I'm not trying to talk to you with all that stank cum crusted up in your beard and your mustache. Go, wash your face!"

"You must have a stank pussy 'cause your pussy juice is mixed up in there, too," he retorted weakly as he headed toward the bathroom. Brick tried to play it off.

Misty could tell his feelings were hurt, but she didn't care. "My coochie does not have an odor. Your foul-ass seed is funking up the whole bedroom," she added maliciously, scowling and fanning her face.

The sound of water running in the sink indicated that Brick was handling his business. Misty looked down at her thighs and recoiled. "Bring me a warm washcloth! Cum is smeared all over my legs. Why you so nasty, Brick?" Then she felt around and snatched her hand back in anger. "Damn, you get on my nerves!"

"Now, what I do?" he called from the bathroom.

"It looks like you shot a gallon of cum. Slimy shit is all over the sheets and everything. I can't sleep overtop of no cum-stained sheets. You have to change this bed linen. Hurry up!"

"Aiight, gimme a minute. I got rid of your cramps and everything, but I can't even get a half-ass thank you," he said glumly. "Brick, do this…Brick, do that…" he complained, mimicking her loud, high-pitched voice.

"Hurry up!" She'd been bossing him around for as long as she could remember. She squinted in thought. Hmmm. She'd met Brick back in first or second grade. He was in the class with the slow learners. She was in the accelerated class. His dumb ass wouldn't know which way to turn if she didn't point him in the right direction.

Brick was six feet four and two hundred and sixty pounds of solid muscle. However, tiny and mighty, Misty was the boss bitch in their relationship.

He entered the bedroom with a soapy, warm washcloth in his hand. A set of sheets were tucked under his arm. He laid the clean bed linen at the foot of the bed and cleaned the crusted cum off Misty's thighs and outside her vagina. Very carefully, he separated her inner folds and cleaned the soft pink flesh. "Aiight, you're straight. Get up so I can make the bed."

"I'm tired," Misty whined.

"You gotta get your lazy lil' ass up if you want to sleep on clean sheets."

Lazily, Misty eased off the bed. "You must not be working hard enough," she informed him as she watched him pull the rumpled top sheet off the bed.

"What! It's two in the morning…you sent me on that appointment. I came home and fucked you, I ate your pussy, I cleaned your pussy, and now you got me changing the bed. What more do you want me to do?" Brick sounded hurt, but Misty's expression held no compassion.

"Yo, nigga," she said, twisting her neck and injecting bass in her feminine voice. "You shot out a gallon of cum. There's no way in hell you should be shooting a big load like that, if you're working as hard as you should." Misty snorted. "But that's on me; I'll take the responsibility for it. I've been too soft on you. But you better believe, playtime is over. You gotta step up your game."

Solemnly, Brick continued making the bed, his head hung low. Misty wasn't moved by the "poor Brick" routine.

"We got bills to pay. You can't hustle a couple times a week and think it's all good. Shit, just gassing up the new truck is costing us a grip. You gotta start bringing in more money and it's my job to push you to make sure you do."

Brick's brows crinkled together. "Baby, I think it's all the shopping you do that keeps us in the hole."

Misty reared back in shock. "What! You expect me to go around looking like a ragamuffin?"

"That ain't what I'm saying."

"Whatchu saying, then?"

"I know you have to keep your gear up. I'm just saying, you shop two or three times a day; sometimes four. Don't you think that might be a problem?"

"No! And you shouldn't either. If shopping makes me feel good, then shut the fuck up and keep that money coming."

"I can take on some part-time work," he said in a meek voice. She gave a loud, derisive snort.

"I could start robbing niggas again," he suggested. "That's an easy hustle."

"Look at me, Brick," Misty said through clenched teeth. He didn't look up. "Look the fuck at me!" she yelled.

Prompted by her tone, Brick looked her directly in the eye. Curled, naked in a chair, Misty glared at him, making him squirm for a few uncomfortable moments. "How long have I been looking out for you—for us?" she asked with strained patience.

"A long time," he muttered.

"How long!" she shouted.

"Since we were kids."

"Don't you think by now, I know what's best for us?"

Brick nodded.

"Do you know how fuckin' stupid you sound, talkin' about robbing mufuckas? First of all, that shit is illegal. I don't know about you, but I'm not planning on doing any more time. Second, robbing niggas only brings in a coupla dollars—it's unpredictable employment. I'm not psychic and neither are you. I can't point out a mufucka and calculate how much he's carrying in his pocket or how much loot he can withdraw from the ATM machine. But the hustle we got going on is bringing in a lot of cheese. I have a master plan that's gonna have us rolling in dough. But you have to cooperate."

"I will," he agreed.

"I'm gonna put up a website, featuring you. After I get that going, we'll be counting so much IRS-can't-tax money, we'll have to hire somebody to set up an offshore bank account for us."

Horror covered Brick's face. "You wanna put me on a website?"

"Do you know how many people we could reach, if your King Kong dong was presented online? The way we're handling things is requiring a whole lot of unnecessary legwork. Once I get the website poppin', the sky's the limit," she said proudly.

"I don't like that idea, Misty."

Misty was momentarily silent. Seething, she looked at him

through narrowed eyes. "Oh, really? I guess you forgot where you came from."

"I didn't forget."

"Nigga, who took up for you when the kids teased your ass in school?"

"You did," he mumbled, looking pained by the unpleasant and harsh shove down memory lane.

"And who was standing next to you, cheering like a fuckin' Laker Girl, the first time you had the heart to go upside a nigga's head?"

"You was, Misty, baby. You gave me the nerve to crack niggas' heads."

"I damn sure did," she snarled. "You were scared of your own shadow until I made you believe you could whip everybody's ass." She stared at him for a few moments. "Did I lie?"

"No, you ain't lie."

"How did me and you—two fourth-graders—manage to beat middle-school niggas out of their lunch money?"

"'Cause you gave me my heart," Brick admitted, looking resigned to having his image posted on a website.

On a rant, Misty sucked in a big burst of air. "So, how come when I got locked up two years ago you couldn't do shit for me or for your damn self? You almost starved to death when I got popped. But as soon as I got out, we started eating again, didn't we?"

Brick nodded, head held low. "True dat. You right."

"I hate to talk about Shane—God rest his soul—but Shane was supposed to be your boy—your best friend, but he didn't look out for you. Shane was all about self—" Misty paused and swallowed. "The only other person he gave a fuck about was his twin, or so he claimed, but after what he did to Tariq, we now know Shane only cared about Shane." Misty and Brick both went silent as they mused over the night Shane Batista's twin brother, Tariq, was hit by a car and killed after witnessing Shane in bed with his wife, Janelle. Shane lost his mind and was never the same.

Misty shook the memory away. "While I was doing that bid, you were ass-out, with nobody you could depend on." Though she talked harshly of Shane, in her heart, she held no ill will toward him. In fact, she hated having to drag Shane's name through the mud just to get through Brick's thick skull.

True, Shane was selfish as hell at times, but he also had a sweet, giving side. To know him was to love and hate him—it depended on how he wanted you to feel. If Shane Batista wanted something—he turned on the charm. If he didn't need shit from you, he gave you his ass to kiss, which was why Misty had fallen hard for him, and had loved him until the day he died. Despite everything, she'd always believed that Shane loved her, too. It was a heartbreaking, soul-wrenching discovery, when Misty found out that Shane had knocked up and married some goodie-two-shoes named Kapri.

Later, when she learned that he'd gotten a divorce and had turned around and married his dead brother's ugly-ass wife, she'd damn near had a nervous breakdown.

When she'd heard that Shane had committed suicide, she was distraught over the loss of that good dick. *Oh, well. Rest in peace, Shane.* Misty returned her thoughts to the present, and gave Brick a scathing look.

"I've been carrying your weight too many years for you to tell me that I'm making a bad decision. One thing I can't stand is an ungrateful nigga."

Brick abandoned the bed-making task and approached the chair where Misty sat. "I'm sorry for questioning your decisions and for acting ungrateful. I know we gotta eat, baby. I'm real sorry."

"Yeah, we gotta eat steak and seafood. Fuck Ramen damn noodles," Misty added with laughter.

Looking pleased that he'd been able to lift her spirits, Brick threw in, "Yeah, fuck Ramen Noodles *and* Cheese Curls."

"That's not funny, Brick. Why'd you have to bring up Cheese Curls? You always gotta fuck up my mood." Her facial expression turned angry; her tone, resentful.

Brick stared at her, wide-eyed. "What did I do?"

"Why you gotta talk about prison food? Damn! You know how much I despise being reminded of that mess I had to eat while I was in jail." She shook her head. "Ramen Noodles and Cheese Curls!" Misty repeated, grimacing as she spat out each word. She cut her eyes at the partially made bed. "Why is it taking so long to change the sheets?"

CHAPTER 3

Misty pushed the gear into reverse.

"You're too lazy to help me with these bags and you're trying to pull off before I'm all the way out of this big, overpriced contraption," Thomasina Bernard complained as she tried to maneuver out of the BMW X5. She held a large shopping bag in each hand.

Misty looked at her fingernails, ignoring her mother's hint for assistance. Nobody told her mom to go buck wild at the Dollar Store. She fiddled with the rearview mirror. Even with the seat adjusted to its highest level, Misty had to sit on a pillow to get a clear, unobstructed view. She'd bought the truck a little over a week ago. It was fully loaded with all kinds of fly gadgets, but she hadn't had time to look through the owner's manual to figure out how everything worked. Having to get Brick back and forth to his appointments and constantly ripping around, taking her mother on endless errands, cut into her free time.

Thomasina slammed the door. "Don't forget about my hair appointment tomorrow morning."

How long did her mother think she was going to mooch off her for transportation? Misty twisted her neck in disgust. "Dang, Mom. Can I get a break from playing chauffeur?" She shook her head. "I'm busy all day tomorrow; you're gonna have to call a cab or take the bus."

"Take the bus!" Offended, Thomasina glared at her daughter through the open passenger window.

Unfazed by her mother's scathing look, Misty sucked her teeth. "I didn't buy this whip so I could cart you all around Philly. You're starting to run shit in the ground."

"Watch your mouth," Thomasina cautioned. "I'm your mother; don't use foul language around me."

"I'm just saying…"

"The registration and insurance card on this truck are both in my name. Neither you nor that dumb Brick has a job or driver's license. If either one of y'all get behind the wheel, drunk or high off that mess you smoke all the time…if you ram into somebody's car, or God forbid, if you run some poor soul over, I'm the one whose going to have to pay a lawyer to unravel the mess."

Misty rolled her eyes. "Why do you always think…?"

Thomasina cut off her daughter's words. "Somebody better do some thinking because you and that ignoramus, Brick, don't know how to do anything except spend money and get high. Let me remind you, Misty, I could lose my home and all possessions because I tried to help your unemployed behind out. Now that you have transportation, do you mean to tell me that you're too selfish to take some time out for your own mother?" Thomasina closed her mouth. She closed her eyes tight and shook her head, as if she were too pained and too overwrought to speak another word.

Misty let out a frustrated sigh. As usual, her mother was being overly dramatic. Thomasina Bernard was gainfully employed with good credit. Misty had promised to provide her with transportation if her mother agreed to put the truck in her name. But Misty had never dreamed her mother's signature on the dotted line would go to her head and make her start acting like she was the primary owner of the luxury SUV.

"This ain't working out, Mom."

Her mother put her heavy shopping bags down on the concrete pavement. Taking in deep breaths, she folded her arms tight. "I guess you want me to call that car dealership and tell that salesman that I changed my mind…you want me to tell them to bring a tow truck and come get this gas-guzzler?"

Misty sucked her teeth. "That's not what I meant. Look, I don't like getting up in the morning. I'm not a morning person and you know it." Misty's shoulders heaved in frustration. She leaned toward the passenger window. "Here, Mom. Take this."

Thomasina stuck her hand in the window. Misty pressed three folded ten-dollar bills into her mother's palm. "Call Mr. Johnnie; he'll give you a ride to the hair salon. For ten bucks, he'll take you there and pick you up when you're ready." Mr. Johnnie was the neighborhood hack.

Thomasina appraised the folded money and then begrudgingly stuffed it inside her handbag. "I don't see why I have to ride to the hair salon in Johnnie's dusty clunker after I took a whole day off from work and sat up in that car dealership, signing one stack of papers after another. You and that no-good Brick are riding around in style and y'all expect me to get around the best way I can. If it came down to me having to stick my thumb out and hitchhike my way here and there, you two selfish asses wouldn't give two shits." Breathing hard, Thomasina rolled her eyes at her daughter.

Hoping to put an end to her mother's tirade, but not wanting to be so rude as to pull off while her mother was still lecturing, Misty turned the volume up a notch, preferring to hear TI rant in his sexy Southern drawl. But Thomasina wasn't having it. She got back inside the X5, reached over and politely adjusted the volume so she could be heard, loud and clear. "Don't get all biggity with me. I'm talking and you're gonna listen."

Misty jerked her shoulders in disgust, but remained in the parking spot. Her mom had missed her calling; she should have been a travel agent and earned some dough from all the guilt trips she loved sending her daughter on.

"You're sweet as honey when you want something, but you're mean as a snake after you get it. That's a very unattractive trait, Misty. When you get down to it, I'm the only person in this world that's going to stick by your side, come hell or high water."

"I know you love me, Mom, but I don't have time to listen right now. I have a lot on my agenda."

"I guess your agenda includes rushing down to that block where Brick sells drugs?"

Misty sighed deeply. "Brick does not sell drugs."

Thomasina snorted. "Well, the way you two are throwing money around, he's got to be hustling something. How the hell did two unemployed, trifling people come up with all that cash money to put down on a truck that costs more than my little row home? Neither one of y'all could come up with one single pay stub to show that car salesman. So, how are you planning on keeping up on the payments that cost more than all my monthly bills put together? Huh, Misty. You must think I'm some kind of a fool. I don't know what you two are into, but I know it's not legal."

"You getting senile or something?" Misty asked, seizing the opportunity to make her mother wince. Her mom didn't like being reminded of her age.

"Senile! I'm only forty-two years old. I'm nowhere near being senile."

"Well, maybe all that hot flashing is making you forgetful," Misty snarled.

"What hot flashing? Menopause is ten years or more down the road. Stop trying to speed up the process."

"Well, you should stop acting like you're old and helpless." Misty paused in thought. "I know what your problem is—you need a man. You know, a new boyfriend—somebody to run you all over creation."

Misty smiled; she'd struck another nerve. Her mom was still feeling the pain from a breakup with her most recent man, Mr. Victor. Old dude bounced and went back to his wife about a month ago. Her mom had been trippin', acting evil, ever since the breakup. Frankly, Misty couldn't imagine shedding a tear over some old dude like Mr. Victor. Dude had that O.J. Simpson-type walk—all bent over and half-crippled, but still trying to inject some old-school cool in every step.

Thomasina was quiet, unable to give a snappy retort. She just huffed up and wiped a few drops of perspiration from her forehead with the back of her hand. Misty smiled to herself. She knew how to break her mother down when necessary.

"Mom," she said with a fake, patient tone. "I told you a million times, Brick is working in construction. He gets paid under the table."

"Uh-huh. Tell me anything." Thomasina pointed her finger at Misty. "You're twenty-three years old and I can't tell you how to live your life." She shook her head. "All that beauty I blessed you with…"

Misty said nothing to dispute her mother, but they both knew her good looks came from her father—Roberto Delagardo—some Latino who'd married her mom, got a green card and then went ghost.

"Girls would give their right arm to be half as pretty as you are, and you're just wasting your looks—running around with that ugly Brick."

Misty checked out her reflection in the rearview mirror. "I still got it going on; ain't nothing changed."

"Looks don't last forever! You served time in prison! You lost six months sitting behind bars." Thomasina snorted. "You sat in jail while that big, ugly mufucka and his friend, Shane, walked around as free as birds. They got you all finagled up in that mess and neither one of them put a dollar on your books." Seething at the memory of her daughter doing time for two grown men caused Thomasina to have to dig inside her handbag, searching for a tissue to mop off the river of sweat that now ran down her face.

Misty smirked. She was the mastermind behind the scam that landed her in jail. But, her mother was right; Shane should have had her back. He should have looked out and made sure there was money on her books. But, Brick…he couldn't do shit; he could barely cross the street without Misty leading the way.

"May his soul rest in peace," her mother continued, "but that Shane was bad news from the start—his pretty-boy good looks didn't fool me. Not for a second. I don't know which one was worse, Shane or Brick…" Thomasina pondered for a few seconds. "I guess Shane was a little better than Brick. Don't get me wrong, that Shane was sneaky as a garden snake, but at least he was handsome. But Brick—" her mother spat out his name. "Ugly and bad; now, that's not a good combination. Shane was rotten through and through—but at least he was easy on the eyes. Like you, Shane had the kind of good looks that distracted people from focusing on his wicked ways."

Misty didn't appreciate her mother dredging up memories of Shane, reminding her of how gorgeous he was. Now, she was going to have to waste more time cruising around the 'hood, looking for somebody who resembled Shane.

Brick was gonna have a fit; he'd already been waiting for the past hour for her to pick him up. "Mom, I'm tryna be nice, but seriously, I gotta roll."

Thomasina inhaled sharply. "The way I kept you dressed, worked two jobs so you could have the best of everything… nobody could have told me…not in a million years, that my beautiful little princess would end up putting her hopes and dreams into a hustler. A big, dumb hustler at that." Thomasina threw up her hands in exasperation. "Brick ain't got a lick of sense, so I don't know how he's handling his business," her mother added scornfully, "but I better not find out that you're out on that block with him. You better not be helping that idiot with his hustle. Mark my words, Misty. He might play like he's half-retarded, but you'll be the one left holding the bag. And the next time you get locked up, I'm not coming to visit and I'm not putting one thin dime on your books. Nope." She folded her arms. "Let Brick take care of you the next time you land in jail."

"The next time? I'm never going back to prison. Are you trying to jinx me or something?" Weary, Misty raked her fingers through her hair. "Are you finished, Mom?"

"No, I'm not finished." Her mother began to wag the finger that was already pointed at her daughter. "Let me tell you something, little lady…if you get knocked up by that scuggly, ugly bear, you better march your tail right to one of those abortion clinics because there ain't a chance in hell that I'm gonna associate myself with a grandchild that's guaranteed to be butt-ugly and retarded. I'd bet good money that Brick can't father nothing but a slew of artistic kids."

"What?" Misty scowled in bafflement.

"You know what I'm talking about. Those artistic kids who won't talk or smile or nothing; they just sit around screaming their heads off if their parents touch 'em or try to show 'em any type of affection."

"You mean autistic," Misty corrected.

"Artistic!" Thomasina insisted. "I saw 'em on a daytime talk show. Those artistic kids can paint and draw; some of 'em can play the hell out of musical instruments—without ever taking a lesson. Trouble is—they don't know when to stop. Them kind of kids can paint and play music for hours on end, if you let 'em. One parent tried to take the paint brush out of her child's hand and the little girl starting screaming like somebody had set her on fire. Now, is that the kind of child you want to bring into this world? Because as sure as my name is Thomasina Bernard, I can guarantee you that any child fathered by Brick is gonna be pitiful looking and it ain't gonna be right in the head." Thomasina tapped her temple for emphasis. "So, I'm letting you know in advance, I'm not babysitting. Don't bring your artistic child over here."

"Rest your mind, Mom. I'm not built to deal with crumb snatchers."

"You don't ever want to have kids? Not even by a good-looking man?" Thomasina's eyes widened as if Misty's admission was unholy. "It's only natural for a woman to want to have at least one child."

"Well, I don't." She smiled at her mother. "Let me help you with those bags," she offered, looking over at the bags sitting on the pavement. Her assistance, however, wasn't an act of goodwill. She desperately wanted her mother to shut up and get out of her whip. Her coochie was throbbing for Shane Batista-type dick.

CHAPTER 4

Aggravation formed in tiny lines across Misty's forehead. Her mother had really worked her nerves. Misty pressed down hard on the gas pedal, fleeing the vicinity of her mother's house. Stressful times like this required a shopping spree or a good fuck. Or both.

She glanced at the time. Too late for shopping; local malls closed at seven. She zoomed down Girard Avenue and made a sharp right onto Parkside Avenue. She zipped past Microsoft's School of the Future with such speed that the ultramodern building became a quick blur. A minute later, she ran a red light and crossed the intersection at Fifty-Second and Parkside Avenue.

Her ring tone blared. Acting like a straight nut, Brick had been making back-to-back calls. She turned off her cell and tossed it inside her purse. Winding the bend on Parkside Avenue, she slowed when she noticed a large crowd and a festive atmosphere outside a city recreation center. The area bustled with activity. It looked like two or three hundred people—men, women, kids— spectators at a late-night, outdoor basketball game.

This special tournament was hosted by the son of an old school baller, some dude who used to play for the Philadelphia 76ers, long before Misty was born. Rumor had it that the son of the old baller had plenty of cheddar and a special affection for Philly. He ran basketball tournaments to show love for the hood rats who weren't getting no brotherly love from the grimy niggas who ran the city—not the black mayor, black congressmen, black city council members, black police commissioner—nobody—none of them niggas gave a shit about anything except getting elected and upgrading their own lifestyles.

From her tinted window, Misty surveyed the situation. On the parameter of the brightly lit basketball court, there was an ice cream truck, bootleg DVD vendors, dudes selling Philly pretzels, young bucks hustling sodas, spring water, Vitamin Water, and cans of brew chilled on ice and stored inside a bright red cooler on wheels. In the midst of the sea of oversized white T-shirts, niggas were hustling an assortment of pharmaceuticals—anything and everything from pills to heroin.

Personally, Misty didn't get down with anything stronger than weed. There'd been a weed drought in Philly lately and the price of the good grade of green stuff was crazy expensive. She did most of her business with a white dude—a college geek. Her connect went to Temple University. The geek had his hustle poppin'. He handled high-grade bud, made deliveries, and his shit came packaged with jokes printed on a label that was sealed on the outside of the cellophane wrapper. The jokes were corny, but they got funny after Misty was sufficiently blunted-up and surrounded by a smoky cloud of the mind-altering drug.

But tonight, after dealing with her mother, she needed some quick, anonymous sex and some weed to help calm her down. No way she could drive all the way to the Northeast to pick up Brick—not the way she was feenin' to get high and get fucked.

She assessed the situation and could tell that these grimy niggas weren't about nothing. The weed and available dick were most likely low-grade.

Misty scanned the crowd. Niggas were out thick. Cars, trucks, scooters, motorcycles, and dirt bikes were everywhere—nowhere to park. Damn! Feeling more agitated by the minute, she drove around in circles, searching for a parking spot. Irritated, she swerved down a sidestreet and parked crookedly in front of a fire hydrant. Fuck it!

Petite and slim and possessing soft features, Misty looked younger than her years. Niggas who didn't know her, always played themselves, thinking she was young and dumb, an easy target—a vulnerable mark. *Sheeet, better think again, mufuckas!*

She pranced across the street, wearing the hell out a tight, denim skirt with ruffles around the bottom and a pink logo Juicy Couture T-shirt that had just hit the stores. Throwing her tiny hips with a vengeance, and holding her face set in a don't-fuck-with-me scowl, Misty stood on the outer circumference of the crowd.

In a matter of seconds, she was surrounded by three young dudes, who looked to be around seventeen…eighteen…nineteen years old at the most. None of the three had been in the game long; she could tell by the look of uncertainty in their eyes. At the end of the night, the three inexperienced foot soldiers would split a meager profit, three ways. *Dumb assholes!*

"Yo, Ma. What's good? My name is Cash Money; you can call me C. Whatchu need?" he asked, gesturing with his hands.

Cash Money was an ashy-looking dude, attempting to appear grown, as he drank from a can of brew covered by a brown paper bag.

Misty disliked him on sight. He needed to rub some shea butter on his mug, his arms, and his ashy elbows. His wrinkled T-shirt was a dingy shade of gray. She felt such disdain for him, she refused to insult her sensitive eyes by shifting her focus to his feet. Against her better judgment, her eyes traveled down to his feet. She sucked her teeth at his trifling sneakers, badly worn down and tilted on a hazardous lean. Misty turned her nose up at Cash Money. "Yo, Ashy Cashy…I don't want nothing you selling!"

"Ashy Cashy!" the other two dope boys repeated, unable to stifle their laughter.

Cash Money gave a shaky laugh, and then looked at his partners. "What I do?" he asked. His arms were outstretched, his facial expression confused and offended.

"You're too grungy-looking for me to deal with," Misty informed him, with a dismissive wave of her hand. "Look at your dingy shirt," Misty said with contempt. "You can buy a bundle of those jawns from the Muslim store for twenty dollars or less. I came through to cop some weed, but if you can't keep your gear up no better than you doing, then you must be slinging garbage."

"Dayum, shawty—chill. Don't hurt 'im," a tall, lanky teen said. His limber body bucked and dipped by strong ripples of laughter that he couldn't hold. "You comin' straight at Troy's neck."

"I can't believe she called Troy, Ashy Cashy," the third member of the trio added.

"Don't be throwing no slurs at me; I don't hustle in my good clothes," C-Money explained. The lack of fire in his tone told Misty he was soft. She sneered at him until he backed up, eyeing Misty warily as if she were an unpredictable pit bull that might get a sudden urge to take a bite out of one of his ashy arms.

"Yo, shawty, go easy on my man. Troy's aiight; he ain't been in the game that long. But fuck all that; I gotchu. Whatchu want—a nic—a dime?"

Licking his wounds, Troy faded farther into the background until he blended in with the masses. The third dude, whose name Misty wasn't interested in knowing, was muscular with a medium build. Definitely not her type, so she ignored him and gave the lanky, handsome, young hustler her undivided attention.

"What's your name?" Misty asked the cute teenager.

"Monroe." He appraised her; interest gleamed in his eyes.

He was a lighter complexion than Shane, but had his height and build. His face was boyish and cute. He didn't have Shane's angular features, his smug attitude, or his dangerous good looks. But, he would have to do. "Let me holla at you in private, Monroe." She turned her back toward muscle boy, indicating that his presence was no longer necessary. But muscle boy stayed posted-up with his bulky arms folded, as if Misty might change her mind and give him some business.

"You wanna get high with me and get in a quick fuck?" Misty posed the question nonchalantly.

Monroe held a straight face. "Yeah, that sounds good."

Misty looked the young buck up and down. His baggy pants hid the size of his jewels, but she sensed by the way he was standing that he knew how to work his back.

Ever since Shane kicked it, Misty had been searching for a replacement. Shane was special and so far, no one had measured up.

Before he lost his damn mind, Shane was her man. He willingly shared her with Brick because he was smooth like that. Brick was leasing the pussy, Shane owned it all: pussy, mouth, titties. And when asked for access to her asshole, she gave up the booty—in the name of love.

Shane used a ton of lubricant, but his inserted hardness hurt like hell. Pain soon turned to pleasure and she began to enjoy it. She had fantasized about having Shane's long, thick dick up her ass while Brick dug out her pussy with his giant dick.

But that fantasy was never realized.

CHAPTER 5

Leaving Muscle Boy and Ashy Cashy behind, Monroe followed Misty across the street. Unhurriedly, Monroe dragged his feet, fronting as if it were an everyday event to be picked up and offered a quick fuck by a fly-ass dimepiece like Misty.

"That's my whip over there." Misty pointed to the small street where her X5 was parked—zigzagged, with two big tires cranked up on the curb and two down on the asphalt street.

Monroe checked out her truck. His mouth relaxed into an easy smile and then stretched into an ear-to-ear grin.

"Yo, this jawn is tight! That was you behind the wheel?" he exclaimed, awestruck. "Me and my boys saw you spin by the court a couple of times. Couldn't see through the tinted windows. We thought the whip was piled up with a bunch of out-of-town niggas, coming through, trying to cut into our business. I had my hand on my heat, ready to spray the windshield with slugs." He laughed.

"Yeah, that's my whip." Her voice held a matter-of-fact tone, but inside she was beaming with pride. "I was driving in circles, trying to find a place to park." She was quiet for a moment. "Yo, there woulda been some serious consequences if one y'all corny niggas shot at me. Shit, all of y'all would be getting bagged up right now, if you woulda put as much as a scratch on my whip."

"You talkin' real gangsta to be such a tiny lil' chick."

"Don't let my looks fool you." She noticed his crew of two, craning their necks, trying to see what she was wheeling. "Too many nosey people around; let's take a ride." Smirking, she dangled her BMW keychain.

"We can stay here. It's cool. Can't nobody see through the tinted windows." Monroe looked over his shoulder, obviously hesitant about putting too much distance between him and his comrades.

Misty ignored him and got inside her truck. Monroe looked over his shoulder, gave the basketball court a lingering look and then got in the passenger seat. Misty reached inside her Juicy Couture bag, took out a bundle. She laughed to herself, as she observed Monroe trying to keep a straight face when he knew he was lusting for some of her paper. "I hope you realize your two boys over there are feelin' some kind of way for being left out. They're feeling jealous enough to turn snitch over a couple bags of weed," she said as she peeled a bill off the top of the stack.

"Naw, they straight; it ain't even that type of party." Monroe darted an eye at the one-hundred-dollar bill. She handed him the money. "Give me five dimes."

"Uh…" He motioned as if he were about to check his pockets, but dismissed the notion. "I don't have change for that," he admitted, embarrassed. "You got anything smaller?"

Sighing, Misty replaced the bill on top of the pile, and then fanned out the money. She located a fifty, passed it to Monroe. She turned the key, revved the engine.

"Aiight, shawty; I'm riding with you. It's your world," Monroe happily conceded.

"You got that shit right." She pressed on the gas pedal. "Roll the blunt while I look for a secluded spot."

"Stop being so bossy!" Monroe tried to frown as he split open the cigar, but feeling pleased with his present circumstances and plush surroundings, his pleasant expression remained in place. He adjusted his seat, reclining it to a position that comfortably accommodated his long legs.

Misty drove a few blocks and then pulled into a deserted street. "You legal?" she asked Monroe, arching her brow.

He scowled and nodded. Insulted, his lips scrunched together as he fired up the blunt.

"You got ID?"

Monroe's scowl deepened. "Who you—5-0 or somebody?"

"I'm not trying to be on *Action News* for molesting a minor."

"You shoulda thought about that before you picked my young ass up." He pulled hard on the blunt. "How old is you?"

"I'm old enough to push this whip." Misty held up her arm in a way that displayed her newly purchased tennis bracelet. "I got five gees draped around my wrist," she boasted. "What else do you wanna know about me?"

"Um…" Monroe paused, looked up, stroking the fine hairs on his chin. "Um…will you marry me?" Both Monroe and Misty burst into laughter. The high was starting to kick in.

"Yeah, we can work something out…" Misty nodded. "When you start ballin' hard enough to put a giant rock on my finger, then we can talk marriage."

Monroe passed the blunt to Misty. "You must think you talkin' to a sucka. I'm the man, shawty," he bragged. "My game is professional. My crew is up in these streets, slinging packs, twenty-four seven. I'm runnin' blocks. "

"You got a crew?" Misty asked. Her lungs filled with smoke, her voice sounded croaky. She slowly released a cloud of smoke. "Who? Ashy Cashy and Muscle Boy?" Misty laughed sarcastically.

"Aw, shit. I'm impressed," she teased. "Nigga, you broke and you know it," she said, her tone suddenly serious. "You ready to hit it?"

"What?"

She tugged up her skirt, revealing a yellow lacey thong. "Backseat or outside—up against that big-ass tree," she said, pointing.

"Outside! You trying to get us both arrested for indecent exposure?"

"I thought you said you was all gangsta and shit."

"In training," he admitted with laughter. "I might need some schoolin.' For real, though…how old are you? 'Bout twenty-three…twenty-four?"

"Twenty-three."

Monroe nodded. "I thought you were about my age, but I should have known by the way you carry yourself, that you were an older woman."

Misty yanked her skirt back down. "You make it sound like I'm pushing thirty or something. You must be underage. Show me some damn ID, or you can walk your ass back to the court."

Smiling embarrassingly, Monroe dug in his pocket and pulled out a Pennsylvania State ID. Misty switched on the interior lights. "Oh, aiight, nineteen—you're legal." Satisfied, she slid into the backseat, fumbled around in one of the rear seat compartments. "Can you fit a Magnum or do you need something smaller?" she asked, after locating a condom.

"A Magnum? Oh, for sure. I can work with that."

"Prove it."

"I can't right now. You playin' twenty questions; made my jawn go down."

Misty hitched up her skirt again and pulled her thong to the side. "Kiss my coochie. I guarantee you'll get a nice hard-on."

Monroe placed a quick peck on Misty's vagina.

"Nigga, use some tongue. Make it wet, so you can get up in it."

Monroe timidly flicked his tongue against Misty's pussy.

Misty sucked her teeth. "Aiight, you starting to get on my nerves." She pushed his head away.

"Yo, I'm not into that. I ain't come out here to grub on no pussy, y'ah mean?"

"After you get me in the mood, I'll do you," Misty cooed.

"Oh, word?"

She nodded. "I know you're inexperienced…"

"That ain't it. I'm not no sucka; I don't give up head that quick."

"Is that right," Misty said, laughter in her voice. She took her thong off and let it drop on the floor mat. "Sit up and rest your head back, lemme teach you a lil' something."

Monroe got in position, then Misty maneuvered into a half-standing position with her groin pressed against his face.

At first, Monroe proved his lack of experience in cunnilingus by giving a clumsy and overly dramatic performance. The way he groaned and theatrically rolled his face around the unfamiliar territory, it seemed like an audition for a porn flick. Worse, he slobbered so profusely that a messy puddle accumulated in her pubic hairs and began to trail down her thigh.

Annoyed, Misty was about to push his head away and slap a condom on his dick. The abundance of saliva he'd smeared all over her pussy could be used as a lubricant for fucking. *If this youngin' can't fuck, I'm gon' have to put his useless ass out of my whip.*

Quite suddenly and most unexpectedly, Monroe got the hang of giving oral pleasure.

With his tongue now in sync with Misty's body rhythm, Monroe provided hot waves of pleasure that hit her so hard, she had to hold on to the overhead handle for support. His tongue, agile and curious, slipped between her folds and found its way to her bud, licking it hard and rough—the way she liked it. Beneath the harsh tongue lashes, her clit swelled, and extended. He withdrew his tongue. Misty cried out, "Don't stop!"

Exchanging his tongue for puckered lips, Monroe made Misty's body hum—sucking and pulling on her glistening pearl while gliding his long, thick finger in and out of her wet tunnel. The dual stimulation he was giving her quickly became too much to bear. Unable to help herself, Misty lifted a leg and wrapped it around his neck, pressing her coochie against his lips.

Having a newly acquired taste for pussy, Monroe extracted his finger and dug his tongue into her pussy, slurping and licking— trying to lap up every drop of her sweetness.

Misty reached down, feeling his crotch. "Let's see what you're working…" Her words broke off as she found an erection that felt almost as long and thick as her arm.

Misty quickly released his neck from her leg lock. On cue, Monroe lowered his pants. Misty tore open the cellophane wrapper and rolled the condom down over his pulsing, heavily veined erection.

She lowered herself slowly onto his long pole and Monroe immediately went to work, hammering hard and fast into her hot spot. The friction heated up the latex condom; her coochie was on fire. Despite the discomfort, Misty couldn't stop. Every stroke Monroe delivered landed on her G-spot. In less than five minutes, Misty exploded.

After her body tremors settled down, Monroe pulled out. "I gotta take a leak."

"Go 'head," she responded, basking in the afterglow of the powerful orgasm he'd given her.

He eased the condom off and pulled up his pants and got out of the truck. "Give me one minute," he said, giving her a wink that promised that the best was yet to come.

"Go over there somewhere," Misty hollered out of the window and pointed to some bushes. "Don't be spraying piss near my rims."

Monroe urinated on the tree that Misty had earlier suggested they use as a fuck-post. With his fly undone, he approached the truck. A look of shock covered his face when he discovered Misty sitting up front, in the driver's seat, skirt tugged into place, as she repositioned the pillow beneath her butt.

"Whaddup? I wasn't finished!" Frowning, he squeezed what looked like a painful hard-on.

"Your dick's still hard?"

"Yeah. I still got about twenty nuts stored up," he said, cutting her an evil eye.

"That sounds personal. You shoulda got it while you were in it." Unperturbed by Monroe's look of hostility, Misty hummed as she adjusted her mirror, smoothed on lip gloss, and finger-combed her hair. "Where do you want me to drop you off?"

"That's real slimy, yo. How you gon' brush me off like that?"

"Look, I don't have all night to fuck around with you. I got shit to do."

"I had to take a piss!" he explained, frustration causing his voice to rise.

"You shoulda took a piss before you got up in my shit."

"My bad. So, whaddup?" He made a sweeping gesture—palms up, arms outstretched. "I know you ain't gon' try to play me. Be nice. Give up some head or something."

"Nigga, you better kiss my ass!" Misty glowered at Monroe. "I'm not obligated to give you shit. We got down on an equal basis. Nobody told your dumb ass to fuck around on some delay shit.

I didn't play you; you played yourself." Misty turned up one side of her top lip. She glanced at the clock on the dashboard. "Whaddup, youngin'? Are you getting in my whip, or are you planning to walk your ass back to the basketball court?" She gave Monroe a smirking smile.

Realizing that acting sullen wasn't going to prompt Misty to relieve his painful erection, Monroe zipped up his jeans and slid in the seat next to her. "Take me back to the court," he mumbled, frowning.

Misty started the engine.

She cruised along, her thoughts on Brick and getting him more work.

"What you did was real cold, yo. How you gon' get yours and leave me hanging like that?"

His whining and complaining was annoying—he was really starting to piss her off, but determining him too big and too fired up to physically eject from her ride, she decided to forego cussing him out and instead, she turned on the charm. "Can I get a rain check? I'll swing by the court same time tomorrow night, aiight?" She gave him a sweet smile.

Displeased with the proposition, Monroe blew out a deep, frustrated breath.

Fuck you, she thought. "We can get together tomorrow," she said and then touched his arm softly. "Aiight, baby?" She'd thrown in a dash of sugar, just to see if her game was tight.

Monroe gave a reluctant nod and then turned his head toward the window. Just before he looked away, Misty saw a glimmer of hope flicker in his eyes. She had to bite her tongue to keep from laughing. She was just messing with his head when she'd promised him a rain check. *You can wait if you want to; but don't hold your breath!* she thought maliciously.

In less than five minutes, Misty was back on Parkside Avenue. She slammed on her brakes and double-parked next to a Benz. She kept the engine running silently, informing Monroe that she didn't have time for any last-minute chitchat.

"So, uh, I guess I'll see you tomorrow night, right?" he asked glumly as he opened the door to get out. When his two cronies, Muscle Boy and Ashy Cashy, approached, he became suddenly chipper. "Aiight, shawty. See you tomorrow. Be safe!" Monroe added in a cavalier manner after he closed the passenger door.

Oh, no this nigga ain't frontin' for his boys. "Hold up," Misty shouted. Monroe turned around, his eyes sparkled with hope. She reached in the back and scooped up her yellow thong and sent it zinging out the window. Monroe raised his hands reflexively. The thong hit him in the face before dropping into his hands. Monroe gawked at the soft yellow fabric and then turned a puzzled gaze at Misty.

"That's a little something to remember me by," she said scornfully.

"Shawty slapped Monroe in the face with her panties," Ashy Cashy ridiculed, feeling redeemed from the scorn she'd inflicted on him earlier.

Misty sped away. The loud scoffing laughter of Monroe's crew became a distant hum; a murmur in the wind.

CHAPTER 6

Brick was furious. Misty hated it when he mustered the strength to ignore her. However, being much smarter than he, Misty knew she'd come up with an idea that would break his resolve. With her eyes squinted in thought, she stepped out of the shower, prepared to seduce her way back into Brick's good graces.

She towel-dried her hair. No blow-drying tonight. Brick loved the feeling of her long, wet hair being dragged across his body.

"Still mad?" Misty asked as she strolled into the couple's bedroom, wearing just a towel and shaking her wet hair; allowing droplets to land on Brick's bare arms. The pungent aroma of weed filled the air. Brick sat on the side of the bed, puffing on a blunt.

"Yeah, I'm still mad," Brick barked, refusing to suppress his emotions. "And stop flicking water on me." He wiped the moisture beads off his arm.

Too angry to further enjoy his favorite pastime, he dropped the blunt in an ashtray, and then flopped down on the mattress, lying on his back, staring at the ceiling.

Slyly, Misty unknotted the towel. Naked, she straddled Brick. "Let's see if I can do something about all that pent-up anger."

"I'm not in the mood," he grumbled.

Misty gripped Brick's wrists, pulled his arms out at his sides, and pinned the big man down. "You're giving me no choice; I'm gonna have to rape you."

Brick didn't struggle; he didn't even attempt to topple the feisty, little dynamo. "I don't feel like playin'," his voice was low, but unyielding.

"I hate it when you're mad at me," Misty complained, releasing his wrists.

"How do you expect me to feel? I'm not feelin' you, so get up off me before I toss your lil' ass."

"Want some head?" she inquired cheerfully.

Brick snorted. "Hell no, I don't want no more head. My jawn's been sucked enough for one night, but you don't care about that. As long as I'm bringing home money, you don't care what happens to my dick."

"Want your balls licked?"

Brick sighed. "I want you to raise up before I get violent." Brick took deep, angry breaths, his massive chest heaved up and down. "How you gon' leave me out in the fuckin' northeast for two fuckin' hours and then lie about having to take your mother shopping? I called your mom. I know what time you dropped her off. Your lil' ass was probably out on a shopping spree. I think you got a shopping disease."

"Aiight, I lied," Misty admitted. "But I swear, I wasn't out shopping; I didn't buy anything today, I swear."

"Where was you at, then?"

Misty brought her lips close to Brick's ear. "I was on my way to pick you up, but I ran into this fine-ass young buck…" She paused and watched curiosity replace the scowl on Brick's face.

"Uh-huh," he uttered. "And then what happened?" He asked hastily, unable to disguise his interest.

"The way dude was walking, I could tell he had a big-ass dick, so I pulled the whip over and asked him if he wanted to go for a ride." Misty cut her eye at the bulge inside Brick's boxers, which was growing larger with every word that came out of her mouth. "I was so horny, I parked in a dark alley—"

Brick inserted his hand inside the opening of his drawers. He pulled out his manhood, which was rigid and already dribbling pre-ejaculation. "What happened after y'all parked?"

"Um…" She looked up in thought and then started putting together a story. "We started out kissing, then dude bit me on my neck…my legs went on automatic, and started opening up."

"You're just making this shit up. You know you were out shopping."

"For real, Brick. I was out there freakin' with another nigga."

"What was his name?" Brick challenged.

"Um…" She pretended to think. "Um, I didn't even ask him his name and he didn't ask me mine, because it wasn't like that. It was all about lust."

"How big was his dick?"

"Big as shit."

"Big as mine?"

"Bigger. Way bigger. That youngin' was packing about twelve or thirteen inches," she whispered. She aroused Brick even more by dragging her mop of damp hair over his broad chest.

Brick moaned, he stroked his meat, shining up his knob with the oozing pre-cum. "Damn, Misty. You supposed to be my girl and you out there, giving it up like a straight ho, making me wait while you were giving up coochie to a total stranger," Brick accused as he held his growing arousal in his fisted hand.

"I'm sorry. I didn't think it was going to take that long, but that young buck spent about an hour eating out my coochie."

"Umph," Brick grunted lustfully. "Did you give him head, too?"

"Uh-huh," she said, using a tiny, meek voice.

"Did you swallow his seed?" Brick roared. His nostrils flared; the hand movement beneath his boxers ceased as he awaited Misty's response.

"No!" Misty protested.

Instant relief appeared on Brick's face.

"I wanted to," she softly admitted. "I wanted him to nut in my mouth, but I had to be considerate of you."

"So what happened then?"

"Well, you know…taking you into consideration and every-thing, I ended up letting him raw dog my coochie. He busted two big-ass nuts."

Brick gave Misty a hard shove. He glared at her as if he were two seconds from killing her. "You let him fuck you raw?"

Misty nodded.

"And he came twice?"

"Yeah, Brick—he came twice. I wouldn't lie about it."

"So, why'd you come home and jump right in the shower?"

Misty shrugged. "I don't know." She frowned. "Don't be mad—I didn't wash my coochie. You know how I do; I washed every-where else."

Brick's contorted expression relaxed into a smile. "You still filled up with dude's seed?"

"Yeah, I said that I didn't wash my coochie."

"Aiight, then, you better not be lyin'." Brick plumped up a pillow and rested his head. He squeezed his manhood again. "Damn, that shit you talkin' got my jawn hard as a rock." He licked his lips and reached for Misty's hand. "Get over here, girl. Mmm. Squat your ass over my face. Mmm. I can't wait to clean out that nasty, lil' pussy."

Misty had to give herself credit; she was on top of her game. Brick believed the dirty talk she'd whispered in his ear was something made up—nothing more than a freaky, graphically detailed fantasy. Well, what he didn't know wouldn't hurt him.

Misty had led him to believe that she'd been faithful to him ever since Shane's death, but she got her freak on occasionally. Sure, Brick gave her orgasms all the time. But, sexin' dudes who reminded her of Shane was the only way she could bust a heart-pounding, body-convulsing nut.

Playing their game, Brick pressed his nose against her pubis, seeking to get a whiff of a musky, masculine smell.

"What's it smell like, baby?" Misty asked.

"Like sweaty dick."

"You like it?"

Brick sniffed deeply. "Love it." He circled his lips around the opening of Misty's tight tunnel. Stretching the tendons in his tongue, he poked and probed, pretending to search for a sticky glob of another man's cum.

Misty held onto the headboard while she winded her hips. "You'll never find another woman like me. You know that, don't you?" she purred.

"Nevah, baby. Ain't nobody like you," he mumbled against her clit, while his cupped hand frantically worked up and down his steely shaft.

"I always share everything with you," she whispered. "Even while I'm out there, freakin', I always bring a snack home for you."

"Thank you, Misty, baby. I appreciate it." With his face buried between her legs, Brick's voice was muffled.

"Taste good?"

"Real good!"

The combined sounds of Misty's soft feminine moans, Brick's heavy breathing and lapping tongue licks, echoed inside the bedroom.

This session should have been taped. Weirdoes paid good money to listen to dumb-ass shit like the sounds of the ocean, the wind blowing, and falling rain; she was pretty sure there were some perverts out there who would pay to listen to the sounds of pussy-licking. She'd charge extra to allow freaks to view some footage along with the audio.

Yes, in addition to his big dick, Brick had a thick, well-endowed tongue. It was Misty's responsibility to showcase Brick's attributes. If she expected a major come-up, she'd have to take their hustle to the next level. The next step would be to videotape a couple of Brick's sex performances, and feature him on a website so he could get the kind of national exposure he deserved.

Of course, she'd have to record in secret. Brick would get camera shy if he knew he was being filmed. Brick could be such a pain in the ass. Knowing how uncomfortable he was about his hustle, Misty would bet a week's worth of income that his dick would go limp and refuse to get hard if he was aware that a camera was rolling.

Fuck it; she'd worry about that later. Right now, she needed to figure out a way to get this nigga off her. It had been a long day. Monroe had worked her over; her pussy was sore and Brick's rough, hungry tongue was adding more aggravation to the situation.

Misty searched her brain for more sex talk. She needed to come up with some really freaky dialogue that would finish him off.

"The next time me and the youngin' get together, I'm gonna let you watch." Misty waited for Brick's reaction. The sound of his rapid hand movement up and down the length of his shaft indicated he dug the change of script. "You can hide in the closet," she continued, in a husky tone. "Keep the door cracked a little bit, so you can peep what's going on. I know your dick's gonna be rock-hard. You gon' leak like a mufucka when you watch another nigga sliding his thickness up my slit."

Painfully aroused, Brick couldn't concentrate on eating Misty's pussy. Irregular tongue strokes were her cue to dismount his face. She sat beside him and whispered seductively in his ear. "After the young buck shoots his load, you can burst out of the closet and kick his ass for fucking your girl and disrespecting your home. I want you to stomp that nigga—knock him out," she hissed.

Brick groaned in ecstasy.

"While he's out cold, you can wrap your lips around my coochie and suck out his salty nut—get it while it's nice and fresh. Wouldn't you enjoy that, Brick?"

"Aw, yeah. Fucking, yes. Stop teasing me, Misty. Bring that mufucka home." Brick's breathing was harsh; his eyes were glazed over. Too worked up to continue speaking, he could only emit garbled sounds.

Misty smiled with satisfaction; her freaky murmurings were driving him over the edge. Brick was seconds away from spurting.

"Ahhh!" he bellowed as a fountain of hot, white lust shot into the palm of his hand.

Misty smiled proudly. She deserved a pat on the back for being such a creative bitch. She knew exactly what to do and say to dissolve Brick's anger. Keeping him dependent on her to indulge his fantasies was one of the many ploys she used to get him to peddle his flesh several nights a week.

Brick allowed himself to be pimped out, but he made it clear that he wasn't pleased with the situation. He griped and complained endlessly about having to sling dick for a living. All his bitching irked Misty to no end. They were living good—so he needed to save his breath—accept his fate and live his life as a happy ho.

Brick made a guttural cry; he rose into a half-hunch as he squirted out the last drops of semen. A pool of cum overflowed from his cupped hand. Misty shot Brick a reproachful glance. The abundance of the load was proof that he wasn't turning enough tricks. He wasn't working to his full potential.

Misty sucked her teeth and glared at Brick. The tables had turned. Brick no longer had an attitude, but she was one angry-ass bitch.

Wearing an apologetic smile, Brick rushed to the bathroom to wash up.

CHAPTER 7

As warm water washed away the glob of incriminating evidence from his hand, Brick stared intently in the mirror. He caught a glimpse of Misty's picture hanging on the wall behind him. The image was beautiful and erotic. Her long hair was trailing down her back. There was another picture beside it; Misty cupping her small breasts. There were pictures of Misty in every room of the apartment. Her beauty was captured and blown up to poster size. She'd mounted her image on every available space, every wall.

He gazed into the mirror, shifted and zoomed in on his awful image. He cringed at the jagged, face-deforming scar. Suddenly, a fast-moving collage of elementary school photographs traveled across his mind, taking him back to times when he looked normal. He nodded and smiled broadly, warmed by the remembrances of his youthful, undamaged face. He'd been a handsome little guy.

Then, a sneaky, invisible finger hit the fast-forward button on the tape of his life. He heard the sounds, saw the swift images as the imaginary tape swiftly raced to the night that changed his life. Brick flinched when he heard the clunk inside his head that indicated the mental tape had stopped moving, forcing him to flash on a memory that was so cruel, so jarring, it wiped the reminiscent smile from his face.

Sparks of anger glinted in the eyes that stared back from the mirror. He touched the ugly, raised formation of skin. The sparks in his eyes flickered to raging flames. Brick pounded the ceramic-tiled sink and suppressed the urge to scream.

His face had been crudely carved when he was only thirteen years old. Bitter tears wet his eyelashes. Brick used to envision numerous ways to torture the man who'd disfigured him. Unfortunately, he would never get the chance to exact revenge; the mufucka who cut him was already dead. Rivaling drug dealers put two bullets in his head. And that was a goddamn, fucked-up shame.

Misty brought the news when he was locked up in the boys' detention center for selling drugs. He'd taken that fall for Misty. He'd always covered her ass.

"Frankie got shot down like a dog in the street. You shoulda seen it, Brick. He took a bullet in the arm—probably only grazed, but he was crying and crawling around, trying to squeeze between parked cars, but those killas wasn't finished with his ass.

"They came up on Frankie like characters in a gangsta flick. One dude pressed his pistol against Frankie's forehead. Snot was running out Frankie's nose while he was praying, out loud. Then the other dude placed a barrel on the back of Frankie's head. Ya boy, Frankie, started boo hooing, real loud, like a fuckin' bitch. He was pleading for his life. Talked some shit about his mother was on SSI and how she depended on him.

"Yo, the killas was like…pow! pow! Put a bullet in the front and the back of his head at the same time. Frankie hit the ground; boom! He ended up with four holes in his head."

Misty had excitedly relayed the news with the expectation that Brick would experience an immense measure of joy—a feeling of euphoria, now that justice had been served. But, Brick slumped into a depression and hardly spoke for the duration of Misty's hour-long visit. No one would have ever imagined the jolt of disappointment followed by a feeling of utter despair that Brick felt upon learning that Frankie, his torturer, the man who'd disfigured his face, would not die the slow, torturous death he'd planned for the sadistic child molester.

"Frankie the Freak," Brick mumbled as he tried to stop himself from free-falling all the way down memory lane. He braced the sink, trying to stop himself, but he couldn't break the fall. His mind travel exported him back to when the molestation had started.

Frankie counted the money that Brick had given him. With a cigarette clenched between his teeth, smoke swirling upward, Frankie cocked his head to the side. "You came up short, again, Lil' Playa." His voice held a solemn warning.

"I know—" Brick gave Frankie an uneasy smile and then looked down at his sneakers. "I'ma make up that money with my next package."

"Who said you gon' get another package? Why should I keep on letting you fuck up my money?"

Brick didn't have an answer for that question, so he shrugged, which turned out to be the wrong answer.

Frankie snorted. "Oh, it's like that? You all nonchalant and don't give a fuck about my money?"

"Nah, I meant to say, I'm sorry and it won't happen…"

"Too late!" Frankie said, cutting off the last word of Brick's apology. Anger flashed in his eyes. "You took something from me, so it's only fair that I should take something from you. Ain't that right, Lil' Playa?"

Brick nodded uncertainly.

"Aiight, then, come on downstairs." Frankie nudged his chin toward the door that led to the basement. "We need some privacy to settle this debt."

Brick's eyes darted in alarm and settled on the sliding bolt on the front door that Frankie had locked in place after Brick had entered.

Frankie yanked him by the arm. "Lil' nigga, I'll break your mufuckin' neck if you try to unlock that door. Do you think I'm gon' let you run out of here, without paying your debt?" He smacked Brick upside the head. "Bring your ass on!" Sending a prayer to the man above that Misty would realize that it was time to take some kind of action, Brick inched toward the basement door that Frankie now held open.

Certain that he was about to be badly maimed or even killed, Brick trembled as his captor led him down the stairs to a dimly lit, unfinished basement.

At the bottom of the stairs, Brick took just a few steps. Hoping for an opportunity to make a run for it, he didn't want to venture too far from the stairs. He stood near the hot water heater, with his hands in his pockets, shifting from one foot to the other.

"Aiight, lemme see what you got." Frankie took a deep puff of the cigarette.

"I ain't got nothing. I swear, Frankie; I gave you all the money I had. Me and Misty can get the rest of the money for you, by to-morrow. For real!"

Frankie tossed the burning cigarette butt on the concrete floor and ground it out with the sole of his boot. "I know you ain't got no money," he growled in disgust. "Look, I don't have a lot of time to play around with you. Now, like I said, you took something from me and I'm gon' take something from you."

Brick had no idea what he had that could be of value. If this was a movie, this would be the scene where blood was spilled. His blood. "Frankie, please…"

"Shut the fuck up!" Frankie demanded. "Pull down your pants." Frankie gestured impatiently.

Positive he'd misunderstood the command, Brick scowled and said, "Huh?"

"Pull your pants down, man; I ain't got time to play with you."

Brick was greeted with a terrifying image of Frankie demanding him to bend over so he could viciously whip his bare ass with a razor strap, a wet ironing cord, or a rusty hanger. He was used to normal ass-whoopings. At home, his foster father had been delivering a leather strap to his ass ever since he was six years old.

But Frankie looked like he had something *extra* in mind. "Why you want me to take down my pants?" Brick stammered.

Frankie's voice boomed like thunder. "Nigga, pull your pants down, so I can suck that young dick!" Frankie's face was a twisted mask of fury.

Brick stared at him, his mouth wide open. Speechless.

Bam! Frankie punched him in the chest, knocked him across the room. Brick fell up against a washing machine.

"Come on, mufucka, throw up your hands! You wanna fight me over your manhood? Come on, let's do it." Tauntingly, he beckoned Brick to try to take him on. Grinning with confidence, Frankie started dancing around like he was Mike Tyson or Muhammad Ali.

In the schoolyard, Brick was the undefeated champ, but there was no way he could go toe-to-toe with a twenty-five-year-old grown man, who flexed boulder-sized muscles that he'd started sculpting while serving time in jail.

But, he could sneak him! Brick threw a wild sucker punch which, unfortunately, did not connect. Laughing cruelly, Frankie hit Brick with a gut shot. Clutching his stomach, Brick gasped and heaved. Frankie waited patiently for Brick to catch his breath.

"Lemme help you out, Lil' Playa," Frankie said, after Brick stopped gasping. He unbuckled the belt around Brick's waist.

Terrified and in disbelief, Brick stood numb with fear while Frankie unzipped his pants. Where the hell was Misty, he wondered. It was her greedy ass who'd gotten him into this mess in the first place. She was outside, hiding in the bushes, supposedly on alert to take some type of action if Brick was in Frankie's house for more than fifteen minutes. Didn't she realize he'd been in there with Frankie for about a half-hour? Why didn't she throw a rock at the window or go knock on a neighbor's door and try to get some adult help?

Brick sighed resignedly as he felt his pants fall past his knees. Knowing Misty, she was out there peeking inside her shopping bag, admiring her new pair of Gucci sneakers—the reason they had come up short. Yeah, Misty was out there gazing at her new sneakers and had lost all track of time, Brick sadly concluded.

Impatient, Frankie stuck his big hand inside the opening of Brick's boxer drawers. "Goddamn, mufucka!" Frankie chortled gleefully. "You ain't even hard yet, and your young ass dick is hanging long. You hung like a damn horse," he praised. "After I swallow your white sap, I'll probably be able to bench press about three hundred pounds or more."

Huh? Brick almost said out loud, but not wanting to rile Frankie into dispensing more body blows, he wisely contained the curious murmur. With his dick hanging free, a confused Brick watched Frankie meander over to a wicker clothesbasket. He pulled out a yellow bandanna.

He's gonna strangle me and chop my dick off after he sucks it!

"You don't need to see nothing." Frankie's voice was a low growl as he blindfolded Brick.

"See, everybody don't know about this trick. I learned it while I was in prison," Frankie revealed, slowly lowering his body. "Drinking the white sap from a young dude gives a man extra energy. White sap is more potent than eating raw eggs; it's a real power boost."

Being deprived of sight and Frankie's warm breath breezing through his pubic hair was sending Brick into a state of trauma. His body shook uncontrollably. "Calm down, Lil' Playa," Frankie said and then ran a moist tongue up Brick's semi-soft shaft. The next sensation was Frankie's puckered lips pulling on the head of his dick, teasing it into an erection. "Yeah, that's what I'm talkin' about," Frankie murmured when he brought Brick to a full erection. "I ain't no faggot or nothing, so don't get it twisted. I suck dick to build muscles and get more strength."

No matter how he rationalized it, what Frankie was doing wasn't right. Brick strained and groaned, tried to command his penis into going soft, but his dick betrayed him. Becoming an agreeable offering, his phallus hardened and lengthened inside Frankie's mouth. Moments later, a rush of unexpected excitement caused Brick's arms to flail. At first he gripped the sides of the washing machine, and then, without meaning to, he cupped Frankie's head. His body was going crazy on him. He couldn't make it stop. His back, his legs, his groin, thrust forward, assisting in pushing his dick deeper inside Frankie's moist mouth.

❧❦

Frankie removed the bandanna after he swallowed Brick's cum.

"Umph," he grunted as he licked his lips. "I ain't never sucked off no white sap from a juvenile before." Frankie furrowed his thick brows. "How old are you?"

"Thirteen," Brick mumbled, feeling deeply ashamed.

"Thirteen! Hot damn, that's what's up! I feel strong as a damn ox already!" Wearing a fierce expression, Frankie bobbed and weaved, jabbing the air if he were in the ring with a difficult opponent. Looking over his shoulder as he continued to shadow-box, Frankie told Brick, "Aiight, Lil' Playa, fix your clothes and take your ass home. I'm 'bout to go out and collect some money. I'm gon' fuck some shit up if niggas be playin' with my cheddar. I ain't for that shit tonight."

Brick quickly obeyed, zipping up his pants, and tightly buckling his belt. He felt unclean. Unconsciously, he smoothed down his hair, as if a neat appearance would make him presentable and perhaps undo the sordid deed.

"So, uh, the next time you come up short, you know what it's hitting for," Frankie warned. "You gon' have to look out for me, health-wise, you know what I mean?"

Brick nodded but promised he would never come up short again. It didn't matter that getting head from Frankie gave him a rush like nothing he'd ever felt before—what he'd allowed Frankie to do was unnatural and nasty. It was a shameful secret, and he vowed to take that secret to his grave.

CHAPTER 8

But, the secret had been revealed. Misty had been peering through a dusty basement window; she'd witnessed the obscene act with disgust and fascination.

When Brick came outside, she ridiculed him. Disregarding the humiliation that shone in his wounded eyes, unconcerned that he'd endured Frankie's wrath to protect her, Misty maliciously hit him with one low blow after another. "How long you been freakin' with Frankie? I can't believe you been a homo all this time!" she shouted, gleeful that she'd uncovered a shameful secret.

"I'm not a homo. Frankie made me do it!" Brick shouted.

"It didn't look that way to me. Your eyes were squeezed up all tight, gripping his head, grinding all on his face. I guess it's over for me and you. You go with Frankie now. Looks like you done fell in love with Frankie," she taunted.

"I don't go with Frankie. I ain't gay. I still go with you. You know, you're still my girl," Brick said in a pleading voice.

"Faggots have jelly babies. You gon' marry Frankie, if one of y'all ends up pregnant?" Misty asked, and then emitted cackling laughter. She didn't cease the torrent of cruel insults until Brick was reduced to sobs.

And violence. In a burst of rage, Brick clutched her by the collar, shook her until her teeth rattled. His face was filled with such blazing fury, he was unrecognizable. "I took that fall for you!" he bellowed like a wounded animal. "How you gon' turn on me, when you the reason why this happened to me?" Brick's voice boomed, his emotional pain rang out with every word. "I'll kill your lil' ass if you ever tell anybody about this."

Stunned, Misty was briefly silent. Brick had never threatened her before, but he looked and sounded serious. "I'm sorry, Brick," she said insincerely. "I was just playing. I won't tell anybody; I promise."

Brick dried his tears with the back of his hand.

"So, what was up with the blindfold?" Misty asked after Brick had gotten control of his emotions. "You looked crazy, serving dude with a blindfold on," she said with a chuckle.

Brick sighed. "Leave me alone, Misty. I don't wanna talk about it, aiight?" Hurt and frustrated, he kicked a stone.

But Misty persisted. "Tell me, Brick, come on," she cajoled.

"Frankie said a real man won't let another man look at him while he's looking out for his health."

"What!" Misty said in a shrill tone.

"Forget it, Misty. I don't feel like talking right now. I'll explain tomorrow. It's late; I gotta get home. You know how my foster father is. Mr. Rodney's probably sitting in his chair, waiting with his belt. I know he's mad as hell. He forgot to whip my ass yesterday. I hope he's so drunk, he forgot about it. After all this, I can't deal with two days' worth of his leather belt."

❧◌❧

Misty never told a soul. It benefited her to keep Brick's secret. And due to Misty's spending habits, the two adolescents continued to come up short and Brick continued to pay Frankie back with his strength-yielding, white sap.

Frankie seemed content with the agreement until the day Misty went buck wild at the Gallery Mall and fucked up the money from an entire package.

"White sap ain't gon' get it, this time, Lil' Playa," Frankie told Brick grimly. Brick, sorting through the pile of laundry inside the wicker basket, searching for the blindfold, looked up at Frankie in bewilderment. "Look at yourself," Frankie spewed. "You digging through that basket of dirty clothes, all desperate, like a dog looking for a bone. You feenin' for this bone—" He crudely stroked his privates. "Bad as I want to, I can't freak with you no more. You done turned sweet, mufucka," Frankie accused, sounding personally offended.

"No, I'm not. I'm not sweet," Brick mumbled in protest.

"Yeah, right!" Frankie scrunched his face in disgust. "Check this out…me, myself—I do what I do for health reasons. I gotta keep my strength up," Frankie explained, poking himself in the chest, "But you—" Frankie shook his head. "I know young bucks don't handle business right. Figured you were trying to be a man about messing up my cash flow—stepping up and doing the right thing."

"I do try to do the right thing. That's why I get down with you, Frankie. I step up to the plate like a man. I give you my white sap to keep you strong. I'm looking out for your health, for real, Frankie." Brick gulped in fear.

Frankie sneered. "Yeah, that shit you talkin' sounds all heroic, but somewhere along the line you done developed a bad habit. When I think back—the way you were so willing to give up your white sap…the more I think about it, the more I realize that you was already sweeter than a Fruit Loop before I started taking your strength."

"Nah, I never got down with a dude before. I had to look out for my girl. Misty's got a real bad habit. She can't help herself. She gotta shop."

"Oh, yeah? Ya girl been stealing my product?"

"No, she don't smoke crack. She got a shopping habit. I swear, she can't help it. She gotta shop all the time."

"Nigga, please. Ain't no such thing as a damn shopping habit. You probably helping her fuck up that money, just so you can get your dick sucked." Frankie shook his head. "Here I am, thinking I'm teaching you something beneficial that you could use later on in life, and the whole time, I was dealing with a young homo. Nigga, I ought to whip your ass for lying to me. Now that you done turned completely gay, your white sap can't help me no more."

"I'm not gay!"

"Whatever. Tuck your shit back in your pants because I don't want it. Drinking white sap from a faggot could mess my system up, have me sickly and weak as a little bitch."

Hurt and confused, Brick lowered his head and slowly adjusted his pants. A few seconds later, Frankie advanced and yanked Brick into a headlock. "You gon' pay for tricking me into fuckin' with your sissy ass."

"I didn't trick you. I'm not a sissy. I'm straight." He croaked out the words. Gagging and gasping, he fought to break Frankie's chokehold, but couldn't. Though Frankie claimed Brick's white sap was tainted, had made him weak, he seemed to possess the strength of ten men as he crushed Brick's face against his bulging bicep.

With his free hand, he dug inside his pocket and whipped out a gleaming knife. Brick went into a wild panic. To no avail, he desperately struggled to pull his head out of Frankie's steely embrace. As if testing the sharpness of the blade, Frankie punctured the skin on Brick's chin. Satisfied, he plunged the knife in, twisting it, brutally chipping chinbone as he pushed it in deeper.

Brick bellowed in agony. Frankie pulled the embedded knife upward, viciously tearing through flesh and chipping at bone. In a state of shock, Brick went limp. He didn't hear the horrible sounds of his cheekbone crunching and cracking. He didn't feel the hot blood splash out over his arms and clothing as Frankie brutally ripped open his face, zigzagging the knife from his chin all the way up to his hairline.

"Brick!" Misty shouted from the bedroom, her shrill voice bringing Brick back to reality. "How long does it take to wash up? Turn that water off, so I can get some sleep!"

Brick pulled his hand away from the curving scar and turned off the water. Tears blurred his monstrous, mirrored image. Frankie had not only fucked up his face, he'd also succeeded in messing up Brick's head; distorting his sexual identity.

Frankie had claimed Brick was gay. Brick didn't know what category he belonged in. Constantly plagued by freaky urges that involved men, Brick decided that although he wasn't totally straight, he wasn't totally homosexual either. He could back up that claim, too.

Sure, he allowed men to suck his dick and, yes, he engaged in sexual fantasies that revolved around men, but he had never performed or had been on the receiving end of anal sex with a man. As much as Misty badgered him and had tried to persuade him to give up some head to clients in order to increase their earnings, Brick flat-out refused.

A few years back, she'd bugged him about showing Shane some love; pleading with him to do it for her. She'd badgered him so badly that Brick finally broke down and agreed to it. But when she threw Shane some hints, Shane had frowned up, clearly appalled. After that, it seemed that Shane had gone out of his way to avoid Misty and Brick.

If Shane hadn't slit his wrists and taken himself out the way he did, Brick was certain that Misty's determined ass would have figured out a way to convince Shane to let Brick suck his dick. Truth be told, Brick would have done it. Misty was in love with Shane and Shane was his nigga. Shane was the only man that Brick would have even considered blowing.

Brick pondered his sexual orientation for a few more moments and came to the conclusion that neither Misty nor any other woman who'd ever sucked on his jawn could give head as well as a man could. *But that's just the freak in me. I ain't no Fruit Loop!*

"Brick!" Misty yelled again. "Bring a washcloth so you can wipe out all this slobber you left between my legs."

"Aiight!" Brick opened the linen closet and sorted through a stack of colorful folded washcloths and selected a pink, fluffy one, which was monogrammed with fancy lettering spelling out Misty's name.

Lovingly, he ran warm water over the expensive fabric and squeezed a few dollops of Misty's favorite body gel. He'd clean her coochie slowly, tenderly—the way she liked it—until he lulled his pretty baby to dreamland.

"Here I come, Misty, baby," Brick said, wearing a ready smile. He was pussywhipped and proud of it. His devotion to Misty's coochie was evidence that Frankie the Freak had not turned him gay.

CHAPTER 9

The day was passing peacefully. No tricks were lined up that evening and Misty had left him with a large quantity of weed—her way of appeasing him while she hijacked their only source of transportation, leaving him housebound for the day.

Misty was on yet another day-long shopping spree. She was on a binge again. Shopping every day, buying up the stores, but she still wasn't satisfied. Most times, she returned home weighed down by shopping bags that she tossed in the closet without even admiring her purchases.

Sometimes, she mistakenly bought the same item twice. Brick didn't mind, though. He enjoyed the solitude. Nothing soothed his soul like being able to fall back, undisturbed all day. He loved Misty to death, but having her out of the apartment was heaven. If he didn't keep her fucked and sucked several times a day, she'd talk his ear off about her latest idea for him to make them more money. Her constant plotting on new ways to market his dick made his head hurt sometimes.

Last night, he'd fucked her extra long and extra hard, using his penis to wear her out and put her to sleep. Just before conking out, she kissed him and dreamily told him she was going to make him an internet porn star. Even in the state just before slumber, Misty was on top of her pimp game, hinting that she'd like to film him in action. He wasn't even worried about it, though. It didn't matter how big his dick was or how long he could last, nobody would pay to watch a porn flick with a disfigured star.

Blissfully, Brick watched hours of daytime TV, rented a couple pay-for-view flicks, and rolled one blunt after another, puffing away until his appetite became ravenous.

True, he loathed tricking, but admittedly his thick inches kept him and Misty rolling in enough greenbacks to meet their needs. And his needs were quite basic. Food, weed, and brew on a daily basis plus a pair of sneakers, a pair of Timbs, a new pair of jeans, every now and then. Brick wasn't into flashy jewelry. In fact, he didn't wear any type of jewelry; not even a watch. Misty rocked so much bling, Brick was satisfied to bask in the illumination of her shine. Brick smiled. Just standing next to his pretty little Misty was a major come-up in his life.

After all these years, he still felt honored to be in her presence. He didn't even mind when Misty openly flirted with other dudes.

"What about him?" dudes would ask whenever Misty flirted in Brick's presence.

"Oh, that's Brick. He's my bodyguard," she'd reply, looking and sounding like an A-list star. On cue, Brick would assume a severe expression and the wide-legged stance of a bodyguard.

Going along with Misty's public role-playing games always assured him of a night of freaky passion. He had to give her major props. Misty was dat bitch; in and out of bed.

A loud growl from his stomach interrupted his musings. Brick called a local deli and ordered a smorgasbord of greasy food.

When the doorbell rang, Brick rubbed his hands together and delightedly opened the door. The delivery person stood in the doorway, heavily laden with a large pizza and three large paper bags filled with side orders. "Hey, my man. What it is? Yo, cuz, you got here quick as shit. That's whassup!"

Happily, Brick unburdened the delivery man of the packages.

Overdosing on weed and food and groggy from too much beer, Brick fell asleep on the living room sofa. The blare of the house phone jolted him awake.

"Damn!" he muttered and reached for the handset, a bleary eye focused on the caller ID. *Thomasina Bernard.* "Aw, fuck that!" he growled. He had no rap for Misty's loud-mouth mom. If Miss Thomasina wanted to speak to her daughter, she'd better hit Misty up on her cell. If Misty didn't pick up, that meant she didn't feel like talking to her right now. Just hearing Miss Thomasina's voice would wreck the remainder of Brick's peaceful day. Following his better judgment, Brick turned off the ringer and curled back into his spot on the sofa. Two minutes later, the muffled but annoying sound of the telephone emanated from the bedroom.

He sat up and stared at the mute phone in the living room. *What the fuck is up with Miss Thomasina?* Maybe something had happened to Misty! Sudden apprehension caused Brick to lunge for the phone. "Hello!" he said urgently.

"Where the hell is Misty?" Thomasina barked into the phone.

Irritated, Brick blew out a whoosh of air. "She ain't home."

"Well, where the hell is she?" Thomasina asked sharply.

"Shopping." Brick's emotionless, one-word response was certain to rile Misty's mom.

"Tell me something I don't know, genius," Thomasina snapped. "Misty picked me up after work. She dropped me off at my line-dancing class and was supposed to come back and take me shopping after my class."

Brick screwed up his lips. He didn't appreciate hearing that Misty's hateful mom was benefiting off his hustle, too. *I'm not good enough for her daughter but my money's good enough for her to spend.*

He wanted to say something sarcastic, but Misty wouldn't

appreciate him disrespecting her mother. Wisely, Brick decided to suck it up and let it ride. Besides, Miss Thomasina's taste wasn't anywhere near as expensive as Misty's. She couldn't break the bank.

"I've been waiting for an hour and twenty minutes. Where could that girl be?"

Deep in unpleasant thoughts, Brick frowned as he ran a finger over his thick scar. It wasn't like Misty to leave her mom stranded. If somebody had hurt his pretty baby, he'd shoot a mufucka, strangle him with his bare hands, stomp a nigga to death. Brick shook his head as a succession of murderous thoughts galloped across his mind.

"Are you going to help me come up with a solution or do you plan on breathing in the phone like a moron?" Thomasina said with chilling hostility.

"Uh, I'll hit her up on her cell and see whassup."

Thomasina made a long groaning sound. "If I can't reach her on her cell, what makes you think you can? I told you her cell is turned off," Thomasina huffed. "Nitwit!"

Brick flinched at being called a nitwit. So far Miss Thomasina had called him out of his name twice in the conversation. He wanted to go off on her, put her in her place, but he kept a civil tongue. "Maybe she turned it back on by now. I'll check on that for you." Brick forced his voice to take on a respectful tone.

"No, thank you," she muttered resentfully. "I'm not waiting another minute for that spiteful heifer. I'm taking a cab. Make sure you tell Misty that she owes me cab fare and a shopping trip." Thomasina hung up.

Brick flopped back down on the sofa. Something was wrong. He could feel it. Too anxious to go back to sleep, he fired up a blunt and cracked open another can of brew.

CHAPTER 10

Misty's weed connect wasn't taking her calls. She'd left Brick at home with damn near a quarter-pound of bud, leaving her with only one blunt. Damn if she was going to be stuck at the mall with her mom without a nice buzz going on.

Desperation forced her hand. After a little investigating, she obtained Todd, her weed man's, home address. He lived in the Fairmount district. Most streets in Philadelphia were comprised of cookie-cutter row homes, but not Todd's house. As she cruised along, she noticed a variety of interesting, architectural designs, all within the same block. She also noticed, to her chagrin, that Todd's charming little block had no parking spaces large enough for her X5. Two streets over, she found a place to park.

Todd didn't like clients showing up at his front door, but Misty didn't give a fuck. Boldly, she marched up to his house, rang his doorbell twice, and then impatiently pounded her fist on the frosted glass pane of the front door. The sound echoed in the quiet, gentrified neighborhood. The door opened. A dark-haired, white guy stood in the doorway, squinting at Misty through eyeglasses. He was a bookworm type, an obvious nerd.

"Where's Todd?" she asked testily.

"Todd?"

"Did I stutter? Don't try to act like you don't know who Todd is."

"Yeah, sure. I know Todd, but he, uh…"

"He, uh, what?" she mimicked.

"Todd got busted," the bespectacled student blurted.

"He got busted?" Misty was shocked. And disappointed.

"Yeah, a few days ago. He had an open case back in Wichita. He got extradited this morning."

"Are you in charge, now?" She reached inside her Juicy Couture bag. "I'll pay double."

Appalled, the nerd recoiled. "I'm not involved in that. Todd and I were roommates. That's all." He dismissed her with an agitated gesture and closed the door.

"Asshole!" Misty muttered a string of nonstop profanity until she reached her SUV.

Nothing lasts forever, she reminded herself. That was a life lesson she should have learned a long time ago. Even though Todd had that good green stuff, the best in the city, Misty should have had a back-up plan. Now, what was she going to do? She checked the time. She still had a half-hour before she had to pick her mom up from her corny, line-dancing class. She picked up her cell and scrolled through the contact list. *Jocko.* Jocko was a Jamaican dude, who had some real good ganja, but his high prices were ridiculous. But, anxious to get high, she called his number. The call went straight to voicemail. *Goddamn!*

Misty continued scrolling through her list of numbers until she reached the name Young Buck. Who the fuck was Young Buck? "Oh! Monroe!" She suddenly remembered. Monroe was the young fool she'd taken on a joyride and tossed him her thong as a keepsake. Misty laughed. His weed was garbage, but being desperate and running out of time, she called him.

As expected, Monroe sounded excited to hear from her and agreed to meet her at the court on Parkside Avenue. Fifteen minutes later, Misty watched Monroe and another tall male approach. Monroe was tall—well over six feet, but his buddy had him by a couple inches.

As the pair grew closer, Misty gasped and covered her mouth. Her heartbeat quickened. The swagger in the other man's walk, his height and body type, were hauntingly familiar. He reminded her of Shane.

"What's good, shawty?" Monroe greeted. His buddy looked a couple years older than Monroe. His attire was fresh, nicely coordinated. His diamond studs were small. Fine as he was, he should have been blinging some rocks.

"Whassup?" Misty muttered, her eyes fixed on Monroe's friend. Amazingly, from the jet-black, tight curls on his head, the silky thick eyebrows, to his big, juicy lips, and down to the cleft in his chin, the man was the spitting image of Shane. His complexion was similar to Shane's, a mixture of brown and red tones; his handsome angular features seemed sculpted from clay.

"Yo, shawty, I ran out of product, but my cousin has a sweet connect."

She looked at Monroe's cousin and nearly swooned as she marveled at his uncanny resemblance to her deceased lover. Misty swallowed. Her throat was dry; she didn't trust her ability to communicate with her typical sass and self-assurance.

"No disrespect to my partner over here." He nodded toward Monroe. "But my lil' cuz just got rid of a batch of dirt."

"Yo, man, I got the block on smash. My product is dope."

"Is that right?"

"Yeah, you know how I do." Feigning confidence, Monroe poked out his chest.

"Fuck outta here. Your shit is dirt. Niggas around here don't care what they smoke."

"That's real slimy, Cuz. I'm putting you down with shawty and now you trying to disrespect me." Monroe kicked a pebble in disgust.

His cousin ignored him and leaned into the driver's side window. "Obviously, someone looking as fresh as you is used to being pampered. I know you don't wanna smoke nothing but the best—" His eyes swept away from Misty's face. He leaned back and checked out the sparkly rims on her truck. "Yeah, I can see you like to live life to the fullest—" He paused, waiting for Misty to react. She nodded. That's all she could do. Dude was putting his thing down, slaughtering her with his flow, his cocky attitude and his uncanny resemblance to Shane.

Experiencing a severe attack of pussy palpitations, Misty shifted in her seat. Squishy sounds emanated from her core. She squeezed her legs together, trying to quiet her coochie down, or at least muffle the dick-demanding noise.

"I have a hook-up with some AK-47. It's expensive, but it's worth the high cost." The Shane lookalike flicked his tongue against his plump, bottom lip, moistening it as he completed the sales pitch.

Misty breathed in deeply, trying to calm her quaking heart. At her current level of arousal, she didn't trust herself to successfully pull off flirty and playful, so she cut to the chase. "My name is Misty. Before I do business with you, it would be nice to know your name." She wanted to sound firm, but her voice came out soft and whispery.

"Aw, my bad, Lil' Bit," he said, spontaneously giving her a pet name. "Let me introduce myself…" He moistened his succulent, russet-colored lips again. "My name is Dane."

Dane! Her head began to spin, her pussy walls started closing in. Her clit grew hard, aching and engorged, stretching out like a dick.

Misty's eyes glazed over before she slumped over the steering wheel.

"What's wrong? You aiight?" Monroe asked, concern registering in his voice.

With her head pressed against the steering wheel, Misty shook her head.

"Do you need some fresh air or something? What's wrong?" Monroe inquired, his face scrunched in confusion.

Wearing a smug look, Dane reached inside the open window and boldly ran his long fingers through her hair. "Ain't nothing wrong with Lil' Bit that a little CPR can't fix."

She felt a twinge of irritation. *Who does this arrogant nigga think he's talking to?* Offended, she raised her head and shook his fingers from her hair. Her burning gaze informed him that he was about to be cursed out for taking the liberty of touching her hair and for making such a cocky assumption that his kiss would be an instant cure-all.

But before Misty could part her lips to express her indignation, Dane bent, stuck his head inside the open window and covered her mouth with his. His tongue, aggressive and sweet-tasting, slid between her lips, searching and stroking, silently claiming ownership of her heart and soul. She tried to pull away but went suddenly limp, weakened by the soft fullness of his lips, and dazed by the heat of his tongue as it seared her lips.

Adrenaline pumped, making her feel dazed. Misty's heavy lashes fluttered involuntarily, her eyelids lowered and then closed, in defeat. Unable to help herself, Misty widened her already parted lips, welcoming—needing his hot invasion. She moaned in sweet surrender as Dane tasted her tongue, licked it, sucked it, heightening her moist yearning with his panty-dropping kiss.

He pulled his lips away. "Mmm," Misty murmured, still under the spell of his kiss. Time seemed to progress in slow motion. She heard the click of the opening passenger door, smelled his manly fragrance as Dane positioned himself in the seat next to her and started pushing buttons on his cell. "My man won't sell anything under a half a brick. Do we need to talk money? You got your funds straight?" he asked Misty.

"I'm good." Misty was well aware of the price ranges for good weed and money definitely wasn't an issue. The problem was Dane. The sensation of falling in love at first sight had her head spinning fast.

"Yo, this is D," Dane spoke into the cell. "I'm gon' stop by and holla at you in a few minutes, aiight?" He snapped the phone closed and glanced over at Monroe, who stood outside the SUV, wearing a dumbfounded expression.

"Yo, cuz, hit me up in a coupla hours. I might have a little something for you," Dane said, gesturing dismissively.

In stunned admiration of his older cousin's silky-smooth take-over, Monroe muttered, "That's big pimpin', yo."

Dane smiled and nodded in acknowledgment of his skills as the younger man walked away. Then he glanced at Misty. "You ready to make a run?" Before she answered, he instructed, "Bang a left at the light. Make another left when you hit Jefferson Street. Park in front of the Rodriguez store."

Glancing at the clock, Misty followed the directions. Her mom was going to flip when she discovered she was stranded at her line-dancing class, but Misty was willing to suffer the consequences of her mom's verbal assault—later—much later. Right now, blazing up a blunt and lying up with Dane was top priority. Her mom was a grown-ass woman and she'd just have to figure out a way to get herself home.

CHAPTER 11

Forty-five minutes later, inside a hotel room, Misty kicked off her sandals, making herself comfortable as she lounged on the bed, ogling Dane in deep concentration as he skillfully rolled a Phillies.

Dane took a hit and passed it to Misty. After passing the blunt back and forth several times, Misty leaned back on the pillow.

"You blunted up?" A devilish smile played at the corners of Dane's magnificent lips.

Too high for verbal communication, Misty expressed her lust with a seductive lowering of her lashes, and the appearance of her tongue, moistening her lips. She was ready. Nipples pearled, coochie warming up and tightening, Misty was down for anything Dane wanted to get into.

Dane released a puff of smoke and placed the blunt in an ashtray. Then he reached over and grabbed handfuls of her hair, drawing Misty close. His lack of tenderness heightened her arousal, made her tremble with burning need. Braced for a bout of sexy hair pulling and ass spanking, she bit down on her bottom lip. But Dane surprised her. After raking his fingers through her hair, he gently pressed his fingertips into her scalp, making circular motions, soothing and exciting her at once. He worked his hands down to her shoulders, kneading her muscles, melting away knots of tension. Within seconds, she felt her upper body relax. But her stomach clenched uncomfortably. That discomfort rushed downward and settled inside her feminine core, where moisture and burning embers were about to dangerously collide.

Boldly, she removed one of his hands from her shoulder and placed it between her legs. As Dane rubbed the thick denim seam in the crotch of her jeans, Misty arched upward and ripped open the metallic snap and pulled down the zipper.

Dane rubbed soothingly, unaware of the friction he was creating between her legs. She hoped he was prepared to get down there and blow if her coochie caught fire and burst into raging flames.

"You a thorough lil' chick." Indulging her urgent desire, he helped her wriggle out of her jeans. He tossed them on the floor and gazed down at his petite prize. "Pretty," he murmured, referring to her sparkly gold, lace-trim, low-rider panties. Misty blushed at the compliment. Her body quivered as Dane rolled the flimsy fabric over her hips and past her legs. By the time her panties dropped to the floor, she was biting down on her lip in hot anticipation.

Dane began squeezing her thighs, massaging upward until his thumbs reached her outer labia. She squeezed her eyes shut, her breath coming in fast pants. Then, his movement ceased as he focused his attention on the curly nest of hair that graced her femininity. Misty twisted and moaned in sexual agony. Impatiently burning for his touch, she gazed questioningly at her fully clothed lover.

"Take your clothes off. What are you waiting for?"

"You in a rush?"

Misty nodded.

"Oh, you on some Bam-Bam shit?"

"Yes! I mean, no!" she exclaimed. She felt off kilter, disoriented by the blazing heat that emanated within her vaginal walls. Her mind scrambled to come up with words to describe her desperate need.

"Shh! Let me do this. Relax, baby. Close your eyes. I'm gon' give it to you hard." He licked those delicious lips. "Is that how you like it?"

She moaned and nodded her head.

"Aiight, then. I'ma knock it out, all night long," he murmured with confidence.

Trembling, Misty did as Dane instructed. With her eyes closed tight, she allowed herself to enjoy the sensation of feeling her cotton top being pulled over her head. Next, she felt hot fingers unsnapping the back of her bra. Now naked, she quivered as she anxiously awaited his touch.

Using just a fingertip, he traced one eyebrow and then the other and then moved down the bridge of her nose. Softly, he outlined her nostrils and the outer ridges of her lips. She couldn't help stealing a taste of his fingertip when he moved his long digit to the center of her lips.

With slow and sensual movements, Dane worked his long finger inside Misty's puckered lips. Hungrily, she sucked his finger with the same intensity and passion she'd put into sucking a dick.

Dane's senses were intensified by the weed. He released a low moan when Misty enveloped his finger inside her mouth. Dizzied by the stimulation of her sucking lips and undulating hips, Dane grunted and dug the fingers of his free hand into her tiny waistline. Worked into a sweaty fever, Misty quivered and sighed.

"You ready for some heat?"

"Uh-huh," she murmured, his finger inside her mouth.

Dane released her waist. "Nah, you're not ready yet."

"Yes, I am!" Misty cried out in distress.

"Aiight, you gon' get it. Be patient, yo. I wanna take my time—do it nice and slow, like Snoop be singing—*A Sensual Seduction*." Dane chuckled.

Desperate for dick, she didn't think anything was funny. She was ready to demand a forceful fuck, but not wanting to chase him away with her bossy nature and demanding ways, Misty deferred to Dane's suggestion. She acquiesced, nodding and inhaling sharp heated bursts of air.

Prompted by the sound of her heavy breathing and urgent moans, Dane's hand traveled downward to the juncture of her thighs. He smoothed his palm over her nest of curls. Misty bucked beneath his touch. Next, he stretched out a long, sinewy finger and ran it along her moistened slit, searching out her hidden pearl of passion. With the bed of his finger pressed against her small, silken knob, he caressed the dewy softness until her clit emerged—hard and slick and throbbing—sensitive to his touch.

Misty groaned and turned her head. "Fuck me, dammit," she demanded. Aching for fulfillment, she spread her legs wide, offering him a visual of the sticky moisture that had gathered inside her dark, needy place.

"You can get it all night. But, this ain't about a quick fuck." He repositioned himself and lay flat on his stomach, his head between her legs. Face-to-face with her pulsing womanhood, he kissed her vagina.

"Suck on it, baby. Please!" Misty whimpered, needing him to do something to relieve her throbbing ache.

Ignoring her pleas, his fingers moved to her clitoris and massaged for a few moments. Then, obligingly, he separated her delicate folds and dipped his tongue into her damp crevice, moaning as he lapped her sticky sweetness.

Her body aflame, Misty writhed and breathed out a long sigh of pleasure.

Dane brushed his tongue against the bud of her sensitive spot. "Oh, yes," she cried appreciatively. He licked her clit and snaked a finger inside her damp crevice, twisting and undulating as he stroked the satiny flesh of her vaginal walls and explored her depths. Misty made a soft sighing sound as her desire bubbled over. Creamy and hot, her passion coated Dane's finger.

He drew in the short length of her clitoris, holding it captive in the cushiony confines of his plump lips. His tongue flicked against the creamy crown of Misty's sensitive bud, torturing her, sending shivers up and down her spine. His tongue and fingers, all over her, licking and caressing a burning, moist trail.

Suddenly, Misty sprang upright. She couldn't take anymore. Her coochie was having a fit. Convulsing, threatening to explode if he didn't stop sucking on it with those big, juicy lips. "Stop!" she protested petulantly. "I can't take anymore. Come on, now. I need you to get up in it." She impatiently patted the portal of her womanhood.

"Aiight, Lil' Bit," he said, rising lazily. Working at a leisurely pace, Dane pulled his shirt over his head, baring a lean and well-muscled torso. He was built all right, but Misty didn't allow her eyes to linger. Anxious to feast her eyes on his swollen, hidden flesh, she offered assistance in getting Dane undressed.

Hastily, she unbuckled his belt, unzipped his pants and wound her hand inside his boxers. Dane was packing! "Damn, baby," she murmured and possessively grasped and freed his bulging erection. At the sight of his bronzed and beautifully sculpted phallus, Misty went breathless; her mouth watered. Unable to resist temptation, she aimed the swollen head toward her parted lips. With loving tongue strokes, she caressed the underside of his dick. "Mmm, delicious," she murmured blissfully. When she felt him shudder, she sucked in his penis and let it marinate inside her warm, moist mouth.

Combining skillful lips and heartfelt emotions, Misty was inspired to give a superior blowjob. At first, her tongue swirled, tickled, teased. Then, she applied suction, making her mouth perform like a clenching, wet vagina.

Dane's erection grew harder by the second. Suddenly hit with a series of body spasms, he placed his hands on the sides of Misty's head, steadying himself. "Yo, that's enough. If you don't stop, I'm gonna bust a nut," he muttered, trying to catch his breath as he withdrew his throbbing organ.

Misty smiled proudly and reclined in the center of the bed. "It's ready; come and get it," she teased, rubbing her sweet spot.

Responding quickly, Dane kneeled inside the V-shaped space between Misty's spread legs. He wrenched up her thighs and yanked her closer. Breathing hard, he guided his gleaming knob toward her moist opening and drove in deeply.

Her walls of pleasure clutched and tightened around his firm thrusts. "Oh, Dane. Oh, shit!" His dick strokes felt amazing, but it wasn't enough. She needed something more; a closer connection. She needed to feel his skin against hers. Lifting up slightly, Misty pulled Dane close and then sighed, as if enraptured when she felt his chest press against her small, firm breasts.

Motivated by the sensation of flesh-against-flesh, Dane pushed hard inside her, pumping faster and deeper until Misty reached a violent crescendo, scratching and screaming, "Goddamn! Oh, shit. What the fuck you doin' to me, Dane? I love you—you pretty mufucka!"

Her pussy pulsed out of control, milking Dane, forcing him to shoot jets of semen. His seed splashed against her vaginal walls and spilled out and ran down the crack of her ass.

Dane didn't respond verbally. Taking panting breaths, he wrapped his arms around her, held her in a tight embrace. "You got my heart rate all fucked up. I'm feelin' you, Lil' Bit. You're a thorough lil' chick," he complimented, nodding his head. "You gotta give me your number—I'm definitely gonna keep in touch."

"What? You're gonna keep in touch?" Misty frowned, wriggled out of his arms and sat up. "I just told you, I'm in love with you. That means I'm ready for us to kick it on an everyday basis. What? You was on some hit-and-quit-it-type shit? I'm not trying to be your mufuckin' booty-call bitch."

With his head propped up by an elbow, Dane gazed up at Misty, his expression serious. "Check my position, Lil' Bit. Yo, I can feel a strong attraction and no doubt, there's some kind of crazy connection going on between us…" He paused and moistened his lips. "But I only come through Philly every now and then…" He fell silent, allowing Misty to absorb his words. "I live in Detroit and I'm heading out tomorrow."

His words hit like a dagger in her chest, making her slump at the shoulders and gasp for breath. She palmed the center of her chest, rubbed it circularly, trying to soothe the ache of such unexpected, heart-stabbing disappointment.

It didn't work. The pain persisted. Her mind raced around in frantic circles. "No, you check my position," she retorted, after finally getting a second wind. "My feelings for you are real. I'm in love with you." Desperate to make him understand, Misty grabbed his hand, clutched it. "You must be crazy if you think I'm gonna let you treat me like a fly-by-night coochie." She stared at Dane.

"Nah, it wasn't even like that. All I was saying was…"

"Whatever! A long-distance relationship is not gonna work for me. I'm not feeling that." She took a deep breath. "I want you. Right here…in Philly…with me." She punched him in the chest. "Ya heard, nigga!"

"Ow!" Laughing, he defensively crossed his arms in front of his chest. "Oh, you a feisty lil' jawn."

"I don't take no shit off nobody," she responded. Her eyes followed Dane's gaze that wandered down to his dick, which looked like it was trying to come back to life.

"Pervert," she teased. Laughing and smacked his arm.

"Yo, cut that shit out. You got issues. I can tell you got a lot of pent-up rage. Don't make me have to calm your ass down."

"Oh, yeah? How you gon' do that?" Misty forced a hard expression on her face.

"I might have to pull out some restraints for your lil' violent-ass self."

"Pull 'em out." Challengingly, she jutted out her bottom lip.

His eyes dropped. His dick was standing at half-mast.

"Fuck outta here." She fell out laughing.

Dane laughed, too. "You asked how I planned on restraining you. My jawn is gearing up—gaining the strength to pin your ass down and keep you in your place."

"You're not getting any more of my good coochie until we get some shit straight."

"Speak your peace."

"What the hell is in Detroit?"

"Home! I'm a businessman. I'm making money in Detroit."

"How much?"

"I'm eating all right."

"Uh-huh," she responded, her words coated with doubt. "So, uh, what kind of whip do you drive?"

Dane looked down. "Right now, I'm in between rides. I was driving a fly-ass truck, but, um, what had happened was…"

Smirking, Misty leaned back. "In other words, your business hit a slump."

"Things could be better."

"So, what's really holding you in Detroit?"

"On the real, I got a couple warrants. Drug cases. Nothing major, but I'm not trying to do hard time."

Misty nodded. "But, check this. Suppose you got pulled over for a traffic violation or some other minor shit while you're home in Detroit. You know the computer's gon' pull up your Philly warrants. So, what's the truth? Real talk, what's holding you in Detroit?"

"Right now, I'm carrying packs back and forth; trying to rebuild my stash. I should have my money right in a minute. Anyway, that's the reason I'm in and out of town. Don't worry, I won't be doing this too much longer—riding a bus for seventeen hours ain't easy on the ass, y'ah mean?" Dane laughed. Misty didn't.

"A mule. Umph. That's a risky business. I can put you down with something more profitable with zero risks."

Dane picked up the blunt from the ashtray and fired it up. "Is that right?"

Caressing the abundant hair on his arms, Misty told him about her one-man prostitution operation, leaving out numerous significant details and promising him a hefty salary if he stayed put in Philly.

CHAPTER 12

Misty reluctantly dropped Dane off at Monroe's house. They exchanged cell numbers. After a lingering kiss, Dane tore his sexy lips away, promising to return in a week—bags packed, ready to move in with Misty. And Brick. Problem was, Dane didn't know about Brick. Not yet.

If she'd had it her way, he'd be setting up housekeeping with her and Brick tonight. Convincing Brick that adding another dick to the mix made good business sense would not be easy. Though he'd allowed her to have sex with Shane, she was going to have to put forth some extra effort when she sweet-talked him into accepting Dane—a total stranger—into their bedroom. She had seven days to work on Brick. Getting Dane to accept the arrangement was a different story, but she'd cross that bridge later.

Right now, her primary concern was figuring out a way to make peace with her mother. Thomasina would not easily forgive being left stranded at her line-dancing class. She didn't want her mother to stop speaking to her. At least, not right now. Misty was ready to implement her new money-making idea, and she'd need her mother's cooperation and good credit rating to set up her internet business.

Driving and listening to the radio, she heard a newsflash that could work to her advantage. Instead of driving home, she detoured to her mother's house. She pressed the doorbell urgently. Thomasina opened the door wearing a bathrobe, her short hair in miniature, plastic rollers.

Misty gushed, "Thank God, you made it home okay. I was so worried about you."

Thomasina glared at her daughter. "I should slam this door right in your face."

Misty looked wounded. "Mom, I didn't leave you stranded deliberately. Didn't you hear the news? Somebody shot a cop and they shut down half the city. I was stuck up there for hours."

"I heard the news," her mother spat. "That cop got shot up in West Oak Lane. You weren't anywhere near there."

"Yes, I was," Misty said with a nod. "Unfortunately," she added in a somber tone. "While I was out killing time, I decided to shoot by this spot on Olney Avenue to pick up some jerk chicken for Brick."

"You're such a liar. I called Brick and he said he hadn't heard from you."

"Mom, why do you always think I'm lying? I was gonna surprise Brick. I couldn't call him because my cell needed charging and I left the car charger at home."

"Umph. You have an answer for everything." Her mother wagged a finger. "Let me tell you something, Misty. One of these days all your lying and conniving is going to catch up with you. Mark my words! You can't flim-flam your way through life without paying a cost."

Misty sighed. "I'm not lying!"

"Yeah, right." Thomasina rolled her eyes. "You owe me cab fare."

"I'm really sorry, Mom." Misty gave her mother fifty dollars.

With lips scrunched in disapproval, Thomasina folded the

money and stuck it in the pocket of her robe. Misty gave her mother a quick kiss on the cheek and turned to leave.

"You still owe me a shopping trip," her mother yelled at her back as Misty hopped inside her X5.

꙳

Snap! Misty took a nude picture of Brick for the new sex site. He was standing with his legs spaced apart, his dick so rigid it resembled a pole of steel.

"Okay, put your arms up and put your hands on the back of your head," she directed.

"What for? I'm not playing, Misty. You better block out my mug before you post this on the website," Brick grumbled as he laced his fingers behind his head and struck another pose.

Snap! "You don't have to tell me. I know what I'm doing! Along with your dick, I'm trying to showcase the muscles in your arms and your broad chest." She sucked her teeth. Brick didn't have to remind her to crop out his face. She wouldn't get any pay-per-click customers if she revealed his sliced-up face.

"Aiight, turn around and let me take a picture of your ass."

"Man, why you gotta be taking pictures of my ass?" Brick turned around reluctantly, his hands shielding his buttocks.

"Move your hands, Brick! Niggas like looking at a hard, manly ass."

"Those tricks better be satisfied with just looking at a picture of my jawn, 'cause I'm not letting nobody put their eyeballs on my ass while I'm working."

"I know! Damn, Brick, why you gotta act so difficult all the time?"

"Because, man! I'm not with this!" he bellowed.

Disgusted, Misty flopped down on the sofa. "Fuck it, then! I'm not gonna keep listening to you bitch and complain!" She slammed the camera on the coffee table. "Fuck it, aiight? We won't eat! I'll tell my mom to turn the wheels in to the dealership tomorrow because we can't afford it. And the rental office can take back the keys to our fly crib. Fuck it, aiight! My brain needs a break from figuring out ways to keep the rent paid up-to-date." Misty's chest heaved angrily. "I don't need this shit. I can take my ass back to my mom's house." Her eyes shot daggers at Brick. "I know one thing—I won't be at my mom's for long. You know, niggas is on me. All I have to do is step outside and there'll be hard-ballers lining up, grateful for the opportunity to take care of me."

Brick looked distraught. "I know, Misty, baby. I know you stuck it out with me because you felt sorry over what happened with Frankie."

"That's true," she agreed. "But, it's not just about what Frankie did to you."

She paused. "I got feelings for you. Why you think I've been taking care of you for so long?"

"I'm sorry, Misty," Brick blurted.

"It's too late for sorry. I already turned my feelings off."

He nodded solemnly. "Please don't turn your feelings for me off."

"Humph! You don't appreciate nothing. I can't understand why you're so ungrateful?" she questioned, her lips curled spitefully.

Brick shrugged. "I don't know," he muttered and cast his eyes downward.

"I don't know," she mimicked, her face twisted in an angry mask. "Yeah, that's what I thought. Your dumb ass doesn't know shit. You're gonna end up homeless, living in a shelter somewhere with a bunch of broke-behind men. How you gonna get high, living in the shelter? And don't even think about ordering take-out. They don't deliver pizzas and shit to no shelters." Misty looked up in exaggerated thought. "Oh, I know what you could do," she exclaimed, with a smirk. "You can charge some poor homeless man five dollars to suck your dick. You won't be smoking and choking on green buds in that homeless shelter. Hell no. A nickel bag of dirt is all you'll be able to cop when you don't have me around to keep shit afloat."

"Misty," Brick whispered, his voice croaked in anguish.

"Fuck you, you ungrateful bitch!" She smacked an ashtray off the coffee table. Marijuana butts bounced and thumped, ashes swirled and fell; the dark dust blighting the shiny, hardwood floor.

Brick rushed to her side. He rubbed her denim-covered thigh. "I'm sorry, Misty, baby. For real. I'm sorry, aiight?"

Wordlessly seething, Misty shook her head and screwed up her lips.

"You know how I am." Brick chuckled. "I was talking shit. I didn't mean a word I was saying."

Refusing to allow Brick to thaw out her icy exterior, Misty turned up the corner of her lip.

"I'll pose for you, Misty," he pleaded. "Pick up the camera. Don't you want to post some pictures of my jawn on your website?"

Misty cut an eye at Brick's flaccid appendage. "Your shit is limp."

"Give me a minute," Brick said, stroking his meat, trying to make it rise. He knew better than to ask Misty for help. He knew she was too angry to let him eat her pussy or penetrate his ear with dirty sex-talk.

Looking disgustedly at his lifeless phallus, she stood up. "You just slowed everything down. I hope you're satisfied. Damn!"

"Baby, I said I'm sorry. I'm gonna get it back up." Brick stroked his penis, but it wouldn't respond.

Misty sighed. "My head hurts. I have to lie down." She swirled around and Brick grabbed her wrist.

"Just touch it, Misty," he pleaded. "You know my dick obeys you."

She gave a huge sigh, sat next to him and unenthusiastically brushed her hand against his flesh. Magically, his dick stood up. Misty turned up the side of her lip, as she removed her hand. "You could at least say thank you. Dang!"

"Thank you, baby," Brick responded quickly, his own hand taking over the job of moving up and down his burgeoning erection.

"Oh! I forgot to tell you…I gotta new man. His name is Dane. He's handsome and he fucks way better than you can," she said spitefully.

He scrunched up his lips in what appeared to be a mixture of agony and ecstasy. "Damn, Misty. That shit you just said hurts me to my heart."

Misty scowled and got close to Brick's face. "So! I don't give a shit, you ungrateful slut."

"Baby, why you gotta call me vulgar names?"

"Ain't nothing new about that. You trippin'. I always call you vulgar names. You love it."

"Sometimes," he said pitifully.

Brick's hurt feelings were causing his dick to go down, so she flipped the script. "I was so hot for Dane, I wanted to get down on my knees and lick his asshole and his balls."

"Oh, baby," Brick moaned, his hand working fast.

"But he wouldn't let me. He just wanted to get his dick sucked. I sucked it the same way I sucked Shane's. You saw me give Shane head plenty of times, so you know how I get down."

"Ahhh!" Brick groaned, his hand moving up and down, jerking off his dick with rapid speed. "Ooo, I love the way you work me, girl."

"The next time I get with Dane, I'm gonna let him fuck me up my ass. He's so pretty, I think he deserves a piece of ass. What-chu think, Brick?"

Brick trembled. He was hunched over, sweating, and breathing hard, while palming his dick. "Yeah, he deserves it, Misty. Aw, shit. My jawn's on fire." His hand strokes were swift and audible. "Don't ever leave, baby. You gotta stay with me. I need you to take care of me. You the only woman who knows how to treat me."

Misty checked out Brick's erection and noted that his penis had grown monstrously large. "That's enough, Brick." She slapped his moving hand. "Stop!"

"Why?"

"I don't want you to cum. Not yet."

Helplessly aroused, Brick reluctantly released his mammoth appendage.

"Don't touch your dick." Misty reached for the camera. "My nigga, Dane has big, juicy lips, just like Shane. I love that mufucka and you're gonna respect our relationship the same way you respected me and Shane."

Brick nodded dumbly. "Yo, Misty, is you for real? This shit we talking is just a fantasy, right?"

Misty rolled her eyes. "Come on, Brick," she barked. "Just play along. If you start asking questions, your dick is gonna get soft."

"Okay, I'm sorry. I'll give dude the utmost respect." The hand he'd used to pleasure his dick inched toward his pulsing member. He wanted to give his firm flesh a tight squeeze, but Misty wouldn't allow him to touch himself.

"I didn't use a condom with Dane," she whispered maliciously. "We're in love, so I let him hit it raw. He filled my coochie up with his cum."

Brick moaned, aroused to the point of agony. "You fucking with my head, Misty. I'm ready to bust." Overly aroused, Brick's breathing was harsh and labored. His dick quivered, pre-cum dribbled out of the small opening in the center of the head.

Misty aimed the camera. "Don't cum. Mufucka. Let me get a picture of that shit."

"Hurry up, Misty. I can't hold it."

Click! She took a picture of his dick, bubbling out pre-cum. And a second later, she captured several images of his dick spurting out his seed.

She patted Brick on the top of his head. "I have an idea, Brick. Let's test your ability to re-up your semen stash."

Still in the throes of post-orgasmic shudders, Brick sat on the sofa, bent over and groaning as he nodded in agreement.

CHAPTER 13

Misty peeled off her jeans and stood in front of Brick. She rubbed the crotch of her gold, lace-trimmed panties. "I got something for you. Come over here and smell it."

Playing his role in the fantasy that he enjoyed, Brick pressed his face between her legs and took a deep whiff. Shocked by the strong and unmistakable scent of male ejaculation, Brick yanked his head up in bewilderment. Misty smiled and pulled her panties to the side. "That nigga has some strong cum, right?"

Confusion creased Brick's face as he assumed a kneeled position. Misty beamed proudly as she presented Brick with her cum-soaked pussy. "Get it, boo. Go ahead and taste it." Following her order, he slipped his tongue between her coochie lips.

"Is it good?" she whispered and caressed the side of his face.

She smelled musky; her taste was a mixture of sweet and sour—the way she'd tasted after making love with Shane.

"Is it good, nigga?"

He nodded and excitedly performed cunnilingus, uncertain if he was role-playing or really ingesting semen. Playing the game was a huge turn-on. It gave him permission to lose control and moan with wild abandon while fervently sucking another man's seed out of Misty's coochie.

She cried out with unabashed abandon, panting, gasping for

breath. Undulating, as ripples of white lava overflowed, she smeared female ejaculation on Brick's face. When she finally caught her breath, she appreciatively noted the thick sheen that covered Brick's cheeks, lips, and the tip of his nose.

"Damn, boo. You look good like that," she said warmly. "You got sperm and pussy juice smeared all around your mouth."

Reflexively, Brick raised his hand toward his mouth.

"No, don't wipe it off. It looks good, boo. That's a money shot!"

He put his hand back down. Misty picked up the camera. "Get sexy for me—lick your lips, Brick."

Helpless to defy her wishes, Brick's reluctant tongue swept across his lips.

Envisioning dollar signs, Misty snapped the picture. "Ooo, that's hot! Yeah, that's good money right there, baby. I'm gonna put a caption under that flick. It's gonna say, *Cum-sucking, Pussy-Eating Lips!* Tricks are gonna love that shot."

Brick's eyes welled with tears.

"Are you about to cry?" Incredulous, Misty stared at Brick.

"Hell, no!" His facial muscles twitched, but he managed to contort his features into a fierce scowl.

"Don't worry, boo. I'm not gonna expose you. I'm gonna crop out your eyes."

"What about my scar? How you gonna get that out of the picture?" His voice cracked. "I don't wanna risk getting recognized, having niggas think I suck cum."

"Damn, Brick. Pull yourself together."

"I'm trying. But, you got me confused. I'm all fucked up." Though he hated giving in, unable to fight the tears, he allowed them to fall.

She sighed. "Listen, Brick. You don't have to worry about being recognized by anyone who knows you. Only freaks who dabble in twisted sex visit my site. I think the scar gives the picture more sex appeal. I mean, think about it. A hardcore dude with a scar, posing with cum smeared around his mouth. Man, that's good money and I'm about my paper. We gotta show the scar. You feel me?"

Head bowed, Brick uttered a consenting sound.

"Are you ashamed of your scar?" Her tone was soft and sympathetic. Her fingers traveled to his face, traced the scar tenderly.

"Yeah, I'm real ashamed of it, Misty," Brick admitted, anguish cracking his voice.

Misty tried to wrap her arms around his huge body, but her arms weren't long enough. She gave up and pulled his head down; let it rest on her lap. His large head and broad shoulders felt extremely heavy on her lap, but she endured his weight. She caressed the jagged scar. "You feel insecure and inferior, don't you?"

"Yes."

"And getting down with men makes you feel like you might be a homo, right?"

"Right."

"Well, only me and you know your secret, Brick. I've never told a soul. Not even Shane."

"I know, Misty, baby."

"If it makes you feel better, I want you to know that I looked up your case—online."

"Whatchu mean?" He raised his head.

"I did some research and you're definitely not a homosexual." She looked down at him. "Feel better?"

"A little bit."

"But—" she added and then paused for several moments.

"But, what?" He sat up straight.

Misty sighed. "You're not gay, but from what I've read, you do have tendencies."

"I ain't got no gay tendencies," he yelled and then covered his face in anguish.

"Calm down. It's not your fault." She peeled his fingers away, removed his hands from his face. "If Frankie hadn't done that freak shit to you, you'd be a normal man. But, you're not and you and I both know it. I need you to stop worrying about it so much. I gotchu, boo. With me, you can explore all your tendencies and never have to worry about being judged. I think I'm giving you a good life. We get paid while you play." Misty smiled. "Feel better?"

Brick gave her a small, forced smile. "But, I gotta ask you something." He looked deeply into her eyes.

Misty tilted her head. "What?"

"Did you really fuck a dude named Dane?"

Misty instantly relaxed. Laughing, she gave him a sexy wink. "Did my coochie taste like cum?"

"It was kind of salty; it didn't taste the way it usually does." Brick eyed Misty suspiciously. "Tell me the truth. Did you feed me some dude's seed or were you just fucking with my head?"

Smiling, she wagged a finger. "If I told you the truth, it would ruin the fantasy."

He thought about it. "Yeah, you're right."

"One of these days, I'm gonna take our little game to a whole different level. I'm gonna bring a nigga home to our bed and tell your ass to move over." Misty cut her eye at Brick's groin. His penis, she noticed, was lengthening as she spoke. "When that day comes, I don't want to hear no shit. Ya heard?"

"I won't say nothing."

"I'm gonna make your fantasy come true. I'm gonna let you

watch while a long-dick mufucka slides his dick deep up in my pussy hole. Can you deal with that?"

"Yeah, I can deal with it." His voice was raspy.

"If it makes it easier on you, if you don't want to look at the nigga, face-to-face, you can pretend like you're sound asleep, you know, like you did when Shane used to hit it. Remember how we played Shane? We let that nigga think he was fucking me on the sly. Man, you used to get rock hard and ram the shit out of my coochie after Shane busted a nut and fell asleep."

Aroused by the memory, Brick's dick quivered and stretched even longer.

"Just knowing you were about to get some sloppy seconds made your dick hard. Those were good times, Brick." Misty smiled wistfully, and then her smile faded. "But the party ended after we let Shane in our little secret. After we admitted that you knew what was up, that mufucka got ghost. That nigga was so slimy, he'd rather fuck me behind your back than act like a man and fuck me right in front of your face." Misty shook her head in disgust.

"Yeah, he was my dawg and everything. But the way he bailed on us was lame." Brick twisted his lips indignantly.

"He fronted on us like we were asking him to get into some type of gay shit."

"I know!" Brick blurted, sounding offended. "I just wanted him to know I was cool with it—"

"Exactly," Misty chimed in. "All you wanted to do was watch. But, see, being the kind of person I am...I believe in letting shit do what it do. If it had gotten to the point where the three of us could have gotten honest about the situation, I know you probably would have broken down and gave Shane some head. You would have done it for me, right, Brick?"

Brick looked up at the ceiling and thought about it, briefly. "If Shane was with it, I probably would have. Not for me, though. I would have done it because that's what you wanted."

"Why you make it seem like you wouldn't suck his dick for your own pleasure? It's not a secret, Brick. I know you loved Shane just as much as I did."

"I dug him, but I wasn't in love with him."

"So, let me ask you something?" Misty gave him a sneaky smile. "If you had a second chance, would you handle things different?"

"Whatchu mean?"

"If you could do it all over again, if Shane was still alive, would you give in to your homosexual tendencies?"

Brick shrugged uncomfortably, not sure how to respond.

"Boo, if we could turn back the hands of time, how far would you go to please me?"

"As far as you wanted me to go."

"I just want to know, if you had another chance, would you let me and Shane fuck you over?"

Brick frowned. He bit down on his lip, looking too tortured to speak.

"It's me, boo. This is between me and you. Let's pretend like he's still alive."

"Okay," Brick agreed, going along with Misty.

"If Shane showed you love and told you he wanted you to be his bitch, would you give up your manhood for him?"

He took a deep, pained breath and then exhaled. "I don't know, Misty. That's hard to call."

Misty sighed.

"Okay, Misty, baby. I probably would."

"What about me?"

Brick looked at her like she was crazy. "I wouldn't leave you. Not for Shane or no other mufucka. We'd be a threesome, like you said."

Misty didn't look happy.

"What?"

"Who would you take orders from—me or Shane?"

"You! Ain't no doubt about that. I do what you say."

A bright smile lit Misty's face. "That's good to know." Hit with an idea, she cocked her head to the side. "I just got an idea for another sweet money shot. Let's go in the kitchen."

Uncertain as to why she suddenly changed the subject, Brick looked perplexed, but unwilling to risk Misty throwing another tantrum, he headed for the kitchen without asking any questions. Trailing behind him, Misty barked orders, "Put on my Betty Boop apron and then I want you hold up a frying pan or something to make it look good. I'm gonna call that picture *Domesticated Bitch*. After freaks click on that shot, they gonna come out of their pockets big time to get with you."

Brick felt deeply unhappy. Admitting that he would have been willing to be Shane's bitch was one thing, selling ass to strangers over the internet was an entirely different matter. He really didn't think he was gay. Sure, he had a slight weakness for Shane. The dude was pretty and masculine at the same time. Strong and sensitive. Brick used to hear Shane crying at night when they were locked up at the juvenile detention center. Crying for his mother. Hearing someone as hardcore and aggressive as Shane, crying like a baby, used to touch Brick's heart. Made him want to crawl in Shane's bed, kiss his lips, wipe his tears away—suck his dick if he had to—if it would have soothed Shane's heart. But he had never tried anything with Shane. The closest he came to being

Shane's bitch was putting his dick inside Misty's pussy while it was filled up with Shane's cum.

"After I snap the first picture, I want you to change poses, then put your foot up on a chair, so I get a close-up of your hairy, hanging balls."

Thinking about Shane gave Brick a monster of an erection. He took the bright-colored apron off a hook on the kitchen wall and tied the strings around his waist. When he turned around for Misty's approval, his dick had started leaking. A circle of moisture dampened the image of the female cartoon character.

"Damn, Brick," Misty snapped. "You need to get some control over yourself, before you bust a nut all over Betty Boop's face."

CHAPTER 14

Something was terribly wrong. Misty couldn't keep her mind on business. Dane was driving her crazy. He'd told her that he was in financial straits and couldn't afford the plane fare to Philly. Wanting his dick in close proximity, she'd quickly sent him money for a ticket by Western Union.

Twelve hours later, while she stood in the baggage claim area of the terminal, waiting for his flight to touch down, his personalized ring tone blared. "Hey, Lil' Bit," he said breathlessly when she answered.

"Where are you?"

"Still in Detroit."

"What!"

He sighed. "Yeah, I ran into some problems. After I get my situation straight, I'll be on the next plane."

"Can you be more specific?" Misty said, extremely irritated by his vague explanation. She pulled off her large hoop earring and pressed the phone closer to her ear.

"I know how you get, so don't stress yourself. I'll be there in the morning." Dane's voice held a tone of amusement.

"What time?" Misty hadn't felt this vulnerable since the days she'd tried to control Shane's activities.

"Yo, I'm not on nobody's time frame. There's a couple flights tomorrow morning. I haven't decided which one I'm taking. I'll let you know when I get to Monroe's crib. Stay sweet, Lil' Bit."

Before she could protest and state that she preferred picking him up, he disconnected the call.

No, that nigga didn't just hang up in my ear! Indignant, Misty pushed the speed dial button and instantly got his voicemail. Huffily, she stuffed her phone inside her purse and stomped through the terminal. Fuming mad, she pushed through the throng of travelers, aggressively stepping on the heels of anyone who made a sudden stop, bumping into people who moved at a leisurely pace, knocking against rolling luggage, and forcing parents to snatch up their toddling youngsters before she steamrolled them.

Inside her SUV, she tried his number again. Voicemail. *Ignorant asshole!* Dane's behavior was unacceptable. But she was helpless to get any kind of control until she had him in her clutches. Once that nigga stepped foot in Philly, it would be a wrap. There wasn't a chance in hell that she was going to let him treat her like Shane had. She'd been given a second chance and she wasn't about to make the same mistake.

She'd never uncovered Shane's weaknesses, but she intended to make it her business to look for Dane's Achilles' heel. And when she did…that arrogant mufucka was going to bend to her will. Fuck trying to be fair and dividing the power equally. Niggas didn't play fair and neither would she.

Unable to stop herself, she called Dane again. *Voice-fucking-mail!* Disrespect of this degree was too painful to endure. She needed healing—medication—a quick fix. Misty pointed her vehicle in the direction of the Pennsylvania Turnpike. Listening to her favorite Keyshia Cole CD, she embarked on the long trip to the designer outlet mall in Reading, Pennsylvania.

❧

Burdened with a plethora of shopping bags from Dress Barn Woman, Lane Bryant, Maidenform, Reebok, and Sag Harbor, armed with an excessive amount of enticements, Misty rang her mother's doorbell.

Thomasina cracked the door, and then swung it wide open. "Well, I'll be damned!"

"I come bearing gifts," Misty said, faking her best, hearty tone as she entered her mother's small, well-kept home.

"It's too early for Christmas, so what's the occasion?" Excitedly, she relieved Misty of some of the bags and set them down on the floor near the front door.

"There's more. I'll be right back." Misty gave her mother a wink.

Beaming, Thomasina shook her head in disbelief. Her child could be so sweet when she wanted to be.

Misty went to the back of the SUV and returned with bags from Bath & Body Works, Corningware, and Factory Linens. A small bag from Zales Jewelers was hidden inside her purse.

Flattered and surprised, Thomasina smiled extravagantly.

"Mom, I'm running late. I can't wait around while you look at all your goodies, but I wanted to see your face when you open this…" Misty fell silent and dug inside her purse. She handed her mother the small package from Zales.

Thomasina gasped after opening the velvet case. Inside was a circle pendant with the word *Mom* in the center. A diamond chip was set inside the letter "*M*."

The pendant was dirt cheap with the chintzy little diamond chip, but her mom was flipping out like she'd given her a sizeable rock. Laughing inside, Misty took the chain from her mother's hands and delicately hung it around her neck. "Even though it wasn't my fault, because I really was stuck in traffic, I know your feelings were hurt and this is my way of saying I'm sorry." Misty's voice went low. "I love you, Mom," she whispered. Then, she laughed and threw in, "Ya heard?"

Thomasina hugged her daughter tight. "Misty, sometimes I think all that beauty you got was a curse. You've been hearing folks talk about how pretty you are since the day you were born. I thought your looks had you messed up in the head. But, maybe some of my ways have rubbed off on you after all. I was seriously starting to think that all you had was your Puerto Rican father's good looks and rotten traits."

Thomasina hugged and kissed her daughter. "There's hope for you. I know it!" She looked down at the abundant shopping bags. "Look at all this stuff; you didn't have to buy me all these presents."

"I wanted to. And don't forget—we're still going out shopping together. This is just the beginning."

Misty had never met her father and didn't give two shits about him. She had no desire to look him up or question him for abandoning her. She thanked him for her looks and her cunning ability to skillfully maneuver in life. She wasn't anything like her mother, but she'd let the old bat believe whatever she wanted to believe.

"I have to pee." Misty headed for the stairs, yelling, "Mom! Check out that lingerie I bought you. With all that line-dancing you're doing, you're gonna have your shape back in no time. I thought you'd want some cute loungewear to entertain your man…when you get yourself a new one. You look real pretty, Mom. That line-dancing is doing something for you."

Thomasina blushed and made a dismissive gesture with her hand. "Hooking up with another no-good man is the last thing on my mind. I'm taking those classes for the cardio benefits."

"Sure, Mom," Misty teased, and ran up the stairs. When she reached the top, she made a quick left turn, slipping inside her mother's bedroom. Stealthily, she crept to a corner near the bed. She eased out her mother's handbag that was tucked safely behind a stack of shoe boxes.

Fearful of robbers, Thomasina never left her bag out in plain view—not even in her own bedroom. With her footsteps and movements masked by the sounds of her mother excitedly rustling through tissue paper, Misty tiptoed to the bathroom. She turned the faucets on full force, muffling the sound as she rifled through her mother's wallet. After locating the credit cards she was looking for, she jotted down the information, and returned the handbag to its hiding place. Elated, Misty bounced down the stairs.

"I have to run, Mom. Hope you like your presents."

"I love them! Feels like Christmas in July. How much did all this cost you, Misty?"

"A couple thou," she said nonchalantly.

"A couple thousand!" Thomasina shouted, shocked.

"Yeah, but you're worth it." Misty gave her mom a quick kiss on the cheek. "I have to go, Mom. See you tomorrow."

"Don't be late!" Thomasina cautioned. "It's embarrassing walking into that class after it gets started."

"I'll be on time. I promise." Misty breezed out the front door.

Sitting in the driver's seat, she looked in the backseat of her ride, and eyeballed her own purchases—Coach, Guess, Kenneth Cole, Nine West, Movado, Enzo Angiolini, The Sunglass Hut, Ecko Unlimited. She'd bought the good stuff for herself.

Shopping for her corny mother had been bad enough. Taxing her remaining strength to hunt down clothes in Brick's big-ass size was absolutely out of the question. There were only two bags for Brick—a pair of boots from the Timberland shop and a Fossil watch.

She squinted inside her purse; her eyes twinkled when they

located the piece of paper with her mom's credit card information. Misty had already obtained Thomasina's social security number and her bank account information when her mom signed for her new X5. The money she'd spent on her mother was a drop in the bucket compared to what she'd be able to earn after she used the required credit card to open an online bank account.

At the bottom of her purse was a second bag from Zales. She peered inside the jewelry case. The diamond studs shone as brilliantly as her smile—the gift was welcome home bling that she intended to give Dane when he arrived in the morning. *Lemme upgrade ya, pretty mufucka.*

⊱⊰

Brick was drunk and passed out on the sofa when she got home. *Good!* She needed some privacy to check the activity on the website. Misty dropped the bags in the middle of the living room floor, and rushed to the second bedroom, which served as her office. She smiled up at a picture of her draped in a full-length chinchilla and skimpy lingerie posing next to her X5. She fondly recalled that day. Though it had been hot as hell on the day of the photo shoot, wearing chinchilla and lingerie was so sexy that she endured the heat.

Dane was so fine; she'd probably include him in the next photo shoot. Shit, maybe she'd let Brick film Dane hitting it. Smiling, she snapped open her laptop and impatiently waited for the computer to spring to life. She logged online, and was shocked to discover that there had been seventeen hundred hits on her sex site. *Brick is a star!*

There were also dozens of emails from both men and women

from all over the country, complimenting Brick's attributes. With her heart pumping with adrenaline, Misty began responding to emails, narrowing down her responses to those who lived near the Philadelphia area. She'd get in touch with those who were willing to travel at a later date. Her emotional shopping binge had cost her a fortune. Funds were getting low and she needed to quickly fatten up her pocketbook.

First thing tomorrow, she'd set up an online bank account. There'd be no more freebies. Freaks were going to have to pay to peek at Brick's jewels.

CHAPTER 15

"What kind of bitch has to pay to fuck?" Brick wondered aloud.

The rumble of Brick's voice seemed a million miles away. Misty's mind was churning away, focused on Dane. His whereabouts, which were unknown, troubled her deeply. She was being played and she didn't appreciate it. She'd sent him money with such regularity that she was on a first-name basis with the Western Union chick.

"Answer my question. What's wrong with the broad?" Brick broke into Misty's thought.

"Nothing's wrong with her. You should appreciate a change in the routine. Don't you get tired of all those sweaty dick-suckers?" she asked curtly. "Or…do you prefer men?"

"Aw, get off that shit. You know I ain't no fruit."

"So, why are you stressing about banging some new pussy? I know mine is the bomb, but I thought you'd accept this job as… you know, a gift."

"I'm just saying, suppose she's working with just one leg or something fucked up like that. Something must be wrong with her. A female shouldn't have to pay for dick."

Exasperated, Misty let out a sigh. "She's a freak, okay? She wants to experience your thickness and she didn't hesitate to pay my steep asking price. If she's an ugly bitch, just use your imagination—think about me. Do whatever you have to do to get your dick hard enough to bang out that paying pussy."

Brick nodded absently. Though he wondered about the steep price Misty bragged about charging for his services, he didn't dare ask. It was cool, though. Misty would tell him how to collect before he went up to the chick's hotel room.

"Now, how many women do you think would be as open-minded as I am? As big as your dick is, I should be guarding it like it's Fort Knox, but I'm not insecure." She reached over and rubbed her palm against his groin. "I know all this belongs to me." She pat the bulge that quivered in response to her touch.

"How many women do you know who trust their man enough to let him go stick his dick inside another female?"

"None," Brick mumbled, head lowered, contrite.

"So, stop complaining. I don't care if that bitch is missing both legs, serve her up for the hour she paid for and then roll out."

Misty popped in her favorite CD. She was hurt and feeling abandoned by Dane. She felt like listening to Keyshia Cole wail and moan about love gone wrong. "Don't eat no pussy," she ordered Brick as she nodded her head in agreement with Keyshia's crooning lament.

Brick looked horrified. "You don't have to worry about that."

"Aiight. I'll punch you in the head if you even think about sticking your tongue up in some strange bitch's coochie."

Repulsed, Brick reared back and snorted. "Stop playing. You know I don't get down like that. I don't even wanna stick my dick inside no strange broad, so you know I'm not eating no strange pussy."

"I know that's right," Misty responded and then grew quiet as she listened to Keyshia hit high notes, shouting out a grieving wail over loving a no-good man. She handed Brick two condoms. "Cover your jawn up nice and tight, let her ride big boy until she pops. If she don't bust in an hour, fuck it. Tell the bitch her time is up. Grab your clothes and bounce."

"Aiight, but you know I'm not used to dealing with no female customers. Should I get the gravy before we get down or after?"

"I told you, she already paid."

"For real? I thought you meant she agreed to pay your steep price."

"No! Her account is up to date and paid in full. She deposited the money in my online account."

"When did you get a bank account?"

"Man, don't worry about it. I got this. You know how I do. I'm always looking for new ways to keep my pimp game tight."

Brick nodded miserably. He hated when Misty referred to herself as a pimp. He preferred to think of them as partners, doing what they had to do to survive. Feeling sad and insulted, he looked out the passenger window as Misty merged onto I-76 West, headed for Valley Forge.

Later, Misty parked at the entrance of the Valley Forge Hotel. She checked the time. "I'll be back in an hour."

Brick gave her a look.

"I'm gonna go find a place to park, but you're running late—you need to hurry up and get to the hotel room."

"I'm not playing, Misty. I don't feel like sitting up in the hotel bar, stuck the fuck out here in Valley Forge for hours."

"I wouldn't do that," she said, sounding agitated by his insinuation. "I'm going to park in the lot and then I'm going to wait for you in the bar." Grinning, she tilted her head to the side. "Who knows, I might get lucky and spot another trick sitting at the bar."

"Man, stop lying. You're not gon' sit around, waiting inside that bar. Your little ass is heading straight for the King of Prussia Mall."

Misty giggled. "Yeah, I am. But I already know what I want. I won't be long. I promise, Brick. Okay?"

Sighing, Brick got out of the X5.

꒰꒱

Brick knocked and waited. On the other side of the door, his client observed him through the peephole. She probably didn't approve of his face. He shrugged, figuring he'd give her a few more seconds to make up her mind, and then he'd bounce on down to the bar and get his drink on. Most male clients were initially turned off by the disfiguring scar, but after getting closer acquainted, they always ended up digging it; stating that the jagged, raised flesh enhanced his masculinity. Made him appear more virile. Edgy. Dangerous.

Brick turned to leave. The door swung open. Frowning in impatience, he swung around. In the doorway stood an unusually beautiful young woman with a copper-hued complexion. Her green eyes, a stark contrast to her skin tone, bore into him. Tall and willowy, she appeared to be almost six feet tall. "You must be Brick. Come in. I've been anxiously waiting for you." She spoke in a crisp voice, with an appealing accent that Brick couldn't quite identify. As best he could, Brick tried to soften his coarse expression as the exotic and refined client ushered him into her suite.

With fluid, graceful movements, she closed and then put the chain on the door. Her soft and glossy, burnished honey-colored hair was pulled into a loose ponytail that hung over a shoulder and rested on her left breast. A smooth high forehead, protruding full lips, and prominent wide nose were almost sculptural African characteristics. This woman of obvious mixed parentage was a genetic oddity, a drastic contrast of European and African features.

She wore magenta-colored, satin boxers and matching camisole. *Sexy as shit!* Picturesque in her stylish lingerie, she appeared to have glided off a page of one of Misty's fashion magazines. *Why she gotta pay for sex?* Brick wondered. He would have done this job for free. On the real, he would have paid a hefty price for a glimpse of the passion fruit hidden between her firm thighs.

"Yoyin," she said, extending a slender hand. Her name, foreign-sounding and exotic, suited her, but Brick didn't trust himself to try and pronounce it. Feeling self-conscious, Brick took her hand, gave it a quick shake. "Brick," he mumbled. He kept his eyes lowered, keeping it professional, concealing his hungry gaze.

"I know your name," she reminded him with a thin smile. Crafting a wider smile would require more effort than the serious young woman seemed willing to put forth.

Brick felt foolish, and out of his league. Admittedly, Misty was the prettiest woman he'd ever known, but Yoyin was not only beautiful, she had a majestic presence that humbled him. With lowered eyes, his attention was drawn to her long, shapely legs and then wandered down to her narrow, bare feet. A platinum anklet dangled above a toe ring, which was topped with a cluster of glittery diamonds. Toenails painted pink hinted that there was a playful nature to this regal and extremely solemn Nubian queen.

Moving with a noble carriage and stately walk—giving off an air of elegance that made Brick feel clumsy and oafish, she turned and glided toward the bed, gracing Brick with her backside, a small, protrusive, bubble butt—another courtesy of Mother Africa.

Yoyin glided over to the dining area. "May I get you a drink? Patron, Hennessy. Whatever you'd like."

Knowing he was prone to cutting the fool if he started drinking, Brick shook his head. "No, thanks," he said, smiling, determined to be on his very best behavior.

"All right. Well, I'm done with the pleasantries—show me the goods. I'm told you have an enormous cock." Yoyin's accent was beautiful. It stirred Brick's manhood.

Brick put his head down, blushing as he undid his jeans. When he looked up, he noticed Yoyin's nipples pushing hard against her satin camisole. In an instant Brick became rigid with desire. He unveiled his most valuable asset. Holding it in the palm of his hands, he proudly offered his large, throbbing manhood.

"Very nice. Your agent should have charged double the price. You're worth it." There was a twinkle in Yoyin's eyes that shone as brightly as the diamonds on her toe. Brick wondered how much Yoyin had paid Misty, but knew better than to ask. The financial arrangements were between Misty and the client. Misty would have a fit if he tried to be all up in her business.

Yoyin quickly shed her girly boxers and revealed the magnificent treasure between her legs.

"Umph," Brick grunted and caressed his length. Her mons, prettier than he could have imagined, was covered by a soft layer of honey-colored hair. She spread her outer labia, flaunting pierced, pussy petals as well as a pierced clit. Her clit was large and rigid. He didn't know if it was swollen from the piercing or if that was its normal size. What he did know was that the sight of her glistening, big clit, made his mouth water, made his dick throb.

An enormous feeling of hot lust washed over him. He longed to bow down in worship at the feet of this unusual woman, who was endowed with an oversized clit and presented a fascinating, bejeweled vagina. Yoyin's genitalia, elaborately decorated with sparkly jewelry, were a shameless dick-tease. "I ain't never seen a pussy blinging like that," he uttered, awestruck. Brick could feel a nut swiftly traveling through his loins as his dick thumped against his hand, threatening to go into convulsions. Frowning, he gave his dick a hard, chastising squeeze. "Calm down, nigga," he told his unruly appendage.

Eager to feel the sensation of Yoyin's numerous piercings sliding against his dick, Brick kicked off his jeans. *Hold up!* he cautioned himself. He'd never engaged in sexual activity with a female client and never could have imagined securing payment from such an extraordinary beauty. Looking upon this momentous occasion with reverence, Brick decided to prolong the experience.

Sure, Misty had ordered him to keep his tongue inside his mouth, but Brick, awestruck by Yoyin's elegant beauty and suddenly hungry for the taste of her exotic passion fruit, was prepared to get down on bended knee and lap her tangy-sweet nectar. And he had another reason to cheat on Misty. Their fantasy a few nights ago had gotten out of control. It seemed so real, he'd cried like a bitch, believing that Misty had finally crossed the line and fed him pussy that smelled and tasted like it had been filled up with another man's cum.

Did his pretty baby really go out and cheat on him with other men? Or did she just tell him what she knew he liked to hear while they were kickin' it in bed? Brick shook his head, uncertain. The way realities had begun to emerge was frightening. No doubt about it, Misty was changing. She was letting her pimp game go to her head. Brick sighed. Did she love him? He couldn't call it. She'd become so unreasonably demanding and unmercifully aggressive, it seemed she'd lost all respect for him. Yeah, she was the boss, always had been. But damn, was he now nothing more than a big dick and a dollar sign?

Brick pushed away the unpleasant thoughts. Misty loved him. She pimped him out, but she did it out of love. Like she said, her job wasn't any easier than his. Having to think up ways to drum up business was a lot of work. He'd be less than a man if he didn't play his part and put a little effort into the tricks he turned.

Yeah, she loved him. Other than Shane having his back in the joint, Misty was the only person in the world who'd ever shown him love or any type of kindness. He could barely recall his mother. Couldn't remember if she'd ever loved him or not.

Misty wasn't out there fucking around on him. He was trippin', losing his ability to distinguish between what was real and what was a sexual fantasy.

CHAPTER 16

"Violate me." Yoyin broke into his musings. The coarse suggestion was spoken softly, a delicate, but urgent whisper. "Ravage my body." She took a shuddering breath. "I know you're strong and quite capable of ramming me, hard! Hard enough to draw blood. I want you to hurt me," she stated simply. "Abuse my vagina," she further instructed. "Give me pain. Can you manage that?" Her question was followed by a long, blissful sigh.

Oh, shit! Yoyin's a freak. Brick should have known that only a messed-up, twisted bitch would spend money to get her fuck on. Disappointment cast a shadow over Brick's face. He'd wanted to inhale her vaginal fragrance, suck her extended clit and press his tongue against the cushiony walls of her warm passageway. He longed to sip her juices and savor her taste before filling her with his thickness.

Being denied the opportunity to exhibit his soft side felt like rejection. This distressed him and his emotions quickly progressed to rage. "Oh, you want me to rough you up?" He advanced toward Yoyin; his menacing demeanor was reminiscent of his past persona, when he earned a living committing strong-armed robbery.

Nodding uncertainly, Yoyin gave a halfhearted consent.

Giving his client what she asked for, he scooped her up, threw her long body over his shoulder, and stomped into the bedroom, caveman-style. He dumped her on top of the bed, climbed on top of her, and scowled down.

Looking nervous, Yoyin scrambled into an upright position. Brick grabbed her long ponytail, wrapped it around his hand and yanked it harshly. "Lay your ass down!" Yoyin gasped in shock. "You bitches don't never want nobody to treat y'all right," he growled, breathing in angry bursts of air.

Yoyin's eyes became wide with fear. "Hey, this is supposed to be a game. Don't you think you're taking it a bit too seriously?"

"You think this is a game? You think I'm a joke?"

With a look of terror etched across her face, Yoyin shot a glance over at the bedside telephone. "I think you should leave." Her voice was shaky.

Brick snorted. "Put me out, bitch!" He looked her up and down with scorn. "You think you a stunna, with your bling and all those charms and shit hanging off your pussy." He gave a scornful chuckle and easily wrestled her down, pinning her into a prone position. "Open your fuckin' legs before I rip 'em off at the hips." Brick was sick of bitches not letting him love them in a tender way. First Misty, and now this bitch, Yoyin, coming at him with sick desires.

Yoyin reluctantly separated her legs, but sputtered a protest. "This is rape. You can't get away with this."

His earlier adoration for Yoyin was now replaced with hatred, and Brick couldn't care less about breaking the law. "Fuck you!" he barked. He gripped his dick, aligned the head with Yoyin's satiny opening. She was surprisingly moist. Brick felt an amazing sensation as his flesh made contact with the metal rings of desire while making his brutal entry. He groaned his appreciation and drove himself in deeper. Yoyin gave a low moan of pleasure and pivoted her hips and lifted her legs, offering herself for deeper penetration.

Brick halted his thrust and rubbed his thumb circularly against Yoyin's horizontal clit ring. Her lips parted, she writhed delightedly. "You like that?" Brick asked gruffly.

She nodded and whimpered a response. Brick tugged on her clit ring. Yoyin winced from the intense flash of pain. "That hurt?" he asked in a husky voice. She moaned and nodded enthusiastically, thrusting forward, her body begging for increased pain.

He jerked the clit ring, and slowly pushed in a little more of his thickness, giving Yoyin measured increments of his penile pleasure.

Writhing with desire, she drew her legs up higher as she moaned loudly. "Don't toy with me," she shouted as she wantonly rotated her pelvis. "Molest me. Fuck me like the beast that you are!"

Beast! Stunned at being called out of his name, Brick ceased movement. He wanted to cry, *"I'm not a beast."* He wanted to howl in wounded protest. But the pretty exotic woman was right. He was a monster with one attribute—an oversized dick. He was Misty's trained circus act, and he could be procured by anyone with a palate for freakish pleasure.

Fueled by blinding rage toward Misty, Brick violently shoved his dick in to the hilt. Thrusting in and out harshly, he accidentally ripped off one of the pussy trinkets, tearing flesh. "Ahh!" Yoyin screamed, and tried to pull away, but Brick held her firmly in place, fulfilling his commitment to molest and violate. His engorged penis, behaving as a flesh-covered, wrecking device, drove in and out with Herculean speed and power, viciously plundering Yoyin's soft, feminine chamber.

Rage sharpened his senses; he felt warm blood dampening his warring appendage. Drooling and panting like something inhuman, he mercilessly plunged until he felt his angry knob press against the pillowed flesh of her swelling G-spot. Yoyin shivered. She cried out, her voice high-pitched and strident, a distinct sound of passion.

Clutching, pussy spasms tightened around Brick's hard male loins. As he surrendered his semen, he released a groan that progressed to a roar. The sound was guttural, and disturbingly animalistic.

Gasping in post-orgasmic breaths, he collapsed upon Yoyin. She wriggled beneath him, also panting for breath. "That was fucking fantastic," she exclaimed.

Fantastic! Had he heard her right? He'd just killed the pussy and she was singing his praises.

"You're smothering me," she said and then nudged Brick's shoulder. He rolled off her and sat up. Two coochie rings, spotted with droplets of blood, lay atop the bed coverlet. He winced at the sight of the dislodged body jewelry.

"I'm sorry about that." Brick felt sincerely ashamed. But survival instincts overpowered his sympathy. *Suppose she decides to call the cops?* He looked around and located his clothes, prepared to dress quickly and make a run for it if a blinding rage replaced Yoyin's state of bliss.

Yoyin, surprisingly calm, snatched a tissue from the box on the nightstand and dabbed at the injured area. "It's happened before." She scrunched up her lips and shrugged. "Be a dear…gather your things and go. The next time I feel dark urges, I'll make sure to give your agent a call."

His services rendered, Brick, dismissed without so much as an offer to use the bathroom, made his way to the elevator and down to the hotel bar. As expected, Misty was nowhere in sight. Instead of irritation, Brick felt relief, and rushed inside the men's room. He grabbed several sheets of paper towels, wet them and pumped on liquid soap. Alone in a stall, he scrutinized his dick. He'd lost it in the hotel with Yoyin. Brick shook his head. Whether she'd asked for it or not, violence toward women wasn't cool and he was shocked that he'd gotten so caught up in it. *Never again,* he told himself as he held his war-weary member and washed away the smell of exotic pussy. Frowning down at the flaccid flesh, he wiped off hardened streaks of blood.

Along with the paper towels, Brick tossed the two unused condoms. What Misty didn't know surely wouldn't hurt her. Feeling somewhat renewed, he left the restroom and sauntered up to the bar. "Two brews," he told the bartender. "I'm not particular. Give me whatever you got on tap." He settled into his seat, prepared for an extremely long wait.

By the time Misty rushed inside the bar, Brick was on his fifth brew and feeling nice. He paid his tab and rose unsteadily from the bar stool.

"I hope you're not drunk."

"I'm cool."

"Are you sure?" Misty handed him a shiny bag. "I had to go buy another damn Betty Boop apron."

"Why?"

"I'll explain in a minute," she said in a conspiratorial voice, cutting a suspicious eye at the bartender. "You have to go back upstairs. I'll walk with you to the elevator."

Brick's stomach sank. "I can't go back up there. That bitch was weird. She told me to get rough with her, and then after I did what she wanted, she started threatening to press charges against me." He swallowed nervously.

"I'm not talking about her. Fuck that talking-with-an-accent slut. She doesn't even live in this country. She's from somewhere in Europe. What the fuck I care about a bitch that can't be a repeat customer? Bitch better not press any damn charges. She paid for you to get rough and I have her email as proof. I'm talking about another customer. Luckily, I had my laptop with me in the whip. I checked my emails and I was able to pull together a quick rendezvous. I talked the freak into checking into a room right here in this hotel." Misty bobbed her head happily. "Your next client is a dude. He liked the *Domesticated Bitch* picture."

"I'm tired, Misty. I'm not feelin' up to it." There was a pleading tone in Brick's voice.

Exasperated, Misty raked her fingers through her hair. "Are you trying to stress me out?"

"No, but—"

"But, nothing. Don't start your shit with me," she warned. "There's a customer upstairs waiting for you; he already paid." Misty jabbed the elevator button. "He's in room 726. When you walk in his suite, don't even talk. Just give him the bag with the apron. He wants to wear it. All you have to do is pull your pants down and let him spread cream cheese on your jawn. That's it."

"What?" A look of revulsion covered Brick's face.

Misty sighed. "The freak said he likes cheese sausage. He wants some cheese on your meat before he goes down on it." Misty shrugged. "Hey, it's easy money. You'll be in and out of there in twenty minutes or less." She scowled in thought. "That Betty Boop shit is such a success. In the future, we're gonna have to travel with a couple of those jawns on hand. I'll be damned if I'm going keep buying the bitches."

The elevator doors opened. Misty gave Brick a pat on his ass. "Go get 'im, boo. Oh, yeah—one more thing…he wants you to turn him over on your lap and smack his ass with a frying pan a couple of times before you let him taste that cheese sausage."

Brick stepped forward, preventing the elevator doors from closing. "I'm not into that spanking shit and you know it. That bitch, Yoyin, made me work her over. I ain't got no more violence left in me."

Unsympathetic, Misty rolled her eyes at Brick. "In this business, you do what you gotta do. At least he brought his own frying pan. That helps, doesn't it?"

Brick stood motionless for a few moments. Defeated, he stepped backward inside the elevator.

Satisfied, Misty gave him an approving smile. "Make sure he develops a strong appetite for your meat. We need as many return customers as we can get." Just before the doors closed, Misty yelled, "Don't forget to grab the apron before you bounce!"

CHAPTER 17

Misty snapped her cell phone shut. *Slimy bastard!* Hard
knots of anger coiled inside her stomach. She'd just been
told by Dane that he was in Philly. In an unnecessarily
arrogant tone, he'd revealed that he'd been in town since early
afternoon and was currently at his cousin's house—smoking weed
and sitting around, bullshitting. Even worse, he told her that he
was going to hang out with his cousin and he'd see her tomorrow.

Oh, hell no, he wasn't! If she had to walk him to her X5 at gun-
point, that nigga was coming home with her today!

She'd been sending him money and waiting for his ass for
almost two weeks and he didn't have the decency to give her his
flight information. She would have gladly picked him up at the
airport and brought him back to her crib.

She wasn't the least bit concerned about Brick's reaction to the
sudden change in their lifestyle. She'd been throwing hints and
mentally preparing Brick for Dane's arrival—preparing him for
life as part of a threesome.

Dane, on the other hand, didn't know what he was getting
into. She'd told him about her pimp game, but she hadn't delved
into the extent of her personal involvement with Brick. Yes,
she'd mentioned that Brick was a little slow and that he pretty
much did whatever she wanted, but she didn't tell him that she

and Brick had been inseparable since childhood. Dane would simply have to adjust. She'd soften him up with the new diamond studs. After she bought him a new wardrobe, lined his pockets with paper, he'd soon see the benefit in keeping Brick around.

If Dane refused to share the bed with her and Brick, then Brick could always sleep in her office—or on the sofa in the living room.

With Dane sharing their crib, there would be ample opportunities for Brick to reap some benefits. He could watch, jerk off to the sounds of their lovemaking, and if things went the way she planned, Brick would be able to join her and Dane from time to time. Mmm, she could just imagine the joy of feeling Brick's tongue slide against her clit, while Dane banged her from behind, doggy-style.

She'd fit Brick in the picture. No matter how many dudes she fell in love with, Brick was her nigga for life. And if Dane didn't treat her right, she'd make sure Brick gave him an ass-whipping that he'd never forget.

Misty rushed around, getting herself together, and then it dawned on her that she was in a hell of a predicament. Her mom's dance class ended at seven. Thomasina would throw up her hands and try to physically fight Misty if she left her stranded again. As small as she was, Misty could hold her own, but truth be told, without Brick's help, Misty wouldn't be able to do shit with her wild-ass mother.

"Brick, I need a favor. I need you to go pick up my mom from her line-dancing class."

His eyebrows rose. "Huh? Come again?" Brick asked, without taking his eyes off the television screen. His shoulders dipped and moved from side to side as he played a football video game. "Fuck that. No! You know your mom don't wanna see me. And

I'm not trying to see her ignorant ass. Why can't you pick her up?" He continued clicking the controller, eyes glued to the screen.

Misty cocked her head to the side, her voice taking on a serious tone. "I'm trying to get our money right. I'm working on a big deal. The client is some important dude. He doesn't want to leave a paper trail, so he wants to sit down and have a face-to-face meeting," she said, making up the story as she went along.

"Yo, Misty. That money deal is gonna fall through if I get locked up. I swear to God, if your mom comes out of her mouth with some real grimy shit, I'm gon' punch her in her head. Real rap. After she calls the cops and gets me locked up, then what? How you gon' eat, then?"

Dang! Brick was coming at her neck. He really hated her mother. She couldn't blame him. Misty quickly went into damage-control mode. When Brick lost his temper and went off like this, she had no choice but to humble herself and calm him down. "Baby, I already talked to my mom. I told her you're picking her up and I also told her to act nice."

"I don't need her to act nice. All she gotta do is stay the fuck outta my face!" he bellowed. "I'm tired of listening to her call me outta my name. I'm warning you, Misty, if your mom can't control her mouth, then I'm gon' act like I can't control my fist. Now, think about it—you sure you want me to give your mom a ride?"

Misty assumed a pitiful expression. "Brick, I don't have a choice. Like I said, she's gonna act right. I promise."

"I've been on my grind all week. All I wanna do is fall back. Can't a nigga chill on his day off?" Fire shot from Brick's eyes as he stared at the screen, pressing hard on the buttons on the controller, like he was trying to break a couple of legs of the opposing team of animated players.

"Look, baby," Misty said softly, "when this deal goes through, I won't have to work you so hard. This new client is willing to sign a ninety-day contract for you to serve his wife," Misty said, lying through her teeth.

Brick frowned, put down the controller and cradled his chin. "I gotta fuck dude's wife ninety times?"

"No! He wants you to serve her up about once a week, and he's willing to commit to a three-month contract. He's paying in advance—big bucks. Cash!" Misty chuckled. "For the kind of gravy dude is willing to throw around, I should let my mom walk the hell home. It would make good business sense for you to join in on the meeting."

Brick scowled. "Why?"

"You know, show good faith by letting you get acquainted with his wife tonight. Give her a sample of what she'll be getting."

Brick furrowed his brows. He hadn't planned on working to-night. He was trying to enjoy his free time. Maybe chauffeuring Thomasina wouldn't be too bad after all.

"But I don't want to piss my mother off. Who knows when we'll need her signature again? Come on, baby. I need you to have my back. You gotta help me out and go pick my mom up from her class."

"Aiight," Brick said, his sour expression revealing that the last thing in the world he wanted to do was be anywhere near Misty's mother. He glanced at his new Fossil watch. "What time should I leave?" he asked with a loud sigh.

"I think you should leave now! You know how traffic is on Wadsworth Avenue. By the time you circle the block a couple times, she'll be ready." Holding a tube of lip gloss, Misty pointed the shiny tip toward Brick. "Please don't have my mother stand-ing around waiting."

Reluctantly, he put his football game on pause. "Don't worry, the sooner I scoop her up and drop her ass off, the sooner I can get back to the crib and finish chillin'."

Misty's eyes darted at the empty beer bottles. "And please don't drive like a maniac."

"I'm not drunk."

"Not yet."

He picked up a can of Budweiser, snapped it open, and guzzled it down. "Now, I'm feeling nice enough to deal with your mom."

"I know she can be real ignorant sometimes, but don't let her get to you. She can't understand what I see in you. But that's our business, right, boo?"

"Yeah, you right," he said solemnly.

"If my mom wants to stop and pick up some groceries or something, just do it. For me." Misty paused in thought. "In fact, I want you to offer to take her grocery shopping or something."

"What?" Brick looked horrified.

"We need to keep Thomasina Bernard in a real good mood. Feel me?"

No! Keeping the peace, Brick gave a head nod, but the thought of walking around a supermarket with Misty's mom was about as farfetched as her greeting him politely.

∂◦⋖

Thomasina approached the X5. Brick tilted his chin in acknowledgment and assembled his lips to form a cautious smile.

"Where's Misty?" Thomasina demanded; her mouth scrunched in irritation at the sight of Brick sitting behind the wheel.

Here we go! Brick's slightly smiling lips quickly curled into a defensive knot. "Didn't she tell you that I was coming to pick you up?" He barely managed to keep the bass out of his voice. While his left hand gripped the steering wheel, his right hand, restless on his lap, balled into a ready fist. He steadied his tone. "She was supposed to get in touch with you and tell…"

Thomasina gave Brick a scathing look and then waved her hand—cutting off his explanation. She flung open the passenger door. "I've been line-dancing for the past hour. How do you figure I had time to talk to my daughter on the phone?" She pulled her cell out of her pocketbook and scrolled through the calls. "She didn't call," she said accusingly.

Brick glanced away. Misty promised to call her mom; she'd given Brick her word. She knew her mom had beef with him. Why would she put him in such an awkward position? *She probably forgot*, he reconciled. "I guess she forgot," he verbalized to Thomasina. Trying to relax, Brick unfurled his fist, and turned the music up a notch. He hoped Thomasina would take a hint. *Be quiet and enjoy the ride*. If she kept running her mouth, she might fuck around and make an abrasive remark that didn't sit well with him. If that were the case, who knew what angry demons he'd unleash on her?

Determined to yak, Thomasina spoke in a voice loud enough to be heard over the music that blared from the speakers. "That girl sure is shiesty. Misty knows she still owes me a trip to the mall. All that stuff she bought me a few days ago was nice and everything, but those were her choices."

Brick shrugged. He had no idea what Misty's mom was talking about.

"Hell, I'd like the opportunity to shop for myself. You know what I mean, Brick?"

Appreciative that Thomasina's anger was not directed at him, he gave a noncommittal nod. That was the best he could do. Thomasina had no idea that her redirected anger had saved her from getting a busted lip and a few missing teeth. Even better, Brick wouldn't have to face aggravated assault charges.

"Something's wrong with Misty," her mother commented.

Brick cut a curious eye at Thomasina.

"I'm beginning to think that being too pretty isn't all it's cracked up to be. Being real good-looking is probably as bad as being real ug…" Thomasina's voice trailed off.

Here we go; this bitch is about to start throwing slurs. Putting his guard back up, he let his left hand slide off the steering wheel and let it rest on his thick thigh, clenched up, ready to go up inside somebody's ignorant-ass mouth.

"I know you know what I'm talking about. Take for example, the way people stare at you on account of that scar…now, that has to make you feel different than regular people. Well, Misty is in the same predicament."

Surprisingly, Brick didn't feel the urge to knock the shit out of Thomasina. Curiosity over what she had to say about Misty's situation pacified his building rage.

"People have been staring and grinning at that girl since the day she was born. Strangers used to approach me and beg for the chance to hold my pretty baby in their arms. Acting like if they held her, some of her beauty might rub off on them. I couldn't even take Misty around my other friends who had little girls. She outshined them so bad, it just didn't seem fair. Think about it? How many girlfriends does Misty have?"

Brick shrugged. "None."

"You want to know why? Because no girl with any amount of

self-respect would want to stand next to a young woman as beauti-ful as Misty. There's not a soul I've ever seen, except a movie star, who can hold a candle to Misty. And we don't have movie stars running around in Philly, so Misty has to be the prettiest thing most people have ever set their eyes on."

"You right," Brick agreed. People did gawk at Misty, stunned that such a gorgeous woman walked among mere mortals. Brick was sure Misty could have been a movie star if she'd gone to Hollywood and tried out for a part. But Misty enjoyed criminal activity much better than something that would require keeping regular hours and following any kind of orders. But fuck all that, how did Miss Thomasina figure he and Misty were in the same category?

Brick cut an eye at Miss Thomasina. Misty and her mom did-n't have anything in common except their height and their sass. Both were short, only five feet or so, but Misty was slender and her mom was short and curvy. Misty didn't get her looks from her mother. Miss Thomasina looked all right and everything, but she didn't look like she was even related to Misty.

Brick knew Misty's father was some Hispanic dude who had used her mom to get a green card, but to hear Miss Thomasina tell it, she sounded like she was taking full credit for Misty's looks.

"Starting from the day I gave birth to her, all Misty ever heard was, 'Ooo! Oh my God! She's beautiful. Can I hold her?' I couldn't even walk through the mall with her when she was toddling around. People always stopped to gawk at us. I had people ask if they could hold her while I snapped a picture. Now, that's where I drew the line. Hell, no, I wasn't letting potential child snatchers take a picture of my child. Brick, I'm telling you, you would have thought Misty was a child celebrity, the way people acted when they saw her."

Brick nodded. He knew exactly what Miss Thomasina was talking about.

"Now, me, myself, I'm the first to admit that I'm just average-looking. I used to blush with pride when people made such fuss over my pretty baby. I sort of felt like the compliments were being extended to me as well."

Brick gave a hint of a smile. "I can dig it." He often felt the same way. Sharing Misty's shine made a mufucka feel good about himself—scarred-up face and all.

"But now I see that all that finger pointing and people gathering around her because of her looks must have given Misty some kind of a complex." Thomasina's tone switched from cheerful to somber.

Misty ain't got no complex! How the hell did her mother figure that being extra pretty had given Misty a complex? Brick had a complex. He was aware that he had low self-esteem issues. But Misty was a stunna and she knew it. She used her looks to get her and Brick where they were today. Miss Thomasina was talking some bullshit now, and Brick started tuning her out, sorry he'd even bothered to give her a few minutes of ear time.

He wanted to turn the music up extra loud, but that would probably make Miss Thomasina mad and then she'd start her shit. He couldn't wait to pull in front of her house.

"I heard something about this subject on one of those daytime shows that I watch while I'm at work," Thomasina went on. "Between you and me, I make it a point to watch more TV at work than I do at home. I don't let those people at the hospital work me like a damn horse. I sit right up in those patients' rooms, catch all my favorite shows." Thomasina chuckled, but Brick disliked the woman too much to put forth the effort to join her in laughter. "Anyway, one of those psychology experts said that studies have shown that being extremely beautiful is as damaging to a person's mind as it is if they were real, real, uh, unattractive. I know people wonder what you and Misty have in common, but ever since I watched that show, I've been thinking that you two are probably two of a kind."

Brick mulled over the affront, wiggling his fingers, uncertain if he should curl them back into a fist. But he decided he could let it go. In their own way, he and Misty were two of kind. He flattened his fist, thinking that perhaps Miss Thomasina had a point. Fuck if he knew and fuck if he cared. He was relieved that he didn't have to fight the urge to whip Misty's mom's ass and fling her out into oncoming traffic.

He merged onto I-76 East. In a few minutes, Miss Loudmouth would be out of the whip and he'd back at the crib, controller in one hand, a can of brew in the other.

CHAPTER 18

The pungent aroma of weed greeted Misty at Monroe's front door. "'Sup, shawty?" Unsmiling, Monroe gave her a half-hearted welcome, poking out his lips, trying to convey that he didn't appreciate being fucked and discarded. "What happened to your fly ride? Did the repo man pay you a visit?" he quipped, craning his neck and turning up his nose at Mr. Johnnie's old Ford. Misty was too angry to feel insulted or embarrassed by Mr. Johnnie's clunker. The beat-up old squatter sat idling loudly. Badly in need of an oil change, a tune-up or probably a new engine, the hooptie groaned as if begging Mr. Johnnie to put it out of its misery and take it to the nearest junkyard.

"I'm on point with the payments; I had to loan my truck out for a minute." Monroe didn't deserve an explanation, but being that she was inside his crib, she didn't want to come out of her mouth the wrong way. At least not before she gripped up his cousin and rolled out.

"Let me hit that." She extended her hand. Begrudgingly, Monroe passed her the Dutch he was puffing on.

She puffed once as she looked around the modest home. "Where's Dane?" she asked, making sure her tone sounded nonchalant.

"He's upstairs taking a shower. Didn't he tell you?"

"Tell me what?" She feigned innocence and took another hit off the Dutch.

"We're about to roll out in a little while."

"Where?" Knowing Dane's planned whereabouts could probably prove useful.

"We gon' holla at some friends and then we're gon' roll up in that new joint on Delaware Avenue. After that, we'll hit up a coupla after-hour spots. Just the fellas, y'ah mean?"

An unpleasant emotion ripped through Misty. Rejection. Instead of being surrounding by a bunch of no-account niggas, Dane should have been proud to stroll up in the new spot with her under his arm. She didn't like being ditched for his cousin and his dumb-ass crew. "Y'all niggas ain't goin' nowhere. Y'all ain't gon' leave the hood," Misty taunted, angling for information.

"Uh-huh. We gon' hit that new spot, Hades," he bragged.

Ah! Good to know. She'd make some calls later and find out what was what and who was running things at Hades.

The squeal of faucets turning, and the rushing sound of running water trickled off. "Dane!" she yelled from the bottom of the stairs. One look at her cute ass, and Dane would dismiss thoughts of partying with a trio of losers.

The bathroom door opened. "Who's that?"

"Misty!" She dashed up the stairs.

"Yo, shawty. That ain't cool," Monroe protested. "You can't barge your way upstairs like that."

Misty ignored him and didn't stop trotting until she reached the top of the stairs.

Dane stood in the hallway, a blue towel wrapped around his waist. Droplets of water dotted his muscled shoulders and well-defined arms. He looked succulent, edible. Hell, he looked totally fuckable. But looking at the big picture, Misty decided to restrain her sexual impulses.

"Hey, Lil' Bit. What it is?" There was a lack of warmth in his voice; his smile appeared to be forced.

She cocked her head to the side and gave him a stony stare. "Nigga, whatchu think it is? How you gon' be in Philly all damn day and not let me know about it until you got good and ready?"

"My bad. But damn, I hope you didn't come up here to start no shit. This is my auntie's crib. She's not gon' be too thrilled if she walks in the door and hears a bunch of arguing and whatnot." Dane pulled the towel tighter. He took a few steps forward; as if he planned to physically toss Misty out of the house.

She hadn't expected such an aggressive reaction from him, but she wasn't about to back down. Standing her ground, she curled her small lips. "I'm not worrying about your damn auntie or this dump." She looked around the drab hallway, with her nose turned up. "I have my own spot and it's laid out lovely. I just came through to find out what was really up with you."

"I told you. I have plans for tonight with the fellas, but I'll hit you up first thing in the morning."

"Yeah, aiight," Misty said, with a smirk on her face.

"Seriously. It's not cool to run up in my auntie's crib like this," Dane chastised. He scrunched up his lips, attempting to look offended, but when he pushed those juicy lips together, Misty's pussy went into a panic. It was an inappropriate time for moisture to accumulate between her legs. She sent a stern message to her vagina, ordering it to behave and simmer down. Yearning for Dane's tasty meat, her coochie became defiant and started to make a ruckus, emitting urgent, slurping sounds.

She'd be in a world of trouble if she let her coochie run the show. Strong-willed and refusing to weaken under the pressure, Misty clenched up her inner muscles, instantly cutting off the coochie chatter. Now, able to communicate with a clearer head, she gave Dane a side-long look, her lip turned up in a sneer. "I really thought you were about your business, but all you wanna do is run around with a bunch of young-ass thugs. Obviously, you think it's all sweet and everything because I kept sending you cheddar. You thought you played me, but you're wrong. Now that I see how you really roll…" She paused and gave him a look of disgust. "Nigga, that *L* I took, ain't about nothing. My money's stacking right now as we speak. So go 'head—do you, because I'm gon' damn sure do me. Feel me? I'm out!" Misty turned to leave.

Dane grabbed her arm. Misty sneered at his hand and then jerked her arm away.

"Nah, see it ain't even all serious like that," he said. Looking uneasy, he again tightened the towel around his waist. "I just got here." He laughed, tried to get her to smile, but Misty glared at him. "See, I promised my lil' homies I'd kick it with them tonight. But, I'm still gon' move in your crib—first thing tomorrow morning."

"I changed my mind," she said, with taunting laughter. "Move in here with your cousin—or take your ass back to Detroit. I don't care what you do."

Dane's Adam's apple bobbed up and down, his eyes flitted back and forth. He looked close to caving under the pressure. "I hope you didn't quit your other hustle, because I don't want to do business with someone I can't trust."

"You think I'm shady?"

"Yeah, I do," she remarked. "Besides, I need a right-hand man who's serious about stacking paper—someone on top of his game. Obviously, you're not my man."

"Yo, I know how to handle mine. I just wanted to have a little fun before—"

"Obviously, we don't have the same philosophy," Misty said, cutting him off. "I believe in putting business before pleasure." A smile crept across her face. She was putting Dane in his place and in the process revealing that he wasn't the man she'd thought him to be. Dane was exactly like his dumb cousin—vulnerable, needy, and greedy.

"Come on, Lil' Bit. You're making a big deal outta nothing."

"Oh, really? It was a big deal for a dimepiece like me to stay posted up at Western Union, filling out forms and sending dough on the regular to an ungrateful nigga."

He ran his tongue across his delicious-looking lips, attempting to seduce her into a more accommodating mood. "After tonight, I'll make it worth your while. I promise." Dane winked and puckered up, implying that Misty was in for a major dick-down and some intense pussy suctioning.

Misty rolled her eyes at Dane. As tempted as she was to take him up on his sexual proposal, she realized she'd come out in a better position if she turned down the offer. Sneering excessively, she continued her rant. "You might think I'm blowing this out of proportion, but I feel like my trust has been violated. I was acting on good faith when I sent you all that cheddar. I gave you enough dough to pay for two or three plane tickets. But you kept jerking me around, feeding me one lie after another. Now that you've finally arrived, you have the nerve to tell me that you wanna kick it with your cousin and his sorry-ass crew? Do you really think I'm gonna sit back and let your broke ass diss me while you go out and party with a bunch of..." She paused, pondering the most insulting names she could call his friends. "Punk-ass, hustling, backward niggas."

"Damn. That's cold."

"That's real. You played me, Dane."

Insulted, his mouth fell open. "My shit is packed—"

She cut him off with a smirk. "Then you played yourself. I hope you have a nice flight back. Peace, nigga!" Feeling victorious, Misty trotted down the staircase.

"Lil' Bit!" Dane yelled. Holding his towel in place while trying to catch up with Misty, Dane was only halfway down the stairs by the time Misty slammed the front door. A few moments later, she hopped inside Mr. Johnnie's clunker, instructing the old man to pull off.

She hadn't expected to have to play hardball with Dane. Had she known, she would have traveled in a real cab or hired a limo or something. Mr. Johnnie's hooptie was fucking with her image. Oh well, fuck it. With a plan in mind, she told Mr. Johnnie to take her home.

CHAPTER 19

Carrying a case of brew, Brick was anxious to get inside the crib, to pop open a can and get his swerve back on. Miss Thomasina was a trip. Misty had to really be on some desperate shit, to put him and her mom together without being close by in case she had to stand between them and play referee. Brick felt it lucky to have made it back to the apartment without having raised his voice or his hand to Misty's loudmouth mom.

Inside the apartment, he was greeted by the scent of Misty's favorite perfume.

"The deal fell through," she said as she came out of the bathroom, pulling a brush through her hair. She was wearing light makeup, glittery lip gloss, her skimpy Versace dress, and she was flossing a lot of carats. Iced out from her earlobes down to her ankles, Misty was blinging as brightly as that rich chick, Yoyin. She must have bought some extra sparkle on her most recent shopping spree because Brick didn't recognize the diamond-encrusted charm bracelet on her right wrist, the rock on her pinky finger or the princess-cut diamond pendant that dangled from her neck. Prettier than the average woman, Misty should have been gracing the covers of magazines. Brick's private responded to her glamour, rising up slightly, jerking beneath his jeans.

"What happened with the dude you went to go see?" He didn't

really care, just wanted to hear her comment in order to gauge her mood. If she wasn't in a rush to get to wherever she was going, there was a strong possibility that he could sweet-talk her into giving him a quickie.

"Fucking around with Mr. Johnnie, I got there too late." Misty looked sad, then suddenly brightened. "But I have another plan in the works. I have to go out for a few hours and chitchat with another potential client."

Brick had to control the urge to pull Misty into his arms, stick his hand up her dress, and pull her panties to the side. He'd love to hit it real quick before she went out to take care of business, but he knew Misty wouldn't go for it. She was looking too glamorous to allow him to rumple her gear or alter her sweet fragrance with the smell of his sex.

Misty cut her eye at the case of beer Brick had set on the floor. "You 'bout to get fucked up for the night?"

"Yeah, I was thinking about it. Why?"

Misty shrugged. "Just wondering if you planned on waiting up for me? You're horny. I can tell," she informed him.

"True, but I can tell you're in a rush. I'll be aiight—I can jerk myself off."

"Yeah, go ahead and handle that. I shouldn't be out too late."

"It's cool. Take your time. Do your thing, baby. I got my brew and my weed. Don't worry about me. Go make shit happen."

Misty nodded, obviously relieved. "Oh, yeah, how'd it go with my mom? I tried to call her but her phone was turned off."

"It was kind of bumpy at first, but we got through it aiight."

"For real?" Misty beamed.

"Yeah, but I wouldn't wanna make a habit of it."

❦

All that line-dancing sure had worked up a sweat. Thomasina tested the running water in the bathtub, turned on the shower and stepped inside. Eager to get rid of the musty smell of dried perspiration, she lathered up a washcloth and began soaping her underarms, shoulders, and forearms. When she reached her thighs, a tiny smile played at her lips. Was it her imagination or was her jelly-like flesh feeling more toned? No, it was just wishful thinking. It wasn't possible to start toning up after only a few classes.

She rubbed the soapy washcloth across her ample behind and then touched it with her palm. It felt smoother, less dimpled. Not trusting the brush of her hand, she squeezed the jiggly flesh. Her ass didn't have the same marshmallow texture that she hated, but had grown to accept. She gave a full-fledged grin. She wasn't crazy. Something was going on. The scale still spoke the same outlandish number, but those line-dancing classes were shifting her pounds around, redistributing her weight.

Her wheels started spinning and then traveled until they landed on an image of her ex-lover's face. The pain hurt like a knife, but the knife didn't cut as deeply as it had when she watched Victor throwing his luggage in the trunk of his car. Leaving Thomasina and showing no remorse. "*Me and my wife are gonna try to patch things back up!*" He'd emphasized the word *wife*, used it like an arrow, aimed at Thomasina's heart.

Rumor had it that there was trouble in Victor's marriage. Gossipers noticed that he hadn't been accompanying his freckle-faced wife to church in the past few weeks. "Maybe he's sick," Thomasina offered, meaning heartsick over dumping her.

"No, he ain't sick. He done started turning up at the bar again," the most recent carrier of tales informed her.

Yeah, well, he'd better not try to come running back to me, Thomasina thought. Her broken heart was on the mend and she'd be damned if she'd take Victor back so he could shatter it to pieces all over again.

The moment she acquired a half-decent figure, she was going to put on something snug and mosey on over to Victor's hangout, The Delmar bar. She'd flaunt her improved body in front of Victor and then shoot him down with a string of insults if he so much as sent a smile her way. If her hourglass figure encouraged him to send her a drink, she'd take a sip and then throw the rest of it right in Victor's face. The hell with making him jealous by being on the arm of a new man. A new man meant new trouble; looking good was the best revenge.

Her muscles ached, screamed to be left alone and not put through any more rigorous line-dancing for at least two or three weeks. Thomasina turned the knob, making the water hotter, soothing her aching body as vengeful thoughts toward Victor helped speed up the healing of her heart.

CHAPTER 20

D ane, Monroe, Ashy Cashy, and Edison stood at the end of a long line of anxious hopefuls waiting to get inside Hades, Philly's newest hotspot.

All heads turned when Misty rolled up. She got out of the eye-catching SUV and tossed her keys to the valet. Having made the appropriate connections and peeled off the right amount of cash, Misty glided past the velvet rope, making it a point to step back and fling Dane a triumphant look before she breezed inside the club. *Fuck with me, mufucka!*

Inside Hades, she checked out the décor. Images of flames adorned everything from the walls and furniture to the uniforms worn by staff. Even the lamp shades and various light coverings were designed in the shape of flames. Cute, in a trashy sort of way.

Later, after being whisked up to the elevated VIP area, Misty stood at the balcony overlooking the action downstairs. Niggas dressed in their finest were out in droves down on the main floor. Sports figures, local celebrities, and ballers mingled in the VIP area. A blinged-out baller had his eye on Misty. She ignored him. With her cell pressed against her ear, she gave instructions to Big Boy, the bouncer. She told him to pull Monroe out of the long line and send him up to the VIP room.

She took the phone away from her ear while the bouncer went

looking for Monroe. Apparently, the big baller thought the end of her phone call meant she had some time for him. When she saw his slimy swagger easing up to her, she turned her back. It felt good to ignore mufuckas. Fuck a baller; she had her own cheese.

"Which one of y'all nigga's name is Monroe?" Big Boy's booming voice demanded. Misty giggled, imagining Monroe shrinking back in dread, fearful that his under-twenty-one status had been peeped before he'd even made it to the middle of the outrageously long line.

"I'ma ax one more time, then all y'all gon' have to start pullin' out ID. Which one of y'all niggas is named Monroe?"

"Tell him your name, man!" Ashy Cashy encouraged. The sound of his grating voice made Misty frown. She disliked everything about the unattractive boy.

"Yo, whaddup, my man?" Monroe piped in. "I'm Monroe."

Misty suppressed a giggle when she heard the tremble in Monroe's voice. He tried to his conceal his trepidation by deepening his tone, and assuming a cavalier attitude, but it didn't work; a crack in his voice revealed his trepidation. *Ha-ha!* she cackled in her head.

"Yo, come with me, man."

"What I do?" Monroe lost his cool; his voice went up an octave.

Big Boy lightened up his gruff tone. "Calm down, my man. Someone sent you a personal invitation. Your party's waiting for you up in the VIP room."

"What about the rest of us?" There was a tinge of desperation in Ashy Cashy's voice.

"Just Monroe," Big Boy responded sternly.

"Yo, Monroe. You gon' dip up in there without us?" Dane asked incredulously.

"Yo, dawg. I know you ain't gon' leave us out here like this?" Muscle Boy sounded irate.

Had Misty thought the situation through, she would have offered Big Boy even more money to videotape the scenario. She would have gladly paid extra to witness the look on Dane's face while he watched Monroe being personally ushered inside the prestigious club. "*Ha!*" she cackled out loud as she snapped her phone closed. She didn't stop grinning until Monroe was escorted up to the VIP room.

Monroe joined Misty at the balcony. "What's good, shawty?" he said with an air of cockiness.

She rolled her eyes and then gave him a long, speculative look. "What's good?" She made a waving gesture. "This VIP treatment— that's what's good, nigga. Don't I get a thank you or something for getting you out of that long-ass line?"

"Oh, yeah; no doubt. Good looking out," he remarked coolly, demonstrating an ability to maintain his composure despite the posh environment and the sprinkling of local celebrities in close proximity.

Misty sucked her teeth as she caught a glimpse of Monroe's dark eyes sneakily darting about, gleaming in appropriate awe of his good fortune. "Whatchu drinking, youngin'?"

"Um, Budweiser?" Monroe posed his selection in the form of a question.

"That's it?"

He touched his pockets. "That's all I can do. I'm kind of light right now."

"Like I said, it's all good. You're my guest. You're drinking on me."

"Yo, word? That's whassup." Monroe's eyes lit up and appeared to spin delightedly inside his eye sockets.

"Finally!"

"Finally, what?"

"You're finally showing a little appreciation." Misty smiled.

Monroe glanced downward. "Aw, you ain't gotta come at me like that."

"I'm just saying—" She stared him down.

"I feel you," he said, nodding. "Thanks."

"That's better," Misty acknowledged and then beckoned a big-titty waitress. The waitress looked all right. Cute, but not spectacular. She most definitely was not competition for Misty. Then again, few were. All her life, her mother, her teachers, neighbors— everyone—either told her in words or demonstrated with preferential treatment that she was the prettiest girl in the world. To this day, Misty knew with all her heart that Beyonce, Shakira, Halle, and Kim Kardashian all rolled into one couldn't touch her beauty.

Swinging her hips like she knew she was hot, the dark-skinned waitress approached Misty and Monroe. Misty was amused by the degree of confidence in such an average-looking woman. In keeping with the red-flame theme, the waitresses wore a tight-fitting, button-down top adorned with sequined flames and a short, fire-red, curve-hugging skirt.

"Hi. I'm Felice," she said, wearing a big smile that attested that she was extremely pleased with herself. Long shapely legs, a tiny waistline, and a set of what appeared to be double-D boobs had Felice thinking she was the shit.

Misty wasn't intimidated by a pair of big titties or a big ass. Shit, that was all the bimbo had going for her. Still, she was irked that Monroe was damn near drooling over the damn waitress when he wouldn't even be up in this dip if it weren't for her generosity.

She peeped Monroe giving the waitress the eye. On the sly, the young buck was giving a subtle head nod, acknowledging appreciation of Felice's body parts. His slimy attempt to communicate with Felice was irritating.

The misbehavior on Felice's part did not escape Misty. She saw the waitress flirt with Monroe, moistening her dark lips, and coyly fluttering her fake lashes.

Uh-huh, I'ma deal with these two slimy bitches, later.

With his eyes glued to Felice's breasts, Monroe slowly pondered his liquor choices. "Um, lemme see…um…gimme a shot of Henny and um…a bottle of Bud."

"Give him a double Henny and a Bud," Misty interjected sharply.

"Thanks, shawty." Monroe smiled at Misty and then his gaze wandered back to Felice's boobs and lingered there.

"Bring me a Gold Digger."

Felice tilted her head in bewilderment. "A Gold Digger? What's that?"

"Goldschlager Schnapps and champagne," Misty explained. "The bartender should know how to make it," she added with annoyance. "By the way, we'll be sitting in my private booth over there." With an arrogant smirk, Misty nodded toward a secluded booth in the back. "But we'll have the first few rounds out here." She gazed over the balcony and smiled. Monroe looked down also. "Enjoying the view?" She winked at Monroe.

Monroe fixed admiring eyes on Misty. "Yeah, the view is all that. But damn, you got us a private booth and everything? Man, I dig the way you roll." He bent down and gave Misty a quick peck on the lips. "You're beautiful, you know that?" Monroe said, smiling.

None too pleased that Monroe's attention was no longer focused on her, Felice took the orders and sashayed away, showing off another physical attribute—her plump, nicely rounded ass. Monroe's dick took notice and thumped inside his pants.

The disrespectful flirtatious behavior that had gone on right under her nose was duly noted. Misty would handle the hot-to-trot waitress and ungrateful-ass Monroe in time. Right now, her mind was on Dane and her eyes were focused on the door.

By the time Dane and his boys trudged in, Monroe was working on his third round of drinks. Misty, however, needing to keep a level head, was still slowly sipping her first gold-flecked drink.

She watched Dane take in his surroundings. When he looked upward, spotting her and Monroe, Misty leaned toward Monroe. "Were you hitting on the waitress?" she asked softly. Monroe shook his head in denial. "Yes, you were! But I'm not mad at you. You can tap that ass, if that's what you want." Misty gestured excessively and spoke louder than necessary, trying to attract Dane's attention.

"Nah, nah. See. It wasn't even about that."

"Don't worry about it, I'm still gonna let you get with me."

"For real?"

"But there's a catch," Misty said teasingly.

Monroe lifted his chin inquiringly.

"You gotta fuck her first. Then you can have some of this."

"For real?" Excitement glinted in his eyes. Then, worry clouded his face. "How? You gon' hook up a threesome at your crib, later on?"

"Yeah, I'll see how Miss Felice reacts after I give her a nice tip."

Encouraged by the promise of a ménage à trois and unaware that his boys had finally gained entry and were all watching, Monroe draped an arm around Misty and pulled her closer. She felt Monroe's member swell against her hip as she glanced over the balcony and smirked down at Dane. *Fuck with me, mufucka!* Her smirk was met by Dane's hostile glare.

Misty enjoyed seeing the fury on Dane's face. Even Ashy Cashy, as if he'd been personally slighted, looked mad as hell. His angry lips were turned down in scornful disapproval. She could feel the heat of their anger rising up to the balcony like a raging fire, but distance and the thumping club music prevented her the pleasure of hearing Dane and his crew's scathing comments about her and the traitor, Monroe.

Monroe towered over Misty. She had to stand on her toes to stroke his cheek and run her finger across his lips. "Been thinking about you, youngin'. I tried to get you outta my mind…" She shook her head regretfully. "But I can't. That night with you was so good; I get hot just picturing your thick private. You're well hung, like a stallion."

"So, if you was feeling me like that, why you push up on my cousin?"

Misty shrugged. "Because of your age. You're only nineteen."

"So what? I'm not a minor."

"You're under twenty-one," she reminded him. "But tonight, your age ain't nothing but a number…" She moistened her lips. "I'm in the mood for some raunchy pleasure—how you feel about that, youngin'?"

"I'm all up in it!" Grinning, he turned the beer bottle up to his lips for another pull.

Misty reached up, fondled his neck. It was an intimate gesture, designed to send tingles up Monroe's spine and put more fire in Dane's jealous eyes.

Ashy Cashy shifted his feet, agitated. He hollered something crude and gave Misty the finger.

"Fuck you!" she mouthed over the blaring music, and also gave him the finger.

Monroe looked down. Shocked that he'd been spotted by his crew, he raised his arms apologetically, as if being in Misty's company was out of his control. Misty distracted him by rubbing her hand over his crotch, causing his length to stiffen. Gently, she circled the rounded head of his dick, rubbed softly until she felt moisture seep through his pants.

Eyes closed, lips slack, Monroe quickly forgot about his friends on the floor below.

Livid, Dane spat obscenities that she couldn't make out. He glared at the illicit lovers with icy disdain.

Putting on a show for Dane and his two irate cronies, she caressed the top of Monroe's hand, which was placed palm down on top of the balcony ledge in clear view. With her fingertips, she invaded the area between his four fingers; enticing his flesh with soft, feathery caresses.

Excited, Monroe's breathing pattern began to change. "That feels good. Damn, shawty, you really know how to get a nigga heated." Monroe kissed Misty, gave tongue, which she gladly accepted and returned the favor. Finally, enough was enough. She broke the kiss and searched the crowd below, straining her eyes to locate Dane; trying to gauge his reaction to the lustful exhibition taking place on the VIP level.

Dane and the two street hustlers were advancing toward the dance floor to get a closer look at a big-behind woman, who was moving her ass and wiggling around like a stripper.

A stab of disappointment sliced through Misty so deeply, her first impulse was to push Monroe away and then cuss him out for slobbering all over her face. But, she had a sudden change of heart. From her peripheral vision, she saw their busty waitress approach.

"Are you two okay?" Felice asked. Her tone held the hint of an attitude.

"We could be better." Misty gave her a wide smile.

Felice eyed Misty's half-filled drink. "Do you want another one?"

Misty shook her head and crooked her finger, gesturing that she wanted to speak privately. Monroe stepped back while Misty slipped Felice some folded cash and whispered an invitation for her to join her and Monroe in their private booth as soon as she could get a break.

Moments later, seated inside the private booth, Monroe tipped his glass toward Misty. "Damn, you smooth as shit," he praised, referring to the interaction between Misty and Felice. "She gon' roll out with us when she gets off tonight?"

"Yeah, she's with it. So, don't embarrass me. If you can't handle two women, tell me now."

"Yo, I can take on five chicks," he bragged.

"Uh-huh. We'll see."

CHAPTER 21

Carrying a tray with two Gold Diggers, two shots of Hennessy and another bottle of Budweiser, Felice joined Misty and Monroe inside the private booth.

"Is it cool?" Misty asked Felice.

"Yeah, I asked for an early break," Felice responded, setting down the tray and then closing the privacy screen.

"That's whassup." Misty gave Felice a wink.

Out of the loop, Monroe looked inquiringly at both of their faces. "Y'all gon' school a brother or what?"

The two young women giggled conspiratorially. "So, how are we gonna work this? I only have twenty minutes," Felice said.

"That's plenty of time, if the youngin' can perform." Misty smiled at Monroe.

"What? Y'all 'bout to get into something right here in the club?"

"Nervous?" Misty challenged.

"Nah, I'm cool."

"Come join us." Misty scooted close to the wall. Felice squeezed inside the booth, sandwiching Monroe between herself and Misty. She turned toward Monroe and pressed her firm, high-set breasts into his arm. "Hey, handsome. You feeling that Henny yet?"

"Nah, I'm feelin' you," Monroe offered, words slurred, eyes flitting lustfully from Misty's face to Felice's big tits. He gazed at the private screen, which he could see through. "What's that jawn made out of?"

"Don't get me to lying," Felice replied. "All I know is we can see out, but can't nobody see in." She smiled. Her full lips separated, showing off dark gums and pretty white teeth.

Misty nudged Monroe's shoulder. "It's playtime; let's have some fun."

"What y'all tryna get into?" he wanted to know.

Felice glanced at her watch. "A quickie ménage."

"A quickie what?"

"Nigga, you wasting time," Misty blurted. "We're gonna let you do both of us. You have twenty minutes to make us both cum."

Felice checked her watch. "We only have sixteen minutes left."

Monroe's dick throbbed excitedly and dribbled a few drops of desire. Getting into a threesome with two banging chicks was like a dream come true. He started to give a few suggestions on how to get the party started, but common sense told him to keep his mouth shut and let the women take charge. He had killed half a bottle of Hennessy, and was struggling with coordination and coherent speech. Misty and the big-titty waitress might change their minds about playtime, if they knew the hard liquor had him twisted.

Allowing his hands to do the talking, he clumsily groped Felice's boobs. Grabbing two handfuls, he squeezed greedily.

"Slow your frisky self down," Felice admonished, smacking Monroe's hands. Misty gave Monroe an evil stare.

Monroe laughed. "My bad. I couldn't help myself." Wearing a boyish smile, he held up both hands in mock surrender.

Felice unbuttoned the tight-fitting top, revealing a white lace bra that contrasted nicely with her sepia-colored skin. She unfastened the front hook, releasing a set of voluptuous breasts. Monroe's eyes bulged in appreciation.

Monroe was twisted; Misty could tell. She quickly went to work before his drunken ass ruined her opportunity to exact revenge on Dane. She extracted a tube of lubricant from inside her purse and then placed her lips close to Monroe's ear. "Suck on Felice's titties and take your dick out for me."

He tried to maintain an impassive expression, but Misty's heated whisper put a crooked smile on his face. Seated between the two sexy women, Monroe didn't know where to start. He turned his head toward Felice. Her bared breasts bounced freely as she shook them against his face. A trembling hand frantically worked on unzipping his pants, while his other hand clumsily palmed a handful of big, cocoa-colored titty.

The lewdness of such brazen, public debauchery aroused Monroe; his erection pulsed inside his pants. Greedily, he took in one of her dark-pearled nipples, captured it with hungry urgency, pulling and stretching the pliable flesh with his teeth.

Finally, his zipper was down, but drawn to Felice's succulent breasts, he returned his concentration to titty sucking and left his engorged dick inside his pants.

Misty displayed the tube of warming lubricant. "Do you want me to jerk you off?"

Monroe, trying to swallow Felice's ripened bosom, refused to be distracted.

Misty popped Monroe upside the head. "I guess you don't need my help, hungry mufucka. Whassup, you wanna grub on the bitch's pussy?"

Monroe made growling sounds that indicated giving Felice oral sex in a public place was a huge turn-on.

"I guess it's snack time," Misty said petulantly, pulling Monroe by his collar. "So get between her legs and get yourself a Happy Meal, youngin'."

Uninhibited by alcohol, Monroe scooted down to his knees. His head quickly disappeared beneath Felice's red skirt. Stirred by the sensual fragrance that emanated from between her legs, a soft groan came from the back of his throat. Passionately, he pulled her panties to the side and began licking, tasting the sting of her tart womanly flavor. Desiring more, he used his thumbs to pry apart her plump, inner lips. "Ooo, shit. You got some big, juicy lips," he murmured. He plunged in his tongue, twisting it, burrowing deeply. He sucked her vagina, sipping softly at first—delicately. Then he slurped loudly, groaning as he lapped, using broad, wet strokes; his widened tongue coated with sugary cream.

Slumped in the booth, her legs splayed, Felice writhed and moaned helplessly as Monroe sipped her thick nectar.

Certain that her loud moans would get them all ejected, Misty slid over and silenced Felice with lips, enticing the waitress to feed from the sweetness of her mouth. Having done prison time, Misty was well-schooled in girl-sex. She pressed Felice's large breasts together, then lowered her head, helping herself to the taste of double mounds of chocolate.

Felice gave a surprised gasp. Overwhelmed, she clenched her eyes tight and drew in her lips, struggling to contain a scream of passion. Misty's lips abandoned the swollen, sensitized flesh and quickly covered Felice's mouth with a firm hand, cutting off the waitress's ardent sounds. "Be quiet," Misty hissed. "You're drawing too much attention to us."

Felice bobbed her head in understanding. Misty removed her hand and returned her lips to Felice's nipple and tentatively flicked her tongue against the ripened swell. Felice, struggling to maintain control, silenced herself by covering her mouth with her own hand as she arched up her chest, presenting her sensitive peaks to Misty's hot lips.

Misty drew in the nipple and lashed it with her tongue. Felice's chest heaved and her lower body squirmed and twisted in wanton response to the dual stimulation she was trying to quietly endure.

Her body jerked, her fists clenched and unclenched as a spasm of unbridled pleasure surged through her.

Misty patted Monroe's head. "That's enough."

Monroe looked up, his expression a mixture of puzzlement and passion.

Felice's lids popped open, her lashes fluttered, her dark eyes gleamed with lust and desperation.

"She's losing it; you gon' have to stick this bitch. Pull your pants down, boo."

"In here?" Monroe sounded terrified.

"Can't nobody see us." She patted the cushiony booth. "Hurry up, before her manager comes looking for her."

Monroe reluctantly lowered his pants to his thighs and took a seat on the soft leather. Despite his wariness, his penis soared upward. Erect, throbbing with desire.

Without prompting, Felice peeled off her panties, pushed up her skirt and raised a leg, prepared to straddle him.

"Hold up, bitch. You can't ride my boo until he gets his jawn covered up." Misty produced a condom, but before unwrapping it, she clutched Monroe's aching member.

Wishing Dane could witness her powers of seduction, she gave a regretful sigh and then worked her lubricated palm up and down his turgid shaft. She gave his erection a hard squeeze, as if testing its ability to remain firm under pressure. She unfurled the condom and slathered it with the warming lubricant.

Gripping Monroe's penis, Misty moved over. "Aiight, bitch. Climb up on this."

Caught up in the frenzy of the moment, Felice found herself experiencing a perverse pleasure in being treated harshly and being repeatedly referred to as *bitch* by a bossy woman.

Monroe pumped dick into Felice. "We ain't got a lot of time, yo," Misty reminded. Extraditing matters, she applied soft smacks to the waitress's shapely, chocolate ass.

The sudden stinging sensation being dispensed by a tiny, feminine hand sent the waitress into body tremors; her hips rolled rhythmically. "Oh, yes! Spank my ass. Harder!"

Incredulous, Monroe's eyes widened. "Damn, boo, you whippin' that ass?"

Misty responded with another loud slap across Felice's round buttocks, sending the waitress into an uproar of heavy breathing and frantic pelvic thrusts. Monroe gripped Felice's shoulders and rammed his dick in deeply.

While Felice rolled her hips, guzzling up as much dick as she could take in, Misty stealthily slid her hand beneath her red skirt and encircled the base of Monroe's shaft, squeezing lightly. Monroe twitched at her touch. He groaned, but managed to keep the volume to a minimum. Misty then caressed the petals that enveloped Monroe's long stem. Felice's labia were fat and juicy. Misty alternated pulling the swollen lips. Felice gave a cry of pleasure when Misty rubbed her knuckle against her clit. Jolted with electrical thrills, Felice rocked awkwardly, struggling to connect her taut, sensitive flesh with Misty's knuckle while trying to maintain a rhythmic ride on Monroe's dick.

With her well-lubricated free hand, Misty cupped Monroe's scrotum, fondled his testicles. He jerked as if electrocuted. "Say my name!" Misty demanded.

"Misty," he murmured as his plunging hotness penetrated deeply. Bucking wildly, Felice met Monroe's heated thrust as Monroe exploded, still murmuring Misty's name.

With Monroe's softening dick still inside her pussy, Felice squirmed, trying to get satisfaction. Misty stroked Felice's swelling clitoris. "Say my name, bitch!"

"Misty," Felice whispered, barely audible.

"What?" Misty rubbed her extended clit.

"Misty!" Felice shouted, her body going rigid before an onslaught of rippling, orgasmic pleasure.

Fuck with me, mufuckas! Misty collected herself. Straightening out her clothes, she rushed away from the tawdry scene, leaving the privacy screen wide open, exposing Felice and Monroe, their clinging bodies, shuddering, half-naked and exposed.

CHAPTER 22

Ten minutes after leaving Hades, Misty's cell chimed.

"We need to talk," Dane yelled over the blaring music inside the club. "How you gon' come between me and my lil' cousin like that? That's real slimy, yo. You know that ain't right."

"That's a matter of opinion." A smile crept across Misty's face. Showing Dane that she had the power to divide and conquer gave Misty the leverage she needed to ensure that Dane treated her the way she deserved. Fuck how good he looked and fuck how much he reminded her of Shane.

"A tit for a tat."

"That's petty. I just wanted one last night with the fellas…" He paused. "Before you put me on lockdown." He laughed, but it wasn't a happy sound.

"Petty? You the one who tried to play somebody like you had a personal ATM machine."

"How you figure that?"

"You took your own sweet time getting to Philly. Didn't keep me up-to-date, just kept asking for more dough like you really thought I was sweet. Then, you get here and have the nerve to try and put me on the back burner."

"Can you accept my apology? Can we talk?"

"No! You've been treating me like I'm some skeezer and I don't appreciate it." She inhaled deeply, conveying her displeasure. "You owe me some dough. I want all my cheddar back. When you pay up, maybe we can talk."

"Man, stop acting petty. What's a couple thousand? You're a big baller!"

"I'm a businesswoman. I want my money. So, don't call me until you get it. Feel me?" Before he could utter another word, Misty hung up.

It had taken all the will power she possessed to disconnect. Dealing with Dane's pretty ass required a steely resolve. The way he made her coochie drip was hazardous to her well-being. She had no choice but to fight fire with fire. If she didn't take control of the situation, Dane would have her handing over all her hard-earned cash. Fuck if she was going out like that! Hell no, she had to play hardball. Shit, she'd learned a difficult lesson when she fucked around and caught too many feelings for Shane.

She had to play it smarter this time around. As she wheeled toward home, her thoughts turned to Brick. He'd been acting strange lately. Drinking more. Looking sad. Seeming pitiful and lost. Like her, he really missed Shane. But fuck all that; Brick better get a grip. She had a new nigga who could put the smile back on both of their faces.

Maybe she shouldn't spring Dane on Brick just yet. She'd bring him home after she had his wild ass under some type of control, and willing to set up housekeeping with both her and Brick. It was a sticky situation, but Dane would simply have to deal with it.

Brick was a soldier. He'd keep them all eating. Dane could either join Brick and help earn his keep—or sit back, relax—and shut the fuck up.

On the real, she didn't want Dane out there tricking. But the way business was booming, she would soon have to add some fresh beef to the repertoire in order to meet the demand. She considered her options as she fired up a blunt. Monroe might fit the bill. He was hungry, good-looking, and well-hung. He was young and manageable… Yeah, she could work with all that.

❧

Empty beer cans surrounded Brick. They were carelessly tossed on the floor, scattered atop the bureau and nightstand. Misty turned her nose up in disgust. Looking a hot mess, Brick was passed out and sprawled on top of the bed. With his hand tucked inside his boxers, mouth agape, drool pooling and dribbling down the side of his face, he was so drunk that he was damn near comatose.

He looked disgusting. Like a big beast. But he was her beast—a well-trained, creature—and having power over big, monstrous Brick made her very happy and kept her pockets fat. She had three jobs lined up for him tomorrow; the first one was at noon. He needed all the sleep he could get. Smiling, she quietly closed the bedroom door and went to her office to check her website, answer emails, and set up appointments.

She clicked on the computer. Blunt in hand, small feet up on the desk, she puffed happily as she waited to see how much she'd made off the pay-per-click flicks of Brick.

"Damn!" she exclaimed, excitedly leaning forward, clicking buttons, scrolling down. "Mo money; mo money." She grinned at the monitor and then began opening email. Hmm. A trick from the nearby suburb was willing to pay thirty-five hundred for a female to join him and his wife for a few hours of couples' play.

Misty sucked her teeth. Did the dumb-ass trick see anyone on

163

the website besides Brick? Where the hell did he get the idea that she had females on staff?

The money was so tempting, she wondered if she should personally handle the job—just this one time. Misty pondered the thought; let it cruise through her mind. She tried to imagine herself selling her goods. Nah, she was better than that! Big pimping was power, but selling her jewels like a low-life ho was degrading. An unthinkable act.

Still, the money being offered was too much to refuse. She puffed hard on the blunt, filling her lungs with smoke, trying to get high enough to get some type of inspiration. Then it hit her. That waitress bitch! What was her name? Felice. Yeah, that big-titty bimbo would be perfect for the job. She'd already proven that she was down for whatever. Misty had only paid her a buck-fifty. Felice had to give her manager a cut out of that small amount. Yeah, Felice was perfect for the job—and like Brick—she was dirt-cheap.

Using one finger, Misty pecked out a response to the email request. Giving Felice the working name Juicy, she listed Felice's physical attributes, putting her plump labia at the top of the list. She told the trick to set up a date and time and then directed him to her online bank account.

No sooner had she hit send than another response came from the trick. He went by the screen name Happyhubby01. He sent a phone number, and said he wanted to talk before he set up an appointment. Ugh! Misty hated it when clients wanted to talk. It was much more convenient to take care of business online. What the fuck was he doing up so late at night anyway? He had better not be a pervert, looking for some cheap thrill phone sex. Muttering profanities, she dialed his number.

"Hi," the trick greeted. "This is Happyhubby01? How's it going?" His salutation dripped with sexual innuendo. The pervert had a raspy voice, like his hand was wrapped around his dick at that very moment.

Her finger was poised to press the button to disconnect the call. She should have known better than to try to work with someone who insisted on conducting business on the phone during the wee hours of the morning.

"I have to tell you, you've made our night. My wife went berserk after reading your description of that humongous vagina. How come you don't have the photo posted? We really wanna see it."

"Uh, I did. A while back. But there was such a demand for her, I had to take the photos down," Misty rattled off the top of her head. "I couldn't meet all the requests for her services. Now I just send her out for VIP's such as yourself." She played along, just in case the guy and his wife were legit.

"Geeze, we'd really enjoy taking a gander at those cunt lips. Can't you send a photo? It sure would be nice to have a little preview before we pay all that money for something we haven't seen."

"Tell you what, if you pay fifteen hundred—a down payment for your erotic adventure—I'll shoot you an email and give you an exclusive showing of Big Juicy Lips."

"Tonight?"

"No. Tomorrow night."

"Why do we have to wait?" HappyHubby01 said, astounded. "But, you want me to pay fifteen hundred dollars tonight? That's absurd."

"You're gonna have to trust me, uh, Happyhubby."

"Chad," he said, personalizing the telephone exchange.

"Okay, Chad. What do you want to do? Juicy has a three-month waiting list. Now I can put your name at the top of the list or you can wait for an opening." Misty listened to Chad's muffled voice while he relayed the information to his wife.

"We'd be happy to make a deposit. My wife is taking care of it right now. So, uh, how soon before we can take a peek at those dark…forbidden…cunt lips?"

"I'll send you the picture tomorrow night."

"What time, exactly?"

"Midnight," she blurted, imagining herself barging in on Felice while the waitress was serving drinks. She could see herself grabbing Felice by the arm and hustling her into the ladies room so she could get a quick snap of her trap.

"Why so late?"

Misty took a deep breath, counted to ten, controlling the urge to unleash vile obscenities on the pervert. "Are you a new visitor to my site?" she asked, sounding terribly harried.

"As a matter of fact, I am," Chad admitted.

Of course he was. The site had been up for less than a month, but hell, Chad didn't need to know that. Misty gave a long, impatient sigh. "Every Saturday I post Midnight Delight, new pay-per-click photos that are available exactly at midnight and can be viewed for only an hour." Wow, sometimes she amazed herself with her ability to think fast on her feet.

Chad's hard breathing informed her that he liked the idea. "I see. Fine. We'll log on tomorrow night and then I'll set up an appointment."

After Misty and Chad said their good-byes, Misty clicked back on her site. She'd made seven hundred dollars during the short time that she'd spent on the phone with Chad. The picture of Brick with her and Dane's passion juice smeared around his mouth was a favorite tonight, beating out the Betty Boop apron flick.

She reached for the blunt, fired it up again. She puffed. She really needed to get in touch with Felice so they could sit down and seriously discuss business.

She checked the time. Fuck! It was a little after three in the morning. Hades was closed. Not wanting to leave any loose ends before she went to bed, Misty called Big Boy, the bouncer, and left a message on his voicemail, telling him to have Felice get in touch with her as soon as possible. "Tell her there's money's involved," she threw in at the end of the message.

CHAPTER 23

Felice called Misty early the next morning. Motivated by the promise of a second income, she excitedly made arrangements to meet Misty. It was times like this that made Misty wish she were two people. She had to get Brick to his first appointment by noon and sit down with Dane for a serious conversation. She intended to give him his diamond studs and dangle the prospect of a partnership as an incentive for him to behave better.

Misty pulled to the curb and sucked her teeth. Felice lived in a rough neighborhood. Derelicts and shifty-eyed street hustlers were out in droves, looking for the next come-up. Hopefully, she could get the photos as quickly as possible. She'd be fuming mad if one of the loitering hood rats figured out a way to get past the locks on her expensive rims. Rocking a sparkled denim short skirt and gold-studded black boots, Misty's arrival at the storefront steps of Felice's apartment building caused all heads to turn in her direction.

Glancing at her diamond bracelet watch, Misty impatiently rang the middle doorbell, which was handwritten with #2 and taped next to the bell. Every few seconds, she craned her neck to make sure her whip was still safe. *Damn thieves always lurking in the shadows trying to steal somebody's shit.*

"Hi, Misty." Wearing a low-cut camisole PJ set, Felice greeted her with a big grin. Her boobs, pushed up to the rafters, were on prominent display for the photo shoot. *Poor child, she thinks she's gonna be modeling lingerie.*

Misty's presence represented money. Dollar signs gleamed in Felice's eyes. "Here you go. This is for you." Misty handed Felice a shopping bag with a Nine West logo.

"Ooo, what's this?" Felice squealed.

"It's a handbag. Hope you like it." She'd picked up the bag on her recent shopping trip at the outlet mall, but after giving it a closer look, she'd decided it looked too cheesy to swing on her arm.

Clutching the shopping bag, she trotted up the steps to her second-floor apartment. Misty sighed. She hadn't planned on climbing two flights of long-ass stairs.

While Felice appraised the handbag, emitting more joyful noises, Misty looked around. The crib was poorly furnished. But what did she expect from a storefront apartment in a squalid neighborhood? Yeah, Felice could definitely use some extra cheese. "I'm in a rush," Misty said abruptly, eyeing her watch.

"Nice watch," Felice complimented. "You stay fly—from head to toe."

"Thanks," Misty murmured, looking annoyed and sounding unappreciative. "Can we get down to business?"

Felice's expression instantly morphed from gleeful to serious. She put the handbag down, folded her hands, and knitted her brows together as she waited for Misty to speak.

"Like I told you, I need to take some pictures for potential clients."

"Is this outfit okay?" Felice struck a pose, pushing out her boobies.

Misty looked at Felice with a straight face. "I need pictures of your pussy."

Felice gasped.

"For my website. That's how I get business." Misty took the camera out her shoulder bag. "My clients are all top-notch. They don't need to see your face…just your pussy. If they like what they see, they'll set up an appointment for a date."

"A date? Like going out to dinner?" Felice asked, looking hopeful.

"Nah, it's not like that. They just wanna fulfill sexual fantasies."

Wearing a skeptical expression, Felice nodded her head.

"So, where can we do this? The lighting's not too good in here." Misty stood. "Where's the bedroom? I wanna check out the lighting in there."

"In the back." Solemnly, Felice led Misty down a short corridor.

Misty was relieved. The lighting in the bedroom was much brighter. Without wasting time, she pulled her camera out of her shoulder bag and pointed to the bed. "This'll work. Take off your bottoms and sit on the edge of the bed."

Felice pulled off the PJ bottoms, but kept her panties.

"Girl, this ain't the time to be shy. You want to get your hands on some extra cheddar, don'tchu?" Misty nodded briskly as she spoke.

"Yeah, but, I mean…it's not like it's every day that somebody comes over to take pussy pictures." Looking self-conscious, Felice shed her panties and sat on the bed.

"Lean back and spread your coochie lips open."

Felice scowled.

"I'm sorry if I seem abrupt, but I'm on a schedule and time is money. I have to download these photos and set up your gigs. Look, if I had time to kill, we'd be sharing a blunt and getting twisted so you could relax. But, I'm making major moves," Misty explained. "Most likely, I'll be able to set something up for you tonight."

"I have to work."

"After you get off."

"How much did you say I can make?"

"Depends. Put it this way, the smallest amount you'll walk away with is three hundred for an hour—sometimes you can get the job done in a half-hour or less."

Felice leaned back on her elbows. "I'm not into no freaky S&M stuff."

"Don't worry. I'm only giving you easy work. Girl, you know I gotchu." Remembering Felice's bisexual tendencies, Misty changed her tone; her next words came out soft and whispery. "Relax, boo. Let me see that pretty pussy. Open it up for me, girl."

Blushing, Felice lay back and spread her labia.

Misty frowned.

"What's wrong?" Felice sat up.

"I thought you had a set of fat-ass pussy lips?" Her lips and nose scrunched up as if she were viewing something foul.

"They only swell up like that when I'm hot. You know…I gotta be aroused."

"Oh, damn!" Misty rubbed her chin in thought. She really didn't have time for this shit. "Aiight, look. I'm not into no oral sex with a female, but if I play with your clit, do you think that'll make your pussy puff up?"

"It might." Felice shrugged.

Misty sighed and sat on the bed. Felice lay back, reached for a pillow and propped up her head. As she separated her thick, shapely legs, she took a deep breath.

The moment Misty's forefinger made contact with the hood of Felice's clit, her juices started to pour. "Damn, girl. You're leaking. That's money. Let me get a quick shot of your coochie dripping cream."

Felice gave a soft moan as Misty aimed the camera and snapped. "Aiight, you know your pussy better than I do. What's it gonna take for me to get some real money shots. I can't be rubbing on your clit all damn day."

"Um. Can you finger it?" Felice asked meekly.

Misty glanced down at her manicured nails. "I don't know about all that. I can give up a knuckle." She shrugged. "Think that'll work?"

"We can try."

"Try my ass. It worked last night," Misty blurted angrily. "It better work, bitch."

At the word *bitch*, Felice snapped open her legs, and spread them wide. "Oh, yes," she moaned. "Fuck me with your knuckle," she pleaded, winding her hips and moaning as she rubbed on her titties and pinched her own nipples.

Misty was furious, but the job had to be done. Mustering the will to do whatever was necessary for the money shot, she gently rubbed her knuckle over Felice's clit and then dug her knuckle into the creamy puddle. Enthusiastically, she pushed in and out, as far as her knuckle would go. Felice's coochie squished and gurgled, hot lust poured on Misty's knuckle, dripped down her hand. Then, like magic, her labia became engorged.

Now pulling her hair, humping out of control, Felice whimpered helplessly, "Do you have a strap-on in your bag?"

"Fuck no, bitch!" Misty withdrew her knuckle and checked the time. Damn, she had twenty minutes to pick up Brick. Disgusted, she snatched up the camera, aimed and started clicking, taking numerous snapshots of chocolate pussy as creamy filling oozed out.

Panting out of her open mouth, Felice reached over to the night-stand, opened a drawer, yanked out a huge vibrator, and clicked it on.

Misty tossed the camera in her bag, and rushed out of the bed-room, leaving Felice writhing and moaning. Over the hum of the vibrator, Felice screamed Misty's name.

CHAPTER 24

Dane took out his small diamond studs and replaced them with the new ones.

"They look good on you," she commented.

"Thanks," he muttered without a trace of gratitude. He checked out his reflection in the mirror and then set his eyes on Misty. "Fuckin' with my cousin was real slimy. I should whip your ass." He looked at her with searing dark eyes. There was a hint of playfulness, but Misty wasn't sure.

"Nigga, please!" Misty scoffed, unafraid. If he even laid a hand on her, Brick would gleefully rip his pretty head off.

"But you're lucky," Dane added. "See, I don't put my hands on a female unless I'm showing love. Ya heard?"

"No, you're lucky," she stated. Her thoughts drifted to Brick. He looked bone tired when she dropped him off at the apartment after his third job that day. His eyes were sad. He'd been looking really sad a lot lately. *Why?* she wondered. He had everything he could ask for. A dimepiece to sleep with; all the comforts of home. Hell, they could go out and party on the regular if he wanted to, but Brick didn't seem to enjoy partying anymore. She looked off in thought. Maybe she was overdoing it—working him like a field slave.

Fuck Brick. He should be grateful that she was able to find him work. His doldrums were starting to get on her nerves. She truly wasn't in the mood for his depressed, sad face. If he knew what was good for him, he'd better not even think about waiting up for her. If he knew like she knew, his ass better rest his head— try to get a good night's sleep. He had a lot of work to put in tomorrow.

"I'm serious about my little cousin, yo," Dane warned, breaking into Misty's thoughts.

Misty gave a nonchalant shrug. "That wasn't about nothing." Misty shook her head. "Trying to get your attention; that's all." Stretched out on the king-sized hotel bed, she cocked her head, waiting for Dane's response. Dane was incredibly handsome. He looked so much like Shane, she found herself staring at him. He acted like him, too. *Cocky bastard.* He was looking too good in his wife beater and jeans. It took all her willpower not to jump up, unbuckle his belt and reacquaint herself with the bulge inside his jeans. It would be so easy to simply give up the struggle of training this nigga and just throw herself into his arms, surrender the pussy and suffer the consequences.

"Yeah, well, you got my attention. I don't understand why you would go after my little cousin; mess with his head like that?"

"He's a big boy." Misty shrugged, unapologetic.

"Yo, Lil' Bit, Monroe is family. If you got beef with me, there's a million other niggas out there for you to fuck with. My cousin is off limits."

"Your cousin is old enough to make his own decisions. Now, whether or not I fuck with his head is up to you."

"That a threat?"

"A promise," she said softly.

Wanting to choose his words carefully, Dane thought about it for a few seconds. "Is that right? Well, let me put it to you like this. If you ever try to come between me and my blood again—"

Misty made a big show of sitting up and leaning forward, eyes fixed on his face, giving Dane her undivided attention. "You're gonna do what? You see me shaking, don't you?" Her expression stoic, she held her hands up and shook them, mocking him.

Dane gave a half-grin, but there was no humor in his eyes. "You got jokes, yo. On the real, though, fuck with mine again and I'm gon' come at you in a way that you won't ever forget. Believe that!" He laughed but there was no mistaking the acid undertone in his voice.

Misty snorted. "Is that weak-ass threat the best you can come up with?"

"I don't talk a lot. My rap game ain't never been tight. I don't have the gift of gab. But my actions have a whole lot of impact, ya heard, Lil' Bit?"

She gave a loud, derisive, snorting sound. "Yeah, nigga. I'm scared to death of you. Aiight, you spoke your peace. Now, let me holla at you about a business matter."

"Go 'head. I'm listening."

"My business is expanding. I can't handle it by myself. I need a recruiter."

Dane eyed her intently. "Oh, you want me to help you with your hustle by letting you pimp out my little cousin and his crew?"

"I wasn't thinking about his crew. But that's beside the point. How you gon' get all self-righteous. You supply him and those other young bucks with garbage they can't hardly get rid of. He's taking a bigger risk by fucking with you. Who knows what could happen while he and those two dummies are out on the streets hustling? Death or jail; it's just a matter of time." She paused.

"Same goes for you. Sooner or later, you're gonna get popped carrying packages. And don't look at me when you get locked up. Yeah, I got bank, but I'm not bailing nobody out of the clink. Shit, I carried packs back in elementary school. I outgrew that dumb shit a long time ago."

"Damn, whatchu tryna do? Jinx my game?"

"You can't win your game. So, are you gon' holla at Monroe or do you want me to talk to him? I already know what his sex is hitting for. He's good. I can have him working right away." Anticipating a jealous reaction, she cut her eye at Dane.

He didn't flinch. "What's my cut?" He looked at her with searing, dark eyes.

"Fuck outta here. You didn't recruit Monroe. I did! I personally test drove that big dick. He's a dumb youngin', but the sex is good." She threw in that zinger just for spite. "When you bring in some worthwhile mufuckas that I can get some decent work out of, then we'll talk."

Dane twisted his face disagreeably. "Nah, Lil' Bit. I don't do business like that." He fixed his grill in a way that would make an average-looking man appear unattractive. But no matter how hard Dane worked on distorting his features, he was still a pretty boy. "I got access to every lil' soldier out there grinding. How much you paying and what's in it for me?"

"Their income depends on what the gig is paying. Different services pay different amounts. Couple hundred for an hour's worth of work. Your cut—" She thought about it. "I can give you five hundred for every recruit and two-fifty for every job he does." She smiled at Dane. "But you don't get paid until the job is done."

"So, what they gotta do? Serve up rich, lonely bitches?"

"Sometimes. But most of my clients are male." Misty paused

and waited for her words to sink in. "I'm working on getting more female customers."

"You want my cousin and them to work with punks?"

"If you say so; I call them valued clients."

Monroe laughed. "Yo! You expect me to go around recruiting dudes to do some homosexual activity? You must be crazy."

"Cool. I gave you a great opportunity. I'll recruit workers my damn self. Or better yet, I can holla at Monroe; find out if he's up to the job. How many nineteen-year-old niggas would turn down an opportunity to get paid to fuck or get their dick sucked?"

Dane squirmed. "You cold-blooded. But, seriously, Lil' Bit, you can't come at those youngins talkin' that gay shit. You gotta ease 'em into that. Start 'em off with females. Once they get used to having their pockets lined, then you can tell 'em that the only work available is with some punks. If the money's right, they'll go for it. They won't like it, but believe me, don't nobody wanna go back to skipping meals once they start eating on the regular." He gave Misty a devilish grin.

"You a shady mufucka." She tossed a pillow at his head. "Why you make me listen to all that unnecessary dialogue when your ass is just as corrupt as I am?"

"What I tell you? I'm a man of few words." He pushed Misty down, roughly pulled her top over her head. He fondled her perky little tits, bit her nipples one at a time through the fabric of her bra, bringing each to hardened knots. Nibbling nipples and sticking his hand up her skirt. Dane's experienced hand roamed under her skirt, seeking her most secretive place. His thick middle finger slid beneath the soft fabric that covered her treasure, traveled upward until he located her sweet spot, rubbing it, until the slow burn of desire made Misty ache with need.

Misty tried to lie still, tried to control her ragged breathing as Dane seduced her with his finger, but she couldn't stop the rumbling moan in her throat or the gentle sway of her hips. She took a deep, shuddering breath, she lowered her eyelids, squeezed her eyes tightly, as if in pain while Dane's finger caressed and explored the place where she craved penetration. His dick was long overdue. She needed it! But she let him have his way with her. Allowed him to toy with her, as he circled and teased her swollen nub with his thumb and separated her pussy petals with his middle finger. Misty brought her knees up and shamelessly tried to spread her legs for him.

"I got control of this," he growled, using a strong arm to cradle her knees and keep her knees pressed torturously together. "I'll tell you when I'm ready for you to spread that pussy open." Misty struggled to get her legs apart, but Dane was too strong. In desperate need for her aching loins to be soothed, she whimpered. "Use two fingers. Please!"

"I got this. Don't tell me what to do." Seated on the side of the bed, he bent over and kissed her forehead. "I gotta slow stroke, before I beat the pussy up. Aiight, Lil' Bit?"

"Okay," she uttered in a lustful whisper.

His fingers continued their hot assault; her body arched and writhed to his burning touch.

Dane continued to play with her pussy, pushed her legs further apart, so his tongue could work its magic between her thighs. Tingles spread up and down her spine. She murmured soft cries of bliss, and then roughly pushed him away.

Unable to bear another second, Misty pushed his head away. She leveled a poisonous glare at Dane. "Stop playin'. I'm been waiting for you for a whole month. I need some dick!"

Dane stood up. Even with the shimmer of Misty's pussy juice covering his smirking lips, his expression was as cocky as ever. He undid his belt. Misty's hungry gaze ran up and down the length of Dane's tall, lean, muscular, body. Stripped naked, his hard-on pointing where she lay, leading the way, he joined Misty on the bed. "Like I told you earlier, I don't need to have the gift of gab. I let my actions speak loud and clear."

CHAPTER 25

Misty woke up in a panic. She sat up, looked at the bedside clock. 4:27 a.m. *Shit!* She'd promised the new client, Chad, that she'd have Felice's, aka, Juicy's cunt shots posted by midnight, but she'd forgotten and had fallen asleep. *Shit!* Her gaze flitted down to Dane. He'd dicked her down good and had made her forget about her responsibilities. *Damn!* As if he'd read her thoughts, Dane squirmed in his sleep; his eyes fluttered open.

"What's wrong, Lil' Bit?" he asked, rubbing sleep from his eyes.

"Nothing, boo. I just remembered something I forgot to take care of. Get your rest. Go back to sleep." Misty threw off the covers, padded naked to the other side of the room. Her laptop sat on the desk, which was situated near the heavily draped window. She clicked on the lamp, sat down and opened her laptop.

"Whatchu doin'? Come on back to bed." Irritated and groggy, he spoke in a scratchy whisper.

"Give me a minute," she said absently, clicking computer keys, leaning forward.

"Hurry up. I can't sleep with that bright light." His words were followed by the sound of rustling sheets and bedcovers.

Misty looked over in the direction of the bed. In the shadows, she could see the outline of Dane's long body, curled beneath the covers, groaning miserably as if the soft glow of the desk lamp was akin to having the high beam of a police helicopter search light shining down on him.

"You're so dramatic." She chuckled. There was something endearing about everything that he did. Even his uncalled-for grumpiness evoked warmth—gave her the fuzzies. It was a good feeling. "This'll only take a few minutes. Okay?"

Dane threw off the covers and sat up. "You shouldn'tna woke me up." He looked down. "My jawn is hard again," he commented. "Hurry up, so I can knock that out again."

With her digital camera connected to her laptop, she downloaded Felice's pussy pictures as quickly as she could. After checking her emails and her bank account, she literally ran across the room and dove on top of Dane.

"Too late." His voice was muffled beneath the covers.

Laughing, Misty tried to pull the covers he had tucked in a tight cocoon around his frame. "Gimme that dick!"

"Go 'head, shawty. I ain't got nothing to give. You took too long. My jawn went back to sleep."

"Wake his ass up!" She tried to yank the bedspread off Dane but couldn't.

"Can't. He's snoring and everything."

Misty laughed. "Gimme that dick. I'm not playing with you, Dane." She sounded tough but was grinning from ear to ear. Dane made her smile. Made her blush. Made her laugh. Fuck it, she was in love.

Finally Dane pulled the covers off his head. "Aiight, come on in here with me. My man down there woke up but he's feeling kinda sluggish, y'ah mean? So, we exchanged a few words and he said if you get on the mic, he might be able to holla back."

Misty fell out laughing, wiggled inside the covers with Dane and slithered downward. Tenderly, she cushioned his length with her lips and moaned with pleasure as it grew hard inside her mouth, sweet on her tongue. Like candy.

❧

A full bladder and a cramped arm woke Dane up. He kissed Misty's pretty face and then eased her head off his pained bicep. Rubbing the tender muscle where her head had lain and apparently had cut off his circulation, Dane slipped out of bed. Not wanting to disturb Misty, he trudged softly toward the bathroom. A sudden sound caused him to look over his shoulder in surprise. Misty, her face the image of an angel, was snoring as loudly as an ex-hausted truck driver. *Damn, Lil' Bit. I ain't think a cute little shawty like you could generate that kind of noise!* Laughing to himself, he closed his eyes blissfully as he relieved himself. His closed eyes conjured an image. Misty sitting at the desk, eyebrows scrunched together. Intense.

Curiosity got the best of him. He shook the final droplets off his dick and crept toward the desk. Stealthily, he picked up the laptop, took it inside the dark bathroom, closed and locked the door.

Illuminating the small enclosure with just the computer light, Dane closed the toilet top, sat down and steadied the laptop on his bare thighs. Bent forward, eyes glued to the screen, he could hear his own excited breathing as he pulled down and then checked every site recently visited in the computer's history.

His eyes bugged out in repulsed amazement. *Look at this shit!* On the screen were three perverted penis poses with the caption, "Hard as Brick, Melts in Your Mouth!" *The dick must belong to that dude she's pimping.* Dane shook his head, thinking the dude had to have a couple loose screws to let somebody take pictures of his jawn and post them on the internet. Scrolling down further, he saw a sight that made his mouth drool. A hairy vagina with puffy pussy lips that was captioned, "Juicy!"

Dane clicked on the link to peep the prices perverts were willing to pay if they wanted to see more. *Dayum! A hundred dollars a click! Lil' Bit was straight gangsta!* But that fat pussy she was promoting was looking so enticing, Dane could understand why mufuckas were willing to come out of pocket to check out the array of pussy flicks. But for a dude like him to spend a buck to just peek at the pussy, shit, that coochie had better be gripping and clenching in 3-D. That jawn would have to jump off the screen like a hologram and let him get all up in it—or at least feel like he was stroking it deeply. Shit, a hundred dollars just to eyeball that shit! Lil' Bit had balls of steel to be asking for that kind of loot. Then again, there were lots of sex addicts out there who'd give up mortgage money for their next high. Lil' Bit was preying on their weakness the same way drug dealers exploited junkies.

Misty's racket was more profitable than Dane had thought. Internet sex trade was kicking out some serious dough. *So, that's why she is able to cruise around in that expensive ride. That's why she is always blinging like crazy and throwing money around like it's water.* While he, on the other hand, was barely making ends meet. The drug game was getting old. Too many ups and downs. Too many grimy niggas trying to get a piece of the same pie. Shit, at twenty-four years old and having been in the game since he was seventeen, he felt old. He thought he had come up when he started carrying packs instead of grinding on the corner. But he was missing meals like a mufucka. The big boss liked to switch his mules up. Work was sporadic—nothing Dane could count on.

Shit, if it wasn't for his baby's mom back in Detroit, he'd be ass out.

Hell, yeah, it was time for a career change.

Intending on getting his piece of Misty's pie, Dane pulled his eyes away from the alluring pussy picture. "Focus, nigga," he chastised, smacking his own face in quick succession. He didn't have time to waste feening for some virtual pussy. The images of sexy pussy had to take a backseat to the pressing matter he had to quickly attend to.

Leaving the security of the locked bathroom was risky, but needing to jot down some information, his shoulders stooped as if to make himself smaller, he dipped out of the bathroom and slunk across the room. Quickly, he grabbed the pen and pad bearing the hotel's logo off the desk. Heading back to the confines of the bathroom, Dane moved as swiftly and as quietly as he possibly could. But he wasn't quiet enough. Misty stirred and wrinkled her brow in agitation as she switched her position. Her unexpected movement rattled Dane so badly, he dropped the pen. He kept an eye fixed on Misty as he quickly retrieved the pen. Pen in hand, he crept backward, very slowly. With every sneaky step he made, he watched Misty, making sure her eyes were closed.

When he eased inside the bathroom, he breathed a sigh of relief, closed and locked the door.

He blew a kiss at the pussy shot. He could grub on that juicy jawn for breakfast, lunch, and dinner. Yeah, whoever had that pussy between her legs was working with a gold mine that he definitely wouldn't mind digging into for some nuggets. His dick, in apparent agreement, throbbed so badly that the veins were popping out, demanding some relief. His dick was hard, but he was more interested in the bank account. Damn, he needed a password to peep how much paper was stacked up in that jawn. He tried a few letter-and-number-combinations, but had to give up when the site shut down, with a message that stated his time had elapsed. *Fuck!* Before closing the lid of the laptop, he gave the big, juicy pussy lips one long last glance.

Back in bed and snuggled close to Misty, Dane couldn't get rid of the image of that fat-ass pussy on the computer screen. Inching his groin up on Misty's behind, he threw an arm around her. She purred in her sleep and started whispering something.

"What?" Dane asked. Curious, he asked again. "Whatchu say, baby?"

Talking in her sleep, she whispered a sexy response. Told him how she liked it and then fell silent and succumbed to a deep sleep. He could handle what she said she liked, only thing was, she called him Shane. *Fuck it.*

He inched behind her again. His weapon prepared itself, thumping against her lean backside. He thought about the images on the computer screen. The dick flicks were disgusting. The dude caught up in those pictures had to be twisted as shit. But that bitch with the puffy pussy. Now, that pussy was on some ol' other shit. No doubt about it, he'd love to get to know it on an up close and personal basis.

His imagination directed his hand movement. With his palm wrapped around his dick, he guided it between Misty's legs, taking the pussy from behind. She squirmed, annoyed that she was being bothered during her sleep, but Dane wasn't trying to take no for an answer. Holding her in place, he imagined his dick sliding between those anonymous, fat pussy lips as he thrust and quickly squirted inside Misty's tight tunnel.

CHAPTER 26

An hour before check-out time, Misty slipped out of bed, grabbed the small containers of the complimentary shampoo and conditioner, and stepped inside the shower. For Misty, the shower was like a sanctuary. A private place for private thoughts. A place where she could work through problems, and often stumbled upon new, creative ideas.

With jets of warm water hitting her body, she lathered her long hair and massaged her scalp. The smoky steam enveloped her, warmed her. She didn't hear Dane come into the bathroom, didn't notice his long, lean body until he slid open the door and joined her. She was about to protest. This was her time! But he kneeled and murmured, "You don't need no soap and water down there. Put your foot up on the tub; let me lick that pussy clean."

Sensations of pleasure and pain seemed to shoot up her coochie at once. "How'd you know?" she whimpered, her leg trembling as she raised her foot and helplessly rested it on the side of the tub.

"I'm your man; I know what my boo likes."

She held on tight to the metal rack inside the stall. "Yeah, but, how—"

His tongue sliced into her vagina like a knife, cutting off her words, making her gasp, as she bent over and grabbed a handful of his curly hair. His tongue snaked between her diminutive folds. His puckered lips sucked softly, as his tongue swished in and out.

This freaky act he was engaged in—cleaning her pussy—using his tongue as a flesh-covered washcloth; it was something Shane used to do to her. How did Dane know about this weakness? How could she keep her wits about her if Dane knew how to break her all the way down?

"I want the truth, Dane. How could you know about this?" she asked again, tears welling. "I hate you! I really do!"

"Yeah. I love you, too," Dane replied, self-assurance coating every word. "It's gon' be aiight." He pressed his lips against her vulva. Smooched, playfully making the kissing sound.

Misty pulled away. "Stop playing. It's not gonna be all right!"

"I gotchu, Lil' Bit." He reattached his lips.

Panting, her body began to shake with the tremor of a building orgasm. "I asked you a question," she murmured between gasps.

He looked up.

"How did you know?"

He smirked. "Lucky guess."

❧

Misty felt weepy while driving Dane back to his cousin's house. Swallowing back the lump in her throat, her mind raced trying to figure out a way to tell Dane that she desperately wanted him to move in with her. And Brick. By the time they reached the brick row house, she put the car in park, turned off the ignition. "Dane, I'm in a situation that you might not understand."

"Try me."

"Me and the dude who works for me—uh, we're in a relationship. Been together since we were kids, so our relationship is more like a close friendship than romantic love."

"Is Brick getting that ass?" Dane's voice was low and deadly.

"Yeah, but it's not what you think."

"School me."

"We're both kinky. We like the same kind of twisted shit. But Brick—" She took a deep breath. "Brick's got issues about his sexual identity."

"Dude's a fag. You fucking a gay dude and let me go up in you raw!" He yanked her by the arm, squeezed hard, made her feel pain.

Misty jerked her arm away. "Brick ain't gay!" She rubbed her pained arm. "He ain't fucking dudes in their ass or nothing like that."

"What, he'd rather take it up his?"

"Fuck no! He likes the way men suck his dick. That's all. That's as far as he goes. I swear."

"So how do I fit into your family life? You think dude will be cool with me moving in?"

"I want you. He doesn't have a choice."

"So, where's everybody gon' be sleeping up in that dip?"

"Together. You on one side; Brick on the other. I'll be in the middle."

"You expect both of us to fuck you every night?"

"Look, the way I feel, Brick could sleep in the spare room, but he's my meal ticket. I can't put him out the bed. Not yet. You gotta bear with. He won't mind taking sloppy seconds after you. He works so hard most of the time, he's too tired to fuck. He eats my pussy and falls right off to sleep."

Dane turned up his lips in a grimace. "You and dude are disgusting."

"We're also eating."

"I don't know, Lil' Bit. I dig you and everything. Shit, I ain't gon' front. I feel like I love you, but I'm not so much in love that I'd let you chump me. Yo, I gotta think on this one."

Misty reached for his hands, her facial muscles twitching. "I'll put him out if you want me to."

"Then, how you gon' eat?"

"You said you gon' hustle up some young bucks from off the corners."

"That's gon' take some time. You can't expect a bunch of wild, young thugs to jump right into this sex game and start making you enough money to live like you're accustomed to. It can work, but it's not gon' happen overnight."

Dane leaned over and gave her a quick kiss. "I'll make some phone calls, but it's hard to get around to where they stay posted up without some wheels."

"After I get Brick situated after I drive him to his gig, I could take you wherever you need to go."

"Nah, that ain't gon' work. It's better if I talk to them young dudes by myself. They won't like talking that kind of business with a female around. I'll run some game—tell 'em they'll be working with me. They don't need to know about you. Let me deal with the corner boys. Feel me, boo?"

She nodded, but she wasn't comfortable with his business plan. "So what are you saying? You want me to buy you a squatter or something?"

"A squatter? Hell, no! How I look approaching mufuckas, telling them I can put them down with some long paper if I'm riding around in a hooptie. Nah, I was thinking, I could hold your wheel when I'm conducting business. Y'ah mean?"

Again, Misty nodded. She bit her bottom lip. It didn't feel right agreeing to let Dane have use of an expensive vehicle that he didn't invest a dime in. But, he had a valid point about meeting the workers man-to-man.

"This truck cost a grip. If I trust you to drive it, I have to be able to keep tabs on you. Now, you're gonna have to get your stuff and move in with me and Brick if you want access to the truck."

"That's fair enough."

"Then, after they start bringing in some real cheese, I'll buy you your own set of wheels. Something fly."

Dane smiled, leaned over and pressed his plump lips against hers. His kiss was so delicious that she opened her mouth, allowing him to slaughter her with his tongue. Captivated by his impassioned kiss, Misty hungered for more. Realizing that she was weak for him, and that she needed his dick close by at all times, she blurted, "Go get your shit, Dane. Fuck it. You gotta come home with me now. Please. We'll tell Brick together. He'll be all right. I promise. He loves me, Dane. He'll go along with anything I say."

CHAPTER 27

Brick absently pushed the buttons on the controller. Every five minutes, he checked the time. It was after twelve in the afternoon. Where the hell was Misty? She never stayed out all night and into the next day like this. It wasn't like her to be this inconsiderate. She could at least let him know that she was okay.

There was movement outside the apartment door. Voices. The clatter of keys. "Misty!" Brick threw the controller on the floor, leapt up, jumped over the coffee table and rushed to the front door. When the door opened, thinking he was seeing Misty and the ghost of Shane, Brick fell up against the wall, his hand protectively covering his pounding heart. "What the fuck?"

"I know, boo. He looks just like Shane, doesn't he?" Misty said, just as casually as if she hadn't stayed out all night. She took a few steps and set her encased laptop on the dining room table. "Brick, this is Dane," Misty proudly introduced. "Can you believe that shit? They look alike and their names rhyme." Her smile was wider than Brick had ever seen it. "Dane, this is Brick."

Dane set his luggage next to his feet, on the floor. He and Brick bumped shoulders, stood back and checked each other out.

"'Sup, man?" Dane mumbled.

"It's all good," Brick said, though his expression and vocal tone contradicted his words. His eyes swept downward and settled on the duffle bag and suitcase.

Brick looked at Misty with an arched brow. "Is he staying with us?"

"For a minute. Dane's gonna be our houseguest, while he helps me expand our business."

Brick puffed up in fury. "Oh yeah? Just like that. You stay out all night, come back with dude and expect everything to be gravy?" Hurt feelings, along with rage, flared in Brick's eyes.

"I know. That was real ignorant of me. I'm sorry, Brick. But I was making moves and I really thought you'd be happy about how things turned out," Misty said, trying to pacify Brick, who looked like he was ready to go into a fit of rage. She couldn't control Brick when he went off like that. It was easier to manipulate him, when he was nice and calm. "Look at him," she said, giving Brick a lovely smile as she waved her hand and toward Dane. "Can you believe how much he looks like Shane?"

Softened by her smile, Brick exhaled. "Yeah, the resemblance is crazy," he admitted, squinting at Dane. "Scared the shit outta me. For a hot second, I thought I was seeing a ghost." He gave a relieved chuckle. "But damn, Misty, you could have warned me that you were bringing dude home."

"I apologize for the misunderstanding, man. I thought Lil' Bit had handled her business."

Brick didn't appreciate Dane calling Misty by a new nickname, but he kept his feelings to himself.

"I'm not the type of dude who would try to come between a man and his woman, yo." Dane bent and picked up his duffle bag. "So, check this out, Lil' Bit. Give me a ride back to my cousin's crib. I don't want no trouble, yo. You told me it was cool. I ain't no home wrecker. Y'ah mean?"

Misty shot Brick daggers. "Why are you acting like this? You know we need his help. As much as you complain about all the work you have to do, I thought you'd appreciate the fact that I went out of my way to find someone who could help take some of the weight off you." She rolled her eyes. "You're so ungrateful; you get on my fuckin' nerves, Brick." She turned and faced Dane.

Dane looked past her, locked eyes with Brick. "I feel you, my man. I wouldn't want another nigga rolling up in my crib either. I only came through 'cause Lil' Bit said you was aiight with it." Dane nodded his head toward the door. "Let's bounce, Lil' Bit," Dane demanded. "I didn't come here to cause a commotion or to disrespect this man's crib."

"Brick!" Misty shrieked. "Have you lost your damn mind?"

Brick's eyes flitted about nervously. If he didn't rectify the situation, Misty would be hell to live with. "Dude can stay. I was just thrown off guard and shit…"

"See, you don't have to go nowhere. This ain't even Brick's fuckin' crib!" Misty reached for Dane's duffle bag, tried to yank it out of his hand, but he pulled it away.

"I said, let's roll," Dane said emphatically.

Misty glowered at Brick. "Nigga, if you don't open your mouth! And you better come correct…"

"Yo, dude, I was just trippin'," Brick spoke quickly. "You're welcome to stay here with us as long as you want." Brick extended himself in false friendship. He even managed to spread his lips into a convincing smile. "If Misty likes it, I love it. That's how we do. It's all good. Unpack your stuff; make yourself at home, man."

Grinning, Misty looked up at Dane. "See, I told you Brick wouldn't be jealous." She glanced back at Brick. "Tell him in your own words, Brick. Go 'head, tell him."

"Jealous! Me?" He snorted. "Never that. Me and Misty been

kicking it since we was kids. I acted the way I did because y'all took a nigga off guard." Brick took a breath and continued his sales pitch. "On some man-to-man shit, I know you gotta feel me, yo." Brick gave a short laugh. "A nigga don't like surprises." He laughed again, put more effort into the sound, making sure it rang out convincingly. "On the real, though, man, it's cool. Me and Misty got an understanding. We cool like that."

CHAPTER 28

"He's telling the truth, Dane," Misty said with a wide smile. "Our relationship is open. Wide open," she added for emphasis. Proving her point further, she stood up on her tiptoes to give Dane a kiss. Dane hesitated; cut an eye at Brick.

"Do your thing, man." Brick smiled as if Dane were being silly to even think he was concerned over a little kiss. While the two love birds fed each other tongue, Brick looked away and gripped his chest. His poor heart felt like it was shattering into a thousand pieces.

Misty made the thumbs-up sign and beamed with pride.

"Aiight, then." Dane set the duffle bag down again. "What we plan to do, man, is take some of the weight off you. You've been holding it down alone, so Misty came to me and asked if I could help lighten the load."

"I appreciate it, man," Brick said, his tone convincingly sincere.

"I'm gon' recruit some hustlers; grip up some dope boys off the corner. Them lil' young niggas out there grinding should be more than happy to put in some work that pays well and provides pussy as an extra benefit." Dane laughed.

Brick chuckled, but lowered his head in embarrassment, wondering if Misty had told Dane that the majority of the clients were male.

"Once I recruit and train those young thugs, you might be able to retire," Dane boasted as if he was the man in charge of the business.

Brick shot a look at Misty, trying to gauge how she was handling the nigga acting large and in charge, but she was smiling up at dude like he was some sort of financial genius. Shit, dude didn't even have his own whip, how the hell was he gon' recruit a bunch of niggas? Oh, well. The only thing Brick could do was go along with the charade. It wouldn't be long before Misty figured out that just like Shane turned out to be, this dude was as slimy as they come.

"I'm gon help Dane unpack. Finish playing your game, Brick," Misty said with an edge to her voice.

Trying to keep the hurt off his face, Brick picked up the controller, started clicking. Eyes squinted in concentration as he blasted figures zooming across the screen.

Dane and Misty went inside the bedroom. At the sound of the closing door, Brick paused the game, set the controller down, rubbed perspiration from his brow as he slumped in his seat, and stared vacantly at the frozen television screen.

Their soft voices, filled with laughter, drifted from the bedroom. He heard the sounds of drawers opening and closing, the clang of clothes hangers. Then their voices dropped to a low murmur. He heard the sound of bed springs, creaking rhythmically.

Brick thought he would die when he heard the familiar sound of Misty's moan. Dane's low groan confirmed his suspicion— Misty and Dane were in there fucking.

Brick put the controller down. He stood up and crept toward the bedroom. Standing with his ear pressed against the bedroom door, an anguished Brick grabbed the wooden frame for support. Did Misty want him to come in and join them? Should he knock or just go in and sit on the bed and wait for her to tell him what to do? Without explicit instructions, Brick wasn't sure how to make his move. Meekly, he gave the doorknob a twist. But the doorknob refused to turn.

"You want this dick?" he heard Dane groan.

He gripped the doorframe so hard, his short fingernails chipped. His free hand, having other business to attend to, wormed its way inside his sweat pants. Aroused by the sex sounds on the other side of the door, Brick unconsciously stroked his penis. Humiliation and agony, combined with overpowering feelings of sexual stimulation, had him bent at the waist, holding on to the doorframe, gasping as his fingers tightened around his swelling length.

"You know I want it." Misty's voice sounded choked, high-pitched—desperate.

"Say, please." Dane's voice was low, guttural.

"Please, baby," Misty pleaded.

Brick had never heard Misty even come close to begging. Not even with Shane. Not with anyone, ever! His swollen member grew harder and longer, requiring two hands to handle its throbbing girth.

"Whose pussy is this?" Dane shouted. Curious, Brick became quiet. He stood stock still. With a glimmer of hope, he held his breath waiting for Misty's answer. Brick couldn't make out her whispered response. The creaking bedsprings muffled Misty's voice. *Tell him, Misty!* Brick shouted in his head. *Tell dude that's my pussy he's fucking! It belongs to me! Tell him, Misty, baby. Please.* Hunched over, his huge penis in his hand, Brick was a peculiar sight as he moaned in sorrow and groaned in sexual bliss.

"Say that shit like you mean it," Dane demanded.

"This pussy belongs to you, Dane," she shouted, like she meant it with all her heart.

"And I don't want no other nigga up in my shit, ya heard!"

"I won't let nobody else hit it. Just you."

The headboard banged against the wall; harsh-ass slaps echoed loudly.

"Oh yes, baby. Slap my ass, pull my fuckin' hair. Tear this coochie up."

Some hot sex was going down on the other side of the door. Brick couldn't control his libido—couldn't make his pulsating dick understand that it was out of line—behaving inappropriately. It was inexcusable for his dick to betray him right now. *That ain't no porno chick; that's Misty in there, mufucka,* he reprimanded his dick, yanking it in anger, trying to bully it into getting a grip. Mad at his dick, mad at the world, he was two seconds from kicking the door down, and pulling that mufucka off his pretty baby. He'd throw that lanky mufucka up against the wall. He'd snap Dane's back. A broke-back nigga sure can't fuck with another man's girl.

Yeah, he could feel his emotions trying to rage out of control. He was about ready to rip the door off the hinges, get in there and stomp the shit out of that nigga; crush the bones in his pretty-boy face. Subconsciously, Brick lifted his foot, picturing himself using his Timberland to shatter all Dane's bones; especially those in his face. Stomp that bitch until his face wasn't nothing but blood and mush. Misty wouldn't be trying to get it in with dude if his face was all fucked up.

"Ooo, you give it so good," Misty shouted in an impassioned voice that Brick had never heard. "Oh, Dane, I can't get enough."

"You sure?" Dane asked, headboard slamming.

"I ain't never giving this away. It's yours. You got my coochie on lock."

Listening to Misty's wailing was beyond disturbing. When Misty and Shane used to go at it, they both kept their voices down, out of respect for Brick. But Misty was screaming at the top of her lungs, shouting a love chant like her ass was possessed.

Conflicting emotions knotted in the pit of Brick's stomach. His libido battled with his heart. His heart was wounded, but his libido was powerful; strong.

A long groan traveled up Brick's throat and escaped his lips. The fornicating couple didn't hear him. Their rambling, pounding flesh, and the creaking bedsprings drowned out Brick's heavy breathing and sexual groaning, as his mighty libido disregarded his injured heart.

Misty moaned louder; Brick's hand moved faster. "Give her that dick, man," Brick mumbled between panting breaths. "Get up in that coochie. Fuck it hard, like I do." Caught up, Brick lost control; anguished groans became loud and audible. Misty and Dane could hear every word. "Fuck her, man! Get real deep up in that coochie! Hit that spot! Make her cum!"

Misty cried out, her voice a strident, high-pitched feminine sound. Dane released a pleasure shout—his tenor note accompanied Misty's music. Brick jerked his dick, fast and desperately. His face contorted, as a white eruption shot out and splashed all over his hand. His ringing baritone added a bottom note to the ménage à trois of sex sounds.

CHAPTER 29

Later, worn out from hard fucking, Dane fell into a deep sleep. Misty unlocked the bedroom door and stepped into the hallway, nude. She sucked her teeth when she discovered Brick stretched out on the floor outside the bedroom. Snoring loudly, his pants gathered around his ankles and dried cum caked on his thighs and his hand, Brick could really look disgusting when he wanted to.

"Brick!" she whispered, not wanting to wake Dane. Brick stirred slightly. "Brick!" she hissed louder, and then gave him a swift kick.

He jerked awake. "What? What's wrong?" he blabbered. Disoriented, his arm flew up defensively. When Misty came into focus, he relaxed and lowered his arm.

"What's wrong with you? Why are you out here, sleeping on the floor?"

"I was listening to y'all. I fell asleep by accident." He wiped drool off the corner of his mouth.

"Look at you!" She pointed downward. "You came all over yourself and didn't even wash up. You're disgusting." She sneered at him.

Brick looked down and frowned at the dried evidence. "Umph," he muttered and shook his head.

"Yeah, we heard all that noise you made. Damn, Brick. Why did you have to embarrass me like that? I'm trying to make a good impression and you out in the hallway jerking off while we're making love. You are so ignorant and rude."

"I'm sorry, Misty. I didn't know. I thought you wanted me to come in and join y'all—like we talked about."

"Brick," she said, injecting patience in her tone. "That's between me and you. Some things have to be kept on the low until the time is right. Dane doesn't have to know about that. Not yet. I'm gonna fill him in—eventually. I hope you're not deliberately trying to mess up my new relationship."

"No! I was trying to help, Misty. You know I wouldn't do nothing to hurt you."

"I don't know," she murmured. "You didn't help when I needed you to get Shane straight."

"Misty, I didn't have nothing to do with that. I don't know why Shane bounced."

"He bounced because he didn't want to come between you and me. You were supposed to tell Shane that you were willing to step back and let him be number one. You knew how much I loved him and you never stepped up to the plate."

"I tried Misty. Shane thought I was talking about a threesome and he didn't want any part of that."

"Whatever!" She gave him a hand flip. "I'm not gonna let you mess this up, you hear me?"

"I'm not trying to mess it up." His head was low and remorseful. She sucked her teeth. Sighed. "Go run my bath water, Brick."

He nodded.

"Wash yourself up first."

"Aiight."

"We gotta talk. On some serious shit, we really gotta talk, Brick," Misty said, her tone ominous.

Brick stumbled to his feet, pulled his pants up. Terrified that he had fucked up to the point of causing Misty to want to put him out on the street. He searched her face, looking for a clue— some hint of what she intended to say. "Hurry up, boo," she said softly. *Boo.* That term of endearment gave him a glimmer of hope. Straightening his shoulders, he walked down the hall toward the bathroom.

Inside the bathroom, Brick stood at the sink washing up. He stared in the mirror. Uglier than ever, he shook his head at his reflection. Misty was going to give him his walking papers, he could feel it. She was going to tell his sorry ass he had to take an early retirement. He couldn't blame her. *With that pretty boy working for her, what does she need me for? She don't need me for nothing,* he responded to his own, troubling thoughts.

Minutes later, he ran Misty's bathwater, poured in her favorite scented bath gel to add some bubbles and hopefully get his baby in a forgiving mood. He gathered her fluffy monogrammed bath towels, placed them on the ledge of the tub.

He thought about his wanton behavior—how he'd carried on so recklessly outside the bedroom door. What the fuck was he thinking? Knowing Misty, she probably had a plan in mind, was going to let dude know about Brick's sickness in her own good time. But Brick had careened out of his lane and fucked up her plan. *You dumbass,* he scolded himself. He'd ruined the good impression Misty was trying to make with Dane.

Misty padded down the hallway. As her footsteps grew closer, Brick became consumed by a sense of impending doom. His heart hammered inside his chest as he envisioned homelessness. Living among bums. Crawling in and out of a cardboard box; scrounging around for food.

"Brick." Misty stood in the doorway, wearing a white terry robe.

"Yeah, Misty, baby?" Too ashamed to look at her face, Brick fixed his eyes on her name, which was monogrammed on her terry robe above her left breast. His eyes lingered on the vibrant pink, fancy-script. He gazed long and hard at the embroidered stitching. *Misty!* He spoke her name in his head, feeling as if he were gazing at her personalized insignia for the very last time.

Choked up, he mentally braced himself for the ax to fall. He bit his lip and looked in her eyes. Feeling ready, he cocked his head to the side. "Give it to me, straight. Whassup, Misty?"

"Oh, Brick, what am I gonna do?" She looked distraught; her words were followed with a sigh.

"Whatchu mean?"

"What am I gonna do about Dane? This is bad, Brick. I'm so in love with him. It's worse than the way I felt about Shane." Misty's shoulders shook, tears spilled from her eyes. "Brick! You gotta help me. Oh, God. I'm in so much trouble." She sagged against the bathroom closet. Brick instantly swooped her up in his arms.

"I gotchu, Misty." He lowered the lid on the toilet, sat down with Misty cradled in his arms. "I ain't gon' let nothing bad happen to you, Misty. I gotchu, girl."

"You can't leave me, Brick. You hear me?"

"You ain't gotta worry about that, Misty. I'd never leave you."

"No matter what?" she asked, sniffling and wiping away tears.

"I'm gon' ride this out. Who knows, you might be able to get him out of your system."

"I don't think so, Brick."

"You never know, Misty." Brick hugged her close as a physical show of support. He kissed her tear-stained face.

"You're right. Anything's possible. But, what are we gonna do in the meantime? You know…while I'm all caught up like this?"

Brick shrugged. "I don't know. We'll figure something out. You know how we do."

Misty pulled Brick's hand up to her lips. Kissed the back of his hand. It was a rare and tender moment. Brick's heart soared. Then she lowered his hand, positioned it between her legs. Knowing what she wanted, he allowed his longest finger to travel inside her core. In and out, he plunged deeply; her pussy made loud, squishing sounds. Misty reached down and withdrew his finger. Held it up for Brick to appraise his finger, which was stained by another man's cum.

He felt his erection building. "Whatchu want me to do?" he murmured, overcome by a hazy sensation. Feeling himself giving in to lust. "If you want me to lick your pussy, just say the word. I'll do it," Brick offered in a pleading tone. He eased Misty off his lap and immediately lowered himself to a kneeled position on the fluffy bathroom rug.

Misty looked down at him and shook her head. "That's not what I want."

"Whatchu want?"

"Give me a bath."

Brick shot up, ready to do her bidding.

"But, not right now."

"Oh!" He waited while Misty looked up in thought.

"Did you wash all that dried cum off your dick like I said?"

"Yeah."

Misty flung off the robe, surprising Brick as she joined him on the floor. "Okay, then. Come and get Dane's sloppy seconds, boo. I want you to get acquainted with Dane's seed. That's a good way to start off a good friendship with him. Don't you think?"

Anxiously aligning the mushroom-capped head of his dick against her moist opening, Brick plunged in to the hilt.

"Do you feel it, Brick? My coochie is filled up with Dane's cum."

Brick growled as he drove in deeper. "Hell, yeah. I feel his nut all over my dick."

Misty lifted to meet his next powerful thrust. He slammed into her; the sound of slapping flesh echoed in the bathroom.

"We living, baby. This is that shit we been fantasizing about," Brick exclaimed, fucking fast, giving it to her as hard as he could.

"Don't I take good care of you?" Misty murmured.

"Yeah," he moaned.

"Are you my bitch?"

What? Brick went silent and slowed his pace. Misty had never referred to him in that derogatory manner. She'd joked about putting that caption under one of his flicks on the internet, said she was gonna call him *Kitchen Bitch*, or something like that. But, she was just playing around; he had assumed. But she'd never, ever called him her bitch. He couldn't respond; didn't know what to say. Trying to be on point with his fuck game, trying to make sure he was serving her right, was difficult while grappling with confusing emotions all at the same time. *Bitch!* His mind shouted in righteous indignation. His dick, however, began to expand. It stretched a little longer, making it clear that it didn't have a problem with Brick being called a bitch. In fact, the way his dick was thumping and pulsing and secreting pre-ejaculation, it was obvious that his dick loved hearing Brick being called out of his name.

He'd always been weak when it came to standing up to Misty. When pitted against overbearing Misty and his strong-willed male appendage, Brick's personal emotions had to be pushed aside. "I'm not gon' front. We both know what it is—I'm your bitch."

There, he'd said it and the words could not be taken back. Oddly, he felt much better. Purged.

Brick arched his back; pulled up Misty's legs. Obligingly, she wrapped them around his back. Aiming for her secret spot, he drove in deep and hard. He knew he'd touched it when she started shaking, whispering his name. Instead of hitting it hard, he pulled back.

"Why you stop?" Misty snarled. "You was just about to hit my spot."

"You confusing me. Calling me Brick. What is it? Am I Brick or am I your bitch?"

"Shut up and fuck me. I'll call you whatever the fuck I want."

Brick took the insult; felt it was deserved. Determined to make Misty feel good, he served long strokes, as he sought to relocate her spot. He hit it. She cried out. He pressed against it; driving her wild. Writhing with carnal pleasure, Misty's vagina clenched as ripples of an orgasm rocked her body. She cursed Brick. Debased him. Called him obscene names, inciting him to release his seed, joining her as she writhed in the final moments of gasping completion.

While Misty lay panting for breath, Brick turned on the hot water faucet, warming her bath. He looked over at his pretty little princess, curled on the floor in a knot.

"You want me to give you a bath?"

"Yes," Misty whispered, hugging herself.

"Come on, baby, let me clean you up." Brick lifted her in his arms and lowered her into the warm, sudsy water.

"I love you, Misty. With all my heart."

"I know you do, Brick. But you can't expect much from me. Not right now."

He nodded. "I don't expect nothing from you. You feelin' ya

boy, Dane, right now. I can dig it. Like you said, we gon' ride it out. In the meantime, I'll keep busy—work hard. Feel me? Go ahead and set up as many appointments for me as you want. Shit, give me some Red Bull and a couple swigs of ginseng and I'm good," Brick said with false bravado. Determined to show love, he washed every inch of her body, inside and behind her ears, between her fingers and toes. When he got to her vagina, Misty opened her legs. With extra loving care, he guided his cloth-covered finger inside her tunnel, twisting it to thoroughly clean every crevice.

Brick felt needed. Loneliness, destitution, and homelessness no longer loomed.

Misty had her eyes closed. She wasn't listening to one word that Brick was saying. Imagining herself preparing a romantic dinner for two, her mind was on soft music and candlelight.

CHAPTER 30

D runk, Rodney had trouble getting his newly acquired key to fit inside the lock. After a few moments of fumbling, the mission was finally accomplished, but the chain, locked in place, would not allow admittance inside the untidy, ramshackle house. Though short in stature—standing at only five feet three inches and slight of frame, Rodney, consumed with alcohol and fury, kicked the door with the force of a big, brawny man.

"Lynette! Open the damn door." Through the opening he could see her slew of kids transfixed, watching television. "Will one of y'all open this damn door?" Not one pair of eyes left the television screen. The only child concerned about his locked-out status seemed to be the son of the crack addict, who lived a couple houses down the block. The boy, Baron Kennedy, came running down the stairs, eager to accommodate.

The neighbor's child was tall for his age. He easily unlocked the sliding chain. Rodney stepped inside and popped the boy upside the head. "What took your ass so damn long?"

"I was in the bathroom, Mr. Rodney."

"Look at this place," Rodney complained, looking around at the dusty, neglected home. He stumbled over scattered toys and other odds and ends that were strewn about. Kicking items out of his way, he staggered to the kitchen. He glared at Lynette Baxter, the most recent woman to share her home, her food, and her bed with him. She wasn't much to look at, skinny with uncombed, knotty hair, but she provided a temporary roof over his head. Until something better came along, Lynette and her brood of crumb snatchers would have to do. He looked around the kitchen, turning up his nose, sneering at Lynette, the peeling paint on the wall, the dishes in the sink, the overflowing trash, and the dirty kitchen floor.

"How come this place gotta look like this? I can't stand a trifling woman." Rodney gave Lynette an extra-long sneer. Yeah, he'd be out of that joint just as soon as he stumbled across better pickings.

Mouth slightly slack, eyes focused on nothing, Lynette mechanically stirred a pot of rice. Milky water boiled over, ran down the pot.

"Woman, you 'bout to burn the house down," Rodney hollered. "Can't stand a junkie, neither," he complained. "Can't you hear?" he hollered. "Turn that burner down before this dump catches on fire."

Rodney bumped Lynette out of the way, turned down the burner. Jolted out of her drug-induced stupor, Lynette peered at him questioningly. "Damn, woman. You too high to be fooling around with fire." He lifted the lid to see what they were having for dinner. "What's this?"

"Rice."

"Rice! That's it? Nothing to go with it?"

"I'm outta stamps."

"You ain't got no food stamps! Sheit! I'm not used to living like this!" He banged his hand on the countertop. From the squalid living room, the volume of the television went up to full blast. "What's wrong with your kids? They deaf or something?"

Lynette scratched and shrugged. "Guess you making so much noise, they can't hear their show."

"Sheit!" he repeated. "And another thing," he said, frowning deeply. "Don't you think you got enough kids running around here? When is that boy's mother coming back for him?"

Lynette shrugged. "Shuggie come and go; she ain't really say when she planned on picking Baron up. You know how she do. She'll turn up. Give it another day or so."

"Whatchu mean, she come and go? We got enough mouths to feed up in here; we don't need one more." He stood, huffing for a few seconds, and then bellowed, "Baron!"

Wide-eyed, the child dashed into the kitchen.

"Where's your momma at, boy?" Rodney gave Baron a long, evil look, causing the child to stutter in fear.

"I...I...she said..." The boy looked down, tearful. "I don't know."

"Whatchu mean, you don't know? I'll be damned. Your mother done dumped you like yesterday's trash."

Losing control of his emotions, tears fell from the child's eyes. "She said that she'd be right back."

"That was over a week ago!" Rodney blasted. "We ain't got enough food to feed your hungry ass for another week or two."

Rodney folded his arms and glared at six-year-old Baron. "Your mother ain't shit; pulling disappearing acts when she knows she got a child to look after." He shook his head. "If your own mother don't give a fuck about you, why should I?"

Weeping and not knowing what to say, Baron shrugged his shoulders.

"Stop making him cry, Rodney," Lynette slurred. "Shuggie's gon' turn up. She's out there doing her thing—getting high. Why you letting it bother you so much?"

"Because!" Rodney huffed. "People with kids need to get high on they own time. I don't see you leaving your pack of kids on nobody. Am I right or wrong?"

"You right," Lynette promptly responded. "But…"

"But nothing. Shuggie's taking advantage because you too soft; you let her get away with too much. I got some words for her when she gets back." Rodney hitched up his pants. "I'm the man of this house now. Ain't gon' be no more getting over. If Shuggie wanna go get high somewhere, she gon' have to take her boy with her."

"She gave me some food stamps," Lynette offered meekly.

"How long ago was that? Whatever she gave you sure ain't helping. Anytime you down to cooking up nothing but a pot of rice, it don't seem like she gave up too many of her stamps. I'll tell you who she gave 'em to—the drug man. Uh-huh, Frankie's probably in Pathmark filling up his shopping cart right now."

Rodney scowled at the unsightly pot on the stove and then turned his hateful gaze on the cowering child as if the boy had personally devoured all the food in the house. "I oughta whoop that ass." Rodney started the slow, torturous process of unbuckling his belt.

"It ain't Baron's fault," Lynette said, giving the trembling boy a sad shake of her head.

"This boy can't stay here and just live off the fat of the land, Lynette. After I give him a good ass whooping for using up my heat, water, and eating up more than his share of the food around here, I want you to call Children's Services and drop a dime on his no-good mother. You gon' have to turn this boy in. We can't keep feeding his ungrateful ass."

"I don't want no social services agency snooping around my

house. No way! Shuggie go out on binges for 'bout a week or so, but she always comes back. That's the truth. You'll see."

Rodney rolled his eyes at Lynette and then fixed his gaze on Baron.

Lynette sighed. "All right then, if it'll make you feel better, go ahead and give the boy a whooping." She flopped down in a kitchen chair, scratching. "I can't worry myself about it." She raised her hands in weary surrender.

Looking from Rodney to Lynette, little Baron pleaded for mercy with his terrified eyes.

"Get over here, lil' nigga." Rodney held the leather belt in his hand.

"Don't beat him too bad, Rodney. He can't help the way his mother acts," she appealed to Rodney.

Rodney stuck his chest out, puffed up. "Oh, now you gon' tell me how to whoop a hardhead child?"

"I'm just saying…" She lowered her head, scratched her arm. "If I let you beat on him, you better not call up social services. I can't have those people snooping around here. We'll deal with Baron in our own way. Okay?"

Rodney grunted a half-hearted agreement, raised his hand high and laid his belt across Baron's backside. At the sound of the first lash of the belt, six pairs of feet stampeded into the kitchen. "Ooo, Baron's getting a whooping," one child said, eyes gleaming in awe.

"Why Mr. Rodney giving Baron a whooping, Mommy?" asked Sharday, the oldest.

Lynette rolled her eyes up to the ceiling in exasperation. "Rodney, this ain't right," she said, rocking and scratching. "The kids were quiet. Now they all worked up. All this commotion is messing with my high!"

Rodney shot a menacing look at Lynette's six children, shook the belt threateningly. "Take y'all asses back to the living room, so I can handle my business in privacy." The children shrank back, but didn't go very far. Watching Baron get whooped with a belt was too interesting to miss.

❧

A year passed. Baron's mother, Shuggie, never did turn up. There were rumors that she'd ended up in the trunk of a drug dealer's car; shot and dumped for neglecting to pay a large tab. No one really knew or cared; except Shuggie's son, Baron. But there was no way for him to solve the mystery. There was nothing he could do.

Rodney stuck around, mainly because he took a liking to whooping the boy's behind. He convinced Lynette to go over to the welfare office and get Baron added to her check. To Lynette's surprise, the county people didn't come nosing around. She was required to file for custody, which she easily got. Children's Services turned Baron over to Lynette without even so much as a household visit. Naming Lynette as a legal guardian was cheaper and more expedient than searching for emergency foster care.

With Baron's contribution to the amount of food stamps, Rodney was mildly satisfied. Baron's situation worked to everyone's benefit; except his own.

Rodney kept the docile youngster in line by giving him a daily whooping. Baron tried to be a good boy, tried to prevent the fiery burn of the belt against his skin. But to no avail. There was no rhyme or reason to ass-whooping time. Baron could be immersed in a favorite cartoon with Lynette's six children, and

Mr. Rodney would stagger in and announce, "It's ass-whooping time," as he unbuckled his belt.

"Ooo, you gon' get it, Baron," the six children would taunt. Instantly, Baron would walk a solemn path toward Mr. Rodney's waiting strap.

Sometimes, the lashes took place downstairs in front of the children, but most times Baron was marched upstairs to Lynette and Rodney's bedroom. "Oh, you don't feel that fire, boy?" Mr. Rodney would blare, applying harder belt strokes if Baron didn't scream loud enough during the assault.

Whooping ass made Rodney's dick angry...hard...erect. After every whooping, he'd dismiss the whimpering child and call Lynette and order her to assume a prone position on the bed. She'd grit her teeth and spread her legs and clutch the bed covers in preparation of a brutal, sexual assault.

When Mr. Rodney was too drunk to give Baron a physical beat down, he used verbal abuse to terrorize the young child.

"You better watch your step, boy. You better do as I say, and do it quick! Shape up or ship out. You's an ungrateful lil' nigga. Keep fucking with me and I'll tell you what's gon' happen to you." At this point, Rodney would twist his drunken face into a detestable contortion. "You gon' wind up right where you belong—outside. Homeless! Out there on skid row living with the bums. That's what happens to ungrateful lil' niggas. They end up living underneath a bridge, inside a cardboard box."

The threat of having to live under a bridge would send the young boy into tremors of fear—tears and awful, wailing. "Please, Mr. Rodney. Please don't throw me out in the street! I'll be good. I promise, I'll be real good, Mr. Rodney," the defenseless child would plead.

During ass-whooping time, hearing such a high degree of begging made Rodney feel big and powerful, inspiring the dwarfed man to deliver hard, revitalized blows.

It was just a matter of time before Lynette and her six children jumped on the taunting bandwagon. "You better wash them dishes before you end up homeless," they'd chant.

Homeless! That word could produce instant results, could get the young orphan moving swiftly, tackling all household chores: cooking, cleaning, laundry—and of course, he remained a human whipping post.

Before long, Mr. Rodney had progressed from alcohol to drugs. Baron came in handy when Rodney was short of cash or owed his dealer money. Baron's services were exchanged for drugs.

"Hey, boy! No school for you, today. Frankie got some work for you to do. Put that book bag down and take your ass on over to his house."

Baron removed the book bag.

Rodney studied the boy's appearance. "Nah, you better keep that strapped on your back. Makes it look good, just in case those truant officers see you. You can tell 'em you late for school. Make sure you don't give Frankie a hard time. Frankie's real good to us, so make sure you show the man some gratitude for giving you work to do," Rodney reminded the child as he fondled a crack vial. "I know you don't wanna end up living in a cardboard box, so get on over there and do whatever he wants you to do. Clean up his yard, wash his car. Try to take notice of the things that need to be done. Make yourself useful," Rodney implored the motherless child. "If I don't teach you nothing else in life, boy, I'm gonna make sure you show gratitude to the people kind enough to take care of you."

৵৵৹

Baron noticed lots of fallen leaves when he arrived at the home. "You want me to rake up the leaves in the yard," he inquired, making himself useful.

"Nah, not today, lil' playa. I got another job for you," Frankie said, studying Baron. "I got some bricks that need to be moved. You're perfect for the job. Ain't nobody gonna suspect a lil' kid of carrying bricks of weed in his book bag."

Shortly after, Frankie started referring to the child as Lil' Playa and sometimes he called him Brick.

CHAPTER 31

Mr. Rodney died of renal failure a few months before Brick got sent to the juvenile center. Brick wept bitterly at his tormentor's funeral. Mr. Rodney had been the only father figure he'd ever known. The violent-tempered man had convinced Brick that he deserved every beating he gave him; he taught Brick to respect him for taking the time to teach him the meaning of gratitude. His own mother had run off and left him like a piece of trash. Mr. Rodney told him he should have been grateful that he and Miss Lynette were kind enough to raise some trash that had been dumped at their door.

"Instead of crying like a lil' bitch, you should be thanking me," Mr. Rodney sometimes said after giving Brick a harsh whooping. Those words were usually followed with, *"Show some gratitude, lil' nigga!"*

❧❧

"Dane and I are gonna talk business when he wakes up. After that, I need some alone time with him, so you can take the truck and drive yourself to your gigs," Misty told Brick.

Brick swallowed the lump of pain that formed in his throat. Bearing Mr. Rodney's words in mind, Brick said, "Okay, thanks."

Masking humiliation, hiding hurt feelings, Brick stood tall. His body language and stoic expression didn't give a hint of the pain that threatened to stoop his shoulders and fill his eyes with tears.

"Don't worry, I'll fill the tank when I get finished working," he threw in. Maybe he'd get some alone time, too, if he acted grateful.

Misty nodded absently, poked her head in the freezer, checking out packs of frozen chicken. "How long has this chicken been in here?" she asked, as she inspected the stickers on the packages, her face tight with concentration as she searched for an expiration date.

"Not that long," Brick responded. "It's still good. You want me to cook dinner for the three of us when I get home tonight?"

"No, that's aiight. I got this. I'm gonna fix a romantic dinner for me and my boo." She blushed and then covered her mouth to suppress a girlish giggle. He'd heard that joyful tinkle in her laughter back when she was dealing with Shane. The only difference was Brick wasn't jealous of Shane. He loved Shane. He was his best friend and Brick was more than willing to share Misty with his main man. He and Shane had an unspoken agreement. Shane knew Misty was crazy over him, but he also knew that taking her away from Brick would tear him to pieces.

Keeping his jealous eyes downcast, he mumbled, "Oh, that's whassup. Have a good time. See you tonight."

❧

Fuck cooking, she'd call a caterer! Hell yeah. She could afford it. She flipped open her laptop, prepared to Google catering services in Philadelphia, but twenty-two unopened emails deserved at least a quick glance. Damn! Juicy had two date requests. One for tonight; the other for tomorrow at six.

How the hell could she get Felice and the trick situated without her whip? Damn.

Irritated by the interruption in her dinner plans, she snatched the phone out of the base. "Hi, Felice. I have two dates for you. One for tonight and one for tomorrow night. The pay is good." Misty pulled the phone away from her when Felice shrieked with joy.

"Girl, this is right on time. I got fired from my job."

Whatever! "There's a slight problem, though. You're gonna have to get there on your own. Catch a cab or something. I'm not obligated to provide you with transportation, you know," Misty said, using a snippy tone.

"Are you gonna reimburse me?"

"Hell no! Do you want the gigs or not. I have tons of other girls," Misty lied.

"Yeah. Where's he located?"

Misty checked out the information the client provided. "He's in Cherry Hill."

"All the way in Jersey!"

"It's just over the bridge."

"I'm not taking a cab to Jersey. Fuck it; you can give that gig to somebody who has a car."

Misty was stumped. She hadn't expected Felice to show any backbone. "Hmm. Look, give a few minutes to work something out. I'll call you back."

Misty called Brick. "Where you at!" she barked into the phone. "I need you to come home right now."

"What's wrong?"

"Nothing. Where are you?"

"Um, I'm on Kelly Drive right now, heading for my next gig."

"With who? Herb?" Misty felt hopeful. Herb was a regular.

Cooperative. She overcharged him on the regular. He was a push-over; a real sucker.

"Nah, I just left Herb. I'm on my way to Dr. Harding's office."

Misty's mind raced. Dr. Harding was an asshole. Obsessive about time. She couldn't trust Brick to smooth things over with Dr. Kenneth Harding. She'd have to handle it.

"Okay, turn around and come back home. I'll call doc and tell him you're gonna be late." Misty clicked off, gritted her teeth and called Dr. Kenneth Harding's cell phone.

"Hey, doc, it's Misty. Listen, Brick's running behind schedule. He's going to be a little late."

"How late?"

"Half-hour. Forty-five minutes," she said with forced nonchalance.

"This is unacceptable. Totally irresponsible. I'm a busy man," he ranted. "I paid in advance and I expect appropriate compensation."

Cheap ass. "Not a problem. Next appointment, you can get the first half-hour free of charge." *You can suck dick on the house, you married pervert!*

Muttering as he mulled her proposition over, the doctor snorted, and then begrudgingly agreed.

Punkass! Misty clicked off the line.

Dane snuck up behind her, kissed the back of her neck. Startled, Misty jumped, let out a tiny yelp. "Don't sneak up on me like that! You scared the shit out of me. How long have you been standing behind me?"

"What's going on, playa? You doin' big things?" There was a teasing light in Dane's eyes.

"Trying, but I think I'm in over my head. I have all this work…" She gestured toward the open laptop. "But not enough workers.

I was planning on fixing a romantic dinner for us while Brick was out working, but there's a change in plans."

"Whassup?"

"I had to reroute Brick; he's on his way home with the whip. I have this chick working for me. She has a gig in Cherry Hill, but she doesn't drive and the dumb bitch refuses to take a cab over the bridge. Isn't that the dumbest shit you ever heard?" Misty snorted. "I didn't buy my whip so I could chauffeur a bunch of mufuckas around. After tonight, she better get herself some reliable transportation."

"I didn't know you had women working for you?" Dane feigned ignorance.

"I don't discriminate."

"Big pimpin', yo. I'm impressed."

Misty smile appreciatively, then her expression darkened. "But everything I've tried to build could fall apart if I don't get some extra help." She whirled around and faced him. "I thought you were going to recruit some of your people for me."

"I am. I didn't know the situation was critical. Didn't you say you wanted to give them some training before they start?"

"Training?" she scoffed. "Standing up and getting your dick slobbered on doesn't require listening to a long lecture or taking a pop quiz."

"True." He chuckled. "But I thought you wanted me to sit down with the young hustlers, tell him how much paper they can make tricking and then, after I get them all hyped and everything, then I kind of ease in the fact that most of the clients are men."

"Why you gotta go easy on a bunch of thugs? It's not like they're too fragile to handle real life. Take my word for it; any dude out there getting his hustle on has had his dick sucked at some point by another man. Female addicts aren't the only ones trading sex for drugs. You used to hustle on the corner; you know what I'm talking about."

"Yeah, I was out there grinding, but I never got down with another man." Dane cringed at the idea.

"Bet you had a whole lot of offers, didn't you?"

"Yeah, I'm not gon' lie. But I'm not a homo; I don't fuck around with men. Never have, never will."

"This isn't about you, Dane. I'm just trying to make a point. Why you taking it personal?"

"I guess I'm homophobic," he said, laughing. "Speaking of homos, whassup with your boy, Brick? He's a fag?"

"No!"

"Bisexual?"

"Hell, no. Brick don't do nothing but get his dick sucked. That's it."

"So, what was the deal with him trying to get in the bedroom earlier today? Was he trying to join us?"

"Not really." Misty chose her words carefully. "We have a special situation. Me and Brick are freaks. That's what keeps us together. He likes to see me getting fucked and I like the idea that he's looking. Feel me?"

Dane shrugged. "Not really."

Misty rubbed her hand up and down Dane's smooth, hairless chest. "It's like this…Brick understands that it's all about me and you now. He's on the sideline. But you have to share sometimes, Dane."

"Share? Whatchu mean?"

"Let him watch; that's all."

Dane ran it through his mind. If having Brick drooling over him serving Misty would get him the password to Misty's bank account, shit, what the fuck. "Yeah, aiight. But dude better not touch me."

"Damn, do you think everything is about you? You're pretty and everything but you don't look better than I do. Brick ain't looking at nobody—male or female—except me. I own that nigga. He lives and breathes to please me!"

Half an hour later, Misty proved her point as she drove Brick to Dr. Harding's office. Dane sat in the passenger's seat. Brick sat in the back behind Misty.

"Just the thought of all the driving I have to do is making my neck start to cramp up already."

Without even being asked, Brick leaned forward and began to massage the back of Misty's neck. His huge hands worked on her neck and shoulders, kneading and massaging until they reached his destination.

"Feel a little better?" he asked, getting out.

"I guess," she mumbled, sounding dissatisfied.

"I'll finish tonight, if you want me to." Brick's eyes were lowered; embarrassed that Dane was being allowed to witness the nature of his and Misty's relationship.

"We'll see. Yo, Dr. Harding is not a happy camper; dude is talking a bunch of bull because we're running late. Please stuff his mouth with a big hard-on, so he can shut the fuck up."

Any other time, Brick would have laughed, but it was embarrassing to have another man privy to his and Misty's game. Shit, Shane didn't even know about their private hustle. Brick could feel that he was being forced into a situation that wasn't working to his benefit. He would be patient for as long as he could, but Misty was putting him in a bad situation. It would be in his best interest if she'd hurry up and get Dane out of her system.

CHAPTER 32

Felice was waiting outside her building when Misty pulled up. Her eyes held a mixture of interest and displeasure as she slid into the backseat, looking Dane up and down.

"Felice, this is my partner, Dane. Dane, Felice," Misty introduced, her tone crisp.

"You didn't mention a partner." Felice's mouth turned down, pouting.

"Forgot."

"I don't feel right discussing my personal business in front of him."

"Get used to it," Misty retorted.

"'Sup, Felice?" Dane turned around, gave her a flirty smile that instantly put her in a better mood.

"Oh yeah, I forgot to ask. Do you pay by check or cash?" Felice queried.

"Cash."

Felice nodded, cut her eyes at Dane as he lit up a Dutch. She found herself focused on the movement of his full, sensuous lips as he pulled on the cigar.

"Here you go, shawty," he said, turning around, coughing as he offered Felice the Dutch. "That's good stuff; should calm your nerves," Dane said in a voice made gravelly from choking on smoke. He cleared his throat. "Being it's your first job and everything, couple puffs should have you feeling nice." His voice was silk, spoken in the confident tone of a man who could sling some good dick.

"Thanks." She puffed deeply, eyes roving from Misty to Dane. Dane and Misty were both hot. Dane was even sexier than the young buck Misty brought to Hades. She wondered if his dick was as long and thick as Monroe's. Hopefully, she'd find out. Misty was looking straight ahead, focused on driving over the Benjamin Franklin Bridge, but Dane's flirty eyes and puckered lips hinted that a there was a possibility for a threesome later on.

Misty pulled into the driveway of a lovely Tudor-style home. Misty and Dane sat in the X5 while Felice sashayed up to the front door. Dane kept his eyes glued to Felice's plump ass. The door opened; Felice turned and waved. Misty honked once and backed out.

"Where to now?" Dane inquired.

"Pick up Brick; take him to his next job. Come back over the bridge, pay Felice and drop her ass off at her spot."

"I was thinking…"

"What's that?"

"Let me hold the wheel after Brick's last job. That way, I can run past some of the corners, run down the game plan and get some recruits."

Misty sighed heavily. "How long do you think it'll take?"

"Couple hours. Depends."

"You know who would be a natural in this line of work?"

"Who? I know you're not referring to me!"

"Naw, boo. I don't share my private stash." She glided her hand across his groin. "I'm talking about your cousin."

"You better have a female client in mind because Monroe's not getting it on with a homo. That's too fucked up. Monroe's blood. How I look trying to play my little cousin like that?"

"Damn, you ain't gotta come at my neck. Well, what about his friends? They blood, too?"

"Naw, they ain't no relation." Dane thought briefly and nodded. "Yeah, Troy might go for it. I'll talk to him."

"Good! There's money to be made and I need some workers, but that damn Ashy Cashy better invest in some body lotion if you're thinking about letting him represent. Make sure you get with him about his hygiene, clean drawers, and all that shit." Misty sucked her teeth. "Ashy Cashy! I'm really scraping the bottom of the barrel now."

"I'm gon' talk to Edison, too. I know Edison can handle the women, but he might have a problem with the homo side of things."

"Who's Edison?"

"You know Edison. Short, muscular."

"Oh! Muscle Boy."

"Damn, you got nicknames for the whole crew. What's your name for Monroe?"

"Big Johnson." Misty fell out laughing.

"Why you have to go there? You know I'm still dealing with the way you tried to turn my cousin against me." Dane frowned and looked out of the window. Suddenly, he yanked his head in Misty's direction. "So, whatchu trying to say? My cousin's dick is bigger than mine?"

Misty scrunched up her face, tilted her hand back and forth. "Y'all running neck and neck."

"See, you trying to make me and my cousin come to blows." Dane gave a short laugh.

Brick was picked up and transported to his last job of the night. Felice was paid and dropped off at her apartment. Misty watched from the truck while Dane stood on Monroe's porch, running it down to Monroe and his two homies. Monroe and Muscle Boy wore neutral expressions but from the look of Ashy Cashy's delighted face, she knew that he could be counted in. *I'm scraping the bottom of the barrel.*

Suddenly, her spirits lifted. Perverts were known to go for pretty much anything freaky. An ashen penis might be a good money shot. With much enthusiasm, Misty honked on the horn.

Dane held up a finger. Annoyed, she pressed down on the horn. Looking irritated, Dane strolled over, making sure to maintain a leisurely pace. "Whassup?" he asked, when he approached the truck. "I'm over there kicking it with the fellas, trying to convince them that there's big money to made, and you laying on the horn."

"If they're not interested, fuck it. I'm not gon' sit back and watch you beg those sorry niggas."

Dane reared back, insulted. "Beg! I'm not begging."

"Look, it shouldn't take more than ten minutes for them to decide whether or not they're interested, so fuck 'em. Go tell Ashy Cashy that I want to have a word with him."

"Yo, I'm not Brick, so don't think you're gonna start giving me orders. Why you trying to be all up in it, anyway? I told you I would handle my end."

"I have an idea for my side hustle." Misty softened her tone.

"Side hustle? Oh, yeah?"

"Yeah, my money flows from different sources. I deal with freaky sex flicks on the side."

Though he knew perfectly well what Misty was talking about, Dane frowned up uncomprehendingly.

"I'll explain later. Right now, I want to capture Ashy Cashy while he's good and crusty. Tell him to get his ashy ass over here."

Dane gave her an evil eye.

"Please," Misty forced herself to say.

"Yo, you got me trippin'. I thought you said you wanted Troy to use lots of lotion before you present him."

"Nah. I changed my mind. Freaks are into twisted shit. His ashy ass will probably bring in a truckload of cash. I'm gonna promote the hell out of him."

Dane gawked at her. "Seriously?"

"Trust me. I know how freaks think."

Dane laughed. The sound came out in broken chords of disbelief. "If you wasn't such a fly-ass chick, I'd think you were full of shit. But I know you're all about getting that paper, so I'm gon' go talk to Troy—on the strength." He shrugged as if amazed at his willingness to participate in a campaign to promote a man with severely dry and ashen skin.

"Tell Ashy Cashy that I want him to take a quick ride with me. It might play better if you stay here with your cousin. Ashy Cashy might be more comfortable taking out his dick if he's alone with me."

"You want me to bring my boy over here so you can look at his dick? I'm telling you, you getting me confused with your boy, Brick."

"You're making this more complicated than it needs to be. Ashy Cashy ain't nothing but a dollar sign to me. You're my partner; Brick is my employee. I would think you'd want to start lining your pockets." She caressed his face.

"Yo, Troy!" Dane called out. Ashy Cashy trotted toward the truck. Monroe's and Edison's curious eyes followed him.

"I'll be back after I pick up Brick." Misty dismissed Dane and turned her gaze toward Troy's questioning eyes. "Get in. We're gonna take a little ride." Ashy Cashy looked at Dane for confirmation.

"Go on, man," Dane encouraged. "She's gon' make it worth your while."

⊰✦⊱

Misty was in luck! Ashy Cashy's dick was long and ashy. Not as thick as she would have preferred, but hell, you can't have everything. She started off the bargaining at fifty dollars and was prepared to go as high as three or four hundred—maybe five. She'd get the money back in no time. Despite his boastful nickname, *Cash-Money* joyfully accepted fifty dollars and he wasn't shy about exposing his goods. Young and virile, his penis stretched out and stiffened the moment he took it out of his pants. Misty snapped away; she even lent a hand and stroked it to speed up the big money ejaculation shot.

"You know, you could make triple what I just paid you, if you work for me."

"Taking more pictures?" Ashy Cashy inquired innocently.

"No, I need you to fuck desperate housewives."

"That's whassup." He nodded eagerly.

"Every now and then, I might need you to let a freaky husband get involved. You know, show him some dick, let him suck on it," Misty said nonchalantly. "It ain't no thing. All you gotta do is cum in the trick's mouth. Can you get with that?"

"Hell, yeah," he said, eyes gleaming. "But the part about the husband stays between me and you, right? I wouldn't want any gay rumors getting started about me."

"Nah, don't worry about it. Everything between me and you is strictly confidential."

CHAPTER 33

Ashy Cashy didn't aggravate Misty the way she'd expected. In fact, he was quite easygoing and willing to provide cheap labor. Misty was thrilled. After getting all the photos she needed, Misty dropped him off at Monroe's house. She honked the horn for Dane.

Dane got inside the truck. "Leaving me here with my cousin was real slimy, yo," Dane announced, reclining the passenger seat to his preferred position. Looking sullen, Dane flipped through Brick's collection of CDs.

"I told you why you couldn't go," she said wearily. "Look, I'm sorry if you felt…"

He turned up the volume, blasting Kanye West, drowning out Misty's apology.

It had been a long day for Misty. Too tired to come up with placating words for Dane, she drove in silence, weaving through traffic en route to pick up Brick from his last gig of the night.

Back at the apartment, she intended to download Ashy Cashy's photos, but Misty lay across the bed to rest her eyes for a moment. Brick flopped down beside her. Within minutes, both were asleep.

Meanwhile, Dane, feeling antsy, angry, and trapped, smoked a Dutch and channel-surfed in the living room. Unable to find anything worth watching, his mind wandered discontentedly. King-sized bed or not, he'd been crazy to agree to stay in the crib with

Misty and Brick. He could hear Brick and Misty both snoring. If he wanted some quick cash, tonight would be the perfect night to ransack the place and jet back to Detroit. But he was in for the long haul. He wasn't leaving until he got the passcode to the bank account. For that, he'd have to gain Misty's trust. But, in the meantime, she needed to grip up an extra bed—put it inside her office. Fuck how big the bed was, he wasn't sleeping in the same bed with another nigga. Fuck was he thinking when he agreed to that dumb shit? He and Brick could take turns sleeping in the spare room. Shit, to get his hands on that bank account, he'd sleep in the office every night if he had to.

Bored, Dane thumbed through a photo album. One page after another, pictures of Misty posing spectacularly. Smiling at club openings, having champagne toasts with sports figures and big ballers. He turned another page. There she was again, stepping out of a limo. He shook his head. *Who does this bitch think she is? The black Paris Hilton or somebody?*

Dane took an angry pull on the Dutch he was holding. He quickly turned the pages and then gawked when he caught sight of a disturbing image. In the midst of Misty and Brick was someone who looked like he could be Dane's twin. Had to be that dead dude—Shane. Seeing the close resemblance between him and Shane, he now understood why Misty was trippin' so bad. She was still in love with the dude in the picture and was trying to use Dane as a replacement.

Dane slid the photo out of its plastic sleeve, held it up for closer inspection. Damn. Dude even had the same dimple in his chin. The shit was eerie. He felt like he was looking at a picture of himself, but had forgotten posing for it. He had a quick bout of shuddering heebie-geebies. He replaced the creepy picture and closed the book.

Other than that lone photograph, every other picture in the house bore Misty's image. The crib was a shrine to Misty. Seeing poster-sized photos of her all over the place was starting to get on his nerves. It was creepy. He had to get out of there; get some fresh air. The walls bearing Misty's likeness were definitely start-ing to close in. Feeling angry…confined…caged, he paced in circles and then strolled into the bedroom. "Yo, Misty," he mumbled, his voice deliberately low. "I have to make a quick run. Lemme borrow the whip and a couple dollars, aiight, Lil' Bit?"

Misty murmured an incoherent response, which Dane took to be yes. Puffing hard on the Dutch, he routed through her purse, extracted some bills and her BMW key ring.

☙◆❧

There'd been no need for pointless small talk. Heated glances and seductive body language had been their only means of com-munication. They'd agreed to get together tonight, but wining and dining wasn't on their agenda. Instead, hot, naked, skin-on-skin bodies thrusting and dueling hips was on their freaky sexual menu. No need to loosen up or get in the "mood" with a puff off a Dutch. Their fiery attraction had been instant and negated the need for anything but hot, carnal sex.

After two impatient jabs on the buzzer, he stood out on the sidewalk, looked up at the second-floor window, and yelled her name. He walked over to Misty's truck, leaned up against it and waited. Curtains flittered open; he caught a quick glimpse of coffee-colored skin. Satisfied, he sauntered over to the storefront door.

Moments later, the door pushed open. The smile in her eyes welcomed him, but her mouth was poked out in displeasure. "Took you long enough," she said, sulking.

"I got here as fast as I could." He slipped inside, closed the door behind him. Inside the dim, confined vestibule, he gave a head nod to her body-hugging, lace negligee. He covered her pouting lips with his kiss, backing her into the mailboxes that lined the grayish-colored wall.

Anxious hands groped her large bosom. Those big, soft titties demanded attention, but his impatient hands suddenly switched direction. Wandering downward, his restless fingers reached and stretched until his hands were wrapped around her voluptuous behind. He held both ass cheeks with reverence, as if gripping a flesh-covered basketball.

"Baby got back," he whispered in her ear, and then nibbled on the lobe.

She tilted her head saucily. "Baby got back and a whole lot more."

"Is that right?" His tone was husky, oozing with desire. An image of her puffy punany blazed across his mind. Thoughtfully, he stroked the hairs on his chin. Was she aware that her pussy was posted on Misty's sex site? If so, what was her cut? Oh, fuck all that; he'd get up in her financial business at a later date. This moment wasn't the time and judging by the way his dick was thumping and jumping, the cramped vestibule damn sure wasn't the place. *Down, boy!* Pressing his dick into obedience, Dane followed Felice up two flights of stairs.

Felice's plump ass and curvaceous body composition was making his dick drip before it made contact with her flesh. Shawty was packed from front to back.

She led him straight to her bedroom, pulled the flimsy gown over her head and tossed it on the floor. Lying on the bed, body splayed, her mocha-toned nakedness beckoned him. Dane didn't know what to do first—strip out of his clothes or greedily fill his mouth with one of her succulent, big tits. He wanted to lick her taut tummy, bite on her inner thighs, flip her over and kiss her round, bouncy ass. Like a child in a candy store, he wanted to taste everything—suck cream from titties, lick chocolate from ass, sip the tangy sweetness that glazed her juicy pussy lips.

"Come on, baby, what are you waiting for?" Felice cooed. She writhed ever so slightly, but the sexy, fluid movement spoke volumes; expressed her desires louder and more clearly than she could ever convey with words.

With his dick becoming more and more unmanageable, indecisiveness was no longer an option. Obeying primal urges, Dane unzipped his jeans, slid them down and unleashed the unruly beast. Jeans and drawers hung around his ankles; his dick in his hand.

She smoothed her hand across her hairy mound and wound her hips, undulating vigorously, wantonly welcoming his dick.

Overcome by lust, Dane fell on top of the pussy. Clumsily, he thrust himself inside, grunting as he pushed deeper, desperately seeking darkness and warmth. He had every intention of serving Felice a series of long, rhythmic strokes followed by a speeded-up pace and intensity, giving the pussy a punishing, a pounding. He had planned to teach this bitch the lesson he reserved for flagrant flirts like her. But her pussy was too much for him. Each time the capped knob of his length dipped into her moist, heated center, her pussy lips puckered up and tightened around his thickness. The dual stimulation—the cushiony softness of those big juicy lips brushing against his dick and the liquid heat that poured over the head of his dick—was throwing him off his game.

Heightening the pleasure, Felice tightly contracted her inner muscles. Dane could feel himself about to lose control. Biting the collar of his shirt, ripping the fabric with his teeth, he tried to gag himself, tried to muffle the sound of the strident falsetto that pushed against his throat. Any minute now—one more pussy clench—it would be all over, and Dane would be cumming like crazy and screaming like a bitch.

Gasping, he buried his face against Felice's neck. "The pussy was banging, yo," he exclaimed between panting breaths. "What kind of pussy is that? Red snapper?" he asked, laughing. His chest continued to heave as he laughed and struggled to catch his breath. Coming to terms with his lack of stamina, his less-than-stellar performance wasn't easy. Trying to play it off, he said, "Yo, that ride was thrilling—like a roller coaster. It ended too fast; I want to get back on."

His pop had put him down with an old school jam, called "Misty." The melody chimed from his cell phone, informing him that Misty was awake and, no doubt, fuming mad. He wanted to ignore the call, jump back in the pussy and step up his fuck game. But evil-ass Misty would be out gunning for him. Or worse, she'd call the cops on his ass for jacking her whip. He had open cases—didn't need that kind of trouble out of the police, so he reached down, grabbed the denim that was gathered around his ankles, patted until he located the phone, and pulled it out of his pocket.

Dane didn't have to worry about Felice coughing, clearing her throat, or making any kind of jealous female noises. Hearing Misty's name crooning from the cell phone, had Felice looking appropriately frazzled, eyes bulged, her hand covering her mouth in dreaded fear.

"I told you that I had to go out and grip up a lighter. I couldn't find one in the crib. Picked up a couple Dutches, too. Yeah, I'm on my way home. I'm right around the corner," he lied.

Dane snapped his phone shut; cut an eye at Felice.

"You gotta leave?" she asked sadly.

"Yeah, but don't worry. It ain't over, shawty. I'm gon' be back for round two."

"When?" Felice's lips curled back into their previous pouting position.

"Soon. Are you working for Misty tomorrow?"

"I'm not sure. She'll call me and let me know." Felice thought for a few seconds. "Take my number."

"Nah, shawty. I don't have any business with your number in my phone. Feel me?"

Felice gave a reluctant head nod.

"I'll roll through tomorrow night. Don't have me standing and waiting around outside. When I ring the bell, get your ass down there and open the door."

Dane was surprised that Felice let him handle things. She should have been cussing him out for shooting off his seed and leaving her hanging until tomorrow.

He washed up and gave her a quick kiss. He'd make it up to her. She wasn't wifey material—damn shame that wifey was waiting back home in Detroit. But she was definitely that Philly bitch. He could never get enough of her big, juicy lips.

CHAPTER 34

Dane said he was right around the corner, but a half-hour had gone by and he still hadn't come home. Resisting the urge to blow up his cell, she distracted herself by downloading Ashy Cashy's flicks. Gnawing on her lip, she worked on her website, trying to keep from worrying about where the hell Dane could be. After downloading the last photo, the phone rang.

Dane! Misty glanced at the caller ID and was let down when she saw her mother's name scrolled across the screen. Sucking her teeth, she snatched the phone from its base. She'd told her mother about Dane and made it clear she wasn't willing to listen to any criticism. She was grown and could do as she pleased. She wasn't trying to hear her mother lecture about her lifestyle. "Hey, Mom, whassup?" she said in a monotone.

"How come you didn't return my call?" Thomasina asked accusingly.

"Um." Misty couldn't come up with a convenient answer.

"Brick didn't give you my message?" Thomasina was gearing up to call Brick all kinds of evil names.

"Yeah, he told me you called. I just forgot..."

"Oh," she said, somewhat disappointed. "By the way, Misty..." Thomasina cleared her throat, preparing to get up in Misty's business. "What's wrong with Brick? He has a strange vibe about him, don't you think? He doesn't seem to have any fight left in him. I've called that boy every name in the book, just to get a rise out of him, and he doesn't have any comeback. Just says that he'll tell you that I called. What do you make of that? Is he on drugs or something? I know he stays high on that weed, but I wouldn't be surprised if this new behavior is on account of him starting to fool around with the hard stuff."

"Oh, Mom. Leave Brick alone. He's not bothering you, so be happy. Some people can't be pleased." Misty snorted. "You used to complain about how he had too much mouth for his own good, called him disrespectful, now you're complaining because he stopped playing your game. What is it with you?"

"Don't jump down my throat. I was just making a comment. An observation. I thought you'd appreciate the fact that I'm voicing a little concern about your man's emotional state. Something's wrong with him, Misty. You better keep your eye on him. He's never been the quiet type. You got that man in there, driving him over the brink. You and your new lover gon' find y'all selves shot up and left for dead. I hate to ask where everybody's sleeping."

"First off, Brick is not my man. We're just friends."

"Okay, well, your close friend isn't acting right. I'm just giving you a heads-up before he flips out, destroys your plush apartment and tears your new man apart—limb-by-limb. Misty, you have to be careful. Brick is usually outgoing; now he's quiet and acts real timid. Something isn't right. Keep your eye on him."

"Mom, there's nothing wrong with Brick! You are the most complaining person I know. I can't believe you're choosing Brick as a target just because he doesn't have much rap for you now. He's probably so sick of getting cursed out that he's just tuning your insults out. You can't blame him for that. That's called self-preservation."

"All right, Misty. So, look, what time are you taking me to my line-dancing class?"

"I thought you quit those classes!"

"I did, but I'm going back. I'm not gonna let a lowlife cheat stop me from getting on with my life."

"Umph. I can't believe you're still trippin' over Mr. Victor after all these months."

Misty had no idea that Thomasina had weakened and gone to The Delmar. After too much drinking, she'd allowed Victor back in her bed and ended up with a brand-new heartache. The only good part was she managed to cut Victor with a pair of scissors. Her scissors-tirade was probably big news at The Delmar. Thomasina had been keeping a low profile since that night; too embarrassed to return to The Delmar and too weak with disappointment to go back to her line-dancing class. Other than going to her job, she'd been staying in the house, mourning. But noticing the softening that had started to occur in her inner thigh area brought her to her senses. No man was worth letting her appearance go.

"I can't do it, Mom. I have too much to do tonight."

"Well, send Brick or that other…" Thomasina caught herself. "No, don't send that other thug. I don't want to meet him. Having to deal with Brick is bad enough, but I think I'm better off not knowing that other one. I'm not going to allow you to shove your ménage-à-trois relationship in my face. It's not normal!"

"I'm not in a ménage à trois," Misty protested. "Me and Brick are buddies. Dane is my man."

"Then why all y'all gotta be living in there together? I never liked it when you used to sneak that evil boy, Shane, in my house. Had him in there sleeping in the same bed as you and Brick."

"Mom, let it go. That was years ago. When Shane crashed with us, he'd sleep on the floor," Misty lied.

"Okay, let's just say that's true. Then that means you and Brick were laying up in bed together—like boyfriend and girlfriend," Thomasina said cunningly.

Misty sighed. "I don't feel like digging up the past."

"Look, Misty, I didn't put my name on those papers expecting to still get around on public transportation…"

"Okay!" Misty shouted. "I'll tell Brick to pick you up."

With her mother's transportation arrangements made, Misty's mind roved back to Dane. He was missing in action with her whip, and she was becoming more and more incensed with every passing minute. Her arms tightened across her chest, Misty paced back and forth.

She heard the ding of the elevator from down the hall. *Finally!* She flung open the door. Like a man returning home from a long military tour, Dane rushed inside. Breathless, he bent down and tightly embraced her. Then he cupped her face, stared deeply into her eyes. "I love you, Lil' Bit. You know I didn't mean to upset you. I was down to my last Dutch, couldn't find a lighter— I started feenin' bad. I asked you if I could borrow the whip and you told me it was okay. You told me out of your own mouth to go inside your purse and take the keys," he lied with ease.

"I don't know half of what I'm saying when I'm sleeping…" Her voice was set at an aggravating, whiny pitch. "I went into a panic when I woke up and couldn't find your ass. I don't want to lose you, Dane." Misty's eyes slid from Dane's gorgeous face down to his crotch; her mouth watering with yearning.

Dane saw the lust in her eyes; heard the desperation in her voice. Felice had drained him; he had nothing left to give. Eyes flitting about in panic, he noticed the open laptop on the dining room table. Hmm. Misty had been working. Lining up gigs. He deserved his share of the business. Thinking fast, he came up with a plan. He winced suddenly, bent over and theatrically slapped a hand against his heart, and then hung his head low.

"What's wrong?"

He gripped his forehead, shook his head as if distraught, and slowly walked over to the sofa. He slumped against the cushion.

Misty rushed over, sat next to him, caressed the silky hair on his arm. "Dane, what is it? Talk to me!"

"I can't lie to you, Lil' Bit. For real, yo. I can't do this. This situation you got me in—this ain't me. I can't be up in this twisted shit. You're already in a relationship with dude. I'm not a fool. I was willing to be one for you but this shit is eating me alive. On the real, I was out there driving around in circles, trying to clear my head."

"Oh, Dane…"

"I kept asking myself… *What the fuck you doing, man? You know this ain't you.*" He lowered his head, covered his face as if in agony.

At a loss for words, Misty rubbed Dane's arm faster, massaging, kneading; thoughts racing as she searched for the right words to give him peace of mind.

"For all it's worth, I dig you, Lil' Bit, but I can't share you with that other man in there." He inclined his chin toward the bedroom where Brick slept.

Misty stopped massaging; dropped her hand in her lap. "What are you saying? Are you going to leave me?" Misty asked with rising hysteria.

"Yeah, boo. I came to the conclusion that I gotta pack my shit. I gotta raise up."

"Dane! Be serious. I told you, me and Brick are just friends."

"You need to tie up your loose ends. I can't deal with this." He swiped his hand across his forehead. "Can you give me a ride to my cousin's crib? I can get my stuff tomorrow."

Wild eyes darting, mouth opening and closing, unable to adequately express her exasperation, Misty summoned tears as a last-ditch effort. "How can you leave me?" she sobbed. "I worked so hard to get you involved in my business. I got your boy, Cash Money's picture up on the website. It's probably bringing in some dough right now."

Emboldened by her tears, Dane twisted his lips in anger. "Yeah, you talk a good game," he said, leaning forward, "but I noticed how you guard that laptop. You keep that jawn close by your side, like it's a cashbox loaded up with money. You expect me to be a headhunter for you and dole out niggas like you're running a slave trade. I'm still dead broke." He leaned back and regarded her coldly. "I peeped the way you went all around me and pulled Cash Money into the game. Whassup with that? You don't wanna give me my breakdown?"

"I haven't made anything off of Ashy Cashy yet. I just put his picture up a few minutes ago. Anyway, what happened to the hustlers you were supposed to get off the corners?"

Dane thought for a few seconds. "It ain't really about the money, yo. I was just saying… It's about this lifestyle. I'm not with this. I'm going back to doing what I been doing. Be my own man, make my own money. Ya dig?"

In full-fledged panic-mode, Misty sidled closer, inserted the tip of her finger inside the cleft in his chin, then she moved her hand past his soft sideburns, raked her fingers through his thick, curly hair. "I'm gonna show you how I run the website. Let you line up all the gigs that come in for Cash Money. You can be his manager. Okay, boo?" she soothed.

Dane shrugged. "Aiight, that's a start. But I'm serious about sharing you with Brick. Until you figure out which one of us you really want, I can manage Cash Money from over at my cousin's crib." Dane stood up.

"I don't want Brick; I want you," she insisted. "But me and Brick have been together for a long time. Brick's my bread and butter. You can't expect me to kick him to the curb."

"Yo, that's on you. Do what you gotta do. I know how to look out for mine."

Huffily, Misty stood up. She stormed into the bedroom. He heard a closet door slam, heard the computerized voice stating, "Entry granted." *Damn, shawty has a stash right here in the crib.* Fuck learning the combination or trying to pick the lock. He and his crew would clean out the place and roll out with the cashbox, crack it open later.

"Here's your cut." She tossed him a stack. He blinked in confusion. "That's for recruiting Ashy Cashy."

"Oh, bet!" Dane counted the bills. Happy for the fat stack of bills and relieved that she hadn't noticed that her purse was a couple hundred lighter, he smiled appreciatively. Missing money was sure to throw up a red flag. He decided to put the money back in her wallet. Yeah, that made a lot of sense. Then he suddenly got mad. He could feel the heat of his anger burning his face. The bitch was loaded. She had so much loot and was so busy worrying about her whip that she didn't even notice that money was missing. Dane's beaming gratitude quickly morphed into a sinister grin. "Aiight, so let's take a look at the website. Let me see what's going on up in that dip."

CHAPTER 35

"Mom," Misty whispered into the phone. "I need a favor. You were right. Brick is really going through something. He's acting all depressed…looking sad. He's getting on my nerves, Mom. I can't even think straight with him moping around here."

"Yeah, and…" Thomasina said suspiciously.

"I need some space." Misty took a deep breath. "I was wondering…for a shopping spree and some extra cash, would you do me a big favor and let Brick stay in one of your spare bedrooms? I'll make it worth your while. Just for a week or two; until I can find him his own spot."

"Are you crazy? Hell no! You expect me to willingly invite a ticking time bomb into my home? You better put him up in a hotel, a rooming house, or somewhere. Why can't he stay with his people?"

"What people?" Misty scoffed. "You know Miss Lynette wasn't his real mother. She just let him stay there for the check she got off of him."

"That's not my problem, Misty. I like my privacy. If wanted a boarder, I'd quit my job and allow a couple no-accounts to rent out my spare rooms."

"Brick won't be in the way," Misty pleaded. "He's real easy to live with. He'll be working most nights. I'll drop him off after work and he'll go right to sleep."

"Yeah, he'll go right to sleep after he smokes a bunch of that weed. I don't feel like inhaling a cloud of illegal substance. I haven't had a severe coughing attack since you moved out of here. Umph! I can't believe I allowed myself to suffer through all that choking. You smoked that mess day in and day out—no consideration whatsoever about my asthma."

"Mom, stop exaggerating. You haven't had an asthma attack since I was a little girl."

"I'm still at risk. Listen, you're my flesh and blood, Misty, and I've put up with a lot of mess from you over the years, but I'm not putting up with any type of nonsense from that mean-ass Brick."

"Brick's not mean. He's really nice. You'd know that if you treated him halfway decent. But, Mom, for real, though—you can't deprive him of smoking; he has to get high to unwind."

"Unwind from what?" Thomasina demanded. "I'm getting nervous about him staying here. Just what is it he does for a living, Misty? I can't harbor a criminal under my roof. The more I think about this demolition mess you claim he's into, the more my good judgment tells me that he's working for the mob. Is Brick a hired killer? For all I know, he could be out there doing killing sprees every night."

Misty giggled. "You watch too much TV. Brick wouldn't hurt anybody unless that person was trying to hurt me."

"Yeah, whatever. But I need to know exactly what he's doing for money. Y'all living all high and mighty and all he does is go out to mysterious places for a couple hours a night. Shit, he's big and ugly enough to be the muscle for some mob boss."

"Mom, I swear he's not out there killing anyone." She followed her statement with more laughter.

"I don't see what's so funny. You want me to harbor a killer—

put my life in jeopardy. For all I know, y'all could be using me to hide Brick from some rival killers. I wouldn't put it past you, Misty." Thomasina sighed. "And I only have myself to blame. You're spoiled and selfish. You'd put me in harm's way in a heartbeat to save your own skin. I don't know, Misty. Something's not right about this."

"There's nothing dark and sinister going on. Me and Brick need some space for a minute." Misty was quietly thoughtful. "Put him in the back room," she blurted. "I'll tell him to crack the window and blow the smoke out, so you won't have to smell it. Please, Mommy?" Misty didn't mind begging or using the "Mommy card" to crack her mother's hard veneer.

Thomasina let out a long breath of defeat. She'd spoiled her child terribly, now she was suffering the consequences. She couldn't deny her pretty little brat if she tried. "Just a week, Misty. I'm not playing. One damn week and that's it!"

"Thank you, Mommy." Misty sounded like a happy little girl. Despite her knowledge that her daughter was playing her like a harp, Thomasina beamed with motherly pride.

"And you can tell that gigolo you're trying to have some privacy with…tell him that he needs to thank me also."

"Why he gotta be a gigolo? Yeah, he got a little hustle in him. That's why we get along."

"Hustle, huh? I guess that's why I haven't heard anything about him working at a job. Guess he's living off you—or should I say, Brick, since Brick's the only one who leaves the house to make a nickel. Only God knows how, but he's making enough to keep you living like a superstar."

"Yeah, Brick's the breadwinner. But just for a minute. Me and Dane have a lot of ideas."

"Umph! I'm surprised at you, Misty. I thought you had more

self-respect. It's hard to believe that you'd let a man live off the money Brick works for. Brick's not easy on the eyes, but he's not lazy and he loves you to death. Like you said, Brick's your meal ticket. Are you sure you want to risk that for some no-count pretty boy?"

"Dang, Mom. You can't be pleased. First, you say Brick is too ugly to be my man. Now, I shouldn't replace him with a pretty boy. Make up your mind. Didn't you say you wanted some pretty grandkids?"

Thomasina was at a loss for words. She really didn't want her daughter getting pregnant by a beast like Brick, but she didn't want her making a mistake she'd have to live with over the likes of some jobless fool with good looks and empty pockets. She wanted her daughter to use her beauty to snag a man of worth; a hand-some man of worth. Misty just wouldn't do right to save her soul.

"You might be over twenty-one, but you're still a child in your mind. You're still ripping and running in the streets; you're not ready to settle down and take care of a child. Lawd!" Thomasina was tired of the conversation. Misty had worn her out.

"You're right about that," Misty agreed. "But I'm just saying, if I did get pregnant it would be by someone like Dane."

Thomasina sucked her teeth. "Why do I keep getting a feeling your new boyfriend has the same trifling characteristics as that no-good Shane?"

"Dang, Mom. Let the dead rest in peace."

"I just wanted to let you know that I wasn't blind to your shenanigans. I knew there was a lot more than just friendship between you and Shane. I shudder to think what all was going on in your bedroom. Umph. You, Brick, and Shane—all sleeping together in the same bed. Just nasty."

"We were not! How many times do I have to tell you, Shane and Brick took turns sleeping on the floor."

"Uh-huh. Whatever."

"Mom, why you trippin'? All that's in the past. But you know what? Dane really looks a lot like Shane. He's a lot smarter, though. That's why I made him my business partner."

"What kind of business? Slinging drugs?"

"You know better than that. We're putting together a business plan—something that's beneficial to people. But I can't give out the details. Not yet. Can't risk having someone steal my creative ideas."

"What kind of business are you in with this man—this total stranger? And when did you start giving a damn about helping people?"

"Since I met Dane. He's a positive influence. For real, Mom. Look, here's the deal…we're starting a dating service," Misty lied. "Hooking up couples. Helping men and women find true love," Misty rattled off the top of her head. "We got the idea because we fell in love at first sight. We just want to spread our happiness around."

"Hmm. Oh, yeah?" Thomasina said sarcastically. "Well, put my name at the top of the list. I could use that kind of service."

"Eeow. I hate it when you talk like that. Act your age, Mom," Misty chided.

"You don't cater to the over-forty set?"

"No! And you shouldn't be thinking about love and sex. Not at your age. I thought you said you were through with men after Mr. Victor broke your heart. For real, Mom. You should move on with your life."

"And do what?"

"I don't know. Join a women's group, or a church or something. Get involved with a charity."

"So, you think my life should be over at forty-two?"

"Not over. But you're too old to be still thinking about having sex with men. It's disgusting."

"I see. So, how's Brick taking all this? You know, being kicked to the curb and all?" Thomasina changed the subject.

"Not well, but he'll be all right."

Thomasina sighed. "You're heading for trouble, Misty. I can feel it. Mark my words. You and a total stranger, living together and starting up a dating service just doesn't sound right."

"After I make my first million, I hope you give me an apology."

Thomasina chuckled. "Speaking of money—how much rent is Brick paying?"

"Um. Fifty a night?" Misty said in a meek voice.

Thomasina did the math. "Three-fifty for all my trouble and inconvenience. I don't think so!"

"All right. Five hundred for the week."

"That's more like it. And don't forget my shopping spree!"

❧

Brick had never been able to understand why Shane had taken his own life. Now, faced with the gut-wrenching fear of being left all alone in this cold, cruel world, suicide seemed like a logical ending. He'd been smoking and drinking all day, but even the highest-quality weed couldn't dull his pain. Swigging down a couple six-packs of brew and swallowing blue Xanies like they were Tic Tacs didn't help the situation either.

On the verge of calling his connect to put him on with some prescription painkillers, merciful sleep claimed him.

But not for long. Misty's petite hand grasped his shoulder and roughly shook him out of the temporary safe haven. Brick raised his head, cracked open his eyelids and surveyed the situation. Two packed duffle bags were in the middle of the living room floor. Through hazy eyes, he recognized Dane's bags. His heart leapt with joy. Dane was leaving!

"You don't have to work tonight, Brick." Misty eased onto the sofa, where he'd escaped inside a drunken slumber. "I packed some of your clothes. I didn't want to put your stuff in my Louis Vuitton luggage, so I borrowed Dane's bags."

Sluggish and sick to his stomach over the news, Brick tried to pull himself upright, but couldn't complete the task. Leaning at an awkward tilt, his eyes pleaded for understanding. "What? You throwing me out?"

"No." Misty laughed as if he was being totally silly. "You're gonna stay at Mom's for a few days. Dane isn't comfortable with you around. He wants some private time with me. I'm sorry, Brick. I thought he'd be able to deal with our situation, but he's so crazy in love with me. I tried to talk to him about how we do, but he refuses to share." She shook her head, her mouth turned down. Then, Misty gave Brick a sneaky smile. "Give me a few days alone with him; I'll make him change his mind." She cocked her head to the side, batted her lashes.

He groaned in anguish, intertwined his fingers, and clasped them against his forehead. "Why you letting that nigga come between us, Misty? Why you doin' me like this?" Brick lamented, his voice cracking.

"Man-up, Brick!" Misty yelled. "Damn. Why you gotta bitch like a little girl? I got this. I'm gon' fix it. I just need a minute to get shit in order. But I can't do shit with you bitching and moaning and getting on my fucking nerves."

"I'm just saying, yo. After all we been through, how did it get to this?" His eyes searched her face, beseeched her to search her soul.

Misty sat down next to Brick, brushed her fingers across his temple. "Love. I fell in love."

"I thought you loved me."

"I do. I love both of you. But he doesn't understand how we flow. So, I'm gonna spend some quality time with him, get him hooked on me like you are. After that, it'll be all good. He won't be able to tell me no."

"But if he ain't with it—our lifestyle—whatchu gon' do, force him?"

"No. I figured you gon' have to make it worth his while."

"Make what worth his while?" Brick reared back, insulted.

"Sharing me. What's in it for him?"

"Fuck if I know."

"Yes, you do. You always knew it was gon' come to this."

Brick dropped his head. "Yeah, I guess I did."

Misty ran her finger down his scar. "It's all good, boo. Sooner or later, it was bound to happen. At least he's a pretty mufucker."

Brick nodded sadly, head lowered, trying to hide his grief.

"Don't be sad, Brick. You'll be doing it for me. Finally getting the chance to see you suck a dick is going to have me cumming like crazy. Shit, my coochie is getting wet just thinking about it." Misty rubbed the lycra-covered crotch of her panties, then roughly pulled Brick's hand to her crotch. "Nice and wet! Mmm. I want you to fuck me right now, while Dane is out on some errands."

"Why I gotta sneak a fuck? You don't care about letting him fuck you when I'm around."

"He thinks it's his pussy. Come on now, take your dick out and hit this before he gets back." She pulled off her panties, kicked them aside.

"I can't; my shit won't get hard."

"Why not?" Misty stuffed her hand inside the slit of his boxers. Sure enough, his penis was soft. "Aw, shit. You outta pocket, nigga. I'm feeling some kind of way about this. My pussy is all up in your face and you got a limp dick?"

"I'm sorry, Misty," Brick mumbled, looking down in shame.

"Fuck you!" She kicked one of the duffle bags in anger as she hastily made her way to the kitchen. "Just remember that you brought this on yourself," she said, fury glinting in her eyes as she looked back at Brick. She grabbed the phone and pushed a button. Shoulders heaving in rage, she impatiently tapped her foot while she waited for her call to connect. "Why you take so long to answer your damn phone?" she barked into the phone. "So, how much longer are you gonna be?" She patted her foot faster. "An hour! Damn, why you gotta take so long? Look, hurry the fuck up—this worthless nigga needs to be on his way."

CHAPTER 36

Dane would have gladly wined and dined Felice, just to get another peek between her legs. The girl had a pussy like no other. And it did amazing things—worked on a dick like a pair of fat-ass lips. Dane was ready to turn his life around; marry the pussy, make it his wife. But with Misty breathing down his neck, calling and checking up on him, he had to find creative ways to get Felice to spend a little time.

After the last sexual fiasco, he was scared to stick his dick up in the punany. So, for the time being, he just wanted to look at it, admire it with his eyes, and then smell it for a minute before sucking the sweet juice out of those scrumptious pussy lips.

So, knowing he'd have to pay to play, he scooped up a trinket out of Misty's overflowing jewelry box. A charm. A tiny gold sandal with glittery straps—something Misty had most likely forgotten she'd even bought.

Misty deserved to get got—she kept making him promises, but nothing had materialized. Fuck that conceited bitch. What happened to the two-carat rocks he was supposed to be flossing? Bitch had game; he was still rocking a carat on each ear.

Lying on her back, knees wide apart, Felice held her tiny present, marveled at the craftsmanship, excitedly examined every exquisite detail. Meanwhile, Dane crouched between her legs, examined

Felice's genital region with the serious professionalism of a doctor. But when he separated her hairy outer lips and glimpsed her puffy flower, he moaned and slumped over, groaning. He gripped the sheets, trying to muster the strength to revisit her soft, feminine domain.

"You really feelin' my pussy like that?" Felice asked. "A lot of niggas admit my shit feels good, but they say it looks strange."

"Fuck what other niggas have to say. I'm not trying to hear about no dick you had in the past. This is my shit right here." He patted her pussy. "Ya heard?" Dane took a deep breath, biding his time before he took another plunge down below.

Felice set the trinket on the bedside table. "All right. Get on with it then. I'm ready." She opened her legs wider.

"I can't fuck you," Dane admitted, looking up at Felice with incredulous eyes.

"Why not?"

"You know what happened the last time. I'm better than that, but I have to get used to you, yo. That ain't no regular pussy; I gotta take it slow."

"Okay." Felice was quiet for a moment. "I have a dildo. You wanna use that on me?"

"Umph," he grunted and grabbed his dick. "That'll work." He gripped his manhood as it grew as hard as granite, but he didn't trust his manhood to hold up under the pressure of Felice's puffy pussy lips. "Hell, yeah. Gimme that dildo. I'ma work you over, yo." He stroked his dick expectantly, while Felice groped under a pillow. She pulled out a convincing dildo. Jet black and rippled with bulging veins and replete with a set of balls.

"We need to lube this up," she said. "I have some K-Y…"

"No, you don't. Let me see you suck it. Lube it up naturally."

"Baby, I don't wanna s…"

"I might be able to fuck you, if you wrap your lips around that black dildo." Dane scrunched up his face, aroused by his coarse words. The frowning expression enhanced his good looks, added more thug to his pretty-boy-ness. The combination of thug and sweet made Felice's tunnel tighten; she was ready to get down and dirty. More than ready to get tangled up in the sheets with Dane, she tongued the bulbous sloped-head, snaking her tongue around it, licking along the synthetic shaft. She was giving a command performance that deserved to be rewarded with some hot, distended flesh.

Oh, hell. Who was she kidding? Getting fucked wasn't the only thing on her agenda. Stealing Misty's man was at the top of the list. If she had to pussywhip him into shape, then so be it.

Misty had it going on and Felice wanted what Misty had. She wanted Misty's fly wardrobe, her shiny whip, her bling and her money stash…she wanted her entire fucking lifestyle. And she figured she could get it, if she could win Dane's heart. As far as she could tell, Dane was the nigga in charge. She'd spotted the thick wad of cash in his pocket the minute he walked through the door. Yeah, that nigga had his money right. Misty was only arm candy. Dane was the type of dude who liked to see his woman flossing, but he was on some low-key shit. No need to flash and shine. Nigga was so fine, big chains and gleaming jewelry would be overkill. He wasn't about gaudy glitter. Nah, all he flossed was a pair of diamond studs in his ears. Felice dug that.

So, what did Misty have over her? She wondered with a frown. *Nothing!* Misty didn't have anything except long hair and a pretty face. Fuck that skinny-ass, no-hips, no-tits, stuck-up bitch. Felice intended to have Dane all to herself. She just had to plan it right.

Let him keep coming around, let him keep sweating her—play hard to get. Dane had a nice operation going on and she wanted a big-ass slice of the cheese. Instead of selling her pussy like a peon, she would claim her seat on the throne—queen bee status— joining the king at his hip while he stacked up cheddar.

Visions of driving around in her own fly whip prompted her to suck in more plastic. She licked and slurped like the rubber dick tasted candy sweet. With an eye fixed on Dane's face, she took in another inch of the supple rubber, sucked the dildo-dick like she expected it to start twitching and shooting out a load of semen.

Dane praised her skills with a low, masculine groan. Then he manhandled his own dick, grasping it, wrangling with it, as he thrust his wide girth into the small opening made by his long, curled fingers. Grimacing, he panted hard, like he was hard-hitting inside a sticky, hot hole. "Suck it, baby. Suck that dick the same way you gon' suck the cum out of mine."

She deep-throated the supple rubber, dragged her tongue across the flesh-like testicle base.

With his hand wrapped around his rigid length, he dove face-first into her dark moisture. He kissed the pussy. Pressed his lush lips against hers with such ardor, he felt his mouth and her pussy vibrating together in passion. He licked the fleshy petals open, and whisked one plump lip with his tongue, and then the other. He teased her feminine nub with the tip of his tongue until it became rigid and engorged. Then it captured the slippery jewel and held it between his teeth, tugging on it, gently making her quiver and cry out. Making her say his name. Her juices spilled out like nectar from bitten fruit, saturating his tongue, refreshing his mouth with its tart-sweetness. He lapped the sweetness that seeped from her dewy core. She twisted and moaned; he sucked harder, dug his tongue in deeper, all the while hand-stroking his aching shaft, working himself up to the point of spilling his seed.

"Lemme fuck you, baby," he gasped, eyes flitting toward the dildo. Felice blinked in confusion. Groaning with sexual desire, Dane eased the dildo from her mouth and held the realistically shaped penis in his hand. Low, guttural moaning passed his lips as he positioned himself between her legs and slid the smooth head up and down her delicate slit, separating her heavy folds, uncovering the creamy moisture, probing until her desire poured out and trickled down the replica of massive manhood.

Fuck the dildo, she could have that anytime. Felice was ready for Dane's hard shaft. "That's enough." She twisted her torso, sat upright, trying to knock the fake appendage out of Dane's hand.

"Relax, shawty, lemme do this." Using the hand that had been stroking his own erection, Dane eased Felice down, held her firmly in place while he penetrated her with the black dildo, pushing it and twisting it rhythmically until she surrendered. Bucking hips and a cry of pleasure indicated Felice's acceptance of the freak fuck session.

Yanking on his hardened loins, Dane felt a familiar sensation swirling in the pit of his stomach. He felt it coursing throughout his veins. His temples began to throb as blood rushed to his head. He sank the dildo deeper. He was beyond rational thought. Working on sexual instinct, he removed the black penis from her pussy and guided it to her mouth. "Suck it for me," he urged.

On command, Felice licked her moisture off the dildo and then puckered her lips around the sloped head.

Dane aimed his weapon at the target, aligned it and pushed inside. "Ahhh!" he cried the moment her bulging pussy lips enveloped the head of his dick. Her lips hugged his aching man-

ALLISON HOBBS

hood, weakening him. Immobilizing him. Preventing him from penetrating deeply. Through gritted teeth, he grunted and growled. He pushed, attempting to insert some of his length while fighting to hold back the inevitable eruption. "Oh, shit!" Semen bubbled in his scrotum and traveled up into the base of his shaft. Lightning bolts of pleasure jolted him, sent him plunging over the crest. *Fuck it!* He let go. Shot out hot jets of semen, felt his seed splashing against fat pussy lips, dripping down into her hairy mound.

Dane was extremely disappointed. His hose was long and firm. He was fully equipped to do the job. Damn shame he fucked around and splattered the outside when his jawn should have been up inside that dip, spray-painting her interior walls.

268

CHAPTER 37

T homasina had never seen a sadder sight. Then again, maybe she had. She hadn't been a very pretty sight after that last go-round with Victor. Whew! That last bout had knocked the wind out of her sails, had her in pretty bad shape. Still, as hurt and fuming mad as she'd been, Thomasina doubted if she looked as broken down, shell-shocked, and dispirited as Brick looked when he trudged inside her living room.

"Get those bags off my carpet. Don't be so damn lazy. Pick 'em up and take 'em up upstairs to the back bedroom," she barked, hoping to incite Brick into firing back.

She was bored. Nothing on TV worth watching. Antagonizing her reluctant new boarder into a heated argument might be entertaining. That damn Misty had put her in this inconvenient bind; she might as well have a little fun. She was prepared to cuss Brick out with all the rage and passion she had stored up after Victor had so cruelly dumped her for the second and final time.

Without a word of his usual sass, Brick trudged upstairs. A half-hour passed. What the hell was he up there doing? She didn't hear drawers or closet doors opening and closing. That bastard better not be up there getting high.

Thomasina stomped up the stairs and found Brick sitting on the bed, staring into space, a pile of blue pills cupped in his hand.

"What the hell?" Thomasina smacked the pills out of his hand, sent them scattering. Brick fell over; his large body hit the floor like a toppled tree.

"Oh, hell! What in God's name is wrong with you? Did you take any of those pills?" She pulled on his arm, but he was dead weight. He was conscious, alert, but unmoving. Staring and moaning. *Oh, goddamn!* Thomasina was going to give her daughter hell for putting her in this position. That little heifer knew Brick wasn't in his right mind; that's why she shipped him out of her cozy apartment. What the hell was she supposed to do with him? Call an ambulance? Hell no! She wasn't about to give her nosey neighbors another exciting show. Bad enough that they'd witness Victor and his best friend, Mason running out of her house, carrying luggage. They'd probably heard all the commotion most recently when she'd tried to stab Victor to death with a pair of scissors.

Her neighbors had had enough titillating entertainment at her expense. If she couldn't get this big brute back in bed, he'd just have to sleep on the floor.

Arms folded across her chest, Thomasina scowled down at Brick, who was positioned in a tight fetal curl. The nerve of him attempting suicide in her domicile. She pulled the blanket off the bed and tossed it on top of him. *Humph!* First thing in the morning, Misty and her new boyfriend better get out of their cozy little love nest and come get this nutcase off the floor and take him to get some psychiatric help.

☙❧

Thomasina had a hell of a time trying to get to sleep. Those blue pills she'd swept up and tossed in the waste bin were calling her name. One pill would guarantee a decent night's sleep. She didn't approve of addictive medication, but after all that drama with Brick, her nerves were shattered. She needed something to calm herself down. She'd called her daughter a million times but that rotten little brat had turned her cell off; wouldn't pick up the house phone either. Thomasina tossed a few more minutes, then found a comfortable position. The sound of footsteps in the hall jerked her upright. *Now what?* She had to be at work in the morning, dammit. She couldn't take any more of Brick's nonsense. Grumbling to herself, she got out of bed, frowned at her sleeping gown, and grabbed a robe off the hook on the back of the closet door. The sleeping gown was too sheer, too low-cut to be worn by a woman who slept alone most nights, but she'd been in a distracted state when she threw it on. Gathering the sash of the robe and looping it in a knot, she trekked toward the hall.

Lawd have mercy! Brick was in the bathroom, door wide open, standing in front of the toilet, urinating and holding a colossal-sized penis.

She should have backed away, given him some privacy, but God forgive her, she was only human—a lonely female who'd recently endured a lengthy sex drought and then a heartbreaking one-night stand. Mesmerized by Brick's large package, she stood in the hallway, her hand covering her mouth in awe. Making her move, Thomasina patted her hair and puckered her lips.

"Feeling better, Brick?" she cooed, surprising herself with her own sultry vocals. She sounded uncharacteristically vixen-like, as if she were well-seasoned in seducing younger men.

Taken off guard, Brick quickly stuffed his oversized manhood back inside his boxers. "Yes, ma'am," he muttered, embarrassed.

"Feel like talking? You know, about what you're going through?"

"Nah, I'll be aiight." He smiled weakly.

"Taking pills...trying to take your life..."

"I know. I'm sorry 'bout that, Miss Thomasina. I was going through something; I wasn't thinking straight. "

"You're only human. I know how it feels to get your heart broken," she said sincerely. Thomasina shook away the memory of Victor and all the others. She'd never been lucky in love. Her eyes went to the bulge in Brick's shorts. *I bet he's good in bed.* She wasn't thinking about love; her mind was strictly on sex. Hot, torrid, no-strings-attached sex. "You had a rough day." She looked up in thought. "You know what you need?"

Brick gave her a skeptical look.

"A relaxing bath." She smiled and twisted the faucets on. Water began filling the tub. She cut a curious eye at Brick's covered package. His dick strained against his cotton boxers; the imprint was long and wide. With all he was carrying, he was more than capable of rocking her to sleep. Smiling, Thomasina dumped a generous amount of bubble bath.

Brick shook his head. "I don't..."

"Let me help you get rid of some of that stress," she said, her suggestive tone leaving no doubt of her carnal desire. She was shocked and slightly amused by her desperate whorishness. Smiling devilishly, she used her hand to test the water temperature.

Her gaze met Brick's. Her eyes sparkled with lust; he lowered his lashes in embarrassment and then resignedly, pulled off his boxers and stepped into the soapy water.

She thought of her daughter and felt no remorse. Misty was trying to play games with her. That little heifer was trying to take advantage of her generosity by dumping Brick on her. Well, okay then. No point in allowing all this virile masculinity to go to waste. She still couldn't deal with the scar on Brick's face, but if she focused on his other cheek, he wasn't a bad looking young man; not bad at all. Rather handsome in a rugged way. Hell, his looks didn't matter; she planned on having her eyes squeezed tight while he pumped her with all that youthful, bulging masculinity.

Thomasina soaped up the washcloth and sat on the edge of the tub. Tense, Brick sat in the bubbly water, his back and shoulders straight. She gently rubbed the back of his neck, ran the cloth across his expansive back, trying to relax him with caressing strokes. Using a soap-slicked hand, she caressed the bunching muscles of his shoulders. "Mmm," she uttered softly, enjoying the feel of hard male muscles beneath her hand. Thomasina massaged his broad, hair-roughened chest, circled his male nipples with her fingertip.

Too large to stretch out in the normal-sized tub, Brick drew up his knees, rested his feet on the ledge at the far end of the tub, his shoulders braced on opposite sides of the spigot, his head lulled in relaxation.

She soaped the hard slab of his belly, tangled her fingers into wiry pubic hair. The closer she got to his phallus, the tighter she clenched her inner muscles together, trying to quell her own building desire.

Large and dark, the smooth, knobbed head of his rod bobbed up and down, creating gentles waves, soft splashes. Suddenly, his stirring manhood burst through the bubbles and surfaced above water. "Miss Thomasina!" Brick uttered in a croaked voice, looking aghast, as if his penis was a wanton entity, acting on its own depraved accord.

Shh!" she hushed him. With a soapy palm, she stroked his straining shaft, giving it permission to swell up—to burst and explode if it needed to. He'd been through hell, fooling with Misty and her new boyfriend, whatshisfacename. If Brick needed to relieve himself of some tension, she'd help him out—she'd get hers later.

She worked Brick over, her hand sliding up and down his swollen staff. In a frenzy of yearning, Brick thrust upward, his hands flailed in wild response to Thomasina's sensual administrations. Needing to grab hold of something, he tugged on the sash of her robe, unwittingly pulled her robe open, exposing her soft sleeping gown. Thin straps slipping off shoulders, deep cleavage, a valley between voluptuous breasts. His eyes wandered downward, where her thick, toned thighs were bared. Her gown was hitched up, giving a glimpse of dark pubic hair.

Naked and wet, Brick rose from the water. Thomasina snatched a towel from a rack, dried Brick quickly. His nude body was pleasing to her eyes. Hard muscles bulging everywhere. She gave an extra special pat to his big dick. It looked good enough to lick, suck, and fuck—all at once, if possible.

His strong arms reached for Thomasina—scooped her up, handling her with tenderness. Cradling her one hundred and seventy-three pounds as if she were as light as a feather, he glided toward her bedroom.

CHAPTER 38

I t was her maturity—her womanliness, that made his nature rise. Touching her curves, her cushiony bosom, her fleshy rump, protruding tummy, and her ample hips, soothed a yearning deep in his soul, fulfilled a desire he hadn't been aware of.

"You can't mention this to Misty," Thomasina whispered.

"I won't," he assured her as he gently placed her on the bed.

He hovered over her, awkward, wondering which approach to use. Was she the type of woman who wanted it rough? Did she want him to plow into her and savagely beat up the pussy? Or should he treat her as gently as he treated Misty? Oddly, big brute that he was, tenderness was his natural inclination. Risking making a fool of himself, he put an arm around her and looked at her, trying to gauge her reaction. The smile in her eyes gave him permission. His mouth found hers. Softly, he kissed her lips, parted her lips. Invitingly, she widened her mouth, welcoming the sweet invasion, encouraging him to explore.

Brick communicated his desire with ardent tongue strokes. His excited hands roamed freely, fingers journeying over her shoulders and down to her flimsy nightgown. Impatiently, he ripped off satin straps, tore through lace fabric, desperate to touch her bare skin. Awestruck by her magnificent female landscape, he gawked, his open palms suspended in mid-air.

Waiting to be ravished, Thomasina held her breath as she lay atop the sheets. She was so hot that she could feel the heat rushing through her veins.

Determined to take his time, Brick feasted his eyes upon her ripened beauty, ignoring the ache in his swelling loins as he took in every inch of mature womanhood.

Slowly, hesitantly, he reached out to touch her. Her eyelids were closed, but she felt the warmth of his hand as it drew near. She shivered when the back of his hand softly touched her cheek. He outlined her yearning lips with the tip of his finger. Thomasina struggled with an overpowering urge to pucker her lips and slurp on his finger.

His hands trailed downward, gently squeezing her shoulders, fondling her breasts. Thomasina gasped and shuddered in sexual anticipation, but Brick took his time, enjoying the velvety smooth texture of her skin. Awestruck by her voluptuous body composition.

Thomasina and her daughter were complete opposites. Misty was small-boned, youthful, and heartbreakingly beautiful, yet she couldn't light a candle to her mother. Thomasina, with her average looks and imperfections, had an abundance of sex appeal that far surpassed Misty's superficial, outer beauty. Enjoying the pleasure of her flesh, he indulged his need to learn the curvatures and contours of Thomasina's nakedness.

He slipped his fingers inside the smooth warmth of her arm pits, then taking her off guard, he raised one of her arms, pinned it against the soft pillow and inhaled the clean, fresh scent. She shivered as his breath tickled her skin. When he kissed that hidden erogenous zone, Thomasina undulated with unexpected pleasure. Brick's hand traveled and roved over every curve of her sacred temple, tenderly stroking her skin.

Having never been able to look beyond her bad attitude, he

hadn't noticed or been able to appreciate her fine attributes. But now, after shedding the lace fabric from her body, he'd also peeled away her tough façade. She was a good-looking woman. Real sexy. Her sensuality was so raw, it pulsed like a heartbeat; making his rod throb with unbearable need.

He cupped her heavy breasts; the luscious orbs spilled into his open hands. He held them with reverence. His thumbs toggled her large nipples until they peaked and became ripe for sucking. Hungrily, he raised the life-giving flesh to his lips. "You got some big-ass titties, Ma," he delivered the compliment with a groan, before taking a taut nipple inside his mouth.

Incited by the guttural sound of the compliment, driven to wildness by the feel of his tongue twirling around her beaded flesh, Thomasina cried out, her arms flailed, scratching, tearing at the skin on Brick's massive back. While his lips clung to her bosom, his hand spiraled down, settled on her paunch, caressed and squeezed the soft pad of flesh. He finger-combed her wild bush of pubic hair, and then stretched his fingers, which seductively meandered toward her soft petals. Gently, he separated the fragrant flower. Breathing hard, he inserted his thick, middle finger inside Thomasina's glimmering pool, swirling the dew until it spit and bubbled over.

He sucked the spicy poontang off his finger while his other hand busily kneaded the ample flesh of her ass. Her butt was so plump and meaty, Brick couldn't hold back his desire to be completely uninhibited—unashamedly freaky. He withdrew his finger from inside her honey-soaked tunnel, and flipped Miss Thomasina over, her plump tummy flattened onto the cool sheets. Her buttocks shook like jelly, causing Brick to unconsciously lift his hand and pop that ass, making it jiggle like crazy.

"Ooo, baby, make it hurt," Thomasina coerced.

But he couldn't. His dick was straining for release, distracting him, preventing him from concentrating. Forcing his mind off his erection, his hand moved down to separate her ass cheeks. His strong hand pried her buttocks open; his eager tongue licked a blazing trail down the crease, zooming in on the tiny opening. Teasing tongue flicks became urgent, pressing, and probing until the tightened center responded like lips opening for a kiss. Hands freed, he allowed her cheeks to enfold his face. Ass licking and finger-fucking had Thomasina squirming and moaning. Her sounds of passion enticed Brick to give her even more pleasure.

"How you want it, Miss Thomasina?"

Confused, Thomasina murmured an incoherent reply. She'd never been asked that question before. And she most certainly had never been called "Miss Thomasina" by a sex partner. *Goddamn!* Her pussy felt like something had been ignited inside, setting it on fire. Enflamed, she could only babble, speaking nonsensical gibberish.

Brick couldn't make out what she was saying, but he recognized pussy talk. He couldn't decipher her exact yearning, but he knew her coochie needed emergency attention. He turned her over on her side and eased between her thick thighs. "Can I taste it?"

She replied with loud moaning. Her supple thighs enveloped his strong jaw line. Brick drew in her female fragrance. "Mmm. You smell good, Miss Thomasina," he groaned in a voice muffled by bushy pubic mound and moist vagina flesh. Inhaling deeply, he felt intoxicated, love-drunk by her aromatic musky scent. He would have happily kept his face buried in her pussy, lapping, licking, and exploring until her pussy bubbled over in an orgasmic eruption, but Thomasina's good-smelling pussy weakened him. Made him want to surrender, lie prone and let her have her way with his face. He couldn't find the words to express his desire for her to take control. How could he tell her he wanted her to plant her ass on his face—smother him with her womanhood; strangle him with an overflow of sexual juices? How could he express his sudden yearning for sweet suffocation?

At this point, Brick's secret desire would have to remain an unrealized sexual fantasy. Thomasina was too far gone to take control. "Baby, eat it," she purred. "Put your lips on it and suck it." Like her daughter, Thomasina obviously enjoyed getting oral sexed. Resisting the strong desire to have his face sat upon and smothered with hairy pussy, Brick gathered the strength to go to work and indulge her. Timidly, he took small licks of the creamy goodness between her thighs. Her nectar was thick and rich, enticing him to want more of the tasty custard. He curled his tongue, using it like a ladle as he scooped up the sugary cream. Hungry for more of her creamy lust, he stretched out his tongue, stroking with the full width and length, feeding on her sex. Moments later, he bunched up his lips and latched on to her love button.

Thomasina's body bucked, her breathing emerged in deep, shuddering gasps.

"Stop!" She tried to disengage from Brick's pleasure-giving lips. "I don't want to cum. Not yet!" Thomasina extricated herself. "I want to return the pleasure." She slithered downward.

But Brick knew his limitations. He couldn't take another second of stimulation. Male clients provided him with enough head to last a lifetime. Right now, he needed pussy. Hot, well-seasoned, mature pussy. Giving a low moan, he demonstrated his desire, gripped Thomasina's shoulders and repositioned her on the bed. Holding his pulsing shaft, he directed it toward her warm haven.

She'd wanted to give Brick oral pleasure, wanted to lick the moisture drops from his swollen dick and then suck him dry. Realistically, she doubted that she'd be able to accommodate the full length of his giant phallus inside her mouth, but she was willing to try.

But Brick's craving could not be sated by oral stimulation. With a gentle tug, he urged her upward. Thomasina felt a stab of regret. Her disappointment promptly changed to gratitude the instant she felt his globular head sliding past her petal-soft folds. She clenched her fist in a spasm of excitement as Brick entered her slick, wet center, easing his oversized hot flesh inside her tight canal, slowly stretching her slippery walls.

She made a soft cry of pain.

"Am I hurting you?" Brick asked, alarmed.

"It's good pain," she uttered.

Brick grunted, slid in a little deeper. He could feel his stomach flutter as he struggled to hold back his wad. With an animalistic disregard for her incapacity to take in the full length of his dick, he pushed it in to the hilt, desperately seeking shelter and female heat. Deeply embedded, he unwittingly located her spot. Thomasina's vocal pitch escalated. She became wild, clawing, crying out, thrashing.

Brick pumped hard, faster, deeper. "Ooo, Miss Thomasina, you got some good, wet pussy. I'm sorry, Ma; I can't hold it. I'm 'bout to bust."

Ma! Thomasina blushed; she didn't know which sounded more endearing and sexually stirring—"Ma" or "Miss Thomasina"? *Both!* She voiced her approval with soft gasps and sought to match his pace, grinding her full hips in circles as they strove to reach an orgasm.

"You gon' cum with me?"

She mumbled something. Unable to speak coherent words or phrases, she relied upon primitive sex sounds, murmured rambling, rhythmic chanting, low and guttural moaning, frantic pelvic gyrations. Her breathing was harsh and labored, her face scrunched up as if in excruciating pain as she struggled to reach a climax.

"You wanna take a break? Do you need some rest, Miss Thomasina?" Brick's face was etched with concern and tenderness.

What a considerate young man. She'd been so wrong about Brick. Misty was a fool to let him get away. "No, don't stop." Brick's sweet concern aroused her; made her pussy become even more revved up. It pulsed in appreciation and clenched in anticipation of a powerful eruption.

Brick felt her coochie's reaction—he felt the temperature change as her pussy interior went from warm to scorching hot. His dick could no longer conduct itself or control the desire for savage behavior. "You ready for me?" He spoke in a husky, urgent tone.

Thomasina moaned a response, and then allowed her body to scream the word, *Yes!* She lifted up, wrapped her legs around his waist and used vaginal muscles to pull in dick. His dick went in so deeply, his balls felt like they had been dragged inside and were now lodged up in the pussy, giving Thomasina intense pleasure, making her thrash, emit high-pitched wails, and cuss like a drunken sailor. Female ejaculation squirted out as forcefully as a man's. "Umph! Your pussy's gushing," he groaned, impressed by the force and volume of her lust. He pulled her closer, groaned in blissful agony and then flooded her satiny confines with his seed.

Wrapped in each other's arms, Thomasina and Brick kissed like lovers. They searched each other's eyes for a reasonable explanation of what had just transpired between them. What had started out on her part as a sneaky, shady, shamefully scandalous sex act—

had morphed into something else. Thomasina was keenly aware that she and Brick had experienced more than just a moment of lustful satisfaction; they had stumbled upon something meaningful—something that could blossom and flourish. Something long term? Should she allow herself even a glimmer of hope?

Brick wondered if it was all in his mind. He bear-hugged her, kissed her again, waiting for her to pull away. She didn't. She kissed him back and then asked, "What's your real name, Brick?"

"Baron. Baron Kennedy."

Thomasina caressed his face; allowed her finger to wander toward his scar. "That's a nice name. Dignified." She nodded. "I'm going to call you Baron from now on. Is that all right with you?"

Nodding, Brick blushed. He liked hearing her say his name. He'd been called Brick for so long, he'd never developed a personality for a man named Baron Kennedy.

"Good night, Baron." She snuggled inside his arms, eyelids fluttering, sweet sleep fast approaching.

"Good night, Miss Thomasina." He kissed her neck, squeezed her and then blissfully closed his eyes.

CHAPTER 39

Hiding his contempt, Dane sucked his teeth softly. Misty was a pain in the ass. Felice's spongy pussy had damn near depleted him, but he'd still managed to serve the selfish little nympho some leftover sperm that was floating at the bottom of his nut sac. But she still wasn't satisfied. Misty was a beast. Insatiable. She kept touching him, rubbing his thighs, hinting for more dick. When she brazenly climbed on top of him, rubbing her pussy against his groin, he'd had more than enough. He felt like snatching her up and throwing her narrow ass against the wall. He yearned to hear the sound of her breaking bones. He was pretty sure he hated Misty. Hated her for her arrogance; her conceit. So sure of herself, she didn't even realize she was getting played.

If he weren't anxious to get out of the house, he'd suck her pussy just to keep her satisfied and thrown off guard, but he didn't have time for a whole lot of unnecessary cunt sucking. There was a pressing matter that needed attending to. Once Misty went to sleep, he planned to sneak the car keys again. He didn't plan on paying Felice another visit. He had a burning question and there was only one person in the world who could provide the answer.

"I'm thirsty," he said, standing up. "You want something to drink?" he asked indulgently.

"Yeah, I want to swallow your kids." She smiled and licked her lips. He returned the smile, but secretly wanted to punch out her lights. Bash her head in, so she'd shut the fuck up and go to sleep. "Whatchu want—juice or soda?"

"I want you," she whined.

He let out a harsh breath.

"All right," she said, sensing his impatience. "Bring me some Pepsi. But, baby," she whined in a nasally tone, "I'm really thirsty for you." Pouting, she poked out her small lips. Her unsuccessful lip protrusion was a reminder of how much he hated kissing her. He refused to even allow himself to mentally dwell on the contempt he felt when slipping his dick inside her paper-thin slit. *Skinny pussy-lipped skank!*

"Aiight. I gotchu." He gave her an insincere wink. He puckered his sexy lips beautifully and blew her a false-hearted kiss. "Be right back." With eyes darkened, he plodded to the kitchen. He poured Pepsi into a tall glass for himself and then set to crushing up a couple of pills—a couple muscle relaxants and an over-the-counter sleeping aid—a cocktail that would put her ass to rest. He hoped the cocktail wasn't lethal, but the bitch damn sure needed some time out. The pretty bitch couldn't fuck or suck worth shit. Hell if he was going to waste any more of his seed on her.

Stepping lively, he merrily rejoined her in the bedroom.

"Here you go, Lil' Bit. We only have a half a bottle left, so if you're just gonna fuck around with it, give it to me. I'll drink the shit."

Desiring to please, Misty took several long sips.

Dane's eyes lit with joy when she guzzled the drink, emptying the glass.

Waiting for her to show signs of wooziness, he ran his fingers through her hair, massaged her scalp, helping her to relax.

"Baby, rub my coochie." She thrust upward.

Impatient, he gave her tiny mound a quick, harsh rub.

"Dang, why you gotta be so rough? Put your finger in it, baby. Play with it." Her voice was slightly slurred as she separated her thighs, offering her deepest regions. Dane was disgusted. Begrudgingly, he lodged his finger inside her tight tunnel and finger-fucked her harshly. Jabbing in and out with increasing anger, until her head lolled and drool pooled at the corner of her mouth.

"What's wrong, Lil' Bit?" He feigned concern as he peeked at her face.

"Nothing," she crooned. "I'm just resting my eyes."

"Aiight, you do that. Keep your eyes closed while Daddy works on that little coochie. Y'ah mean?"

"Uh-huh," she whimpered as he sneakily withdrew his finger.

"Don't stop," she moaned in weak protest, her eyes fluttering as she fought to keep them open, struggled against the pull of sleep.

"I gotchu, Boo. That's enough finger-fucking. Me and you 'bout to get into it. You want some dick, don'tchu?"

"Uh-huh," she moaned, dragging out the last syllable. "That's what I really need," she slurred sleepily.

"Aiight then. Close your eyes and get ready. We 'bout to rumple up the sheets and shit in a minute."

Misty murmured softly, smiled dreamily as Dane grabbed her laptop and tiptoed out of the bedroom. *Sleep tight, sucka!*

He would have loved to hop in Misty's whip and steer it straight to Felice's crib. That slut presented a challenge. He had to get back with her and prove that he could conquer that pussy.

Unfortunately, he didn't have the time to tackle the poontang at the moment. He was on a fact-finding mission, and after he got the information he needed, he had other business to attend to—personal and money wise.

He pulled out his cell. "Yo, Felice! I'm gon' slide through later on tonight—around two or three. Listen for the door and keep that thing hot for me." He frowned at his cell. "Yeah, I got something for you. Don't worry about it—it's a surprise." Dane snapped the phone close.

Minutes later, he pulled the X5 into the back of Ziggy's Barbecue Joint. His father, Marshall Newman, worked for Ziggy. He swept and mopped the inside of the place, carried large bags of trash and garbage to the commercial-sized waste bin. In between cleaning and garbage-toting treks, his father could always be found throwing down hard liquor in the back of the joint.

As expected, there he was, guzzling whiskey straight from a bottle concealed inside a brown paper bag. His mother claimed his father's good looks had blinded her to his bad characteristics. *What good looks?* Dane wondered as he approached his bleary-eyed, haggard-looking father.

"What's good, Pops?" he asked, his mouth giving the impression of a warm-hearted smile. Inwardly, he sneered at his bum-ass father. His old man had on a T-shirt, with the name *Ziggy's* practically obliterated by dirt, grime, and caked-on barbecue sauce.

"Look who the cat dragged in," his old man said sarcastically. "I know that ain't none of yours." His father nodded toward Misty's truck.

"Naw, I borrowed it."

Looking relieved that his son hadn't struck it rich, his father nodded, then took another swig. "Whatchu want?" The drunken man eyed his son suspiciously. "You can tell your greedy mother that you're too old to be still coming around hassling me about back-owed child support."

"Mom ain't thinking about you. She's remarried." Dane gave his father a fierce scowl for slandering his mother's name.

"Oh, yeah?" His father chuckled. "What fool did she hoodwink this time?

"Hoodwink? She still got her looks. My mother's smart and hard-working. But you already know that. Right, Pops? You wouldn't have left a stupid, defenseless woman to raise your only child, would you?" he said sarcastically. He clenched his teeth to keep from throwing some hard body shots at Pops, but if he let go of years' worth of pent-up anger, he'd probably kill his worthless father.

"Simmer down. I was just having fun." Marshall chuckled. His laughter, however, was without mirth. It was a spiteful, disrespectful, croaking sound.

"I gotta question for you." Dane narrowed his eyes.

"Yeah?"

"How many other brothers and sisters do I have?"

Marshall reared back, face twisted in disgust. "How the hell would I know?"

"Did you ever knock anyone up while you were married to Mom?"

"What the hell is this about?"

Dane slid the photo out of his pocket. Handed his father the picture of Shane and his brother, Tariq. His father squinted at the picture. Dane took a lighter from his pocket, flicked it, illuminating the photograph. "Anyone look familiar?"

His father continued squinting. His face twisted into a frown. "I'll be damn. That tall, skinny fella…" He tapped Shane's image. "He looks just like I used to. Looks like I spit that one out, but damn if his mother pulled my coat. I never saw this boy before."

"Yeah, he looks like me, Pops. Like he's my twin," Dane interjected. "You wanna tell me about it. Do I have a twin?

"I don't know this boy," Marshall insisted. "Do you think your mother would give away her own flesh and blood? Boy, stop talking crazy. You ain't got no twin."

Dane sighed in relief, leaned close to his foul-smelling father and pointed out Tariq. "That's his twin right there."

"Hmm." Marshall gave the picture back to Dane and then stared off into space. "Lemme tell you something, son," he said, when he came back down to earth. "Some of the best pussy in the world can be found locked inside a mental ward."

"Here you go…talking about that nut house you used to work in…" Dane blew out a burst of aggravated air. "I know all about it. That's all you ever talked about when I was growing up. Bragging about it, like working in a mental hospital was something to be proud of. You wasn't no doctor, Pop! You wasn't nothing but hired help," Dane blurted, angry and frustrated.

"You right, I didn't have no fancy job title. But a young thug like you don't know the reward of earning a paycheck—putting in a honest day's work."

Dane's chest heaved in exasperation. "Man, what's that old job of yours got to do with the question I asked you? Damn!"

"I was gon' get to it, but if I can't tell it the way I want to, then forget about it. Go 'head on about your business."

Dane sighed. "Aiight, Pops. Run it down. Tell me all about the crazy house you worked in."

His father shifted his body, stretching out his legs comfortably as he sat on a metal folding chair. "Schizophrenic pussy is the best pussy I've ever had."

Dane grimaced.

"I ain't lying. Schizo pussy…" He paused. "That's what we used to call it," he reflected fondly. "It don't have no phony airs about itself, son. Nah, that pussy is raw and unrefined. Wild pussy! Uninhibited. It grabs a hold of a dick and pulls it in—all the way down to the balls. Fucking schizo pussy is like trying to stay in the saddle when you sitting on top of a bunking bronco. I done had my share of women, but ain't no pussy can compare to the dick ride given by the mentally unsound." His eyes closed dreamily. "You listening to me, boy," he barked, snapping himself out of his perverted reverie.

"I'm not tryna hear this shit. I just wanna know if you—"

His father made a snorting sound. "I know whatchu thinking. You think your old man is talking shit. Yeah, I'm feeling a little tipsy. I ain't gon' lie about it; your old man ain't feeling no pain. But this ain't drunk talk. I know exactly what I'm saying. That job I had at the mental hospital provided me with unlimited crazy pussy."

"That's bullshit."

"You ain't gotta believe it. But I swear by God, I had all the sex I wanted. More than I could handle most of the time. See, I had to help restrain patients. Help hold 'em down. Back in the day— way before my time, the doctors used to give the crazy people something called a lobotomy."

"What?" Dane scowled in revulsion.

"A lobotomy. It's an operation on the brain. I heard about it, but I ain't never witnessed it, like some of the older fellas I worked with claimed. They told me there was a traveling psychiatrist who would give—"

"Man, come on. Get to the point. Am I related to the dude in the picture?"

Marshall continued as if Dane hadn't said a word. "So, anyway, they said the traveling psychiatrist would come in and do ten to twenty procedures in one day. Had patients lined up, performed surgery on 'em, one right after the other. Some say the man was sadistic; others claim he was a visionary—ahead of his time. Fact is, he figured out a way to do cost-effective, quickie brain surgery."

CHAPTER 40

The grimace on Dane's face spoke volumes. "Quickie brain surgery? How the fuck he do that?"

"He'd knock the patients out with electroshock and then insert an ice pick underneath their eyeball."

Dane couldn't help from squirming at the idea of a sharp instrument anywhere near his eyeball.

"He'd take a hammer and drive that ice pick up into the frontal lobes of the brain. Then he'd wiggle it around to make sure he was hitting every dark corner of their violent, depraved minds."

Dane felt nauseous. "Seems like that would have killed 'em?"

"Nah, it calmed 'em down. Calmed 'em real good, from what I heard. Those mental patients didn't make much of a ruckus after they had ice pick surgery."

"That's fucked up." Dane felt violated by having to listen to his drunk-ass father rant and talk trash. He doubted there was even a thread of truth to what his father was saying, but didn't feel like arguing. He wanted information. He didn't know why it was so important to know, but it was. He always wanted a brother to run around and wreak havoc with. For his own peace of mind, he needed to know if their uncanny resemblance was a quirk of fate or if the deceased Shane Batista had been his brother by blood.

"But the mental health department…the feds or somebody came in and put a stop to lobotomies. So, by the time I was working there, those days were long gone. Most were made to relax with medication—Thorazine and whatnot. Those that didn't respond to the medication had to be held down with leather restraints." His father produced a reminiscent smile. "That's where I come in the picture." He took a deep, rejuvenating breath. "They needed young, strapping fellas like myself to wrestle with 'em and hold in place, and help cuff 'em to metal tables. Problem was you couldn't keep those people cuffed up twenty-four hours a day. So, me and several others were called on and told to use what we were blessed with to keep the ladies nice and calm." He gave his son a meaningful wink; his eyes roamed down to his groin.

"Now, you're lying."

"My hand to God. The doctor hisself gave permission to me and a few others. Told us we could sex down females as long as we kept it among ourselves and confidential. Doctor told us, don't think of it as rape; think of it as therapy."

"Aw, man. That's sick."

"I think banging an ice pick up in their skull is sick, but once upon a time, the medical profession thought it was therapeutic."

"So, you was up in the crazy house raping bitches?"

"No, I gave therapy sessions." Dane's father laughed hard. It was loud, shoulder-shaking, knee-slapping, coughing-up, phlegm-rattled, raucous laughter.

Dane glared at his father.

"Why you looking at me like I'm wearing a shit suit? I did my job well and received extra perks. See, back in those days, they didn't have hidden security cameras all over the place, taping niggas while they were giving behind-the-scenes therapy sessions. Shit, working in a crazy house could make a nigga lose his own good mind, if he didn't have a way to relieve some of that job-related stress."

"Did you know a woman—last name, Batista?"

"Puerto Rican bitch?"

"I'm not sure."

"Puerto Rican bitches were okay to work with, but the doc was as prejudiced as they come when it came to us black men sticking our dicks up in the white patients." He frowned at the memory. "White women were off limits to us blacks." He tapped his hand with his forefinger, indicating his brick-red complexion and then shook his head at the shame of such blatant racism. "Humph! That man sure didn't want a bunch of black dicks up in those white schizos. You wanna know something? A lot of interracial mingling went on behind closed doors. We figured what that doctor didn't know, didn't hurt him." Marshall gave a burst of raucous laughter. "The joke was on the doc and the hospital—every time one of those crazy white women pushed out a half-black baby." There was more knee-slapping laughter, followed by a bout of phlegm-filled coughing.

"Wasn't none of that DNA mess. They didn't investigate workers. They just blamed the patients, said they were all hot for each—too crazy to be separated by race. The kids got put up for adoption. Foster care and whatnot."

Dane always knew his father was slimy, but he now realized he was worse than slimy. The man was bona fide crazy and he could only pray he'd hadn't been contaminated too badly. He didn't want to end up an alcoholic, talking about his glory days of raping and pillaging schizophrenic women in a nut house. Damn, his pops was worse off than he'd thought.

Still holding the picture, Dane pointed out Tariq.

"So, you admitting that you fathered these brothers?"

"Hell no! That yella one ain't none of mine."

"They're twins, Pop."

"I wouldn't give a shit. That yella boy looks just like ol' Roger Smallwood. Roger was a high-yella pretty boy. If memory serves me, Roger went in and calmed Marguerite down right after I did my work on her. He didn't want to, though." Marshall scowled. "Damn, sissy!" he snarled. "That's probably why he had the last name Smallwood. You get it?" He laughed hard, coughed up and spit out phlegm. "Nah, he didn't wanna tussle with that wildcat, Marguerite. Even after the long hard ride I gave her, she was still spitting and clawing. Me and the other fellas pushed Roger in the room with her; made him stand up like a man and take his turn. A woman like that needed two or three strong backs to calm her all the way down. The rest of us couldn't give her no more therapy until our dicks recharged."

"So, you expect me to believe that a woman can have twins by two different men?"

"Damn straight. Those boys ain't identical. The mean-looking one is most likely your brother. But, that sweet-looking boy is the spitting image of Roger Smallwood. I know my own blood when I see it. Boy, we come from a long line of fierce Cherokee Indians. We made out of Cherokee and African warriors. There's no white blood mixed up in my veins. I can't make a male child who looks as soft and sweet as a girl. That yella twin ain't none of my seed." Marshall took a deep, satisfying breath. "Now, when can I meet my son?"

"You can't."

"Why not?"

"He's dead. Killed hisself."

Disappointment contorted Marshall's face.

"Yup, your son, Shane is dead and gone," Dane informed him with a large measure of satisfaction as well as a modicum of sorrow over the personal loss of the brother he'd never known. "His twin is dead, too."

"Umph!" His father uttered in disgust and turned the bottle back up to his lips. He took a long swig. "What about Marguerite? How she make out?" He looked hopeful, like there was a possibility for a spur-of-the-moment hook-up.

"She's calm. Peaceful," Dane taunted, deliberately fucking with his father for abandoning his parental responsibilities without a lick of remorse.

"Say what?" Marshall reared back in shock. "You mean to tell me that spitfire is actually taking her meds?" He gave a snort. "I'll believe that when I see it. How can I get in touch with her?"

"Can't."

"Why not?"

"She's in her grave." Dane glared at his father. "It don't get more peaceful than that, Pops."

"Damn!" His father spat out the word and then kicked out his foot, angry and regretful at having lost his last shot at schizo-phrenic sex.

CHAPTER 41

Claiming illness—a high temperature and cold sweats, Thomasina Bernard stayed home from work for two days in a row. Yeah, she had a fever all right. Love fever. She felt flushed just thinking about her hard-muscled, young lover lying in her bed. *Umph!* She smiled as she flipped pancakes in the skillet. Another pan contained scrambled eggs and cheese, bacon was crisp and waiting inside the microwave. Cooking for a man felt good—felt as natural as if she'd been doing it her whole life.

This morning, she'd really tried to get out of bed and get herself ready for her job, but after making love twice before six a.m., she didn't have the strength or the will to put in a day's work. "I'm still sick; can't make it in," she told her boss, using the convincing, throaty tone of someone not feeling up to par.

She replaced the phone in the base and two strong arms instantly wrapped around her waist. "You still sick, Ma?" Brick whispered, his lips nipping and teasing her ear. "Want me to make it better?"

She blushed, kissed one of his iron-hard arms. "If I keep messing with you, I'm going to wind up dead. The coroner's gonna take one look at me and say this woman was obviously loved to death." She broke out laughing.

Brick didn't find it funny. "You know I wouldn't hurt you."

"I was just kidding, Baron."

"I know, but I don't even like you to play with the word *death*."

"All right. Who would have ever thought you had such a sensitive side?"

"I'm sensitive when it comes to you."

He seemed to have swiftly and seamlessly transferred his love and adoration from daughter to mother. How was that possible? Brick had issues. Inevitably, Thomasina would have to start peeling away layers of his psyche and try to get to the bottom of the matter. Or maybe she wouldn't. Being realistic, she had to accept that his presence was only temporary. She hadn't heard a mumbling word from her trifling daughter, but it was just a matter of time before Misty turned up to collect her meal ticket. She lived off the money Brick made from doing only God knew what. Dark clouds loomed, threatened to take away the sunshine from Thomasina's work-free day. *Lord, please don't let me find out Baron's a hired killer*. She wouldn't put it past Misty to have him out there maiming and murdering for her own greedy purposes.

Thomasina pushed aside the dark thoughts and allowed herself to bask in the joy of having an unselfish, long-lasting, and youthful sex partner.

Diving under the covers, she drew Brick's large, swelling phallus inside her mouth. Becoming skilled at oral sexing his enormous dick, she ran her tongue up and down the length of his shaft, swirled circles around the smooth head, moaning as she tasted his chocolate sweetness, sucking until she heard the harsh groan of masculine satisfaction.

&ᕤᕤᕤ&

"Breakfast is ready," she sang the words.

Brick bounded down the stairs and strolled into the kitchen, wearing jeans and a wife beater that displayed his bulging muscles. Feeling good—better than he'd felt in years, he bounced over to the spot where Thomasina stood in front of the stove. He palmed her butt cheeks, uttered a low moan and then proceeded to fondle her big, round ass while kissing the back of her neck. "Mmm. The grub smells good…you smell good…that ass is looking good. I'm in love, Ma."

"How is that possible?" Thomasina giggled and motioned for him to take a seat. He reluctantly tore himself away from her and pulled a chair up close to the kitchen table.

She set a plate heaped with breakfast foods in front of him. Brick dug into the scrambled eggs. "Yo, this is banging. You can burn, Ma." He nodded his head as he threw down on her home cooking, something he hadn't had in years. A sudden dark feeling came over him. It didn't seem right for her to miss work to stay home and keep him company. It was real fucked up to be grubbing on food he hadn't bought. Brick put his fork down. "You need some money, Miss Thomasina?"

She cocked her head in surprise. "Where'd that come from? Boy, hush and eat your breakfast."

"Seriously, I have a couple hundred on me to help out with food and whatnot."

"What's wrong?" She stared at him, her eyes focused on his scar; surprisingly the jagged cut no longer repelled her. She could look beyond it and see his good looks, his loving and trusting spirit.

"Misty already paid for you to stay here. To be honest, I was thinking about giving the money back." Feeling embarrassed and slightly off kilter, Thomasina turned her gaze away from Brick.

"Even if you decide that this isn't what you want…if you and Misty get back together—"

"I'm not going back to Misty. I'm through with that life. I've been doing a lot of thinking since I've been here and I figured out something about myself."

"What?" Thomasina was curious.

"It feels good to be treated nice. I never knew how it felt to be treated like I'm special."

"You are special." Thomasina raked her hands through her short, thick hair. "Good sex feels like love, I guess. That's probably our only connection."

He cocked his head to the side. "It feels like love to me. All I ever knew was mad, sad, scared, and lonely."

"You've never been happy?"

Brick shook his head. "Back when I was a kid, I used to think I was happy if a day went by and my foster father didn't whip my behind."

"What about Misty? Weren't you happy before whathisface came into the picture?"

"I worshipped the ground Misty walked on; I put her up on a pedestal, treated her like a queen. I didn't mind how she treated me. I was grateful to be with her. So, I can't blame Misty. Plus, that's the way I was raised. My foster father told me to be grateful for whoever took care of me."

"But Misty didn't work or take care of you."

"She taught me the ropes. I was grateful for that."

"Do you still love Misty?" Thomasina figured he did, but she wanted to hear the words straight from his mouth.

Brick nodded. "Yeah. I'll always love Misty. She gave me my heart."

"What?"

"She took me under her wing, taught me to defend myself and how to make money for us."

Sorrow clutched at Thomasina's heart. Her daughter had manipulated this sweet soul and she had personally treated him with enormous disrespect. Pounding it into his head that he wasn't good enough for her selfish daughter. "There's been a lot of hostility between us—in the past. And I'm sorry, Baron. I really am."

"Yo, I ain't been no saint. I had plenty of harsh words for you, too. I apologize as well."

"Deep down, I always knew that my child was corrupt down to her core."

"She's not all bad. Misty's spoiled," Brick said in Misty's defense.

"And I'm the one responsible for her spoiled, rotten ways." She waved her hand, silencing him before he could defend her daughter again. "I don't want to know what Misty had you out there doing to earn all that money; I really don't." She shook her head emphatically. "But whatever you were doing has got to stop. Right now. Today!"

Brick reflected on Thomasina's words. "I can't let Misty take the blame for everything. See…" Brick inhaled, gathering his thoughts.

Thomasina shuddered. *Please, Lord, don't let this man tell me he's a hired assassin.* "I said, I don't want to know. The past is the past. Me and you…we're going to move forward. Together. We'll take small steps. No point in making a whole lot of promises. Let's just treat each other good and see how far this can go."

Brick smiled—wide and broad, making his scar even more pronounced. Thomasina didn't care. She wanted him—scar and all.

"First thing tomorrow, I'm going out to look for a job. I never had a regular job before. But I'll flip burgers or do whatever I have to do to take care of you. Y'ah mean?" As Thomasina beamed over the thought of a young strapping man coming home and paying some of the bills, Brick's mind wandered to Misty's fat stash. He'd never asked her for much of the money he'd brought in—a couple dollars here and there. She owed him and right about now, he could use some of that cheese. He looked at Thomasina. "I don't want handouts. I can hold my own." Brick shrugged. "I can do better than that. If you let me be the man in your life, I'll take good care of you."

Thomasina had never heard sweeter words. She couldn't help from blushing; she imagined a deep, red color blazing across her brown skin. Then reality hit. "What about Misty? She may not want you anymore. But knowing about me and you…" Thomasina shook her head ominously. "She's not going let you go easily."

"I don't owe Misty anything. Being her mother and all, I guess you feel like you're doing her wrong. I can't tell you how to feel but I do know that Misty is happy; she's really in love," he remarked without a trace of bitterness.

Thomasina searched his face. "Are you using me—you know—trying to get revenge?"

"No, ma'am." Brick shook his head.

Thomasina inhaled, closed her eyes as she squeezed her vaginal muscles. She loved the way Brick switched it up, going from speaking intimately, calling her baby and then addressing her respectfully as ma'am. Mmm. The dichotomy was unbearably sensual.

"On the real, Misty did me a favor. The way we was living—it was starting to wear me down. She wasn't happy. I wasn't happy."

"What do you need to be happy?" Thomasina sincerely wanted to know.

"It don't take much." He looked up in thought. "I want to experience real love. Does it exist?"

Thomasina shrugged; hell if she knew. She'd been used and abused in all her relationships—truth be told, she'd never experienced real love either.

"Besides wanting to be loved, all I need is weed, booze, food, and sex," he said, laughing. "But, I'm gon' work on some of those bad habits. Gotta get 'em outta my system. I don't know if you noticed, but I ain't smoked no weed or drank a brew since I been here. Now that's a miracle." He gave her a wink. "It's all because of you," he added with a grin.

His words warmed her; melted her heart. But she needed to stay focused, keep her wits about her. Happily ever after hadn't happened to her and it wasn't likely to start now; especially not with her daughter's ex-boyfriend. "A few nights ago, you were miserable, tried to end your life." She assumed a serious expression and crossed her arms in front of her chest. "So, let's be honest about our relationship. Misty put us together because she was feeling inconvenienced. She'll call you back when she's good and ready and I doubt if you'll be able to tell her no." Thomasina's eyes swept downward in shame. "I spoiled her something awful. Made her think her looks were all she needed to get somewhere in life. Being average looking myself, I enjoyed all the attention of having such a beautiful daughter. But I ruined her. The way she is…selfish and inconsiderate—it's really not her fault."

"You shouldn't blame yourself. Misty's a grown woman. Grown-ups have to be responsible for their own selves," Brick commented wisely. "I thought you said we could take small steps—toward a future together."

Thomasina tilted her head questioningly.

"Well, right now, all we need to focus on is me and you." He reached out, pulled Thomasina on his lap. "I know I'm a big boy, but you put enough food on this plate to feed a couple of troops."

Thomasina looked at his plate: bacon, eggs, pancakes, sausages, grits, and toast. Brick forked up pieces of pancake. "Here, baby, help me eat some of this."

She sat uneasily, moving her hips around trying to adjust her ample butt and hips into a comfortable position. Brick carefully guided a forkful of pancakes toward her mouth. "Open up," he coaxed and then ate the pancakes himself, as if proving to a young child that food was indeed good. "Mmm," he said, prodding Thomasina to sample her own cooking. "Eat, boo. You gotta stay in shape. You know I like all that baby phat." He patted her hip, squeezed her thickness, murmuring sounds of appreciation.

She gave a girlish giggle. The sound so surprising, she covered her mouth and then removed her hand and self-consciously parted her lips. Brick fed her and then kissed her on the cheek as she chewed. In no time at all, Thomasina grew comfortable and began to enjoy the attention Brick was giving her. When he picked up a breakfast sausage and slowly slipped it between her lips, the sexual imagery was instant and powerful. As if they'd been simultaneously shot in the loins by Cupid's arrow, their eyes locked in lust. "We can finish that later," he told her. Utensils clattered as Brick pushed the plate away. He scooped Thomasina up and speedily headed for the stairs.

Carrying her in his arms, Brick glided up the stairs. Thomasina was literally floating in the air. With her arms wrapped around Brick's neck, she stealthily pinched her wrist. I'm not dreaming, she assured herself as her muscled young love gently lowered her onto the bed.

CHAPTER 42

Dane, Monroe, and Troy zipped to Narberth, Pennsylvania, where a high-paying, kinky couple waited for Troy to deliver his ashen-covered goods.

Troy sat in the backseat, fidgeting. Dane passed him a Dutch to calm his nerves.

Troy passed it to Monroe. "You up for this, man?" Monroe asked, pulling on the Dutch, his eyes glimmering with mocking amusement.

"I got it." Troy straightened his shoulders.

"Yo, make sure you hit 'em up for a big tip. They didn't tell me the wife was gon' be in on it until a minute ago."

"Aiight." Troy bit his bottom lip nervously.

"Tell you what, yo. Since you so nervous and everything…"

"I'm cool," Troy protested.

"Well, I think we should roll up in there and double-team that freaky couple. You let dude knock you off and I'll pitch in and put wifey to bed." Monroe rubbed his crotch. "With all this, shouldn't take but a few minutes to make her cum."

"Man, you ain't going in there." Dane shot Monroe a scorching look.

"Why not? I could use some extra cheese. Y'ah mean?"

"Man, chill. Troy got it." Dane craned his neck. "You cool, man?"

"I'm aiight. I can do this."

"You don't sound convincing," Dane spat. "Nigga talk a bunch of shit, but when it's time to put out, he ends up with the jitters."

"I ain't got no jitters."

"Well, bounce, nigga. Stop wasting time—get out the whip and go put some work in."

Troy eased out of the back of the X5. Shoulders hunched, hands tucked in the pockets of his jeans, Troy plodded along the cobblestone path that led to a magnificent stone and stucco home.

"Damn," Dane muttered, watching as Troy was admitted inside.

"What?"

"I hope that nigga remembered to keep his legs, knees and his dick ashy."

Monroe's jaw dropped.

"Shit, this would be a helluva time for that nigga to start using lotion."

"Fill a nigga in. Whatchu talkin' about, man?"

Dane gave Monroe a cocky smile. He slid his seat back, reached behind and retrieved the laptop that was perched on the backseat. He handed it to Monroe. "Pop it open and crank it up. I'm gon' let you peep some shit. Fill you in on how that little bitch was making all that cheddar."

"You already told me. You said she be pimpin' mufuckas."

"That's only part of it. The bitch be charging mufuckas to peep the sick-ass pictures she got posted up on her website. Man, Lil' Bit ain't no joke. She got flicks showing niggas' dicks spurting out cum; she got big, burly niggas posing like bitches in aprons and shit. Freak mufuckas been paying her top dollar to peep that freak shit. She even got a bitch with the fattest pair of pussy lips you'll ever see splattered across the screen."

Thinking about the waitress at Hades, Monroe reared back, shocked.

The wallpaper—multiple images of Misty—appeared on the computer screen. Monroe handed it to Dane, who moved his seat back even further, giving himself more elbow room to navigate the website.

He clicked and scrolled and then pointed the screen in Monroe's direction.

"Whose ashy dick is that?" Monroe wondered aloud.

"Ya boy, Troy. Lil' Bit promotes him as Ashy Cashy; there's been a big demand for his long, ashy dick."

"Yo, man. That's disgusting. How much paper he pullin' in for this shit?"

"Why you wanna know?"

"Just curious. Y'all getting money; I want some, too. My dick is bigger and longer than his. I'd be rolling in dough if I was in on this."

"Man, stop playing. How I look, pimping you out? Be patient; I told you, I gotchu."

Monroe eyed Dane suspiciously. He patted his empty pockets for emphasis and then slouched in his seat, muttering discontentedly.

"Peep this cunt flick," Dane exclaimed, changing the subject. "Yo, I guarantee, you ain't nevah seen a pussy like this one."

Monroe gazed at Felice's crotch shot. "I been all up in that," he said, unimpressed.

Dane's heart stopped. "You got with Felice? When?"

"I told you about it. Me, her and Misty. We worked it, three-way—that night at Hades."

Fire lit up Dane's eyes. "You ain't say nothing about no waitress."

Monroe frowned. "Yo, nigga. Fall back. Why the fuck you care where my dick been? Yeah, I hit it. So what?"

"I'm just saying, how you gon' keep that type of info to yourself?" Dane's voice came out a little shaky, showing vulnerability, giving Monroe an edge.

Monroe leaned forward, a scowl on his smooth, hairless face. He tapped the computer screen. "Man, I super-soaked that ho!" He guffawed loudly, shoulders rocking, head lolling, Nikes stomping the floormat in time with the rhythm of his laughter.

A half-hour later, Troy bounced up to the whip, grinning. "Yo, that shit was dope." He pulled a wad out of his pocket. "Check out the tip. Three bills, yo."

"I get half," Dane mumbled.

"I know," Troy responded, looking back and forth from Dane to Monroe, noticing the tension in the air. No one bothered to respond to his questioning look. Monroe stared out the passenger window and had his hand stuck out, demanding his cut.

"Damn, man. Can't you wait 'til I get some change?" Troy scowled at Dane's outstretched hand.

"Don't play with my money, youngin'. I got change."

Troy handed over the three bills. Dane pulled off. "Your next client is in Roxborough, somewhere." He sucked his teeth. "I hate driving in Roxborough—all those narrow-ass, two-way streets. Shit is crazy. Ain't none of them streets wide enough to be two-way," Dane ranted. "Plus, I get corny-ass Roxborough and Manayunk confused. I probably should use this GPS system to get us there in time." Dane pushed a couple buttons. "Fuck, I don't know how to work this." He sighed. "Y'all know?"

"Nah, man. I ain't with that GPS shit. So, um, what's up with my change?"

"I gotchu—when we finish up, tonight." Dane twisted his face in annoyance, picked up speed and whipped through the dignified motorists cruising along Narberth's Montgomery Avenue.

"Yo, dawg. Don't be breaking speed limits up around here," Monroe cautioned. "These suburban cops be bored; they be looking for shit to pin on a nigga. I ain't trying to spend the night in the joint, man."

"Man, stop whining. Fuck these suburban cops. They living good up here in whitey world—shit, I'm trying to get mine."

"I know that's right," Troy agreed. "But, yo. Why I gotta wait 'til the end of the night? I'm trying to get mine, too." He gave a heavy sigh. "That's what the fuck I get for trying to come at you, all honest and shit."

In the middle of traffic, Dane slammed on the brakes. Monroe was hurled forward; his chest hit the dashboard. Motorists screeched to a halt, trying to prevent slamming into the SUV. Dane was oblivious to the chaos he'd created. With scrunched-up lips, he whipped his head around and cast an evil look at Troy in the backseat. "You thinking about holding back? You thinking about trying to cheat me?"

"Nah, man," Troy sputtered, squirming under Dane's hateful gaze. "I was just saying—"

Dane nodded at Monroe. "Yo, man. Monroe's over here, trying to get off the bench—says he's ready to jump in the game. If you not happy, just say the word."

"I'm cool, man."

"Aiight, then. Stop complaining; shut the fuck up."

Wordlessly, Troy stretched out his legs and slumped against the back of the leather seat.

Monroe eyed Dane. "You driving this wheel like you crazy."

Dane frowned. "So."

"So? You're using my license. That jawn is nice and fresh. I ain't trying to get my shit suspended before I even get my first wheel."

CHAPTER 43

Dane navigated his way to Roxborough. Troy was in and out in less than twenty minutes. "Yo, I need a break," he complained as he slid in the back of the truck. "I'm hungry." Troy winced and rubbed his stomach.

"How much you get?"

"Oh! Dag, I forgot." He dug in his pocket and pulled out a fifty.

"You holding out, dawg?"

"Nah, man. It ain't even like that. Dude said he paid online."

Dane couldn't dispute that. Troy didn't even know about the internet situation. "So, why he come up all cheap? Was your shit ashy like I promised, dude?"

Monroe broke out laughing. "Y'all crazy. Talking about Troy's crusty ass, like it's something special."

"My ass ain't crusty."

"So, what's the deal? Shed some light. Why your jawn gotta be ashy in order for you to get with these tricks?"

"Man, shut the fuck up," Dane snarled. "At least Troy's making money. You riding shotgun, waiting to go shopping, trying to sponge off his tips."

"Fuck you, man. In fact, take my ass back to West. I can be making moves on the block instead of riding around with you while Troy's putting in work with these freaks."

"I ain't no freak," Troy muttered from the back.

"Man, I ain't talking about you." Monroe sucked his teeth. "Yo, Dane. Take me back to West, man. I ain't feelin' all this disrespect and shit."

Dane ignored Monroe. He pointed the SUV toward Center City, where Troy's last client lived.

"I can't keep busting nuts without no food or nothing. I gotta have something in my stomach, yo."

"You a pain in the ass, Troy." Dane pulled into the drive-thru lane of a nearby Burger King. He ordered and paid for burgers and fries, tossed the bags to Troy and Monroe and then floored it to the last job of the night.

ॐ

After splitting tips, Troy and Dane were left with six hundred dollars apiece.

"Fifty-fifty ain't gon' get it, man. Starting tomorrow, I'm gon have to raise my cut to sixty percent. Ya feel me, dawg?" Dane slowed up and then stopped in front of Troy's house on Farragut Street.

Troy heaved a sigh as he dragged his tired body out of the X5.

Zipping to the closest ATM, Dane inserted the new ATM card, which was issued in Monroe's name. He withdrew the daily limit. Grinning, he dropped a pile of bills in Monroe's lap. "Truce, man. There's plenty more where that came from; I'll get some more loot in the morning, when the bank opens," he explained.

Monroe nodded and pocketed the money without bothering to count it.

"You still mad about Felice?"

Monroe frowned. "Hell no. Wasn't no love between us. I hit it…" He shrugged. "That's it. Why you trippin' over that ho?"

"It ain't about her," Dane said, sneering. "It's the pussy. That jawn is crazy and I can't hang. That shit got me feeling like less than a man," he admitted. "My shit starts squirting as soon as it touches those fat pussy lips." He shook his head, his expression a mixture of confusion and agitation. "So, you handled your business and rode it out, huh?"

"Man, I was messin' witchu. When she gripped those lips around my dick, I was like…fuck it… I pulled out and skeeted all over that fat pussy. As long as I got mine, what the fuck did I care about that ho? On the real, though, I think your girl, Misty, finished her off."

"Fuck outta here!" Dane was genuinely surprised.

Monroe shrugged. "Man, fuck both of them bitches. I was twisted that night; I can't half remember what went down. Why do you care?"

"Ego, I guess. I ain't never encountered a pussy that I couldn't whip," Dane said, laughing. His laughter stopped as he gazed in thought.

"What's up? Whatchu thinking about getting into?"

"Felice's expecting me to drop by tonight. We gon' roll up in that piece and surprise the bitch. I been fucking around on some bullshit, trying to handle that wild pussy by myself." He reached under the driver's seat and pulled out a plastic bag stuffed with neon green buds. "I'ma offer her some of this killa, get her in the mood for some freak shit."

"Damn, man. You was holding out?" Monroe shot a glance at the green buds.

"You think I was gon' share my high-quality weed with Troy's dumb ass?"

"I can dig it."

Dane passed the bag of weed to Monroe. "The Dutch is in the

glovebox. Roll it up." He clicked buttons, turning off Kanye West and switching to Ne-Yo. "Felice thinks she's all that, but Misty…" He shook his head. "Man, that lil' mufucka's a trip. Bitch got blown-up pictures of herself plastered on every wall in the crib. For real, yo. That bitch is crazy. She even got pictures of her stank ass and little-ass titties posted up in the bathroom."

Listening quietly, smiling and shaking his head, Monroe split and emptied out the contents of a Dutch. He let the tobacco fly out the passenger window, then worked on rolling up a fat stogie with precision and fine craftsmanship. "So, what's the deal? You wanna double-team her?"

"Whatever it takes."

"How's that gon' play with Shawty? She gon' be aiight with that?"

"Is she gon' have a choice?" Dane asked, his expression deadly. "Pullin' Trains.com—that's gon' be the name of my new website," he bragged. "I'ma put you, Edison, and Troy on that shit. I might join in, too, every now and then."

"Pullin' Trains.com?"

"Yeah, nigga. Bitches be having all kinds of smut fantasies. And I know how to fulfill their needs. I'm gon' have y'all wearing masks, or have bandanas tied around your faces. Trick-bitches gon' pay a chunk for a rape fantasy. To get a train pulled—whew!" Dane shook his head. "Man, that's gon' cost them bitches a grip."

"Yo, that's gangsta." Monroe gave Dane his props. Dane took a hand off the steering wheel, offered it. Monroe slapped Dane's open palm in admiration and approval of his get-money skills.

❦

A powerful urge to urinate sent Misty to the bathroom. Her

bladder felt painfully full. Sitting on the toilet, she smiled, closed her eyes and released. *Ah!* The moment the wet sheets connected with her skin, she sprang awake. "Oh, shit," she muttered and attempted to jump up, put distance between herself and the piss-stained sheets. Woozy, she fell back and lay in the soaking urine. "Brick!" she whimpered. "Brick, the bed is wet," she called out in a louder voice; garbled speech. "Come and change these wet fuckin' sheets," she muttered in agitation. In a stupor, her mind too fuzzy to remember that she'd fired Brick in favor of Dane. In her current groggy state, she forgot Dane existed. All she remembered was Brick, her lifelong and faithful servant. She lifted her head, impatiently waiting to hear his heavy footsteps, rushing to rectify the awful situation.

"Damn, Brick. What's taking you so long?" She twisted away from the drenched area, scooting over to a drier spot on the bed. "Brick! Hurry up," she murmured before falling back into a deep, drugged sleep, having no memory that she'd evicted Brick; that he was at her mother's house and was at that very moment, contentedly banging Thomasina, giving her all the love he had stored up in his heart—filling her deeply with his enormous pleasure-giver.

Misty had no clue that Brick's sheet-changing, cum-licking, eating-pussy-on-demand, selling-dick days were officially over.

CHAPTER 44

Dane's knees weakened; his dick pulsed the instant Felice opened the door. "Damn!" Dane blurted out, but the utterance was not a compliment. The black stretch lace, strappy, thong-back teddy with a snap crotch she wore displayed her curves and big boobs in a way that gave her an unfair advantage before the party even got started. The black and silver whore heels she was rocking didn't help his dick dilemma either.

"Where's my present?" She stuck an indignant hand on her sexy hip.

"In the ride," Dane quipped.

"Go get it." She gave him a coy smile.

"You sure?" He sounded amused.

"Yeah, I'm sure. You promised."

"Aiight, peep this...Misty ain't trying to hook you up with no more gigs."

"What?" Her head whipped toward him, her eyes narrowed in skepticism.

"Have you heard from her lately?"

"No, I keep getting her voicemail. But I know she's gon' hook me up in a minute. Shit, I lost my job over that bitch."

"For real?"

"Yeah, they caught me on camera with her and some young buck while I was on the clock."

"Damn shame. So, how'd you get along with the young buck?"

"He was cute." Felice shrugged indifferently.

"Is that right?" Dane's voice took on a low tone.

"He had a big-ass dick, too," she threw in. Then, remembering her financial condition, a scowl creased her face.

"Did he bang out that coochie longer than I can?"

"What?" Her thoughts were on making ends meet.

"Did the young buck make you cum?"

"Nah, baby. He ain't have nothing on you," she cooed. "But, look…being that I'm in a financial bind…"

"You ain't gotta sweat nothing; I gotchu." He dug inside his pocket and extracted three bills that he'd gotten from Troy earlier that night. "Here you go. Got more for you tomorrow, if you act right."

"I'm always sweet to you."

"I need you to be extra sweet tonight. Is that cool?"

Felice nodded and smiled enthusiastically, knowing she'd have Dane exploding in less than ten minutes.

"You're in demand with the customers. Did you know that?" She shook her head.

"Misty didn't like that. She made me lose money behind being jealous of you," he lied easily. "So, being that I always put business before pleasure, I had to fire Misty's lil' ass for making bad decisions." He softly stroked Felice's chin. "If you play your part right, you might end up with Misty's position. Yeah, I had my baby girl living a lavish lifestyle…"

Aw, yeah. This shit is on! Felice was ready to suck, fuck and even give up some butt—whatever. Top bitch status and all its trappings was swiftly moving in her direction. She lifted her fluttery fake lashes, her hot gaze connected with his. Lust shone in his eyes…along with something else.

"That young buck, Monroe was bragging…"

"I didn't know you and Monroe were friends."

"Closer. He's my little cousin. Well, we're not related by blood, but we call ourselves cousins. Anyway, the young buck been bragging that he banged out your pussy, said he made you cum two… three times—"

"That's a lie…"

"Whatever. I need you to prove a point for me."

"Okay." Felice got an instant image of a new, laid-out apartment and new wheels. It was time to raise up out of the ghetto.

"I want you to do me and my boy…together. But you gotta make sure you cum for me; even if you have to fake it. You feel me, shawty? I can't have that youngin' thinking he can fuck my woman better than I can."

"You want me to fuck both of y'all?"

"It's up to you." He held his palms up nonchalantly. "He's outside waiting to hear from me. Should I invite him up?" Dane pulled out his cell phone.

Felice fidgeted, folded her arms across her big breasts and then forced calm into her voice. "Yeah, you can invite him." She felt suddenly exposed in her barely-there teddy. She wasn't emotionally prepared to have two pairs of male eyes appraise her, two sets of hands touching her, or two dicks alternately prodding and plunging inside her. On second thought, *Mmm.* Her sex walls tightened in anticipation. She drew in a breath of air to compose herself, but couldn't stop the tingling sensation or the shivering goose bumps that accompanied the idea of getting dick from two pretty mufuckas. Felice was proud to take Misty's spot—top bitch in charge.

❧❦

A Dutch was passed around, shots of straight Hennessy guzzled down. Felice couldn't recall how the sexual aspect of the party had gotten started, but somehow they'd all ended up naked and in her bed. She lay on her back, Monroe beside her, lying on his side, his head resting on the pillow next to her. He squeezed one of her breasts, hungry lips pulled on her protruding nipple.

At the foot of the bed, Dane spread her legs wide. "Your puffy pussy looks good, baby. Big juicy lips—red and wet," he groaned, trailing a finger up her slit, separating her swelling inner lips.

Curious, Monroe twisted around, maneuvering downward, positioning his long body in a way that tangled the three bodies, but enabled him to view the blossoming vulva. Aroused by her rose-colored petals, Monroe groaned and raised his hips, offering Felice his lengthened shaft to nurture with her warm mouth. Felice obliged. Grasping his length, she dragged her tongue across the smooth head of his dick, arousing him to harsh shuddering and heavy breathing. Slowly, she licked her way down to his balls. She recalled how Misty had worked on Monroe's nuts at Hades. Misty's thumb, along with Monroe's dick, was inserted inside Felice's hot pussy. Misty's other four fingers curled around his nuts, bringing both Felice and Monroe to a powerful, screaming orgasm.

Stroking his dick, Felice licked Monroe's scrotum, figuring she might as well knock him off quickly so she could really throw herself into the thrilling tongue job Dane was giving. Sucking up pussy juice, while racking his tongue across her clit, was wonderfully torturous. Clit licks made her bud harden, had it sticking out like a mini-dick. She let go of Monroe's dick, reached down groping for Dane's head, yearning to guide his lips to her clit, but Monroe's body was a barrier between her hand and Dane's head.

Frantic, she tore her mouth away from Monroe's taut scrotum. "Suck it," she cried out in desperation. Her fists clenched around Monroe's dick, her hips writhed pleadingly. Dane ignored her clit, but continued licking her velvety slit. His fervent tongue sloshed quickly, probing deeply. Giving in to a more acute and carnal urge, he reached upward, stilling her moving hand by covering it with his own, and brushing her hand away from the throbbing appendage. Dane ceased eating pussy and put a tight grip around Monroe's dick. "You like fish better than dick?" Dane barked, hand swiftly stroking Monroe's long, hard rod.

Monroe flinched. "Hell, no, man. You know what I like."

What the fuck! Felice gasped in shock. She looked downward. Proving his words truthful, Monroe buried his face in Dane's crotch, drew Dane's thickness into in his mouth, sucking dick just like a bitch. Meanwhile, Dane gave Monroe a hand job with a palm that was lubricated with juice from Felice's wet pussy.

Suddenly, Felice was given a shove so hard, she landed on the floor. Hurt and confused, her coochie unattended, she crouched by the side of the bed. With her chin resting on the top of her hands, she watched in horny horror while the two men curled in the sixty-nine position, gave each other head. Her vagina, callously abandoned, throbbed with need.

CHAPTER 45

Where the hell is he? Groggy and sore after lying in bed, sleeping off and on for the past four days, Misty stumbled around the bedroom. The stench of urine filled the room. Judging by the hardened, dull, yellowish stain on the sheets, she'd fucked around and peed the damn bed. Now, what kind of shit was that? And where the fuck was Brick? His ass should have been looking out for her. What happened? Had she gotten drunk? How could Brick be so trifling? The linen needed to be stripped and the pissy mattress needed to be scrubbed. Why would he let her lie around in pee-stained sheets? And why did her head hurt so badly?

Bumping into walls and furniture, she staggered around the apartment, searching for Brick. She stumbled into the bathroom, splashed cold water on her face, trying to clear her head, trying to make sense of things.

She had to find Brick. Now, where did Brick and Shane hang out? Wait a minute, something didn't feel right. *Shane is dead!* She dropped her head; sorry she'd recalled the death of the love of her life. *But, hold up!* She'd found a new Shane, hadn't she? *Yeah!* Shit was starting to come back. Her new man's name was Dane. She remembered him teasing and pleasing her coochie with his finger…Misty shook her head. Shit wasn't adding up.

Where was Brick while she and Dane were freaking? *Oh!* She suddenly, remembered. *I took him over my mom's.* Flooded with relief, Misty reached for the phone and called her mother.

The call went to voicemail. "Mom!" Her voice sounded scratchy, she cleared her throat. "Tell Brick to call me as soon as you get this message. It's real important."

She hung up and attempted to piece together a plan. She would hook up with Brick. She was too drowsy to drive. Brick could drive her to Monroe's crib so she could find out what was up with Dane. Hmm. She scratched her head. Dane had taken the keys to her ride before. She peeked through the blinds in the kitchen, looked down to where her whip should have been parked. It was gone.

The sneaky bastard was driving around in her whip. What the fuck was wrong with him? She wondered how long she'd been asleep. She squinted at the phone, watched the date scroll across, and was shocked to discover that four days had gone by.

He must have drugged me! That realization infuriated Misty. She picked up the phone and stabbed a button with her finger. She got his voicemail. "Bring my fucking truck back before I call the police!" she snarled into the handset. Fuming, she walked in circles, paced, sat down, jumped back up.

Where the hell were her mother and Brick? Her mother probably had the TV volume up so loud, she couldn't hear the phone. She called her mother's house again. She picked up.

"I shouldn't have picked up. I should do you the way you do me and only talk to you when I'm good and damn ready. Do you know how many messages I've left on your phone?" Thomasina said, agitated.

"What's wrong? Why are you screaming in my ear? Dang!"

"Oh, cut the innocent crap, you little criminal. You stole my identity and now I'm in all kinds of hellish trouble. I'll tell you one thing, Misty, if you call my house again, I'm going to turn your ass in. Career criminals shouldn't be mingling with the public. If you weren't my flesh and blood, I'd have you arrested and locked up for the rest of your natural life," Thomasina fumed, her voice trembling with rage.

"Mommy, stop screaming at me. My head hurts. I think Dane drugged me." Her mind raced as she tried to figure out a way to placate her mother. "I didn't steal anything from you. What's going on?"

"What's going on?" Thomasina shouted, ignoring Misty's pleas for a lower tone of voice. "I received a statement from some internet bank. I can't believe my own child stole my identity."

"No, I did…"

"Misty, stop lying. You opened a bank account in my name and then turned around and transferred all the money in someone else's name."

Misty's heart leaped in her chest and began banging in terror. "I didn't transfer anything."

"You deposited over two hundred thousand dollars in a bank account…"—Thomasina drew in a deep breath—"in *my* goddamn name," she shouted. "How could you do something like that to me?" Thomasina's voice cracked.

"I'm sorry. I didn't know you'd be mad. But don't worry. I didn't transfer any funds. The money should still be there." Her eyes darted about anxiously.

"Do you realize the kind of trouble you've caused? What the hell am I supposed to do? The bank reports large deposits to the IRS. And another thing…where's your truck? The expensive truck that's also in my name?"

"I'm not sure," Misty mumbled, feeling dumb.

"Well, let me break the news… The insurance company called and said they found the truck stripped and abandoned. They said it's no good to anybody. I tried to get in touch with you, but I couldn't, so I told those insurance people to go ahead and sell the remnant of the truck. I told them to go ahead and sell it at auction; they ain't gon get much money for a remnant of a truck."

My truck! Sold at auction! Her mother's news report grew more horrific with each word she spoke. She knew how things worked in the streets. Dane had taken her truck to a chop shop and bought it back at auction—all legal and shit. Her good life had swiftly turned into a grim nightmare. Misty felt the room spinning. She was hungry, dehydrated, but she had shit to do.

"You better clean up your act," her mother yelled into the phone. "I'm not about to do any time for you. I don't have the money for the IRS. When they come knocking, you better believe that I'm gonna sing!"

Misty felt awful; she would have never knowingly brought this kind of trouble down on her mother. She didn't know that internet banks reported to the feds. She thought her sex scam was tax-free. Hell, she couldn't keep up with every damn rule in life. How the fuck was she supposed to know?

She had to get to the bottom of this mess. With the phone tucked between her shoulder and her head, her eyes shifted around, trying to locate her laptop. It was nowhere in sight. "Tell Brick to pack his shit. I'll be there shortly. Don't worry, Mom. I'm gonna get all this shit straight. I'll call you right back."

"Don't call me back and don't bring your ass over here until you come up with every dollar of the tax money that's owed to the IRS," Thomasina yelled before hanging up.

The laptop was gone. She'd given Dane too much information

about her business. More than likely, that slimy mufucker had stolen her bank account. But she had some extra stash in a cashbox. She rushed to the closet in her home office. Her heart dropped. There was an empty space where the cashbox should have been.

Dane was the scum of the earth, and had no decency, no scruples whatsoever. Sure, Shane had scammed plenty of female suckers— but he'd never tried to con Misty. Misty and Shane had been partners in crime, with mutual respect for the game and for each other. No matter how close the resemblance, Dane and nobody else could ever replace Shane.

An idea hit her, pulling her thoughts away from Shane. She could get online with her Blackberry! She hurried to her bedroom closet, swung open the louvered doors. Her eyes gleamed joyously at her Louis Vuitton shoulder bag hanging on a hook. She scrounged around inside. No Blackberry, no money, no nothing! Desperate, she pulled handbags and purses from shelves, yanked others off hooks, looking inside and tossing the beautiful, useless objects in scattered piles on the floor. The bedroom became a sea of designer leather. Prestigious logos, dangling haughtily and declaring their value, mocked her. She rushed to her marble-topped, cherry hardwood, Asian-style dresser, flipped open drawers, rooted around. Her jewelry—all her bling—gone!

Dane was a ruthless nigga. Tears of betrayal welled, but there was no time for tears. Wiping her eyes, her mind searched for a way to get her hands on her next buck. Fretful, she brushed fallen hair from her face and anxiously gnawed on her fingernails.

As soon as she got access to a computer, she'd get Felice back to work—Brick, too. In no time, she'd rebuild her empire. Lesson learned—pretty niggas with big dicks are bad for business.

She'd rebuild bigger and better. She'd get her mother out of

IRS debt in no time. Misty frowned at the audacity of Dane. That scheming mufucka had placed her in a world of trouble. Angry, she kicked a pile of designer bags. She scooped up a cute Juicy Couture bag and sent it crashing into a lamp.

Calm down, Misty, she told herself. Her heart rate slowed down and when her thoughts became clearer, sharper, she decided to take a badly needed shower, put some clothes on, get a cab and go get Brick. Damn, she didn't have money for a cab. She'd have to call the hack man, Mr. Johnnie. She shook her head. She hated riding in his dirty-ass hooptie.

Brick probably had a nice-sized stash. He never went anywhere or spent much of his pocket money. Brick would help her work through this mess. Together, they'd track Dane down. Once they located the scamming bastard, she'd sic Brick on his ass. Brick would love fucking up Dane's pretty face. He'd stomp that nigga in the head until his brains oozed out. *Fuck with me, mufucka!*

❧

It had only taken a few days for the chop shop to strip the X5 and abandon the carcass on the street. In cahoots with the insurance company, Dane bought the truck back at auction, registered it legally in Monroe's name. Later, the truck was reassembled with its original parts.

Grinning, Monroe sat behind the wheel of Misty's former truck. "Thanks, man." Lips puckered, he leaned over and gave Dane a quick kiss. He moved closer, threw both arms around his lover's neck. The two gorgeous men held each other in a tight embrace, lips locked, tongues dueling during an impassioned kiss.

Dane pulled back. "Yo, sexy, stop that. Always trying to work a mufucka up."

Monroe smiled and licked his lips.

Dane's expression turned serious. "Aiight, so dig, the first thing we gon' do when we hit Detroit is find you a spot. Something tight. Expensive furniture. Y'ah mean?"

"And a pool," Monroe added.

Dane nodded. "Ain't no thing. I'll find you a spot with a pool. But money don't last forever, man. As soon as we get settled, we gon' have to send for Troy and Edison and get the business rolling in Detroit. But, we gotta keep our shit on the low."

"I know." Monroe frowned, agitated at the reminder.

"We gotta handle shit right. You gon' have to find yourself a shawty, move her in and shit. Y'ah mean?"

Monroe looked down, eyes saddened. "I feel you."

"You know how it is. What my wife don't know won't hurt her. I got my lil' daughter to worry about. If it wasn't for her, I'd be out and wouldn't look back. I hate that niggas can't keep their mouths shut. Running they mouths and writing books and shit, got females stressing, looking at niggas sideways—suspecting every mufucka with a good friend is on the down low." Dane rolled his eyes.

"It's the truth, ain't it? I mean…it seems that way to me. Most niggas I know like getting it on with another brotha. Most do it for recreation. They don't even take it seriously. And even though you and me took it to the next level don't mean we're punks or nothing."

"I know that. But how we do is supposed to stay behind closed doors. Some shit is best kept in the dark. Y'ah mean? Niggas get loose lips when they get caught with their pants down. Once their bitch gets hip, then they start giving up all the tapes, trying to drag everybody down. Punk asses need to speak for they own damn selves—need to leave innocent mufuckas out of the mess. It's stressful trying to keep a bitch out of your business. Nigga don't need a spotlight shining down on him while he's trying to juggle two lifestyles."

Monroe nodded. "Yeah, mufuckas talk too fuckin' much. Yo, did you peep Felice's face when she saw how shit really was?"

"Man, I wasn't sweating that stank ho."

Monroe laughed heartily. "At first I thought she was heated, but she wasn't mad; that freak wanted to join in."

"I was just using shawty—trying to conquer the pussy so I could steal her from Misty—put her to work for me. But I realize, bitches be too much trouble—falling in love, trying to ride the dick to death. Fuck them hoes," Dane stated with contempt.

"Yo, dawg. Can't no skanks come between us. Not my wife or no other bitches, ya heard? I'm one step ahead of suspicious mufuckas. Throw 'em off track by saying we cousins."

"Yeah, that shit be working. Edison and Troy don't even know about us."

"Like I said, I got this, man. As long you play your part...me and you...man, we can go on like this forever."

"Sounds good. Sounds real good." Monroe stroked his crotch and looked at Dane with lust in his eyes. "Keep talkin' sexy, nigga. You gon' make me pull over and let you handle some of this."

"Ain't no thing. Take your jawn out then. I'll suck it for you. Can you handle that while you're driving?" Dane challenged.

"Who you think you dealing with?" Monroe asked with much bravado. "Damn right, I can handle it. I ain't no chump."

"Aiight, then, whip your shit out."

Monroe quickly unzipped his pants, carefully pulled his hardening penis out of his pants. Dane took one look at Monroe's long, sturdy member and quickly buried his face in Monroe's lap.

❧❧

The sound of the crash was deafening; like an explosion. Pedestrians and motorists gaped in horror at the BMW X5, which was tightly wrapped around the bloody trunk of a tree. One man was trapped inside the carnage, wedged behind the wheel, his bloodied head and torso jutting outside the windshield. The image was surreal, like a grotesque work of art. The other man had shot out the passenger door. His mangled body was entangled with metal and tree bark. Both were obviously deader than dead.

Hands moved in synchronicity, reaching inside handbags, pants and shirt pockets, extricating cell phones to snap pictures and videotape the newsworthy tragedy.

CHAPTER 46

"I'll be right back, Mr. Johnnie. I lost my wallet, but my mom has the money to pay you."

"Okay, take your time," the older man replied good-naturedly. "Say hello to your mother for me."

Misty bolted out of the car and rushed to her mother's front door. She rang the bell, pressed it repeatedly, but her mother refused to open the door. "Mom!" she yelled, knocking on the door as hard as she could.

"Brick!" she screamed, using her foot to pound against the sturdy wood door. But her dainty sandal proved to be an ineffective weapon to kick down a door.

All the commotion prompted Mr. Johnnie out of the driver's seat. The old man shuffled around his wreck of a car and leaned against his battered vehicle, arms folded as he watched with interest, wondering if Misty would get inside and get his money. Nervously, he mopped his sweaty brow, hoping he hadn't wasted precious gas carting Misty around.

Patting her foot impatiently, she pulled out her cell phone and called her mother. No answer. Desperate, she began to gather small stones and tiny pebbles, aiming them at the upstairs windows, all the while alternating between yelling for her mother to open the door.

Misty was causing a commotion; making a spectacle outside her mother's house. Before long, the neighbors began to open blinds, part curtains and soon began streaming outside. One particularly nosey neighbor came out carrying a folded lawn chair under her arm. She lit up a cigarette, popped open a can of Pepsi, plopped in her chair and turned toward the action.

Thomasina peeked through her blinds. She was appalled that Misty was out in front of her house, acting the fool, giving her nosey neighbors something to talk about for years to come.

Determined to put a stop to the spectacle, she stomped downstairs, Brick on her heels. "Don't say nothing, Baron. Let me handle her little butt."

Thomasina swung open the door. "You know better than to bring all this nonsense to my front door!" Thomasina was breathing hard and sweating.

"Why ain't you open the door? Dang, Mom. I just came to pick up Brick." She glanced at Brick, confused. "Where's your stuff? I told my mom to tell you to pack."

"He's not going anywhere with you," Thomasina bellowed, mopping sweat from her forehead.

"Stay outta my business," Misty shouted.

Thomasina flung her shoulders, placed a hand on her hip, prepared to launch into a verbal tirade.

"Come on, Miss Thomasina, calm down. Don't get your blood pressure worked up," Brick said. The concern in his tone spoke of an alignment with Misty's mother.

"Since when do you care about my mother's blood pressure? Now, you trippin'. Nigga, get your shit so we can be up out of this dip! Damn, why you wasting time? Hurry the fuck up!"

Thomasina rushed toward Misty, balled fists raised in the air. "What did I tell you about using foul language?"

Brick grabbed Thomasina; his hands encircled her waist. Misty's eyes widened at the intimate gesture. "Come on now. Ain't gon' be no fighting." He rubbed Thomasina's shoulder soothingly.

"You don't understand, Baron…It's only but so much I can take off of Misty. Cuss words in my presence is something she knows I don't tolerate."

"Baron! Why you calling Brick by his first name?"

Still attempting to calm Thomasina, Brick's hand moved circularly in the middle of her back and worked to her hip area, rubbing and patting, obviously familiar with Thomasina's body parts.

"Y'all fucking?" Misty screeched. She covered her mouth with both hands, eyes bulging in disbelief.

"Me and your mom…" Brick started.

"Are you fucking my mother?" She spoke through clenched teeth.

Brick met her horrified gaze. He looked her straight in the eye. "Yeah, we're in a relationship. You said you and me were over."

"I did not! I said I needed some space. Temporarily. Brick, how could do something like this to me?" Misty swung on Brick. He grabbed her wrist. "Mommy, you should be ashamed of your old ass self—trying to take what's mine just because you can't get a man."

Thomasina got close in Misty's face. "He told me everything…"

"Don't go there, Ma," Brick interjected.

"Oh, I'm going there! You're the one who should be ashamed. Taking advantage of him; putting him out there; making him do unspeakable things."

"She didn't make me…"

"Baron!" Thomasina held up a silencing hand. Brick closed his mouth. "What you did to his mind—to his manhood—is cruel and malicious. But I plan to straighten all that out. Once me and him are married …"

"Married! I'm not letting Brick marry you," Misty said with disdain.

"You don't have no claims on me, Misty," Brick said, standing by Thomasina's side. Misty flinched. Brick had never stood up to her before. If she could get him away from her controlling mother, she'd be able to talk some sense into his head.

"Brick," she said softly, tears pouring from her eyes. "She's using you to get back at me. Don't let her do this. She's old and desperate; she's trying to brainwash you."

"Am I old and desperate?" Thomasina asked Brick, her hand on her hip, her tone and expression coy.

"No, Ma. You sexy. Sexy as shit." He rubbed her behind, right in Misty's face.

"Oh, I'm gagging!" Misty spat.

"Gag all you want to. Once I get Baron on my insurance plan, he's going to be getting a whole lot of psychological treatment. He's getting some cosmetic surgery, too—to get that scar fixed."

"I love your mom. We didn't plan it. It just happened," Brick explained.

"Ain't shit happen. You don't know what you're talking about," Misty insisted. "You don't love her; you talking shit. You belong to me."

"He doesn't *belong* to you!" Thomasina piped in, her voice filled with disdain. "He's not your personal plaything, he's not a pet, or some object you bought from the store. If you can't respect our relationship, then stay the hell away from here."

Misty's face crumpled. "Please, Brick. Don't do this to me. Not when I need you the most." She inched closer to Brick, her expression pleading, beseeching him to come to his senses. "I'm sorry for whatever I did to hurt you. But fuck all that..." Misty caught herself. She backed up, expecting her mother to try to smack her for cussing. "Come on, Brick. You know how we do. Forget her; it's time to bounce."

"It's over between us, Misty. I'm serious. You made your decision to mess with Dane and I made mine. Like she told you…me and your mom…we're getting married. There's nothing you can do to change that," Brick said adamantly.

Misty covered her ears, shutting out Brick's blasphemous spiel. Unable to convince Brick to see things her way, Misty opened her mouth and released a bone-chilling scream. "I can't stand this; you're killing me, Brick! You can't marry my mother. I don't want you to fuck my mother. Do you hear me? Stop fucking her! Stop fucking my mother; stop fucking my mother!" Over and over, she shouted the decadent proclamation, rousing the neighbors' curiosity, provoking them to band together and murmur excitedly as they moved en masse, stomping across her yard, trampling Thomasina's flowerbed. Huddled close to the front door, the group of nosey neighbors enjoyed better sound quality and with the door cracked open, they were provided a bird's-eye view of the scandalous goings on behind their neighbor's closed door.

Thomasina slapped Misty and then gripped her up by the collar. "Have you lost your mind?"

"You can hit me all you want, just give me my man back. Please, Mommy, don't take him from me. I need Brick."

A chorus of shocked gasps sounded outside the house. Thomasina shut the front door. Furious, she grabbed Misty by the shoulders and tried to shake some sense into her. Misty screamed louder, infuriating her mother. "Shut the hell up, you rotten little bitch!" Thomasina snapped and knocked Misty into the wall. Misty slid down to the floor and cried like a little girl.

"That's enough, Miss Thomasina. You gon' end up killing her." Brick pulled Thomasina away from her and used his hulking body to block her from launching another attack.

Mr. Johnnie hobbled up the pathway as quickly as his arthritic body could move, shuffling past the discontented neighbors, who, deprived of entertainment, now murmured threats to call the police to break up the disturbance. He made it to the front door and finding it unlocked, Mr. Johnnie limped on in.

"What's going on, Thomasina? Sounds like somebody's getting killed in here. Your neighbors standing outside, saying they 'bout to call the police over this disturbance."

More mad than embarrassed, Thomasina looked down at Misty and blew out an angry breath. "Get her, Brick. Take her thieving ass outside. You can drop her ass out on the curb, for all I care."

"Don't touch me!" Misty kicked out her feet when Brick approached.

"You gotta respect your mother's house, Misty. You gotta roll out." He scooped her up, hoisted her up in his arms. Thrashing and twisting, kicking and cussing, Misty was carried out of her mother's house and deposited inside Mr. Johnnie's dilapidated car and locked inside.

"How much I owe you, Johnnie?" Thomasina asked, wiping sweat, chest heaving, as she peeked through the blinds. "Good," she muttered to herself. Brick had Misty trapped inside the car and was standing guard, waiting for Johnnie to come out and take her home.

"Ten dollars total for the ride back and forth."

"Okay." Thomasina routed through her purse and handed him a ten. "You better hurry up. Drive off before she kicks out one of your windows. I'm already deep in debt. I don't want to fork over another dollar on account of that spoiled girl."

CHAPTER 47

The room was quiet. The curtains were closed, the lights turned low. Though it was two-thirty in the afternoon, the hushed, tranquil atmosphere mimicked early morning calm. Brick lay curled next to Thomasina in her hospital bed. With an arm draped over her shoulders, he watched closely as she slept. After all she'd been through, she looked serene, so beautiful to his eyes. Brick smoothed her hair near her forehead, lovingly kissed her cheek.

Eyes closed, she felt his kiss and smiled, too weak to verbally acknowledge his loving presence. Pushing out a baby at forty-three years old wasn't as easy as it had been at nineteen when Misty was born. Carrying Brick's baby had damn near killed her.

The baby stirred and began to whimper. Brick sprang to his feet and lifted his son from the bassinet. Thomasina tried to prop herself up on her elbows, but was too weak. "Is he all right, Baron?" she asked softly.

Brick brought their son over, laid him next to his mother. "See, he's fine. The little guy's hungry." Brick reached for a bottle, picked up Baron, Jr. and began feeding his son.

Thomasina beamed proudly. "He's so handsome. He looks just like you."

Brick blushed. Nestling the baby, he briefly set down the bottle and unconsciously touched his cheek, his fingers searching for the raised flesh that had disfigured his face. But instead of an ugly scar, his fingers caressed smooth skin. *Handsome!* Brick didn't think he'd ever get used to hearing that word associated with him.

The syncopated rhythm of heels clicking against tile broadcast Misty's arrival before she stepped through the door. A lovely, wafting fragrance announced her presence before she spoke a word.

Just an hour earlier, Brick had been awakened by the shrill ring of the telephone in Thomasina's hospital room. Brick lunged for the phone before it could disturb his sleeping family. Rendered speechless when he heard Misty's voice on the other end asking to speak with her mother, Brick hesitantly awoke Thomasina and handed her the phone. Tears had welled up in her eyes as she listened to her prodigal daughter's apologies and pleas for reconciliation. It had been very difficult for Brick to hide his distress when Thomasina invited Misty to the hospital to meet her little brother.

"Congratulations, Mommy. Congrats, Brick," Misty said cheerily, holding out an elaborate bouquet of spring flowers. "This is Troy," she said, introducing her young escort.

"Whassup, man?" Brick said.

Troy nodded, took a seat and silently fiddled with a cell phone.

"Here, Troy. Put these flowers over there." She pointed at a table near the window. Troy jumped to it. Brick smiled to himself and shook his head. Misty would never change.

Brick moved off the bed, giving Misty room to kiss her mother. "I miss you, Mommy."

"Oh, Misty, sweetie. I miss you, too." Overwhelmed with emotion, Thomasina dabbed at her eyes with the back of her hand.

"Let me hold my little brother," she said to Brick. Brick placed the baby in Misty's arms. She pulled back the receiving blanket.

"Look at him! He's so handsome." She looked up at Brick and passed the child back to his father. "You spit him out, Brick," Misty remarked, gazing at his improved, handsome image.

"Thanks," Brick murmured, and gave an uneasy smile. He lowered his head, busying himself with rearranging the blanket wrapped around his son.

"I wanted to let you know that I'm ready to take over your payments to the IRS," Misty told her mother.

"Oh, sweetie. It's over and done with. I went to my congressman. His office handled it; they discovered that some man named Monroe something or another had committed that fraud. He's deceased and so the IRS dropped the case."

Troy's head shot up at the mention of Monroe's name. He and Misty locked eyes.

"Do you know him?" Thomasina asked, sensing tension in the room.

"Used to. He was a friend of Troy's," Misty said, the timbre in her voice, pained—mournful. "Hey, it doesn't matter," she said, suddenly snapping out of her somber state. "He's taking a long dirt nap now. Guess he and his boy, Dane, got what they had coming," she said in a chillingly cheerful tone. *Fuck with me, mufuckas!*

Brick and Thomasina exchanged a glance.

"Misty, honey," her mother stammered, "no one deserves to *die* over stealing money."

Misty begged to differ. "An eye for an eye," she stated coldly.

This was supposed to be a happy occasion. Thomasina refused to get into a moral discussion with her long-lost child. She said a quick prayer for her cold-hearted daughter, hoping Misty didn't have a hand in causing that Monroe fellow or anyone else to meet an early demise.

Changing the subject, Misty looked Brick up and down. "Brick, I can't get over your face—how handsome you look. You're all buff. Your muscles look bigger than they were," Misty complimented.

"Little bit of cosmetic surgery, ya know, and weightlifting." He rubbed his face proudly.

"I took health pregnancy classes at the YMCA. Baron went with me; he worked out in the men's weight room while I was in my exercise class," Thomasina explained, puffed up with pride. "Once I get back on my feet, we're going to work out together, so we can both stay in shape. But that's enough about us..." Her eyes roved over her daughter's expensive clothing and sparkling jewelry. "You look good, honey. You sure know how to land on your feet." Thomasina gave a soft sigh. "I'm so glad we can all get along without any hard feelings."

"Mom, you should know me by now. As far as I'm concerned, there's not a problem in the world that money can't cure."

"That's a matter of opinion, Misty, but I don't want to debate it. I love you. You're back and that's all that matters."

"I love you, too, Mom." Misty cut an eye at Brick. "You too, *Big Daddy*."

"Stop playing, girl," Brick said, blushing, eyes downcast.

"We're an odd family, that's for sure," Thomasina said with a chuckle.

Misty noticed that her mother was wearing the *Mom* pendant she'd given her over a year ago. "Mom, you need to be flossing something better than that old thing. You have two kids now, so I'm gonna get you a new pendant with two diamonds repping me and my little brother."

Thomasina caressed the pendant that hung from her neck. "I'm happy with this one. Just having you here, sharing in this occasion, is the best present you could give me."

"But, I wanna make up for all the pain I caused you." She glanced at Brick. "You too, Brick—I'm really sorry for the way I treated you." Her brown eyes held him in a lingering gaze.

"It's all in the past," he said uncomfortably, dropping his eyes. The lifestyle he'd led with Misty seemed far away and long ago. The reminder was unpleasant. He'd redefined himself, improved himself. His name was Baron Kennedy—husband, father, and wage earner. Brick was some other dude. Baron intended to keep Brick in the past where he belonged.

Giving birth had knocked the wind out of her sails. Thomasina closed her eyes, resting peacefully in a room filled with love. Brick put his sleeping son back in his bassinet and cuddled next to his wife.

Misty joined Brick on the bed. "I love you, Mommy," she whispered, kissing her mother's cheek, and stealthily patted Brick's arm. Brick inched closer to his wife, wrapping his arm around her, as if holding on to a life preserver.

Thomasina gave a blissful sigh. Eyes closed, and resting peacefully, she didn't take notice of Misty's persistent gaze that set on her husband's unscarred, handsome face and then leisurely roamed the length of his hard, muscular form.

❧❧

Playing a game on his cell phone, Troy ignored the family reunion. He dared not tell Misty to speed it up, but he wished she'd hurry. How many times did she plan on telling her mom that she was sorry and that she loved her? *Dag, give it a rest.* Besides, from his vantage point, her mom looked sound asleep and Misty seemed to be whispering something to her mom's frowned-up husband. *Whaddup wit dat?* Damn, he hated hospitals

343

and all this family bullshit. Troy squirmed in his seat. He yawned and stretched out his long legs, throwing hints that he was ready to bounce!

Ever since Edison quit working for Misty, Troy was working around the clock. Misty had promised to take him shopping and treat him to dinner at Red Lobster. Sitting up in a hospital room was a fucked-up way to spend his rare day off. Boss lady should be spending this time recruiting, instead of wasting time on some lovey-dovey family shit.

Troy sighed. Man, he'd be glad when Misty hired some extra help.

About the Author

Allison Hobbs is a national bestselling author of *Pandora's Box*, *Insatiable*, *Dangerously In Love*, *Double Dippin,'* *The Enchantress*, *A Bona Fide Gold Digger*, and *The Climax*. She lives in Philadelphia, Pennsylvania and is working on her next novel. Visit the author at www.allisonhobbs.com

EXCERPT FROM

The
CLIMAX

BY ALLISON HOBBS

AVAILABLE FROM STREBOR BOOKS

Chapter 1

To the observer, it seemed Terelle Chambers was locked inside herself, unaware of her surroundings. Her caregivers at Spring Haven Psychiatric Hospital hand-fed her, manually moved her limbs, and even toileted her, but they treated Terelle dispassionately as if she were an inanimate object—something that required care. Her affliction, persistent catatonia, had robbed the young woman of even a glimmer of her former personality.

Aside from occasional sorrowful whimpers and anguished moans—fleeting echoes of a tormented inner world—Terelle had not uttered a coherent word in two years.

However, although she appeared to have retreated from the outside world, Terelle was keenly aware of touch, taste, smells, and sound. Her thoughts and memory were jumbled and disjointed but she was able to distinguish among the smells and voices and even the touches of the doctors and nurses who briskly performed their duties on her behalf without emotional attachment.

Awakened by the sound of footsteps approaching the bed where her rigid body lay, Terelle was instantly comforted by the feelings of compassion and love that emanated from the person who had entered her room and was now standing over her.

Saleema, she thought as a smile formed in her mind. She would have greeted her dearest friend with a hug if her unmoving arms and clenched, contracted fists would agree to such a gesture. She wished she could remember how to speak the word, *hello*, but the technique required to form clear and audible words escaped her.

Terelle inhaled deeply, trying to draw in her best friend's fragrance. But instead of the pleasant hint of Saleema's perfume, Terelle recognized a masculine scent. She gasped in alarm.

Long thick fingers tenderly stroked her cheek, calming her. The fingers inched upward and caressed the soft hair that curled at her temples. Terelle knew this person—this man. She recognized his touch—his essence. Was she still asleep? Was she lost inside a dream?

The squeal of the bedrail being lowered sounded much too real for this to be a dream, but in her heart she knew a dream was all this could be. Terelle's lashes fluttered as she struggled to raise eyelids that felt too heavy to lift. The struggle ceased when she felt the weight of his chest pressing down upon her breasts. He kissed her cheek.

"Terelle," he whispered her name. "You gotta get better, babe." He squeezed her closed fist. "This ain't the way it was supposed to go down." His voice caught. She heard him taking in deep breaths. She felt his raw emotions. His sorrow. And his love. "I miss you."

Marquise! Terelle wanted to look in his face, but she knew if she opened her eyes, he'd disappear as he did at the end of every dream. She could only be with Marquise during slumber, so she allowed herself to relax, praying to remain blissfully asleep forever.

"I know you got the strength to come up outta this," he said, stroking her hair. "You can't give up. We still can have a future together. Me, you, and Keeta."

Markeeta! Oh God, my poor baby. She'd been enjoying the time spent in dreamland with Marquise long enough. It wasn't right for her to remain in her inner world just to be with him. She had to get well for Markeeta.

"You can't give up like this." He caressed her arms and her hand and then leaned down and kissed her lips. The sensation of their hearts beating together nearly took her breath away. When she felt his lips touch hers, Terelle easily accepted that her life on earth had ended and she was finally reunited with her beloved. No dream kiss could feel like this. Had she died—was she in heaven?

"All that shit with that other broad wasn't about nothing. Didn't you listen to the message I left on your answering machine?" His voice sounded choked. "I gotta go," he said suddenly and then abruptly pulled away.

Wait! Don't leave me, she wanted to shout but couldn't get the words out.

"I love you, girl. But I can show you better than I can tell you," he told her, speaking words that were uniquely his.

Oh, Marquise. I'm not dreaming. It's you. It's really you! Tears moistened and unsealed Terelle's closed eyes. In an act of sheer determination, she willed the muscles in her neck to cooperate. Forcing her head to turn, she managed to catch a fleeting glimpse of a very tall man pacing quickly toward the open door. *Marquise!*

His name was on her tongue, but she couldn't make a sound. From the depths of her soul, she drew on the memory of the mechanics required to produce coherent sound. She tried to shout his name, but the sound that issued from her lips was an unintelligible whimper. Determinedly, she tried again and this time his name came out in a loud and clear shriek, *Marquiiiiiiise!*

But instead of being comforted in Marquise's loving arms, Terelle was held down by several pairs of strong hands, trained to restrain the chronically mentally ill.

The next day Saleema Sparks sat at Terelle's bedside. Saleema gazed anxiously at her best friend, but Terelle did not acknowledge her. As usual Terelle was mute and wore a blank expression.

Holding Terelle's limp hand, Saleema pleaded, "Talk to me, Terelle. Why won't you say something? The charge nurse called last night. She told me you spoke. She said you screamed for…" Saleema swallowed. "She said you screamed for Marquise." She squeezed Terelle's hand imploringly and gasped when she felt a slight movement in Terelle's fingers. Saleema's eyes, shining with hope, flashed upon Terelle's face.

Terelle's vacant look was replaced by a grimace as she struggled to emit sound.

"Terelle! You're back! I know you are. Oh, my God; I gotta get a nurse," Saleema said excitedly as she pushed herself forward, prepared to rise. Terelle's fingers wiggled urgently.

"No?" Saleema asked. "You don't want me to get the nurse?"

One side of Terelle's face twitched as she uttered a gurgling sound. Saleema looked into Terelle's eyes. Terelle blinked rapidly. "Okay, I understand. You don't want me to get a nurse. But I don't know what to do. Are you in pain?"

"Maaar," Terelle uttered with great effort.

"Markeeta?" Saleema said, nodding. "She's fine, Terelle. Keeta's beautiful. Four years old and smart as a whip. I've been taking real good care of your baby. I love her like I would my own but I make sure she knows you and…" Saleema's voice faltered. "I show her pictures of you and her daddy," she said in a voice filled with emotion.

Tears slid down Terelle's cheek. "Oh, my God. You're crying. But that's a good thing," Saleema said as she snatched a tissue out of box on Terelle's bedside stand. She wiped the tears from Terelle's eyes. "Your tears mean that you hear me. You understand everything I've told you." Tears now welled in Saleema's eyes. "Oh, Terelle. I missed you so much." She bent down and gave Terelle's prone body an awkward hug. "I'm so glad you're back." Then Saleema, unable to keep her emotions in check, began to sniffle. She reached over and grabbed another tissue to wipe her own eyes.

"Maaarq…," Terelle said again. Saleema knew all along that her friend was referring to Marquise. But instead of acknowledging Terelle's attempt to speak her deceased fiancé's name, Saleema spoke animatedly about Terelle's daughter, Markeeta.

Exhausted from the effort of trying to speak, Terelle closed her eyes. Saleema sat holding Terelle's hand until her friend drifted off to sleep. Looking back at Terelle with concern, Saleema quietly left the room.

Saleema barged into the charge nurse's office. "I want Terelle to have speech lessons."

"Well, she's been evaluated and unfortunately, despite her break-through last night, Terelle's still not responsive. I'm sorry," the nurse said sincerely. "Terelle is not a candidate for speech therapy."

"Excuse me!" Saleema held up her hand in an exaggerated motion, which informed the nurse that she was not pleased. "The last time I checked, my name was written at the bottom of the check this hospital gets for taking care of Terelle Chambers. Don't get it twisted; I'm not asking for anything. If she can't get speech therapy here then I'll take her to another hospital—a better one." Saleema whirled around and strutted away.

"Ms. Sparks," the nurse blurted. "I didn't mean to offend you. I'm only reporting what the speech therapist wrote in her evaluation note."

Saleema stopped abruptly, turned around. "You people told me that Terelle would never have meaningful or conscious interaction with her family or friends. That's what the doctors said, right?"

The nurse nodded.

"Wrong! My girl is interacting her ass off—blinking, moving her fingers—trying to communicate with me. So do your job. No more tests. Call in a speech therapist who knows what the fuck she's doing—"

"Ms. Sparks, that language isn't—"

Saleema held up her hand. "Don't be criticizing my language. I can talk any way I want. The way y'all misdiagnosed Terelle, you shouldn't even be concerned about no cuss words. You better hope I don't call my attorney and have him slap this place with a malpractice suit."

"I'll have another speech therapist evaluate Terelle."

"No, I'm not trying to hear that," Saleema said, wagging a finger. "No more evaluations, no more tests. The next time I come up in here, that therapist better be doing her job; I want her working with Terelle and giving her some real speech lessons. Ya heard?" Deliberately in-timidating the now obviously frazzled nurse, Saleema threw out her arms in a flagrant combative gesture, glowered at the nurse, and then sashayed out the door.

After reading an article on DNA, Kai Montgomery had an awakening. She'd come to realize that the narcissistic and unscrupulous conduct that had ultimately led to her unjust incarceration was not her fault. Her bad behavior, she'd learned, was genetically inherited. Her biological mother, a conniving and completely immoral human being, had passed on defective DNA. Her mother had diligently visited her long enough to deceive Kai into believing she could help her get the justice she deserved. Once she'd obtained her daughter's banking information, the bitch absconded with the money Kai had stashed in a safety deposit box.

Now equipped with a clearer understanding of herself, Kai decided it was time for an abrupt halt to the martyr persona. She would no longer passively accept her prison sentence. She'd been behind bars for two years and quite frankly, enough was enough. Sure, she'd done some vile things to a lot of people, but it wasn't as if they didn't deserve to feel her wrath. Spending the rest of her life in prison for a murder she didn't commit went beyond poetic justice.

She did not kill Marquise Whitsett, yet she was convicted of the crime and sentenced to life in prison. Kai refused to rot in jail for the rest of her life. Doing time was hell. Everyone thought that prisoners' needs were met by the state. That was a crock! Survival behind bars was dependent upon financial security.

Kai's adopted parents provided her with money to make purchases from the commissary, but what they gave was just a drop in the bucket compared to what they owed her. She'd deal with them one day. It was only a matter of time before she got out and got even!

Her scheming birth mother had informed her that her adoptive parents felt so embarrassed by the scandal of her murder conviction, they'd disinherited her and skipped to southern California. Providing her with only a post office box in Santa Barbara, her crafty parents made sure Kai could never contact them directly.

Someday, someway, she'd find her neglectful parents, but in the meantime, her thoughts of exacting revenge on people whose whereabouts were unknown were frustrating and unsatisfying. So she turned her thoughts to her most recent sex partner, a hot male prisoner named Mookie. Mookie reminded her of Marquise. Like Marquise, he was a real rough rider—tall, with a deep dark complexion, handsome features, and best of all, Mookie was well hung. *Mmm!* Just thinking about Mookie made her kitty purr.

With intense sexual images running across her mind, Kai wrote Mookie a graphic note. It was time for another rendezvous. Knowing just the person to make the delivery, Kai folded the crude lined paper, ripped from a composition notebook.

Kai found Taffy in the kitchen stuffing her face instead of stacking trays. "Whassup, Taffy," Kai said. She'd had to adapt to prison life, including speaking the vernacular.

"Hey, Kai!" Taffy's round face swelled into a big, expectant smile. A while back, Kai had considered riding Taffy's tongue, but there were some gross rumors about the girl that made Kai steer clear. Anyway, Mookie was handling things now and quite frankly she was bored with having her pussy licked.

Taffy had finally taken a hint and stopped pestering her, but Kai knew the pathetic pig still had the hots for her, so she had to conceal her contemptuous superiority and handle the situation delicately. "I need you to get a note to Mookie for me," Kai said casually. "He's supposed to be hooking me up with a big-time attorney to handle my appeal."

"I thought you didn't have no money for a lawyer," Taffy said suspiciously.

"I don't. Mookie told me that the lawyer would take my case *gratis*," Kai said, slipping into her natural pattern of intelligent speech. But remembering that she was talking to a damn-near retard, she explained, "Um, the lawyer will work on my case for free. He'll accept a few favors for pay." Kai gave Taffy a conspiratorial wink. "You know—I'll have to give up some booty," she further explained. "I wrote dude twice but he ain't wrote me back yet." Damn, Kai hated talking like an uneducated idiot, but when in Rome…

"Uh-huh," Taffy said, inhaling food instead of chewing it.

"You know, Mookie has a cell phone," Kai continued, sensing Taffy required more detailed information. "I want him to make a call to that lawyer."

Men in prison had it going on. Their thuggish attitudes and muscular bodies had everyone from fat lonely girls on the outside to female inmates as well as correctional officers on the inside drooling over them. The women in their lives made certain male inmates kept their gear up and had access to cigarettes and drugs, and plenty of money on their books. Many male inmates even had internet access. Nurses and social workers were always willing to exchange sex with the gorgeous hunks for a little computer time.

Female inmates, on the other hand, had to pretty much scratch and scrounge and eat a lot of pussy for material gain. Fortunately, though Kai had been on the receiving end of oral sex with women, she'd never reciprocated. Thanks to the pittance she received from her parents, she'd never had to.

Forcing Kai to keep her company while she ate, Taffy changed the subject, and Kai had to endure the delay.

"Did I ever tell you we used to be able to work in the kitchen with the men?"

Kai shook her head, knowing Taffy was going to tell her a drawn-out tale.

"Yeah, girl, we used to work side-by-side with the men until this chick got pregnant by one of the male inmates. After that they had to separate us."

Why is she telling me this? What the hell do I care? Kai wanted to slap the shit out of Taffy, but instead of showing annoyance, she wore an impassive expression.

"Anyway, that chick sued the state for millions."

"Millions?" Kai lifted a brow. Sounded like something she would have done but she wouldn't have enjoyed having to get pregnant for the money. Getting an abortion would have been on the top of her list, but still, she knew she would loathe the idea of something growing inside her. Yuck!

"Yeah, that bitch got a fat bankroll off the state," Taffy said as she wiped sweat from her forehead with the back of her plump hand. Her other hand shoveled food into her mouth. Her eyes kept darting to the back of the kitchen, where several workers rattled pots and pans.

Taffy was a tray runner, a job that required her to distribute food trays to the female inmates. Overweight inmates like Taffy loved having that position because they were able to eat the food from the extra trays. Tray runners picked up the food trays from the men's areas of the correctional facility also. Though separated by a metal gate, the tray runner was able to pass the men notes from female inmates. A tray runner could make exchanges of cigarettes and even drugs, all for a price of course.

Kai toyed with the note in her hand. "Look, if you get this note to Mookie, I can get you a perm kit or something."

Taffy glared at Kai, and Kai was immediately sorry she had blurted out the offer of a perm kit. According to prison gossip, Taffy was so broke when she first came in that she ate some girl's foul-smelling pussy in exchange for a perm kit and ended up having to get treated for gonorrhea of the throat.

"Mookie ain't even here no more!" Taffy spat, her moon face etched in animosity.

"What do you mean, he's not…" Kai couldn't continue. Feeling a sudden bout of nausea and vertigo, she backed against the wall to steady herself.

"Your man Mookie is the one who got that girl pregnant. It took her a couple years to get the money. But she's a rich bitch now. She paid off Mookie's restitution. I heard she picked him up in a fly-ass Maybach yesterday. Bitch rode up to the gate with their little son strapped in a car seat. Yeah, Mookie and his bitch is two thorough-ass niggas. The bitch played the system and Mookie played *you!* Big time," Taffy added with her face twisted in a sneer.

Kai gasped. She took in so much air, she choked. Coughing, she clutched her chest while tears burned her eyes. It was outrageous that someone as intelligent as she had been outsmarted by an ignorant thug. A poorly educated, practically illiterate convict and his ride-or-die chick had conned the system. Gagging and coughing from the shock of the unwelcome news and feeling humiliated beyond belief, Kai couldn't keep her thoughts from turning to Marquise and his ghetto-trash girlfriend, Terelle— the psycho bitch who had really killed him.

"Need a drink of water?" Taffy inquired. Her darting eyes gleamed with something Kai couldn't quite detect. Was it triumph? A second too late, Kai recognized that it was malevolence that danced in Taffy's eyes.

As if on cue, two female inmates emerged from the shadows. Their smoldering hostility was almost palpable.

Knowing she was about to be ambushed, Kai opened her mouth to scream. But Taffy threw her heavy body across the table, then reached out and clamped a beefy hand over Kai's mouth, muffling the sound.

The three women, undoubtedly brawlers from birth, easily dragged Kai's bucking and thrashing body into a secluded pantry. Kai kicked and twisted to no avail. Amid institutional-sized canned goods, large sacks of flour, and corn meal, Kai was pinned down. Taffy removed her hand but it was instantly replaced by the dry and calloused hand of one of her brutal assistants.

"Did y'all know this bitch thought she was too good to have sex with me?" Taffy asked her cohorts. She folded her arms across her chest.

"For real?" one of the women asked, sounding personally offended.

"Whatchu gon' do 'bout this stuck-up bitch," inquired the other inmate. "I say she needs her face fucked up real good."

Eyes wide with terror, Kai shrank back. Taffy glowered, her folded arms tightening as her anger mounted. Now filled with a sufficient amount of rage, Taffy sauntered over.

Kai wondered whether the crazed inmate would draw a crudely formed dagger or brandish a butcher knife or some other dangerous form of cutlery accessed from the prison kitchen. Trembling in horror, she imagined the pain and agony of having her beautiful face carved and disfigured. Oh, Jesus! She needed help. Where were the fucking C.O.s?

But instead of hovering over Kai with a shank, Taffy began to peel off her prison-issued uniform. "Bitch, I ain't nevah want to eat you out. I was just messin' wit your head. I heard you was a freaky bitch so I was runnin' game so I could get you somewhere by yourself."

Kai blinked in confusion.

"Oh, don't get it twisted, bitch. You real cute and everything, I could fuck the shit outta you— but see, I'm loyal to the 'hood." Taffy pounded a balled fist against her heart. "Bitch, I represent southwest. That shit that went down with my niggas wasn't cool. I grew up with both of them," she said, emphasizing her last words with three powerful punches to her open palm.

Both of whom? And what the hell had gone down? Kai would have asked if she were permitted to speak.

In response to the baffled look in Kai's eyes, Taffy replied, "Marquise and Terelle! Them was my niggas, bitch. You killed Quise and fucked Terelle up for life."

The information that passed Taffy's lips was far worse than Kai could have ever imagined. The chubby tray runner had never let on that she knew Marquise or Terelle. Kai had never suspected that the woman had a personal vendetta against her. The conniving food addict had listened with feigned compassion when Kai first met her and had professed her innocence.

Trumped again by yet another vulgar hood rat, tears of defeat fell from Kai's eyes and wet her captive's hand. Were all the inhabitants of the ghetto educated in the school of treachery and deceit?

The hand that covered her mouth pulled away and balled into a fist. As quick as a lightning flash, a pair of knuckles crashed against Kai's face. "This crying bitch got her nasty snot all over my hand," the rough-skinned inmate told the other two. Using Kai's abundant head of curly hair, the inmate wiped the mucous off her hand.

Kai's mouth was uncovered and wide open but she couldn't scream. Her jaw felt unhinged. She was certain she saw stars. But her ordeal was far from being over. Taffy had taken off her prison garb and now squatted over Kai's face.

"Crying ain't gon' do you no good," she informed her struggling victim. "My girl told you she was gon' fuck up your face, but she forgot to add that *I'm* gon' *pussy-fuck* that pretty face."

As Kai feebly fought against her attackers, she instantly regretted having wasted so much time doing cardiovascular exercises in the prison gym. She preferred being slender and fit, but at this moment, she could have used some extra strength and would have gladly welcomed a set of powerful arms that rippled with manly muscles. If this travesty wasn't an isolated event, if a series of horrific physical confrontations would take place for the duration of her prison experience, she'd have to incorporate heavy weight-lifting into her workout routine.

Grinning, the ugly inmates held her down firmly. As Taffy's vagina hovered over Kai's face, the stench of sweat and urine was so overpowering, it curdled Kai's stomach. "HEEEEEELP!" Kai tried to scream, but the word came out raspy and slurred.

In an instant, Taffy lowered her putrid pussy, connecting it with Kai's open mouth. Intertwined in Taffy's pussy hairs were bits of toilet paper that stuck to Kai's tongue. Thick, smelly secretions oozed from Taffy's rank vagina and into the mouth that Kai was unable to close.